A LIFE SINGULAR

PART ONE; VOLUME ONE

BY
LORRAINE PESTELL

A Life Singular Part One; Volume One Copyright © 2020 by Lorraine Pestell. All Rights Reserved.

All rights reserved. No part of this book may be reproduced in any form or by any electronic or mechanical means including information storage and retrieval systems, without permission in writing from the author. The only exception is by a reviewer, who may quote short excerpts in a review.

Cover designed by Shawline Publishing Group

This book is a work of fiction. Names, characters, places, and incidents either are products of the author's imagination or are used fictitiously. Any resemblance to actual persons, living or dead, events, or locales is entirely coincidental.

Printed in Australia

First Printing: March 2020
Shawline Publishing Group

978-0-6487335-1-5   A Life Singular Paperback

978-0-6487335-2-2   A Life Singular E-book

For Jackie, Taryn and Ashleigh, my three amazing iTrack mentees...

Huge thanks to Bradley Shaw and Jennifer Zabinskas from Shawline Publishing for showing faith in my writing and for their valuable advice and assistance. I'm also grateful for the loyal band of readers who have encouraged me to continue with my life's work.

Sale proceeds of this book series will be donated to EdConnect Australia and The Smith Family for the ongoing support they deserve.

REVIEWS FOR A LIFE SINGULAR

There is so much happening in what is a beautiful story about life and love. Even more appealing than your typical love story is how the author has embedded into the storyline some of the more difficult social questions that we often avoid addressing, making it more intellectual than your typical love story. I can't wait to read the next book in the series!
Jenny, 5 STAR review

Contemporary Fiction with Love & Loss - A Life Singular Part One is the first book in the Life Singular Drama. This is a love story that deals with social issues of today including mental illness and loss of a spouse. It is captivating, yet emotional. Sad yet lovely. A truly real story that could be taken straight out of today's newspaper headlines. Highly recommended extraordinary read!! **5 STARS, Anonymous Goodreads review**

I'm always looking for quality series as I like being able to continue on with the story. In this book, the first book of the series, the author sets the stage for what is to come. I've also read the 2nd book but there will be no spoilers given. The only thing I'll say is the author does a good job of letting you think one thing and then doing a really nice twist when you definitely don't expect it. It kept me on my toes throughout the story. If you're like me and like solidly written stories with plenty of details and no lags, I think you'll become a fan of the author and move straight into each book that follows the one you are reading. I've just finished the second book and found the quality of writing to be as good as this one. If you are looking for a good series – put this author on your list... **Diana L 5 STAR review**

A great read by a great author! The description for this book hooked me instantly and I began reading the second I downloaded this book. This was a great read with zero lags. A good portion of this book centred around finding the person responsible for a high-profile murder and then the subsequent court trial. It was hard for me to put this book down at night as I wanted to know what would happen next. I definitely recommend this author as rarely does a book keep me as interested as this one did... **Beverly Clark, 5 STAR review**

A Wonderful Series Begins Here! There's a strong romantic element at the beginning of this story that really sets the stage nicely for the reader to understand the two characters (Jeff and his wife Lynn). When there is a tragic turn to their 20-year anniversary, the author smoothly takes us into the mystery of what happened and also the matter of how one person moves on after a tragic loss. The characters are well created and there is plenty of details to give this story the layers needed to keep one reading. The author has the ability to move the reader through the emotions being experienced – from love to anguish to feelings raked raw – the reader has his finger on the pulse of what is going on (said and unsaid) with each character. This book definitely hooked me on wanting to know what would happen next and I'll say now – I liked the second and third book too... **Wilson R 5 STAR Review**

TWENTY YEARS ON

'Y'know what I like about coming here, angel?'

Lynn smiled at her husband's playful wink. 'You're going to say nothing ever changes.'

'I was,' Jeff shook his head. 'How'd you know?'

The black Land Rover Discovery turned into the unmarked lane towards the vast Benloch property's private entrance, where the couple's shared observation shone as false as it was true. On the face of things, remarkably little had changed in the twenty-three years since the songwriter and his muse first drove his ageing, rust-bucket of a Ford Fairlane along this narrow track, too fast over the gravel and kicking up dust behind them.

Heavy electric gates rolled aside as soon as the sensor identified the vehicle. Its driver, as ever, couldn't resist a well-timed gun of the engine. The extra momentum slewed the lumbering beast around the corner to arrive at the barrier, which barely escaped a helping hand from the roo-bar.

'Well, that's changed for a start!' the beauty countered. 'In the old days, you'd have tried to run me over while I punched in the code.'

In the back of the car, Kierney dug her brother in the ribs. 'Hey, wake up. We're here.'

For a moment not understanding where he was, Jet grunted and opened his eyes. He had flown in from the UK that very morning, having started his journey home from Cambridge University some thirty hours earlier.

The lad had spent his first Christmas away from the family, permission for which was negotiated carefully when he found out an exquisite Russian archaeology student was staying in college over the holidays. As it turned out, he confessed to his father over the telephone, the scheme had been an almost total waste of time and he regretted not coming home to Melbourne as planned. The girl hadn't been anywhere near as exquisite as he had hoped, leaving the young buck to beat a hasty retreat from her room first thing on Boxing Day morning.

The nineteen-year-old sportsman had received a sympathetic hearing from his dad, who must have then shared the juicy snippets of information with his mother, judging by the knowing smile she dealt him later in the day. Jet didn't mind. He was pleased to be back *en famille*, even if it did mean his kid sister was on hand to give him a hard time.

Within a few minutes, the neo-Georgian mansion and its selection of outbuildings came into view, and the car slowed to a standstill close to the row of garages. Stretching and groaning as if they had aged fifty years since leaving home, the teenagers opened their doors and slopped out onto the driveway.

'Grab this, please,' Lynn asked her son, pointing to a large, black suitcase.

While Kierney lifted the straps of two smaller bags over her shoulder, the young man lifted his parents' case out of the car as if it weighed next to nothing, his six-foot-four-inch frame beginning to fill out as he headed towards the end of his teens. He carried his own bag in the other hand and a folder of paperwork under one arm, stopping to kiss his grandmother in the doorway as he passed through into the house.

'Aren't you tired?' Marianna asked. 'You mustn't know what time it is, dear.'

'Sorry? What time is it, Grandma, did you say? All the better to eat you with, I s'pose. Nice to see you. Happy Old Year.'

Using the porch wall to steady his own load, a case of assorted fine wines stacked on top of a slab of beer that was warming up way too fast for his liking, Jeff freed a hand to clip the top of the larrikin's head and leaned over to kiss his slowly-shrinking mother-in-law.

'Best to just ignore him,' he told the elegant lady. 'He thinks he's funny. We haven't got the heart to tell him the truth.'

'Good morning, Jeff,' the gracious woman laughed. 'Twenty years. Can you believe it?'

'Absolutely not. Feels like forty.'

'Papá!' Kierney shrieked from behind him. 'That's so mean! You think *you're* funny...'

The handsome man twisted his head round and grinned at his daughter. 'I mean I wish it were forty,' he quipped.

Once inside, and with everyone suitably greeted and the beer bottles plunged into an esky filled with ice cubes, the Diamond family disappeared straight upstairs to unpack for their New Year celebrations. The air-conditioning system made sure the temperature in the homestead was comfortable, and sparkles of sunlight glistened on the outdoor pool down below, enticing the couple as they stood on the balcony and breathed in the cornucopia of country aromas.

Jeff checked his watch. 'Are we all having lunch together, d'you think?' he asked. 'Or can we just relax for a while?'

To his delight, Lynn stepped closer to wrap her arms around her favourite sex maniac, a suggestive look on her face. She was wearing a new perfume, and it turned him on; just a hint of mystery about the woman he knew so well. He had missed out on their usual morning liaison earlier that day, since mother and daughter had left home before dawn to collect Jet from the airport.

'I have no idea,' his wife answered, her hands unbuttoning his shirt and stroking his chest and stomach on their way to his belt.

Jeff kissed her with wanton lips. 'What are you doing? This is your parents' house.'

Sighing, Lynn pulled away, standing down from her tiptoes and leaving him crestfallen. 'You're right,' she replied, folding the parted sides of his shirt front over his torso and patting them together. 'I should go downstairs and help Mum.'

'Cool,' he scoffed. 'Go on then. Don't let me stop you.'

Strong guitar-playing hands slipped inside his wife's blouse and began to fondle the underside of her breasts through the silky fabric of her bra. She leant into him, their bodies drawn together by an unseen force.

The billionaire turned around to lock the bedroom door. 'I'm sick of living dangerously,' he smiled, seeing her blue eyes flash their approval. 'Take me to bed, you goddess of perpetual torment.'

Jeff steered his dream girl towards the bed which had been hers since she was fifteen years old, and they made love with an intensity built up over the last two spectacular decades. They had grown together, fused by passion, maturing as lovers, artists and leaders. In fact, their children were now already older than Lynn had been when she first invited her dark-haired mystery man to the family farm for the weekend.

'How many songs have you brought with you for tomorrow?' the blonde star asked, caressing his back as they moved in unison.

'Songs?' he gasped. 'Now what are you talking about? Jesus!'

The lithe woman laughed. 'OK. Sorry I mentioned it.'

'Too right. Is there something special going on this weekend then?'

Eyes only half open, Jeff arched his back and kissed his wife's forehead. He loved how she toyed with him this way. Then without warning, he whipped them both over so that he lay on his back, with Lynn's long, golden hair falling over her shoulders and breasts.

'Can you believe it's twenty years?' she asked between moans of feverish delight.

'Nope. I still remember being in this room for the first time. Don't know why, but it almost feels like we're taking more of a risk now. Can I make you scream like I did back then?'

'I hope so,' Lynn sighed, lying down onto her man's stomach and feeling an orgasm closing in.

'Scream so your mum and dad can hear,' the musician urged, his breath hot on her face. 'Scream loud enough for them to know how much you love me.'

'Oh, I do love you. More every day. I've loved you forever.'

Imbibing his wife's pleasure with all his senses, the forty-three-year-old came in a huge rush moments afterwards, locked in a soulful kiss. They lay motionless for several minutes, each lost in memories of their time together, their hands idly wandering over each other's tingling flesh.

'Two,' the rock star announced, breaking the silence.

Lynn glanced across. 'Two songs? Damn! I've only got one.'

'No worries, angel. Par for the course,' he teased. 'I'm used to it. I had four but dumped a couple 'cause that would've been just too embarrassing for you.'

The beauty sat up and dealt her husband's chest a spirited slap. 'It's quality not quantity, mate. Anyway, I thought we might disappear to the dam tomorrow morning. Early, if we can get away with it. Would you like that?'

Jeff rolled his eyes in ecstasy and squeezed the champion's tight obliques. 'Would I like it? Ah, lemme think on that for a second...'

'I don't want to take things for granted,' Lynn shrugged, 'even after twenty years.'

'No?' the songwriter laughed, easing her gorgeous form onto the mattress and heading towards the bathroom. 'Go right ahead, angel. Take me for granted. I've been waiting a long time to be taken for granted. I'm all for new experiences at my time of life.'

Lynn smiled. She was ecstatic to see her husband so contented. She knew how much it meant to him that the Fabulous Foursome were together for their special occasion. He had gained an extra spring in his step as their year's work commitments were gradually crossed off the schedule, and a glint had returned to his all-seeing eyes. 1996 was set to be a phenomenal year for the whole family. Every year had been so, and each more phenomenal than the last.

Downstairs, Kierney had gone in search of her cousin, Jazz. She soon found her lazing by the pool along with the younger of her two brothers. Having spent time with each other over Christmas, there was little news to catch up on, except that Jet had arrived home. They lapped up the dark-haired girl's tall tales about her brother's many romantic escapades.

True to the Dyson family tradition of assigning apt nicknames as children, Jet had grown into his early and it hadn't let him down yet. Ryan "Jet" Diamond was Bart and Marianna's eldest grandchild, followed closely by Sonny, Bart Junior's eldest son. Bruce was next in line after Kierney, leaving Jarradie "Jazz" as the youngest, only recently turning the corner into her teens.

Already a prodigious tennis player in her own right, Jazz lived vicariously through the exploits of the willowy, eighteen-year-old gipsy, Kierney. They had recently been told that a sixth grandchild was expected in six months' time; the first baby for Lynn's much younger sister, Anna. It was exciting to think of a new arrival after so long, and the two girls swapped name ideas, hoping it would buck the trend of male firstborns.

By the time the anniversary couple had changed and reached the pool, almost the whole clan was assembled. The only missing person was Bart Senior, the head of the Dyson dynasty and the man largely responsible for putting Australia at the top of the sporting world. Even now, at sixty-three years of age, his dedication to the Olympic movement and his determination for the national team to succeed meant his family rarely saw him, even during the holiday season.

'So, Mum...' Lynn asked. 'What would you like us to do? Can I help with lunch?'

'Shortly, dear,' Marianna responded. 'You guys relax for a bit. There's not much left to do.'

'Congrats, you guys,' said Lynn's elder brother, who had moved over to sit with the billionaire singer-songwriter. 'A day early, I know, but happy anniversary, mate.'

'Cheers, Junior,' Jeff nodded, impersonating his father-in-law's booming voice with surprising accuracy. 'Remarkable achievement.'

Frolicking in the water, the shoal of teenagers turned as one, erupting into raucous laughter when they realised they had been fooled. Lynn came over to greet her brother with a kiss and to receive her share of the congratulations. Sinking onto a vacant sun-lounger between the two men, she opened her book and feigned ignorance of the major milestone.

'Come on, sis',' the footballer pressed. 'Tell us what it feels like to be an old married woman!'

'It's great, thanks,' the stunning athlete grinned, surveying the happy scene. 'Where's Jetto?'

'Oh, I expect he's fallen asleep upstairs, dear,' Marianna posited. 'We'll wake him before lunch. He'll be starving after such a long journey.'

Jeff looked over towards the pool, hoping to catch his daughter's eye. She was too far away to hear the conversation, unable to share his furtive humour. There could be any number of reasons for the young man's temporary absence, virtually none of which were suitable for sharing with their grandmother.

Lynn shook her head in mock exasperation. 'He'll be checking his e-mail,' she replied, watching a repeat performance from the handsome lothario at her code for the cricketer arranging hot dates for the remainder of his Australian visit.

That evening, the Dyson family hosted a New Year's Eve party in the function centre behind the grand homestead, spilling out into the courtyard gardens. The event was a regular fixture in the family's calendar well before the forever couple tied the knot, predominately as a thank-you to their household and farm workers. However, since their elder daughter's marriage to a bad-boy dubbed "The Australian Elvis", it had been adapted to embrace their anniversary as well.

The Diamonds had vetoed the customary extravagance this year, preferring a simple, subdued celebration where they need not be the centre of attention for once. 1995 had been an outstanding year for the superstars, and they had attended enough swanky parties the world over to be thoroughly bored with dressing up to the nines and reveling in sycophantic praise.

The family was also conscious of Junior's recent divorce. Despite an amicable separation from Julie, the forever couple was sensitive to the fact that he was still adjusting to sole parenthood. He had admitted to Jeff only the previous week how disappointed he was in himself for failing to make his marriage last.

With the house bursting at the seams with leftover party guests the following morning, the hustle and bustle of a breakfast barbecue was too much for many heads and stomachs, including Jeff's. Staring into the bathroom mirror, he examined his bloodshot eyes and the extra grey hairs he could have sworn had appeared overnight on his head, chest and arms. He watched as his reflection rubbed the tattoo on its right pectoral muscle and glanced down at the real thing on his left.

'Happy anniversary, mate,' he wished the bloke in the mirror, dipping his razor into the hot water.

Off to Coldwater Creek this morning, the celebrity's fuzzy mind reminded itself. *¡Excelente!*

This secluded setting on the Dysons' Victorian farm had always been the couple's special place. They had passed many happy hours there, writing songs together, waxing lyrical about the meaning of life and worshipping each other's body in splendid isolation. Hangover notwithstanding, the vision of his dream girl lying naked on a picnic rug beside the deep dam aroused him in an instant.

Lynn frowned and shook her head at his obvious excitement when the superstar returned to the bedroom. 'Part of you's already left for the dam, I see.'

'Maybe,' he grinned, throwing on a T-shirt and some shorts. 'S'pose we have to get through breakfast first, yet again. You're always so mean to me, making me wait like this...'

His wife finished tying her hair up, flicking her ponytail as she crossed the room. They met halfway between the dressing table and the bed and kissed, but she snatched her fingers away as he grabbed her hand and pressed it against his predicament.

'The suspense is killing you. I know and I'm sorry. It'll be worth the wait, I promise.'

'Jeez, woman! You always say that,' Jeff moaned, putting on a sad face. 'One year we'll have to go straight over there as soon as we wake up and see if you're right. If the sex is still good, I'll finally know I've been duped all these years.'

'And if it's not?' the blonde temptress asked.

The world-changer shook his head, knowing full well that sex between them could never be anything but wonderful. 'Yeah, well... That's where my argument sort of collapses.'

Breakfast over and heads beginning to clear, Lynn and Jeff piled their regular collection of chattels into a ute and picked their way over the deep, dry ruts. They followed the paddocks' fence-lines until they reached Coldwater Creek, as they had in all weathers since they first met. An extensive catalogue of hit records had been incubated here, and many a grandiose scheme was hatched under the blazing summer sun. Moreover, they were fairly sure their son was conceived in this idyllic spot, or at least they chose to think so.

Twenty years of marriage was a laudable stint, the lovers agreed in the crisp country air. Twenty years with the same partner, never once wanting anyone else, was no mean feat, particularly surrounded by the showbusiness world's unrelenting supply of temptations.

In all this time, they had never grown tired of the songs one wrote for the other, nor the hare-brained ideas their partnership spawned. They had no doubt that sharing such uncomplicated moments in this natural oasis had helped the hardworking celebrities shoulder the pressure of staying on top of their games.

For this particular special occasion, Jeff submitted one slightly ironic lyric and another more optimistic and romantic. These original pieces had been set to music and recorded before Christmas by an up-and-coming British singer whom he had signed to their label, and the prolific songwriter was pleased with the results.

And for her husband's gift, Lynn's theme was also nostalgia, with heartfelt messages and a simple melody. She produced the song in their studio while Jeff had been away in Europe in the weeks prior to the hectic holiday season. While his lover sang, picking out a lean accompaniment on the acoustic guitar, the happiest man on Earth lay back in the sun and listened with his eyes closed and his heart wide open.

Making love in the fresh air, with always the faint possibility of being discovered by a farm worker or some local *Daundwurrung* or *Woirurrung* people intent on a cooling swim, the pair of Diamonds immersed themselves in their private commemoration. Ahead was another mammoth twelve months which would see the family dispersed ever further across the globe. Regardless, they were looking forward to the new year with great excitement for the challenges upon which all four were embarking.

Jet would shortly head back to the UK to continue his second year at Cambridge, and Kierney was impatient to start her first semester at Sydney University. Turning eighteen this coming February, their daughter was itching to obtain her driving licence, which in her mind was the last obstacle standing between her and independence.

Several successful artists were blocked into Lynn's diary to record new albums and to have their music crafted by one of the most highly respected arranger-producers in the business. She was also due to complete an ambitious film project as a gift for her husband. It was supposed to have been finished in time for their special occasion. Given how hectic the year had turned out however, the personal endeavour had fallen behind schedule for worthy reasons.

And if these commitments didn't render her quite busy enough, now the children were practically self-sufficient, she was keen to explore new ways of influencing the country's governing classes beyond the years of effective activism afforded to the Diamonds' social justice agenda by her very public profile.

And for Jeff, this would be yet another year when too many hours would be spent on aeroplanes or locked securely behind hotel room doors in every corner of the globe. There would be no touring at least, since the "Live On Earth" concert series had finally concluded in Los Angeles a month ago to enormous acclaim.

Instead, he hoped to devote more effort to the peace negotiations he was spearheading in the Middle East, Northern Ireland and his beloved Africa, while in the background working on a plan to pare down the travelling and to focus on developing both his golf swing and his wife's career.

'The change'll be good for us, I think,' his beautiful best friend ventured, stroking the hairs on her stallion's chest and abdomen. 'Change is as good as a rest, they say. Do you need a rest?'

'Sex is as good as a rest,' the larrikin quipped, keeping his eyes closed and relishing the undivided attention. 'Old Italian proverb.'

The patient woman sniffed. 'Of course it is. Attributed to?' she asked, only too aware that she was massaging his ego as much as his skin. 'Rudolf Valentino? Or Casanova?'

'That'd make it an old Spanish proverb.'

Taking his beautiful best friend by surprise, the know-all grabbed her wandering hand and pulled it to his lips. Both sat up and embraced once more for luck, knowing that time was passing and their presence would be required back at the house.

Lynn's appreciative smile ignited his passions again. 'So I suppose you were Casanova in a former life too?' she murmured between kisses.

'’Spect so,' Jeff shrugged with more than a hint of macho conceit. 'If you say so, angel.'

The couple dressed and gathered up the rug and water bottles, ready to return everything to the ute's sun-baked tray. Lynn slotted the old guitar into its case, where it would stay until their next visit, while her husband turned the car round. Time to yield to the present and their precious offspring. No matter how many times they came to this unspoilt spot, it never lost its ability to nourish their souls.

'I *am* getting tired now,' the billionaire philanthropist confided, bumping the tyres over crumbling sandy furrows until they reached the lane that led to his in-laws' homestead. 'It feels like I've been around for three hundred years already. I reckon I'm turning into a self-satisfied fat cat at last.'

The blonde laughed without inhibition. If there was something she knew for sure, it was that her indefatigable world-changer was simply incapable of turning into the complacent egotist whose spectre had tormented him all these years.

'Yeah, right,' she teased. 'So you're going to cut up your frequent flyer card? I'd pay a lot of money to see that. What makes you think I want you hanging round the house anyway?'

Jeff chuckled. 'Oh, is that how it is now, after twenty years?' he returned the favour, swinging the vehicle into the garage. 'Easy fixed! I'll hang around someone else's house instead.'

The corners of his wife's mouth drooped. 'Alright then. You win, Felix.'

With their picnic gear stowed back on the garage shelving and the guitar swinging between their joined hands, the devoted pair trudged across the gravel path and entered the luxurious farmhouse through the rear door, preparing to reunite with the rest of the clan.

A LIFE SHATTERED

Lynn and Jeff celebrated the latest landmark in their youngest family member's journey to adulthood on the 15th of February 1996, less than a week after her birthday. She had arrived at the restaurant on Beaconsfield Parade in her own car, brandishing her brand new driving licence and a large floral bouquet for her mother.

'Let me see!' the proud father fuelled her excitement, taking the plastic card from her waving hand and examining the photograph. 'That's not you. It's a fake.'

Kierney stuck her tongue out and snatched the licence back. 'It's not! It's real,' she insisted, passing it to her mother for verification. 'Let me see yours. Let's see if your photo looks like you.'

Her dad obliged, removing his wallet from his back pocket. It was a humid summer's evening in Melbourne, and the famous family had risked a table outside in the restaurant's casual dining area overlooking the bay. Other patrons sat nearby, doing their best to ignore the celebrities, who in return were doing their best to be ignored. Somehow, neither party ever quite succeeded at this game, and certainly not in their home town.

Before handing his own licence across, the forty-three-year-old looked at the mug-shot which was now over five years old. He held it up to his cheek for the women to adjudicate.

'Which me do you prefer? The 1990 model or the current model?'

His wife smiled, adoration gleaming in her blue eyes. 'The current model, of course. Distinguished and sophisticated.'

'Grey and wrinkly,' Kierney countered, eager to examine the detail on her dad's licence and comparing its format to her up-to-date version.

Jeff scoffed. 'OK! I know who's paying for dinner tonight. Somewhere between the two responses would've been nice.'

While waiting for their drinks to arrive, Lynn telephoned Jet in Cambridge for Kierney to pass on her good news. He didn't answer, so they left a quick message and focused on the menu. One after the other, they imparted their own driving test memories and shared the feeling of elation each remembered on passing.

'Sounds like being able to drive legally on our own was a long time coming for all of us,' the sportswoman reflected, turning to her husband. 'Do you remember those lessons you gave me out on the deserted roads near the airport?'

'Yep,' Jeff nodded, scowling at a rare unhappy memory. 'In our blue period, you mean. We were so damned short-tempered with each other...And then, after all that, your first licence was your Californian one.'

'That's right. My God! That test was absolutely pathetic!' Lynn laughed, casting her hand around as if describing an open space. 'Here's a car park. If you can drive once around without hitting any other cars, you pass.'

'Wow! Was that it?' Kierney yelped, astonished. 'Were you driving for ages before you got your licence too, Papá?'

Coughing and gazing around to check no-one could overhear, the comic answered. 'Um, yes, Your Honour. I bought an old wreck of a car when I was sixteen, but I didn't drive it much. Couldn't afford the petrol. Still an amazing feeling to finally get my licence though. Proof that I was a *bona fide* citizen, I guess.'

The teenager smiled. 'Yeah! That's exactly how I feel too. A passport doesn't make you autonomous, because I've had one since before I could walk or talk. At least with a driving licence, it proves someone thinks I'm responsible enough to be in charge of my own actions.'

'Listen to us!' her mum chuckled. 'We're all so similar. It's fascinating how being responsible is so much part of our ethos. Other people shirk responsibility until they die.'

'*Viva* apathy!' Jeff toasted, raising his empty beer bottle as their meals arrived at the table. 'I hate the world but I can't be bothered to change it, so I'll just spend the rest of my life moaning.'

The trio swapped more automotive stories over dinner, laughing and joking like the tight-knit bunch they were. They made plans for Kierney to drive down from Sydney to meet them at Junior's farm in Narrandera for the Easter weekend, which was the next scheduled Dyson shindig.

'You can bring someone if you like,' Lynn invited their daughter. 'Are things OK with you and Dylan? You seemed a little distant on your birthday. Are you still going out with him?'

'Yeah. Technically we are,' the young woman confirmed. 'I'd rather come on my own though, to be honest. I want to enjoy being *en famille* before getting completely dragged into uni' life.'

'Sure. That's cool,' her dad said, leaning over and kissing her temple. 'It'll be great to be together in the wilderness for a few days. Just us, as an antidote to all the madness. Bloody oath, we're going to be so busy by then, angel. Shame Jetto's not here. But hey, Kiz...Exactly what does going out with someone technically entail?'

Lynn grinned as she waited for the youngster to come up with a suitable retort, knowing how alike the two dark-haired Diamonds' brains worked. It was proving more and more difficult to embarrass the children these days, given their rapidly increasing levels of experience with the opposite sex.

'Oh, you know...We get cosy every now and again,' the eighteen-year-old explained with a shy smile, 'in a technical way. But then we do our own thing when we want to.'

Jeff shook his head. 'That makes no sense at all, *pequeñita*, but I'll let you carrying on living in your misguided reality.'

'Oh, whatever, Papá,' Kierney pouted. 'I don't meddle in you guys' sex life, so I'll thank you not to meddle in mine.'

'Sounds like a fair deal,' her mother agreed. 'Did you want us to check anything out for you in Sydney this weekend?'

The youngster shook her head. 'Thanks, but I can't think of anything. I can ring you if I do. Are you staying at the Blakes'?'

'Not tomorrow night, but at the weekend we are,' Jeff answered. 'We've got to help Celia convince Gerald to stop drinking.'

'Oh, why? Is he sick?'

'Yep,' her dad nodded again. 'The usual old people's afflictions: blood pressure, heart problems... All sorts apparently. He needs to stop smoking and drinking so much.'

'Unfair, isn't it?' Lynn added, gazing out across the bay. 'You reach the autumn of your life, and your body starts denying you all the pleasures you've earned during the hard-slog years.'

'*Exactement*,' her husband agreed. 'Still, it's a choice. Keep going at the same pace so you go out partying, or slow down and gradually bore yourself to death.'

Kierney laughed aloud. 'Yuck! Neither of those options sounds very appealing. Somewhere in the middle perhaps? Please give Uncle Gerald my best wishes.'

'We shall. That's kind, darling. Everything in moderation,' Lynn offered, mimicking her own mother. 'For all these new fad diets and ideas for healthy living, that old adage still works the best.'

'Christ!' Jeff exclaimed. 'Enough of this sensible talk, Grandma. Between us, we sound like the Grim Reaper, warning everyone to steer clear of danger. It's old man Blake's choice, as long as he makes it knowing the likely effects on everyone and not just himself.'

The teenager's mobile rang from inside her handbag.

'That'll be Jet,' her mum assumed.

'Hey! Thanks!' Kierney exclaimed into the phone. 'Yeah. It's awesome! Thanks for ringing back. How's things over there? We're having dinner in Port Melbourne, on the bay. It's very hot. Ha, ha! Tough luck!'

The handset was passed around each person in turn. Luckily, by this time, there were no other patrons around to disturb. The Trinity College undergraduate was envious of the summer weather and sorry to be missing out on their celebratory dinner. The new university term having started in earnest, his workload was mounting, already almost halfway through his degree.

'See ya, son,' Jeff shouted over the wind and traffic noise. 'Talk soon. Have fun at the weekend and stay safe.'

Kierney slipped the telephone back into her bag. 'So he bought that bike in the end. I knew he would.'

'Yes,' her mother replied. 'He said he managed to negotiate the price down, so the guy must have been keen to sell it to him. Hope it's not ready to fall to pieces.'

The songwriter nodded, leaning back in his chair and savouring the small amount of wine left in his glass. Their son had been eyeing up a second-hand Triumph motorcycle since before the end of the previous term. If the bike were to break down, it would serve as a useful lesson in resourcefulness for a young buck unpracticed in the art of *caveat emptor*, but he wasn't game to voice this opinion right now. Lynn preferred less punitive learning devices, and all records indicated she was right. Both children were fully automated these days, self-sufficient and confident. Not a bad job done, he thought.

The handsome musician winked at his guardian angel. 'We have no purpose now,' he rued. 'Parental pasture looms. Where shall we retire to, angel?'

'No!' the teenager cried out. 'Don't retire! I still need you.'

'Eh? What total crap!' her father objected. 'Kizzy, you haven't needed us since you were out of nappies. Get outta here!'

'I *have* needed you. Just don't go too far away then. Driving distance only.'

With dusk descending on Port Phillip Bay, Lynn went inside to pay their bill, and the threesome left the restaurant, crossed the road and walked hand-in-hand along the promenade towards Station Pier. The *Spirit of Tasmania* had docked in the last hour, disgorging its stomach contents onto the local roads.

Another, much larger ocean liner was moored alongside it, dwarfing the ferry that ran daily between Melbourne and Devonport on the apple-shaped island state to the south. Passers-by waved and shouted cheerfully to the famous family, receiving smiles and waves of acknowledgement in return.

'Hey!' Kierney piped up. 'I forgot to tell you... You guys remember Youssouf Elhadji, don't you?'

Her father turned and nodded. 'Ah, yeah? Did he reply to your message?'

'More than! He wants to record something new with me. *And* he's become a Goodwill Ambassador for UNICEF. Can you believe that?'

'Wow! He's not even thirty yet, is he? That is amazing. Well done!' Lynn praised. 'But when are you going to fit a recording session in with everything else?'

The proud teenager giggled. 'Oh, I don't know yet. July, probably. At mid-term break, depending on my exams. I could visit Jet and meet him in London. What do you think? I can hardly ask him to come here, can I?'

'No. Not really,' Jeff agreed. 'London or New York. Or what about Paris? I'll see if I can come with you.'

'Thanks. I'm more interested in talking to him about the United Nations,' their ambitious daughter explained, 'so New York would be perfect. He could show me what he does there, if that's allowed. I might even marry him.'

'Oh, might you?' her dad echoed in surprise, opening the passenger door for his wife. 'No wonder you want to leave Dylan behind at Easter. I didn't know you had the hots for him. Isn't he already married? Technically?'

'I don't even know,' Kierney swooned. 'Most likely. *N'importe pas.*'

'Right,' Lynn smiled at the youngster's free and easy attitude. 'We'll leave that one in your capable hands. See you at home.'

The parents drove off before their daughter pulled out of her parking space up ahead, not wishing to put any pressure on her early driving career. Jeff couldn't stop himself from checking his rear-view mirror every few seconds, making sure the little silver hatchback with its red probationary plates was still following them. His dream girl caught his eye and scolded him gently. Letting Kierney spread her wings was truly the hardest thing for the doting dad.

'Shit! I am so old,' he groaned. 'How can our little girl be thinking about getting married? It's just not *kosher*, baby. Now I know how your parents felt.'

'What goes around comes around,' his empathetic wife sighed, stroking the tight sinews stretching along her husband's left forearm as his hand shifted gear in the sleek, dark grey sports car. 'My mum tried to tell me you'd behave just like Dad if you ever had your own daughter.'

'Did she? When you were sick that day in our apartment? While I dueled with your father for your hand on the balcony?'

'Yes. That fateful day,' the beautiful woman confirmed. 'I remember not being too convinced. I told her that at least you'd ask your daughter what she wanted first.'

'No way! That's not going to happen,' her husband denied with a half-smile, shaking his head. 'I'm going to put my foot down. No free thinking allowed 'til she's at least twenty-five.'

'Come on! You'd love to have Youssouf Elhadji as a son-in-law.'

The songwriter nodded, turning his head to the left and grinning at the wise woman. 'I would so! Awesome!'

Lynn chuckled at his impersonation of their exuberant girl-child, lost in fond recollection of the head-strong beau who swept her own innocence away in a maelstrom of passion and nightmares.

After a few more minutes winding through Melbourne's sparse evening traffic, the couple turned into the car park of their city apartment building. To their relief, Kierney pulled up behind them before the gates had fully opened, in her silver Volkswagen independence machine.

'Kizzy, we're leaving,' Jeff announced, knocking on his daughter's bedroom door. 'Can I come in?'

'Yes,' the youngster called out, swinging her legs off the bed to meet her dad with a kiss at the door. 'Right now?'

'Ten, fifteen minutes, tops,' the smartly-dressed businessman affirmed, his eyes alighting on a series of verses written on a single piece of paper. 'What's this? May I read it, please?'

'A-course ya can,' Kierney joked. 'It was inspired by Auntie Lena, after that dinner we nearly didn't share in Sydney last month. Hope you don't mind the subject matter.'

The young woman disappeared into the bathroom, leaving her father hypnotised by a very adult song lyric which lamented the disdain often levied upon sex workers for taking cash for their time, as opposed to the jewelry, cars and comfortable homes that more refined gold-diggers were known to opt for. The words conjured up some callous images, making him shiver, particularly when he homed in on the unfeeling monotony of such a lifestyle.

If this song was his sister's story, it was not one Jeff recognised. Had Madalena really opened up to this extent to her niece that evening? He doubted it. If she had, he was sure the teenager would have told him sooner. Throughout their very separate lives growing up in Sydney's neglected western suburbs, the Diamond siblings had evolved into vastly different people as a result of the wounds inflicted in their formative years. The young lad had gained a surfeit of emotional intelligence, determination and self-awareness, whereas his older sister had closed her heart and mind to any outside influences, whether subconsciously or otherwise.

Deep in contemplation, the forty-three-year-old jumped as the bathroom door clicked shut behind him, and he felt his daughter's presence at his side. 'This is really good,' he said, flapping the page in front of her face. 'I love the last verse, even though you shouldn't be so cynical so young. Mamá'd try to discourage you from thinking this way, but I'm too much like you to get away with it anymore.'

Kierney giggled, accepting the lyric sheet back and placing it on the desk. 'True, *y gracias*. Chip off the old block. I'm glad you like it.'

'I do, baby. Very much. *Pero digame...* Did Auntie Lena really talk about some of those things? Like she longs to be touched by someone who cares? It just doesn't sound like my sister. Are you sure you had dinner with the right whore?'

'Papá!' the teenager shrieked, slapping his arm. 'I'm not that stupid. It's not Auntie Lena's story. We talked about working girls *generalmente*, and she told me stuff about people she knew. It was interesting, how different women deal with being a prostitute. That's all.'

'Cool. Good enough. But why d'you want to know so much about that seedy life?' her father enquired, keen to lighten the mood before his departure. 'United Nations lost its appeal?'

'Perhaps!' the young woman teased, batting flirtatious eyelids. 'I'll need some pocket money while I'm going through uni'. It's the oldest profession, isn't it? I was always told the professions are reputable careers.'

The rock star rested an affectionate hand on top of his daughter's untidy mop of long curls and shook her head until her whole body wobbled. Laughing at the oldest trick in the book, she reached both arms around his waist for a hug. A few years ago, he would have held her at arm's length while she tried in vain to punch his ribs with flailing fists, but she chose to cuddle into him these days. Kierney Diamond loved her papá best of all.

'Enough with the smart remarks, *hija mía*. If you need pocket money to get through uni', our combined songwriting careers must've definitely hit the skids,' her billionaire father scoffed. 'Mamá'll bail you out. She's good like that.'

Kierney smiled, chasing him back to the kitchen. 'The last line did come from Auntie Lena though.'

'Did it?' he responded in amazement. 'The "fine line" reference? I didn't know she thought that way. Who was she referring to?'

'Oh, no-one in particular. Maybe Michelle? She said that women who get married to rich men so they can have kids and nannies and never work again are selling sex just as much as prostitutes do, and I see her point. Is that mean?'

Jeff stopped and turned to this gorgeous creature who went out of her way never to hurt anyone, even with the truth. She knew the answer to her own question. He could see it in her big, brown eyes.

'It's a song, not an affidavit, *pequeñita*,' he smiled, pointing to her heart. 'As long as you understand that in here...'

'I do.'

'I know you do. And generally, for the record, I agree with you,' the philosopher added. 'It is a really fine line, as your lyric says. I suppose people can get addicted to jewellery shopping and being presented with a new car every year every bit as easily as they can get addicted to drugs and drink. Jacinta might fall into that category, and she'd certainly think we were being mean to say so. Tammy too, for that matter. They're both pretty much ladies of leisure these days, courtesy of their husbands' big, fat portfolios.'

Kierney laughed. Her dad was referring to his long-suffering manager's sisters, whom he had known since he was a boy. Michelle was her mother's best friend from school, and she and the feisty Madalena had been bridesmaids at Lynn and Jeff's wedding twenty years ago.

'Michelle's not part of the "thin line" brigade though,' Jeff continued. 'We shouldn't discount unpaid work. Mish serves on a few non-profit boards, like Mamá does, and she takes care of heaps of our legal stuff *pro bono*. She actually works pretty hard, I reckon, but Auntie Lena wouldn't understand that sort of work. You have to dig up roads or stand up all day as a supermarket checkout chick before Lena thinks you're working.'

Kierney looked ashamed, causing her father to sympathise with her flourishing conscience. He didn't need to labour the point. The pair walked into the kitchen where Lynn was clearing away their breakfast.

'*Buenos días, Mamá,*' she chanted, kissing her mother. 'When are you back?'

'*Buenos días,* darling. Tuesday, mid-morning. We're planning to go straight to the house. What are you doing today?'

'Don't know yet,' the eighteen-year-old frowned.

Jeff scoffed. 'What? Question too hard? Come along, for Christ's sake, get with the program! Don't you know the ins and outs of your diary off by heart by now?'

It was a running joke between father and daughter that her mum's planning standards demanded much more rigour in comparison with theirs. Somehow, she was able to retain every appointment in her head, along with those of the rest of the family and even some of her friends too. Dark-haired Diamonds didn't do detail, which was always a source of frustration for the super-organised, blonde beauty.

Kierney shrugged. 'Terribly sorry. I'll try to get all the spontaneity out of my system before you return.'

'Good thing too,' Lynn mocked, giving her daughter a hug. 'Enjoy yourself this weekend, and don't forget to ring if you want us to do anything for you while we're in Sydney.'

'I shall and I won't,' the teenager responded, making a swift scan of the kitchen. 'What about here? Is there anything I need to do?'

'Nope,' Jeff shook his head. 'Everything's under control. Just drive carefully and don't go getting married before we get back, OK?'

The women both laughed, sharing sympathetic glances at the uneasy father figure. After final kisses goodbye, Kierney stood in the hallway in her pyjamas until the lift doors closed on her parents, on their way to the airport; yet again.

The commuter flight to Sydney was uneventful but crowded, and the Diamonds had been forced to hang back to avoid the throng at baggage collection. It took them nearly an hour to reach the rental car counter. Cathy Lane, their trusty administration wizard, had arranged an energetic Mercedes AMG sports car for the couple's brief stop in Sydney, and it was husband versus wife to be the first to drive it.

The silver dart sped towards the Central Business District, weaving through traffic as best it could. The superstars were due to attend a charity luncheon at eleven-thirty, deciding first to check into their favourite boutique hotel, The Pensione on George Street. Jeff pulled into the semi-circular, covered driveway at speed, negotiating the curves expertly and coming to a halt centimetres from the kerb. The doorman was impressed, and then startled out of his wits when the passenger door opened and out stepped none other than Lynn Dyson Diamond.

The tall, elegant lady signalled to the valet that her husband wouldn't require him to park the car. 'He knows where to go,' she told the open-mouthed fan. 'He's like a boy with a new toy in that thing. I'm sure he thinks it's a go-kart.'

The stocky young man gave a tentative snigger and opened a door to one side of the revolving entry to let the sportswoman pass through into the lobby. As she approached the reception desk, she was greeted by a row of waiting smiles. The staff were eager to see their special guests again.

'Welcome, Ms Diamond,' the receptionist marked "Miriam" effervesced. 'How are you today?'

'Very well, thank you. A bit stressed. It took ages to get here from the airport this morning. Jeff's bringing the luggage around from the car park. How are you all?'

Miriam swooned. 'We're good, thanks. And thank you so much for choosing to stay with us today, Ms Diamond,' she added, dripping with sincerity. 'It's lovely to see you and your husband again.'

One half of the hotel's VIP contingent was handed their keys and a pair of envelopes which had been delivered for the couple's attention. She turned to watch the same doorman wheeling a trolley towards her, ready to transport the luggage up to their room. A telephone rang on the counter, and one of the other receptionists answered it.

'Excuse me, Ms Diamond,' Hannah called out, seeing the celebrity walking away. 'There's a phone call for Mr Diamond.'

'Oh, OK. I'll take it,' Lynn replied, turning back. 'Thanks very much.'

Miriam instructed her more junior colleague to transfer the call to a courtesy telephone in the lounge area, next to a comfortable leather couch. The reception staff watched their guest closely as she walked across the tiled flooring, self-assured in a tailored suit and high heels. It was the first time the younger employee had seen Australia's favourite lady in the flesh, and she understood the others' jealous awe at once. To think the Olympian was now forty years old! It was hard to believe the nineteen-sixties child-star had children already in their late teens.

Lynn Dyson Diamond was everything most women wanted to be: tall and slim, with shining blonde hair and a tanned, radiant complexion. In whispered tones, the receptionists remarked to each other that they had seen photographs of Anna Dyson's wedding two years earlier, at which today's guest had been the Matron of Honour. Despite their eleven-year age difference, one could scarcely tell who was the younger.

'Please take a seat over there, Ms Diamond,' Miriam invited, pointing towards the telephone. 'The call will be waiting for you.'

The celebrity did as she was told, mouthing an inaudible thank-you. Lifting the receiver to her ear, she sank into the sumptuous cushions and crossed her long legs, at once stately and casual.

'Hello? This is Lynn Diamond.'

A gruff, nervous voice snuffled at the other end of the line, asking again to speak to Jeff Diamond.

'No, I'm sorry. Jeff's not available. This is Lynn Diamond. Can I help you instead?'

But there was no further conversation. With the faintest of whistles, the celebrity's head was whipped back against the wall behind the couch by an invisible force, and she exhaled suddenly.

Elsewhere, the reception staff continued about their day's business. Nobody noticed the trickle of blood running down their attractive guest's forehead, where a bullet had penetrated her skull. Her eyes were open and staring over towards the hotel entrance, as if searching for her husband. She was frozen in time while the world carried on as normal around her.

A while later, something made Miriam look up and check on the telephone call taken by her distinguished patron. She screamed at the top of her voice, causing everyone within earshot to stop in their tracks and follow her frightened gaze. Pandemonium broke out in the lobby as staff and guests cottoned on to the alarming incident.

Outside, Jeff reached the revolving doors leading into the hotel from the driveway, only to be bombarded by loud cries and the sound of a man shouting orders. With a suitcase in each hand and the parking ticket clamped in his teeth, he stopped to put the docket and receipt in his wallet, wondering what all the noise was for.

'Everyone please keep calm,' the hotel manager's authoritative voice commanded, wild eyes looking from one side of the lobby to the other. 'No-one leave the building, please.'

As the well-known musician grasped the handles of each bag to make his way through the grand entrance, a short, middle-aged man began to push the revolving doors from the inside. The natural leader stepped back out and met the other man as he was ejected into the open air, ending up face-to-face on the pavement.

'Did you hear the instructions from inside, mate? We'd better stay inside. What's going on, d'you know?'

Quite clearly agitated, the swarthy individual spat a few curt words at the songwriter. Confused for a moment, Jeff had trouble recognising the language as Spanish.

'¿Qué dices, hombre?' Jeff asked, towering over him.

'Quería matarlo Ustéd, pero es mejor así,' the terrified foreigner muttered under his breath.

The billionaire's height and strength were too much for the smaller man to contend with, and he found himself being directed back through the revolving doors towards the commotion. A member of staff wearing a security guard's uniform had been watching the pair and stepped in to take control of the fugitive from their impressive guest.

The linguist replayed the incoherent sentence in his head. What had this angry jerk said to him? Something about killing him but that it was better this way... What did he mean? And did "Ustéd" refer to an anonymous person inside the hotel or had he directed this statement to its intended object?

'What's happened?' Jeff demanded of the man in uniform, beginning to panic as he saw a familiar figure walking towards him.

'Mr Diamond,' the hotel manager said in a weak, reedy voice, his face as white as a sheet. 'Come this way, please.'

The hotel's famous patron looked from the southern European man and the security guard to the smartly-attired manager whom he knew fairly well. He began to feel dizzy and nauseated. No, surely not...

'Where's my wife?' he demanded. 'Where's Lynn?'

The noise inside the foyer was frenetic, and the area had taken on a surreal ambience that reminded the celebrity a little of a film set. But no-one was making a movie here. Something serious had clearly occurred, the prospect of which filled him with foreboding. He had the feeling he would not be playing the role of innocent bystander for much longer.

'Karl, take Mr Diamond's bags to his room, please,' Chris Nichols was now at the star's side, his shiny lapel badge sporting The Pensione's logo. 'Mr Diamond, please come with me.'

'Why?' the visitor asked, watching the doorman wheel his belongings away. 'What's going on, mate? Where's Lynn?'

His eyes desperate to find the woman he adored, Jeff noticed the concierge's team had erected a type of barrier at the far end of the lounge area. He tried to remember the normal layout, yet his muddled, swirling thoughts drew a blank.

'Will someone please tell me what's going on?' he asked again, to anyone listening.

In the absence of any answers, the forty-three-year-old's anxious mind strung the circumstances together itself and came to the worst possible conclusion. Pushing past Nichols, he strode towards the small crowd now gathered around the temporary screen.

Another valet tried to prevent him from going any further, but Jeff Diamond wasn't the type of man who took no for an answer. He sidestepped everyone's valiant efforts to prevent him from seeing what he knew by now he didn't want to see.

Reaching the barrier, the superstar's head swam. The sight that met his eyes after one more stride confirmed his worst fear; the one he had been dreading for so many years. Legs buckling underneath him, he struggled to maintain his equilibrium, and his stomach churned wildly.

Thirty pairs of eyes drilled into him, and the weight of thirty-one heavy hearts charged the atmosphere. Deliberately avoiding any interaction, the tall, good-looking Australian stepped forwards to where the love of his life sat, the telephone receiver still resting in her lap.

People all around were crying; some wailing out loud. Their shock at finding the nation's favourite celebrity mother with a gunshot wound to her head was quickly mixing with the distress of watching her husband of twenty years come to terms with the heinous tableau. The situation was too much for several people, who collapsed and fainted in their neighbours' arms.

'Lynn,' Jeff whispered, crouching down beside his wife's crossed legs and placing his left hand on her knee. 'Angel, what happened?'

Chris Nichols lunged forward after the distraught songwriter, grabbing at his upper arm in an effort to pull him back from the crime scene. Jeff grunted and shook his shoulder, dislodging the man's hand.

'Mr Diamond,' the hotel manager urged. 'Come away, please. The police are on their way.'

Watching on, he realised it was clear from the sympathetic reaction of those encircling the much-loved stars that popular opinion was against him. Tearful women seemed to form a line of defence, protecting their idol's privacy while he came to terms with the terrible situation.

Jeff took a few seconds to survey the frozen body as thoroughly as his emotions would allow, willing with all his might for it to move. A flick of an eyelid, a twitch of a finger... Now would be a very good time for his dream girl to wake him up from this horrific dream, as she had done so many hundreds of times before.

Instead, his saviour sat mute and motionless. To a collection of gasps and sobs from the throng behind him, he picked up her hands and stared at the bullet hole in her forehead that had extinguished her life.

Desperate to preserve the area for the upcoming investigation, Nichols again instructed the crowd to move back while he attempted to persuade his famous guest to withdraw. His words continued to be ignored.

Time stood still, and the cries and murmurs of the onlookers rang in Jeff's ears. He lifted Lynn's hands to his mouth before laying them back down into her lap.

Not enough, he concluded. His dream girl deserved more than this. The performer leant forwards and kissed her inanimate, red lips, already much colder than he remembered.

The staff did their utmost to steer the crowd away, but no-one was interested in moving until the celebrity was ready. Jeff became aware of sirens in the distance above the incessant whispering, which even on a good day followed him wherever he went. Tears started to flow from his eyes and down his cheeks as the reckoning finally hit home. Lynn's side of this story would forever be lost to those who cared.

A hysterical woman rushed forward and threw her arms around the heartthrob's shoulders, bawling and screaming. Instinctively, the empathetic man stood up and span around, embracing this grief-stricken stranger.

He found himself staring into glazed, bloodshot eyes which undoubtedly reflected his own. 'Thanks,' he murmured, pushing her away from his chest and searching for a volunteer in the crowd to rescue him.

The doorman led the woman away, leaving Jeff to turn back and catch hold of his wife's vacant, blue pools of boundless love. He perched on the edge of the couch next to her, being careful not to leave fingerprints anywhere. He knew enough about ballistics to assume that trying to revive her was futile.

Having given up trying to extricate the grieving man from the obscured area, Chris Nichols marshalled his staff to lead people out of the foyer. He ran across the tiles to meet two arriving police officers and brief them on what had taken place.

Jeff reached out to stroke Lynn's hair, taking deep, slow breaths to bring his heart rate under control. It was a relief to be close to her again, but the trickle of blood from the hole above her right eye was a ghastly reminder of how she had met her fate.

Jeff also noticed that the front of her suit jacket was stained red at waist level. He shook his head in a mixture of agony and confusion. Whoever this small Spaniard was, and why ever he had sought to shoot this perfect creature, he had done a superb job.

'Fucking bastard,' he murmured, staring into Lynn's lifeless eyes and willing them to blink.

The intellectual considered it strange that the barrage of unpleasant odours didn't bother him more. Glancing up at the blood stains running down the wall, he thought he would have found the whole experience utterly revolting.

He shouldn't be surprised though, since he had reacted the same way when cleaning up after his mother's violent death. It was something that had to be done, so his teenaged self had knuckled down and got on with it. Back then, the macabre activity had helped pass the time while his mind and body processed the shock. How long might the trauma last this time?

Staring into the deep blue eyes again, Jeff held his lover's icy left hand and brushed her wedding ring with his fingertips. It was obvious that the blood on her blouse hadn't come from the bullet in her head, but he couldn't face the repulsive task of locating any others. That was the Coroner's job, and he was welcome to it.

'You promised me you wouldn't do this,' he reminded his eternal lover, tears rolling down his cheeks and dropping onto her skirt.

He went to pass his hand over her eyes, intending to close them. At the last minute however, he decided he preferred them the way they were and diverted his fingers. By leaving her eyes open, he could delude himself she was still with him. His beautiful best friend seemed at peace, still with the faintest of smiles on her paling face.

Out of sheer habit, he ran two loving fingers down a translucent cheek, pallid, chill and desiccated, and a turgid teardrop dropped from his face and burst on an impassive face.

'I'll love you forever, *mon amie*. Together, forever, wherever, OK?'

Two fresh-faced constables had arrived and were rushing to cordon off all but a narrow walkway through the hotel's lobby, leaving just enough space for arriving and departing guests to pass between the lifts and the entrance.

Distracting himself with happier thoughts as his emotions overflowed again, he wondered which room had been reserved for their stay tonight. He had asked Cathy to arrange for a single red rose to be placed on his lover's pillow. His wife often did the same for him, but instead of a flower, her gift would be humorous: a toy or something edible.

Convinced by now that the soul he had been mates with for so long had vacated this wounded body, Jeff forced himself to admit the time had come to let go of her physical incarnation. With one last kiss on her lips, the fingers of his left hand brushed her eyelids closed. She looked peaceful, and he sensed somehow that they had exchanged a silent farewell.

A pair of plain-clothed detectives now stood close behind him. The grieving man had tracked their approach out of the corner of his eye. They too scarcely believed what they were seeing, confronted with the same shocking scene.

The world's greatest lover stood up and drank in the beauty of this exquisite woman who had shared over half his life. 'Thanks for everything, angel,' he murmured. 'I love you so much. See you soon.'

The police investigation was clearly underway, the star realised. He could hear a deep, authoritative voice telling bystanders that under no circumstances were they to answer any questions from journalists or reporters. Several people asked questions, and others whispered and pointed as they caught sight of the revered celebrity.

'Mr Diamond,' the higher-ranking officer addressed the rock star. 'I'm Detective Inspector Robert Fisher.'

Jeff shook the man's extended hand. 'G'day.'

'I'm very sorry for your loss,' Fisher continued, embarrassed by his own emotional reaction. 'Tragic loss for us all. Come this way, please.'

The bereaved husband turned back to where his beautiful best friend sat, his head throbbing with unspent emotion. 'Not yet. I'm not ready to leave her.'

The senior detective moved to take hold of Jeff's elbow, only to have it snatched from his fingers. 'We need to secure the area, sir, and ask you a few questions, if you don't mind.'

Wiping the latest surge of tears from his cheeks, the superstar sighed. He did mind, but what was the point? Taking one last look at his only true love, he followed the inspector and his offsider across the lobby and into a room behind the reception desk.

A few stunned employees tried their best to serve complimentary beverages, answer questions and pacify distressed guests all at the same time. All eyes tracked the washed-out celebrity as he slipped into the sanctuary of the back office. For the first time in many years, he felt completely helpless and totally alone.

'Please sit down, Mr Diamond,' DI Fisher requested, signalling towards an armchair.

'Jeff, please,' the tall man replied, doing as he was told. 'I have a question for you, before we get started, if I may…'

The veteran investigator studied the well-known visage as its owner struggled to utter the phrase he and his partner had agreed together, hoping they would never have cause to articulate it.

'Lynn planned to donate her organs. I think we can safely assume she's not coming back, so at what stage do you guys take her wishes into account?'

'That's a very good question,' the senior detective replied. 'It's good of you to think about such a thing at this time, sir. The paramedic team'll be told when they get here, though I doubt whether the circumstances of her death and the time it'll take to process the scene will make this possible, I'm afraid.'

Fisher stood up and left the room, reassuring the impressive Australian icon that he would relay this futile instruction straightaway. He figured the Coroner would require the body to remain intact, especially in what would inevitably turn into a high-profile case. Another set of vital organs lost to the ever-lengthening waiting list of worthy recipients.

From out in the foyer, Jeff's attention was drawn to the familiar ring-tone of his wife's mobile. The distinctive tune brought with it a renewed wave of grief, along with the sudden realisation that he should let his management company know that lunch was off. His own handset was in his leather jacket, which he had last seen on a baggage trolley, draped over their suitcases.

He turned to the red-haired receptionist who was hovering in the doorway. 'I need to make a phone call, if that's OK?'

Miriam nodded, tears spilling down her cheeks again. 'Yes, of course, sir. There's a phone over there. Dial zero for an outside line.'

She pointed to a desk on the far side of the office, shuddering with a sickening feeling of déjà-vu. Jeff crossed the floor and dialled the number for his public relations manager. After a few rings, a woman's voice answered.

'Cath, hi. It's me,' he announced, sounding much calmer than he felt. 'Yeah. In Sydney. Listen, I need a huge favour. No. Actually, nothing's OK. Is there someone there with you? Good.'

Assembling the facts he now had to put into words made the billionaire cry again too. The more junior detective slipped out of the room while the bereaved man made his call, lingering awkwardly behind the reception desk. Desperate to stifle his emotions, Jeff continued, anticipating this to be one of the hardest messages he would ever have to deliver, and a trial run for the even more gruelling version he must shortly impart to his children.

'Cath, there's no easy way to tell you this, so I'm sorry.'

'Sorry? Pardon? No easy way to tell me what?' he heard from the other end of the line. 'What's wrong?'

Her boss took a deep breath and swapped the receiver to the other ear while he wiped his eyes. 'Lynn's dead, Cathy.'

'Dead? No! She can't be. How? When?'

Jeff looked at his watch. He had no idea how or when.

'Fuck, I don't know,' he cried. 'About half an hour ago maybe? We're in The Pensione. She was shot in the head.'

By now, Stonebridge Music's marketing manager was weeping too. 'No! Oh, my God, Jeff. It can't be true. That's terrible, Jeff. What about you? Are you alright?'

'No,' the morose songwriter sniffed. 'Can't say I am. Listen... Please could you let the Childlight Sydney people know to make our excuses at lunch today? Don't tell them anything specific. Just say something like "unavoidably detained".'

The habitual showman found himself laughing, instantly filled with self-loathing. How could he crack a joke at a time like this?

'Use your imagination, Cath, please?' he grunted at the capable administrator. 'And then close the office and go home. I don't know when the news'll break, so just go home and do your best to forget about it.'

'Forget about it? Jeff, how do you expect me to forget about something like this?' Cathy pleaded. 'Are you sure there's nothing I can do?'

'Look, I can't talk now,' Jeff told her, fighting to maintain his own composure. 'I'm sorry. I don't mean to be rude. I need to ring the kids and deal with the police. I'll call you back later. Thanks, Cath.'

The star didn't wait for his assistant's reply and terminated the call, leaning heavily on the desk to catch his breath. The pair of detectives immediately re-entered the room, thereby eliminating all sense of perceived privacy.

'Jeff, would you like some tea or coffee?' DI Fisher asked.

'Yeah. Jesus Christ! Coffee. Thanks. That'd be great. What happens now?'

'Please sit down. And please call me Bob. This is Detective Sergeant Andy Waters, and we're from the Major Crimes squad at Surry Hills. We'll get that coffee on the go.'

Jeff nodded to Waters, who had the demeanour of a man completely out of his depth. The pair sat down and stared at the floor in silence, waiting for the superior officer to return.

'SOCO's here,' Fisher informed his colleague. 'That's Scene of the Crime Officers, Mr Diamond. Sorry.'

'Cheers. I know,' the civilian raised his hand. 'And it's Jeff.'

It was a long time since the former Sydneysider had found himself this close to a police operation, yet the terminology was etched indelibly into his brain. He wondered whether the older detective might remember his father's case but chose not to bother to find out today.

DS Waters left the room, presumably to supervise the SOCO team. A tray of coffee was brought into the room by one of the scared receptionists, who said nothing and avoided everyone's gaze.

'Thanks,' Jeff said, watching her scurry away. 'It's tough on these guys. Do they all have to stick around?'

'For the moment, yes,' Bob affirmed. 'We need to at least have a brief chat with each potential witness, and then we'll call everyone into the station to provide a statement over the next few days.'

'Was the guy I caught trying to leave...'

The musician broke down again. It was difficult to come to terms with the probability of having apprehended his own wife's killer. He who was descended from one murderer had fallen victim to another. Miss Irony, his old flame, seized his heart with both imaginary hands, keen to declare her finest hour had come.

'Jeez. Sorry,' the dejected man growled, taking a deep breath and running his hands through his hair. 'Was he the bloke who shot her?'

'Certainly a suspect,' Fisher nodded. 'We have him in custody already.'

'Am I a suspect?' the superstar asked, instantly regretting such a rash question.

'Not at this stage,' the stone-faced detective answered. 'From what we can gather so far, your wife was asked to take a phone call a minute or so before the gun was fired. It's too early to draw any conclusions. It appears the two events may be linked, but we don't have any information as to who made this call.'

A trap, the intellectual thought; premeditated. He kept quiet, deep in contemplation as he sipped the hot, sweet coffee. Despite his denial, something in Bob's tone seemed to suggest a scent of suspicion wafting his way.

Abruptly, he lifted his head and addressed the policeman again. 'Christ! I need to phone my daughter. D'you mind?'

DI Fisher shook his head, stood up and headed for the door. 'Of course, Jeff. We need to ask you a few questions as soon as you're ready. While things are fresh in your mind.'

Shit! The former bad-boy knew this tactic well, and it filled him with shame. They obviously hadn't satisfied themselves that he was the innocent party in this situation. He hadn't had to fight for his freedom for many years and wondered whether he still possessed the guile to outsmart these trained investigators.

'Would you mind asking someone to track down my jacket, please?' Jeff called after the senior officer. 'My mobile phone's in one of the pockets.'

The inspector raised a hand in acknowledgement and continued down the corridor. Jeff struggled to remember where Kierney had been going this morning. It was now that he realised the benefit of paying attention to everyone's schedule, yet the person who would undoubtedly have this information to hand could no longer tell him.

Dialling the number for the family's city apartment, his fingers hovered over the button, preparing to hang up before the answering machine message began. He couldn't bear the idea of hearing his wife's voice.

When it became clear that no-one was in, Jeff pressed down on the switch hook and exhaled, hunching over as if he had taken a blow to the stomach. After pausing to gather his thoughts, he dialled another sequence of digits which he hoped would connect him to Kierney's mobile.

'Hey, Kizzo. *Soy yo.*'

'Hi, Papá!' his daughter sounded delighted to hear from him. 'What's up? Good flight?'

Relieved that he had guessed correctly, Jeff's eyes immediately began to sting again. He was about to scatter all the goodness from this gorgeous creature's day. How could anyone be so cruel? His brown-eyed girl, with her infinite compassion and enthusiasm for life, was seconds away from discovering she and her brother were a parent short.

Must he tell her over the telephone, or could he convince her to board an aeroplane without knowing why? She would do so simply at his request, but that wasn't treating her with the respect she deserved.

'Where are you, *pequeñita*?'

He had to tell her straight, hoping she had some friends around her. There was no alternative. Lynn and he had always been up-front with their children and had sought nothing less from them in return.

'Are you OK?' Kierney replied, hearing a strained tone in her father's voice. 'You sound weird.'

'Yeah? I am weird, gorgeous. You know that. But listen... Are you alone?'

'*Sorta-kinda.* I'm in the studio working on some songs with Dane and Eddy. Why?'

'Jesus, Kiz,' Jeff blurted between involuntary sobs. 'I need you to get on the next flight here, please. Something terrible's happened, and we need to be together.'

'Why? What, Papá?' the teenager asked, frightened. '*¿Qué ha pasado?*'

'Christ Almighty! I can't believe I'm having this conversation with you. Life's gone totally to shit. *La mamá está muerta.* She's dead, baby.'

There was silence from the other end of the telephone line. Several seconds passed when neither father nor daughter made a sound, yet they understood each other perfectly. Jeff waited for a response, feeling slightly more stable now the news had been shared.

'How?'

'Someone shot her in the head, angel,' he groaned. 'That's all we know. I was parking the fucking toy car they gave us. She took a phone call in the hotel foyer and now she's gone.'

The father was sobbing again, slumped on the couch with his head in his hand and the receiver stuck to the side of his unshaven face in a mixture of sweat and tears. He could hear Kierney weeping and a man's voice in the background asking if she was alright. Good, he thought, at least their sound engineers were there to help her out.

'Papá?'

'*Sí*, I'm here. I'll ring Gerry and ask him to meet you at the airport. And Grandpa too.'

A shudder ran down his neck. That was a call he wasn't looking forward to... His head ached with abject fear. Why was he always the one who had to break the bad news? It was just like the old days. How did a man tell a father that his daughter was shot dead while he was parking the car?

'You ring Gerry, and I'll ring Grandpa,' Kierney suggested, sounding heart-wrenchingly like her mother: business-like and in control.

'Absolutely not,' her dad overruled, although sorely tempted to be let off this most dreadful of hooks. 'I can't possibly leave you to pass on such a shithouse piece of information. That's my responsibility, gorgeous. I'll call them both now, and then you ring Grandpa in about fifteen minutes. Is that OK?'

'OK, Papá. *Comprendo.* Don't worry. I'll be up there as soon as I can. I can go right now. I don't need to bring anything, do I?'

'No. *Nada, nada.* Just yourself,' he sniffed. 'Just you. *Gracias, pequeñita. Te amo.*'

Ending the call, the desperate man sat staring into space, wondering how this dreadful day might unfold. Where was their luggage? Would they allow him to see

Lynn again? Should Kierney see her mother in this state? Would she even want to? When would he be able to tell their son the terrible news?

Fisher cleared his throat to attract the superstar's attention. 'Sorry, Jeff,' he began, 'but DS Waters and I need to ask you some questions about your whereabouts at the time of the shooting.'

'Sure. What d'you want to know? I'm not sure my memory'll be able to give you anything too clear right now.'

His head pounding with the pressure of having to concentrate his curdling mind, the celebrity rewound and replayed the morning's events for the two detectives. With each sentence, his heart sank deeper and deeper into the depths of despair.

'I'd dropped Lynn outside the entrance while I went to park the rental next-door, as we normally do when we stay here. A small gesture of chivalry on my part, that's all. The world's most beautiful woman shouldn't have to traipse through dank and dirty car parks. And trying to save a few minutes' time in a busy day too, I guess.'

Waters' pen scratched across the pages of his notebook, capturing as much information as possible while his boss pieced a sequence together on his own timeline. They would need evidence of the couple's luncheon invitation, their flight details and room reservation. Dictating Cathy Lane's number from memory, Jeff assured them she was a much more reliable source than he was, even at the best of times.

'I'd like to know how you identified the man you apprehended as the shooter before you'd even got into the hotel?' the inspector changed tack suddenly.

The celebrity inhaled, knocking his head against the wall above the couch in frustration. 'Jesus Christ! What are you insinuating with this question? I didn't identify him as anyone. It was a complete effing coincidence.'

'Did you speak to him? Can you remember what he said to you?' Bob asked.

Jeff took a restorative breath and stubbed out his cigarette, staring at the detective's pen, which was poised above his notepad. Leaning forward, he fixated on the patterned carpet for a few moments before formulating an answer. He could visualise the man's face well enough and set about reconstructing their short confrontation. He recalled noticing its look of astonishment as the pair met outside the revolving doors. It made him smile.

The senior officer shuffled his feet. 'What's funny?'

'Sorry,' the intellectual lifted his gaze. 'It's just such a bitter irony, isn't it?'

'What's that?' Fisher stiffened, twisting the barrel of his ballpoint back and forth.

His interviewee smiled. 'Well... You go somewhere intending to kill someone, kill the guy's wife instead and then get caught by the very bloke you set out to kill in the first place. That truly must've been a "Life's a bitch" moment, don't you reckon?'

The inspector remained serious, his professional duty overruling any sense of humour he might earlier have revealed. 'This is not a joking matter, Mr Diamond. You're still in shock. We could do this later.'

'I'm not in shock. It's only my warped mind,' the bitter man contradicted. 'I know how people's brains work. I heard someone... Chris Nichols, I suppose... shout for no-one to leave, so I stopped him leaving. The guy spoke to me in Spanish.

'At first I didn't hear him because there was a racket coming from inside the building and the doors were creaking their way round, so I asked him to repeat it. He then said something like, "I wanted to kill you, but this way's better," which I'm guessing is pretty much what he said in the first place.'

Jeff paused to flash his dark eyes at the older detective. It was his impression that under different circumstances they might enjoy each other's company. Now however, they were only making things worse for each other.

'I wanted to grab the bastard's arm and shake the words out of him,' the widower continued, sickened by the recollection, 'but thought better of it. Lucky I had my hands full with our luggage, otherwise I might've done. I have PTSD, by the way, Bob. I've learnt not to go with my instincts. Just so you know...'

'Yes,' Fisher nodded. 'I think I read that somewhere about you. Post-Traumatic Stress Disorder. Quite a few of my old uniform mates suffer from the same thing. Nasty business. Anyway... Please carry on. Did you say anything else to him? Or him to you?'

'Nope. Don't think so. I might've leant into him a bit 'cause he looked scared. Then he did a one-eighty and went back into the hotel. When we got inside, I left him with the security guy. Neither of us said anything else to each other. That's all I can recall.'

The forty-three-year-old fiddled with his black jet-stone ring, so long on his finger that he hardly knew it was there. He swivelled it around on his finger and then, chuckling at the reflex action, did the same thing with his wedding ring on the other hand.

'Fuck,' he muttered under his breath.

No more beautiful best friend. No more marriage. Family in disarray. How quickly life could change.

With some relief, he saw his mobile had been left on the coffee table while he had been facing the window, speaking to Kierney. Cursing under his breath at the missed calls he would now have to return, he picked it up and selected his business manager's name from the list of numbers.

'Lord Sparkle, how goes?' Gerry Blake's greeting was as bombastic as ever. 'Aren't you in Sydney today?'

'Yes, mate,' his most important client replied. 'They've had phones up here for a while now, you idiot.'

'That's enough, you smart-arse. What can I do for you? I was just heading downstairs for a coffee with the lovely Fiona.'

'Mate, I need your help, please. It's an emergency. I need you to get to Tullamarine as fast as you can and fly up here with Kierney.'

'Fly to Sydney? Why? What sort of emergency? Is she OK?'

'No, mate . None of us is OK.'

'Why? What do you mean? What the hell's happened?' Gerry demanded, sensing this was not the usual hiccough in proceedings for his long-time buddy.

'She's dead, mate,' the songwriter answered, dispensing with any fancy euphemisms or decoration.

How many more times would he have to say these words? Jeff felt his heart pounding in his chest.

'Jesus, Mary and Joseph,' the suave executive murmured. 'Who's dead? Lynn? Tell me this is some practical joke you're inflicting on me.'

The successful Melbourne accountant found it impossible to believe his most important client's words could be true. He and his new lady had only met up with the forever couple for dinner a few nights ago, and now it appeared some sort of disaster had struck.

'Oh, I wish, mate. Fucking hell! It's chaos here. Police everywhere. I think I caught the bloke who did it, trying to leave the hotel.'

'Holy shit! You *are* serious. Lynn's been murdered? How did it happen?' his manager asked, his voice muffled now. 'Oh, my God. No way…'

Jeff could hear his old friend crying too. Lynn was loved by everyone. It was important to remember this fact. He wasn't the only one who would be devastated by her death.

'A clean shot to the head,' the celebrity recounted with surprising detachment. 'Sitting in the hotel lobby, answering a bloody phone call.'

'Christ, mate. That's fucked. How are you going? Are you OK?'

'No. Not the best,' the younger man sniffed, grateful for his friend's innocent question. 'Can you go to the airport, please, mate? I spoke to Kizzy about five minutes ago. She said she'd go straight there. I need you to go right now 'cause I don't want her to be on her own for too long. I've got to contact old man Dyson too, if I can get hold of him.'

'Sure thing, mate. Of course. What's Kizzy's number? I'll see if I can give her a lift.'

'No need,' Jeff replied, forcing a smile. 'She got her licence. Yesterday.'

Gerry allowed himself a chuckle too. 'Shit! Did she really? Already? That makes me feel very old.'

'Yep. Tell me about it. Anyway, I've got to go. There's a posse of policemen wanting to question us all. I'd better get off the phone.'

'Right-oh. We'll see you as soon as we can. Hang on in there, mate. Does Cath know?'

'Yeah. We had to cancel our lunch thing, and I told those guys to go home. It'd be good if you can ring her too, at some point. She was pretty gutted. Cheers, Gez,' the seasoned campaigner rambled, once more slipping into autopilot. 'Thanks heaps.'

The call crackled and then fell quiet. Jeff leant forward, elbows on knees, and his shoulders began to shake violently as delayed shock set in. His mind flashed back to the other evening, when his forty-six-year-old buddy had introduced Fiona in person for the first time.

All four had been in high spirits, he and Lynn keen to share in their fun-loving friend's new joy. They were also just back from New York, where the chart-topping performers had received yet another recording industry award for the "Live On Earth" album.

The rock star's numbed mind tried to picture his better half smiling at the pair's drunken banter. He remembered how, drinking coffee back in Gerry's luxurious bachelor pad after dinner, he had circled his arm behind her and squeezed her so close. She nestled into him, as she always did, because she knew how much he liked it. They had made love that night, as they always did, with the slow-burning passion of two people who had worshipped each other's body for a lifetime or more.

Dismissing these pleasant thoughts with great reluctance, Jeff dragged himself back to the horrible reality which had befallen them. Time was ticking by, and there was no way he wanted Kierney to speak to Bart Dyson before he had. His heart raced, and the blood vessels throbbed in his head as he selected some choice words for his father-in-law to absorb. How would he react? Which important meeting was about to be disrupted? Where was he, even?

The widower stood tall and scrolled through the contacts in his phone, searching for Bart Dyson's office number. He was gripped with fear at the prospect of breaking the news to the imposing Olympian. Walking over to the door and closing it, he pressed the green button and took a few deep breaths.

'Dyson Administration,' a bright voice answered. 'How may I direct your call?'

'G'day,' Jeff croaked, forcing his vocal cords to function normally. 'It's Jeff Diamond. Is Mr Dyson in the office?'

'Oh, yes. Hello, Mr Diamond. I'll put you through to his PA,' the operator responded.

The line clicked twice and was picked up by Penny, Lynn's father's executive assistant. The musician took another deep breath and repeated his question.

'Oh, Jeff. It's lovely to hear from you,' came another cheerful reply. 'Bart's in a meeting and has asked not to be disturbed. I can ask him to call you back as soon as he's free.'

'No,' the son-in-law countered. 'Sorry, but this is more important, Penny, actually. It's urgent that I speak to him right now, if you don't mind.'

Hesitation in the woman's voice made him even more nervous. 'Oh, I see,' she faltered. 'Is something wrong?'

'Yes. Something's very wrong,' Jeff threw his head back in frustration. 'Please ask him to come to the phone. I really need to talk to him now.'

'Very well. Of course. I'll see what I can do,' the well-spoken woman complied, picking up on an unusually insistent tone from the great man. 'Hold on, please.'

The frantic caller had no choice. He held on for what seemed like an hour, going over and over some glib lines which seemed so inadequate to describe the tragedy. He had broken out in a cold sweat, just like in the old days, and the handset slipped in his hand.

'Jeff, how are you?' the sportsman blustered. 'I gather you need to talk to me urgently. What's up?'

Momentarily tongue-tied, the younger man rocked back on his heels to stop himself from falling over. He who was seldom lost for words found himself struck dumb. As he pieced an opening sentence together, he felt his legs weaken under him.

'Bart, I have some terrible news.'

'Terrible news?'

'Yes, sir,' Jeff nodded, exhaling through pursed lips. ''Fraid so. Lynn and I flew to Sydney this morning for a charity function, and some bastard took a shot at her in the lobby of the hotel. I can't believe I'm telling you this, but Lynn passed away at the scene.'

Bart Dyson didn't reply. The delay was terrifying, compelling the musician to continue the conversation. As he had told his daughter, this disagreeable task was his responsibility.

His conscience played him a memory of Lynn clowning around with the children in one of her many lessons on good manners: when one's wife is shot while one is parking the car, one cannot shirk one's duty to inform her parents, no matter how much one might wish to stick one's head in the sand...

'We think we caught the gunman,' the lonely man spoke into the mouthpiece, switching the telephone to the other ear and drying his palm on his trouser leg. 'We don't know who he is or why he did it, but she's dead. Stone fucking dead.'

'Jeff... Are you... Oh, God,' a much frailer version of the usual ebullience eventually squeezed into the caller's brain. 'Oh, my God. Why? Why would anyone want to kill Lynn?'

The bereaved superstar couldn't hold back the tears any longer. 'I have no idea, sir. I reckon he meant to get me. I caught the fucker trying to leave the hotel. He was a bloody nobody. A runt carrying a gun. I don't know why he was there or what his motive was, but he told me he wanted to kill me. But he didn't, did he? He killed your perfect daughter instead.'

'Oh, my God,' the older man repeated.

'I'm sorry, Bart. So, so sorry to have to tell you this.'

Having surmounted the worst of his initial shock, the Olympian's voice resumed its louder and more forceful timbre. 'Oh, for God's sake, Jeff. Don't apologise to me. She was your wife. Bloody hell. This is a day I've always feared. Where the hell do these lunatics come from? And why do they single out the people who do the most good? She's the mother of your children, Jeff. Oh…'

The songwriter slumped down onto the sofa and rested his aching back against the firm cushion, listening to his father-in-law sobbing. This was a day he had always feared too, and one for which they had put every conceivable contingency in place to avert. Every conceivable contingency except always allowing the valet to park the sports car…

'Jesus fucking Christ,' he hissed, cupping his hand over the mouthpiece.

'Excuse me?' Bart croaked. 'Sorry, Jeff? I missed that.'

'No. Nothing, sir. Are you able to get on the next flight up here? Gerry's meeting Kierney at the airport. I don't want her to fly on her own.'

'No, no. Of course not. I'll leave straightaway.'

'Thanks a lot. Have you got Gerry Blake's number?'

'Yes. I'm sure we do somewhere. And I have Kierney's too.'

'She'll be ringing you about now,' his son-in-law added, his voice husky again as an image flashed into his mind of his little lady preparing to talk to her grandfather about a wholly grown-up topic. 'I'd appreciate it if you could ring her first, if you can.'

'Definitely, Jeff. No problem. I'll organise to leave in the next ten minutes. Oh, my God. I have to speak to Marianna too. Two children gone now. Jesus fucking Christ.'

The widower had to laugh, but did so as kindly as he could. He didn't recall ever hearing the fine pillar of society use any form of vulgarity before, and it sounded peculiar, even under these extreme circumstances.

'That's exactly what I said earlier,' he admitted, 'when you didn't hear me. Fucking Jesus, fucking Christ, eh?'

The older man chuckled too. 'Indeed. You're a good man, Jeff. I'll be there as soon as I can. Don't worry about Kierney. We'll look after her. Just look after yourself.'

'Cheers, Bart. That's great. Safe flight. And I'm sorry again. *Adiós.*'

With his head once more in his hands, the celebrity terminated the call and wept with renewed anguish. He was not a good man, regardless of his father-in-law's endorsement. He had let someone's daughter die. In fact, over the course of his life he had let three people's daughters die. And here he was, waiting for his own innocent girl to arrive and make him feel better; something he deserved even less than the compliment.

Forcing himself out of the depressive spiral already taking hold, the modern-day philosopher wondered what this nameless gunman had hoped to accomplish by killing either of them. Who was he, this Spanish-speaking bloke who had appeared so ordinary and unassuming? Was he a lunatic, as Bart suggested? Or perhaps he was championing a cause. What had they done to push him to such an extreme measure?

Through the blur of memories and questions, Jeff slowly became aware of the two detectives loitering at his side, along with the hotel manager.

GONE

The staff at The Pensione had been looking forward to seeing the famous couple in their hotel again. A celebrity endorsement was always good publicity of course, not to mention the buzz that the odd spot of stardust added to the routine of a day's work.

The Diamonds' booking had been made several weeks ago, and the team had rehearsed a number of ad hoc conversation pieces in case they found themselves in a lift together or delivering room service. Now was not the time for formalities and protocol however.

Chris Nichols reached across and rested a hand on his guest's arm. The trembling man was grateful, this simple gesture steadying his nerves. Even though it had been over a quarter of a century since his last brush with the law, policemen still put him on edge. With instinctive good grace, he stood up to resume the interview.

Before Jeff had a chance to offer an apology for holding up proceedings, the sergeant requested he stay seated, and the detectives made themselves comfortable on the couch across from him. Andy Waters was younger than the victim's husband, probably by ten years. Fisher was older by about the same margin. All four men gazed at each other, stunned to the core by the morning's awful event.

'Jeff,' Bob opened, 'I can see this is extremely difficult for you.'

You don't say, cursed the bitter adolescent inside the billionaire's head, whose outer shell urged the senior officer to carry on.

'We receive training on how to deal with next of kin in violent crimes. We're taught how to counsel the bereaved, but in truth, we know full well we can't relate to what you're going through. You're a public figure as well. Everyone knows you and your lovely wife. Loves you both, I should say, for everything you do. I think it's important that we try to make things as simple as possible.'

'Thanks,' Jeff sighed. 'You won't get any objection from me on that score.'

Fisher was right. They had no idea how he felt. In fact, right at this moment, they were making him feel like the prime suspect. He was also beginning to feel particularly cold and could do with his jacket. Had they impounded it? Nothing was clear anymore.

He shivered, retrieving the squashed packet of cigarettes from the breast pocket of his shirt. 'D'you mind?'

The trio opposite shook their heads, and Chris went to collect an ashtray. A woman dressed in a green paramedic's uniform knocked on the open door and entered, boldly at first, then stopped short when she came face-to-face with her idol. Sensing the woman's indecision, DI Fisher rose to his feet and walked her out again. They exchanged a few hushed sentences before the inspector came back full of purpose.

'The Coroner's people are ready to examine your wife's body, Jeff,' he stated. 'Just letting you know what's going on. Then DS Waters and I'll take a statement from you.'

Taking the unlit cigarette out of his mouth and returning it to the open pack, the songwriter jumped up, noticing the fracas in the foyer had subsided. Pretty soon, there would be no trace of anything unusual having happened here this morning.

The hotel had a business to run, and the show must go on. A whirlwind of fury whipped through his body. How dare they? This was his dream girl they were dealing with. What made them think they could pick their way over Lynn Dyson Diamond without permission?

'I want to see her again first,' he barked, shaking the cramp out of his legs, 'if that's OK.'

Before anyone could stop him, the celebrity left the room and strode over to where the love of his life still sat, surrounded by evidence labels and tiny plastic bags.

DS Waters ran after him. 'Mr Diamond! Jeff! Stay clear of the crime scene, sir.'

The striking figure lurched to a standstill and accepted defeat in front of amazed onlookers. All he wanted to do was to scoop Lynn's body up in his arms. What would the examiners find? The thought of her suffering excruciating pain in the last few seconds of her life caused a loud roar to rise up from deep within, startling everyone from their trance.

Pulling the door closed behind him once everyone had returned to the office, Bob Fisher spoke. 'Take your time, Jeff.'

The celebrity nodded. For some unknown reason, his grief-stricken mind flew back to the stupendous afternoon when his nineteen-year-old dream girl had turned up at his apartment after informing her parents that she intended to choose him as her partner for life in spite of their vehement reservations about his suitability. That same evening, she had accepted his request to move in with him.

How awkward it had seemed during those first few hours as a *de facto* couple! Feeling a little calmer already, Jeff tried to summon another happy moment in their extraordinary life, speculating whether a person's stored experiences were erased upon his or her last breath. Or whether, as he ardently hoped, Lynn might still be able to summon their shared happy moments too. Their wedding, for example, where they had vowed eternal love in front of their families, friends and a slew of dignitaries whom they hardly knew. What a fantastic day that had been too! The happiness had shone from his new wife's eyes while singing to each other after exchanging rings.

Memory after sweet memory crowded into his head: the births of their amazing children; the many tours endured and holidays enjoyed all over the world; and the various significant birthdays spent in the bosom of their family. Then there was the "Together, Forever, Wherever" campaign which had set the world's imagination alight and the fundraising coffers filling; and very recently, their quiet day at Benloch, where twenty years of blissful marriage received private salutation in bare, balletic beauty under the gum trees at Coldwater Creek.

His true love had left him. Unintentionally, he understood, but she had left him nonetheless. The superstar felt voided and abandoned, sensing the walls caving in around him. So his debts hadn't been paid after all... And if he weren't careful, Gravity the Troll may soon come out of retirement. The dealer of so many years of depression would be limbering up right now, already preparing to dance at his saviour's wake.

The spared soul didn't blame his *regala* for leaving him. He had always suspected such gifts to be transitory. If he hadn't been playing boy-racer with that stupid Mercedes, his body would be lying dead in a hideous garbage bag instead of hers. Their misfortune was neither of their faults.

DS Waters knocked on the door and opened it, and the two officers entered. Fisher sat down while his subordinate offered the victim's husband a cigarette, which was accepted with anxious fingers.

'What a bloody mess,' Jeff grumbled, dragging hard and raising his eyes to the ceiling as he exhaled.

Andy Waters grunted. Patches of sweat spreading over the front of his blue shirt, he also appeared to be struggling with the day's events. Constant coughing gave his nerves away, and he avoided eye contact with the famous humanitarian who was admired by almost everyone he knew.

A complex dogfight of emotions was tearing the widower apart as the initial shock began to give way to the fear of what lay ahead. He tried to work out how long it would take for Kierney, Gerry and Bart to arrive. He couldn't remember what time he had called them, but it seemed like an eternity ago.

The air-conditioning was blasting out an Antarctic breeze, so he heaved himself up and pointed to a thermostat on the wall. 'D'you think we could turn this up a little warmer, please?'

'Yes. Go ahead, sir.'

'Hurry up, Kizzy,' he muttered as he adjusted the thermostat.

The seasoned campaigner was fed up with having to cope with disaster on his own yet again. He wanted to cry, yell and be sick all at once, but he did none of these. Instead, he poured himself another cup of tepid coffee and gulped it down. As the dizziness overtook him, he almost fell back onto the couch, leant his head against the wall and closed his eyes, desperate for a modicum of self-control to pacify his crazed mind.

You've come a long way, chico.

It was funny how life always managed to trip him up, ebbing and flowing in random circles. He had written songs about this too. Shit! His fate was only following instructions. The tormented composer jumped as his telephone sprang to life in his back pocket. Reaching behind him, he pulled it out and checked the screen, his mood improving as soon as he accepted the call.

'Hey, gorgeous.'

'Papá, it's me,' Kierney's greeting was tentative. 'Are you OK?'

'Yeah. Now I am. How about you?'

'We're fine, thanks. Confused and shocked, but OK-ish. We've landed, obviously.'

'That's good to know, obviously.'

The young woman giggled at their customary banter. 'We'll be with you in about twenty minutes, but we weren't sure which hotel you're in.'

This first contact from his gipsy girl overwhelmed the grateful father. He thought he heard a croak in her voice, as if she were trying not to cry, yet she was as calm and dignified as always. His daughter was turning into a classy lady of late, just like her mother.

'The Pensione. It's on George Street in the CBD.'

'Oh, cool. *Gracias*. That's what I thought,' Kierney responded cheerfully. 'Do you need us to bring anything?'

'Nope. Just get here as soon as you can, please, baby. I need you. Is Gerry with you?'

'Yes, and Grandpa.'

'*Bueno, pequeñita*. See you soon. Thanks for checking in,' the widower waited for his lifeline to say goodbye before ending the call and returning his attention to his inquisitors. 'Did you find the weapon?'

'No. Our officers are sweeping the area,' Waters jumped in, watching further colour drain from the superstar's face.

'Didn't anyone hear the shots?' the intelligent man asked, his mind imagining the gun abandoned, plunged into the soil of a planter somewhere in the hotel. 'Must've had a silencer, I guess...'

The superior officer glared at his colleague. 'We're unable to disclose any of these details as yet. Were you aware he was carrying a firearm?'

Jeff looked up. 'No. I was only asking. Am I a suspect now? Too curious for my own good. Should I be asking for a lawyer?'

Fisher coughed. 'Mr Diamond, please stay calm. We're not ruling anything out at this early stage. There are often more people involved in a murder than the person who carries out the crime.'

'You think I had my wife killed?' the distraught man threw his hands in the air, ash falling from his cigarette. 'Jesus! That's so bloody ridiculous, but I guess you need to cover all bases. What possible motivation could I have? She was everything to me. I'm sorry, gents. My wife has a bullet hole in her head. Doesn't take Einstein to figure out there was a gun involved.'

'Alright, Mr Diamond. You're correct, but please remain calm,' Fisher returned to his script. 'Can you tell me if you or your wife have received any death threats lately?'

Jeff shrugged and rolled his eyes. 'Yeah, sure. Apologies, but it's bloody ridiculous to hear I'm implicated in any way. Lynn and I get death threats all the time, so does her family. Goes with the territory. There's a lot of jealous people out there. Statistics'll tell you something like this was bound to happen, after JFK, John Lennon, *et cetera*. Y'know, we...'

The star paused. There was really no point in going into detail.

'Nothing specific we were aware of, no.'

Another round of coffee arrived, this time with a platter of sandwiches too. The hotel's special guest asked the waiter if he could rustle up a bottle of whisky, a request which at first met with fright rather than assent. The young man backed away, muttering that he would seek permission.

'Why are you in Sydney, Jeff?' Bob Fisher continued his questioning.

'To present an award and a sizeable cheque on behalf of one of our charities, at a lunch where we should be in less than an hour's time,' the philanthropist shook his head in disappointment, checking his watch. 'What a failure that'll be for them. We were the guests of honour. And after that, we were due to spend the weekend with some old friends in Mosman.'

Jeff didn't care to remember why they had flown to New South Wales, since the whole experience had changed beyond recognition. He saw an image of Celia and Gerald Blake running out to the car with open arms, eager to console him and Kierney. The elderly couple would know by now, he guessed, because Gerry would have rung ahead and told his parents the terrible news. So their plan for a relaxing weekend spent cajoling an ageing man into moderating his unhealthy habits was destined to turn into a series of desperate ploys to raise everyone's flagging spirits.

If only something more urgent had arisen this morning and forced a change of plan... Jeff wondered how long the dowdy Spaniard had been plotting to kill him. If he hadn't succeeded in pulling the trigger today, presumably the gunman would have switched to "Plan B" anyway. And for how long had they managed to evade "Plan A"?

A bottle of blended Scotch and some glasses were placed on the coffee table. The superstar lifted his eyes in thanks, offering a glass to the detectives. Knowing neither would accept, he poured a large measure for himself, swallowed it down and then straightaway poured another. The smooth, amber liquid nipped at the back of his throat, and he revelled in the fleeting pleasurable sensation.

Voices could be heard outside in the reception area. Jeff jumped to his feet and ran out of the room without a word, followed in haste by Fisher and Waters, who watched on as he took a young woman into his arms.

Kierney Diamond was almost as easily identified as her parents. Growing slender and taller in the last twelve months, and with waves of glossy, dark hair, she was a picture of teenaged beauty. She and her older brother were adored by Australia's youth for their accessibility and lack of pretension, and also because they behaved like normal teenagers. Bob Fisher's own children's bedroom walls had been adorned with posters of the photogenic foursome for years. Youngsters everywhere considered them role models, a responsibility the Diamond and Dyson families were known to take seriously.

Seeing father and daughter clinging to each other in despair was more than the hardest of hearts could endure. Fisher wiped tears from his eyes and shuffled forward to introduce himself to Bart Dyson, who stood to one side, mesmerised by the miserable reunion.

As stoic as ever, the elder statesman greeted the officer in his typical diplomatic and gracious manner, before beckoning to Gerry Blake. The senior detective recognised this new arrival as the agent who had often been pictured with the Diamonds. Shaking the tall businessman's hand warmly, Bob led the others away from Jeff and Kierney, to join DS Waters and Chris Nichols in the office.

As the loyal Irishman passed by, he gave his old friend a couple of quick pats on the back of his shoulder. Extending his right arm behind him as he held on to his daughter, the songwriter let his manager grasp his hand with both his own.

The bereft father hugged Kierney so hard. 'Why?' he kept saying, over and over again. 'Why?'

The young woman was sobbing too. She had spent the last few hours hoping that what her papá had told her over the telephone was untrue. Yet seeing him in this state and accompanied by police, she knew the worst must have happened. She held onto him tightly too, neither bothered by the attention they drew.

On her way through the hotel's entrance hall, the eighteen-year-old had noticed a section of the foyer cordoned off, assuming it to be the scene of the shooting. Her head was full of questions. How had a man with a gun managed to hide himself in this open area? What kind of security measures did the hotel claim to take to protect its guests?

'¿Donde está la mamá?' Kierney asked after a long pause.

Jeff stared down into his daughter's beautiful brown eyes, sunken and bloodshot. Blotches of pink on her cheeks betrayed the heartbreak she was doing her best to conceal from the outside world.

'In there,' he pointed to her left, where yellow plastic screening shielded the crime scene from view. 'There are people from the Coroner's office doing untold things to her, and all we can do is wait.'

It wasn't too hard to work out who was supporting whom while the pair of dark-haired Diamonds made their way behind Reception again.

'How does she look?' his daughter whispered. 'Can I see her?'

'Sure, *pequeñita*. We'll all get to see her again soon, I'm sure. She doesn't look too bad considering she's got a hole in her forehead, and there's a lot of blood on her back. I'd guess there are other bullets too, but no-one's telling us anything so far.'

The consummate gentleman saw no point in sharing his cynical views, nor the fact that her father was currently one of the key suspects. He abandoned his usual impeccable manners and chose not to invite the new adult to cross the lobby ahead of him through the narrow channel, and she was glad not to have to go in first.

A party of Japanese tourists whooped with delight at coming face-to-face with the famous celebrities. Appealing for autographs and photographs, the group was disappointed at the star's uncharacteristic brusqueness when the duo walked straight past without stopping.

'They'll know why soon enough,' Kierney put what they were both thinking into words. 'News travels fast.'

The brave pair smiled and gave several shallow bows as they made their way back to Reception, behind which the rest of their contingent was seated in the same small office. Kierney sat down in an empty space beside Gerry, hoping there was enough room for her papá to sit next to her. DS Waters had relaxed at last and was handing everyone fresh mugs of coffee.

Bart Dyson stood to embrace his son-in-law. 'Are you alright, Jeff?'

'Yeah, thanks. I guess so. It's good to see you, sir. How're you going?'

'Shocked,' the resolute Olympian responded. 'DI Fisher here tells me you caught the bloke you think was the gunman.'

The skin around Lynn's father's eyes was sallow and puffier than usual, and he seemed to have aged since the pair last met. Since around ten o'clock that morning, Jeff estimated with a sigh. At sixty-three years old, the sporting hero who had become affectionately known as "Big D" was still a fine figure of a man, although leaner than when in his prime. He kept himself supremely fit, and his towering frame and full head of sandy-grey hair gave him a distinctive and distinguished air.

The Dyson patriarch thought the world of his children and grandchildren, even though he rarely admitted it to their faces. He was a proud man, reluctant to show much affection. Against all expectations, he had also grown fond of Jeff Diamond over the years, respecting his achievements enormously. They not only equalled his own but had often surpassed them, and his farsightedness and compassion for the less fortunate were humbling even for the elder statesman.

And now, gazing from the grieving husband to his devastated daughter, the impact of this high-profile murder was beginning to sink in.

'I'm so sorry,' Jeff said, seeing the tears well up in Bart's eyes as they hugged for a second time. 'I should've been here. It should've been me, I know. Lynn wasn't meant to die today.'

Gerry Blake remained in the background, preferring to let the family members deal with the situation at their own pace. He had consoled Kierney during the hour-long flight from Melbourne and speculated at great length with Mr Dyson about his daughter's untimely demise. Only two nights ago, he and Fiona had listened to their jet-setting friends wax lyrical about their recent trip to New York and describe how they had celebrated their younger child's eighteenth birthday.

Watching his best mate coping with this precipitous loss was agonising, not only because the executive knew how much the forever couple loved each other, but also because he knew the songwriter was bound to shoulder the blame for yet another super-sized catastrophe in their complicated universe.

Everyone sat in silence, drinking their tea or coffee while they waited for someone else to take control. The packet he was carrying now empty, the widower remembered the supply he kept in his coat, the whereabouts of which were still unknown. As absentminded as the rest, he reached into his daughter's handbag, searching for the pack of cigarettes which he knew would be secreted at the bottom, hidden well enough to evade detection by teachers or coaches.

'D'you mind if we smoke?' he asked the dour assembly.

Andy Waters pulled some cigarettes from his own pocket and offered them around. Was he flirting with Kierney? Jeff's radar rarely let him down, and the thought made him glow inside. He would have done much the same thing under similar circumstances... Bart and Gerry both declined, although at this precise moment, the latter was a heartbeat away from breaking his long-standing resolution.

The pack passing over her head on its way, the new adult's eyes flicked upwards. Ruling it inappropriate to mention anything, she rested back against her dad's side. Sniggering at the transparency of her body language, he took the lighted cigarette out of his mouth with his right hand and moved his arm around the youngster's shoulders until his fingers hovered in front of her face. Noting her grandfather's glare of disapproval, Kierney accepted in silent gratitude and snuggled into her papá still closer.

Jeff lit another cigarette from the hidden source he had unearthed in his daughter's bag and glanced over at his manager, hoping his old friend knew how much he appreciated his support. Even though Blake & Partners' success was largely built on the back of the Diamond fortune, Gerry was a formidable businessman. He had been instrumental in many of the well-timed, strategic investment decisions made during the rocker's stellar career. As best mates, their journey together had been stupendous, and the billionaire looked forward to thanking the indomitable one for dropping everything for him today.

Notebook nowhere in sight, Bob Fisher stood to attention and signalled to his colleague to do the same. 'We're about done here,' he announced. 'We'll be in touch to complete our interviews and to let you know how things are progressing with Forensics. The court will require a post-mortem, which takes a few hours to organise. I assume you'll want to take Ms Diamond's body back to Melbourne for the funeral.'

Jeff and Bart exhaled as one, looking at each other in consternation.

'Yeah,' the bereaved husband replied with a grimace. 'We need to start thinking about all that shit, I guess. Jesus effing Christ, I can't deal with this now. I flew up here this morning with my wife's body, in all its glory, sitting right next to me. And now we have to fly down again with it in a box in the cargo hold. Fuckin' 'ell! Don't know about you guys, but it's suddenly all got very final.'

Kierney put a hand on her dad's thigh to console him and watched his knee jump ten centimetres in the air. She had heard about this reflex action from her mother, when she used to describe his symptoms of old. Here they were all over again.

'Sorry, Papá,' she yelped. 'We'll help you with everything.'

Jeff kissed her flushed cheek. 'Baby, I'm sorry too. I didn't mean to freak you out. We'll get through this.'

The two detectives shuffled round in a circle to shake everyone's hand, and DI Fisher handed a business card to each person. Bart Dyson followed them out, seeking answers to some of the questions he hadn't been able to ask while the Diamonds were in the room. His son-in-law noticed them divert into the office next-door and wondered what they might be discussing. Clearly, the old paranoia was back with a vengeance too, along with his cramping legs and compulsive fury.

'You OK, mate?' Jeff asked his manager, who sat dazed and downcast on the other side of the room. 'Thanks heaps for being here.'

'Oh, no worries, Jeff,' Gerry answered. 'I'm utterly effing stunned. I just can't believe it. Is she still where it happened or have they taken her somewhere?'

The executive's normal authoritative demeanour had been temporarily suspended, bringing the consequences of this morning's disaster into sharp relief for the billionaire. He hadn't heard such an uncertain tone from his wingman since their teenage years.

'Yep,' Jeff nodded. 'She's resting. It's a tiring business, getting shot.'

Kierney moaned an objection. 'Oh, for God's sake! Please don't joke about this.'

'Sorry, Kiz. I know,' her father apologised. 'I'm not joking really. It's just bloody hard to know what to do or say. Life as we'd planned this morning is over, and life in the future is unknown. I think we're going to have to live in this *crapacious* sort of no-man's-land until the powers that be tell us what to do.'

Gerry nodded. 'I agree. It's like finding out your meeting's been cancelled but there's no licence to enjoy the free time. Christ! What a terrible state of affairs. You're looking remarkably composed, considering.'

'Am I?,' the rock star replied. 'Y'know, Gez, I'm surprising myself, to tell you the truth. Every now and then, I get a burst of uncontrollable anger or dissolve into a tearful heap, but mostly I'm just numb. Completely fucking numb. Good, I suppose, under the circumstances, but it's bound to smack us hard later.'

'Well, if there's no reason to stick around here,' his manager suggested, 'we might as well drive up to Mum and Dad's. I rang them from the taxi. They're shocked too, mate. Goes without saying. Mum told us to come over whenever we're ready.'

'Cheers, mate. I'm not going anywhere 'til I know what they're doing with Lynn. I want to know where she is at all times. And our suitcases are somewhere in the hotel too. I presume they were taken to whichever room we were supposed to sleep in tonight.'

The Irishman leapt to his feet, pleased to have a task to perform. He was the family's problem-solver after all. This was why they paid him the big bucks, although he now found himself with an irrepressible urge to retire.

'Leave that to me, mate. I'll track your stuff down.'

'OK, thanks,' Jeff smiled, turning to his daughter. 'What d'you want to do now, Kizzo?'

The teenager shrugged. She seemed to have contracted to little-girl proportions, with a lost expression on her face. Her father was filled with sympathy, thinking back to the grown-up behaviour they had seen from her only last night, so proud of her new driver's licence and her upcoming partnership with Youssouf Elhadji.

'I don't know, Papá. Stay with you, that's all.'

'Sure. We'll all stay at Celia's tonight,' the star decided, stroking her cheek. 'I couldn't bear to stay here. Could you?'

Kierney shook her head. 'No way. Where do you think they'll take Mamá?'

Her father groaned. 'To the morgue, I suppose. She's not in her body anymore anyway. I'm sure her soul's flying around at this very moment, searching for a peaceful place to watch us from. What's left over there's only a reminder for us all.'

The young woman burst into tears, and so did her dad. They hugged each other while the outbursts played out. Gerry returned and, seeing them locked in an embrace and with their heads buried against each other's shoulders, wheeled round and walked out again. He had arranged for the couple's luggage to be brought down from their room, so he reverted to the concierge's desk to hire a car to take them to his parents' home on the harbour's northern side.

Meanwhile, Bart Dyson had concluded his discussion with the detectives, meeting the efficient businessman in the reception area.

'They're not doing too well in there,' Gerry said. 'I was going to leave them alone for a while.'

The sportsman poked his head round the door and was relieved to see the father and daughter chatting and reasonably composed. Jeff motioned to his father-in-law.

'It's alright,' the older man reported back to the family's manager. 'Come on in.'

The grandfather had his own news to impart, addressing the others with a customary frankness. 'Apparently, the people from the Coroner's Office are about to arrive to transport Lynn's body.'

The grieving husband blanched. Having barely managed to convince himself there was nothing else he needed from the majestic vessel which used to hold his soul-mate, he was now reluctant to pass up another opportunity to remind himself of her.

'No,' he decided, against his better judgement. 'I guess we have to trust that no harm'll come to her. Though I can't think what more harm there could be... Sorry, Bart. Really I am. Jesus Christ!'

'Jeff, forget it. It's a bad day for all of us. I'm not the best at showing my feelings. People tend to think I don't have any.'

The widower sniffed, smiling at Big D's self-deprecation. He saw him and raised him.

'Unlike me.'

The stalwart chuckled. 'Yes. Unlike you and the rest of your family. Kierney, you're looking more upset now, but you were very mature on the 'plane; patient and polite with everyone. She's a fine tribute to the two of you, Jeff. Your son too.'

While they waited for the Coroner's team to wrap up, the philosopher's dulled mind searched for meaning in the madness happening around him. He felt detached from the world and keen to get some time alone with his gorgeous gipsy girl, who was now the closest bond he had to his absent wife. They needed to make contact with Jet too, once time in the UK had reached a reasonable hour. No point ringing him in the middle of the night. It wasn't as if knowing sooner would make any difference.

Three people in overalls emerged from behind the barrier, wheeling a trolley and accompanied by DI Fisher. Two women and a man, all dressed in dark green from head to toe. They dealt well-practised polite nods as they passed the weary superstars. What made people choose such a job? These people had been staring and prodding at every inch of his wife's body, he contemplated with disgust.

Jeff nodded back. 'G'day.'

'Mr Diamond,' one of the women replied. 'We're very sorry for your loss. What a terrible tragedy. How are you holding up?'

The forty-three-year-old felt like one of those toy dogs people kept on the parcel shelf of their car. It appeared that his entire repertoire of communication had deserted him, leaving only arbitrary head movements. A terrible tragedy indeed, and soon the whole world would know about it. This would be their next hurdle; at some point he must front the media. After leading such an open public life, he could hardly retreat from their fans now.

The handsome celebrity leant against the wall, at a loss for something to say. 'Numb,' he stated again for the record. 'Disbelief, more than anything.'

He took his father-in-law's arm, only to have it yanked out of his hand rather roughly. Fair enough, the negotiator understood. Was Bart imagining, as he was, Lynn's body being hoisted onto the trolley. With nausea building in his stomach, the curious man wondered if they would still be able to see her face.

They couldn't. The body-bag his wife had been placed in, identical to the one he had seen his father wearing over a decade ago, was standard New South Wales Government Issue and zipped closed.

The older man let out a sigh, followed by a long moan. Jeff wondered if he was thinking about his younger son, who had passed away ten years ago. Now another child had died out of sequence. So unfair. He reached for the big man's arm and was permitted to hold on to it for a few moments this time. The two men's eyes met and exchanged a silent message.

The mournful party followed the trolley towards the front foyer. Without warning, a photographer broke through the security cordon and was now sprinting across the lobby's tiled floor with a reporter in hot pursuit. The doorman chased after them, caught derelict in his duties. This new commotion brought the hotel manager out from behind Reception, and he moved to intercept the rogue journalists.

'Sorry, gentlemen. I'm going to have to ask you to leave,' Nichols called out, standing in their path and raising his arms. 'This is a private matter for the family. Please turn around.'

The photographer continued to snap away. Jeff and Gerry both walked over to him, their combined twelve-feet-seven-inches proving enough to make him stop. The former Sydney Grammar rugby captain held a large hand out, palm upwards, summoning the cameraman with his fingers.

'Empty it, please,' he shouted with menace, pointing to the camera. 'Mr Diamond'll be making a public announcement in a few hours. Until then, we'd be grateful if you'd mind your own business.'

The camera duly opened, a reel of film was dropped into the executive's outstretched hand.

'Well said, mate,' Jeff agreed, patting his friend on the back. 'Thanks, guys.'

Gerry was pleased to have fulfilled a worthy function again, as if it restored him to his rightful status. The two interlopers departed as swiftly as they had arrived, but their incursion served as a timely reminder that there was no way the Diamond media machine could maintain its silence for long.

'Sir, we're going to be staying with the Blakes tonight,' Jeff turned back to Bart 'I'm sure you'd be welcome to stay there too.'

'No, thanks,' the elder statesman replied, shaking his head. 'We'll stay in town. Marianna's flying up now, and she'll want to find out what's going on. I'll give you a ring later on.'

'OK. Whatever you think's best. We'll need to hold a press conference soon. That'll be a blast.'

'Undeniably,' the Olympian sighed, daring a smile at his son-in-law's oddball humour. 'Is Gerry organising it? I'd like to participate if I can.'

'Sure. We all can. It's what Lynn would've wanted.'

The hackneyed remark delivered a jolt to both men. It was the first time for either man to acknowledge that the skilled and respected organiser was no longer directing the show.

They looked up to find Kierney walking towards them, closely followed by Gerry, minus his tie and jacket. The man who took care of the wealthy family's every move had the little-boy-lost air about him again, shocked at the sight of the trolley carrying the body-bag.

'Would you like to have a look before Mamá goes?' the concerned father asked the teenager.

The young woman thought for a moment before declining, her face pale. 'No, thanks. I'd rather remember her some other way.'

'Yeah. Good idea,' Gerry agreed, putting his hand on the young woman's shoulder. 'Me too. I doubt if they'd allow it now anyway.'

The Coroner's driver was ready to go. A black van stood idling in the driveway, and the doorman opened the side door to let the trolley pass through. They all watched their loved one being slid into the rear compartment like a pallet of fruit and vegetables. The doors slammed shut, and the vehicle pulled away without fuss.

The widower closed his eyes as a bout of dizziness overtook him. His legs gave way, and he found himself sinking to his knees on the polished alabaster with only his daughter's slender frame within reach. He sobbed uncontrollably as Kierney crouched down and put an arm around his shoulders.

'*Papá, levantate.* Let's go,' the young woman urged, anxious not to create too much of a spectacle and encourage any more unwanted attention.

Gerry walked over and took hold of his distraught client's wrist, pulling him up to his feet. 'Get up, mate,' he encouraged, jangling two sets of keys. 'Let's get out of here. We'll get Mum to fix us some lunch, and then we can discuss what to do next. There's no need for us to stay here any longer.'

'Fucking hell, Gezza,' Jeff replied, selecting autopilot mode once more. 'This is a fucking nightmare. I don't care. Whatever you want. I'm useless. I can't think straight.'

Lynn's father accepted one set of car keys, unable to be persuaded to join the others at the Blakes'. Kierney hugged him tightly, making a final attempt to convince him, before her dad asked her to desist. Bart needed to deal with his daughter's demise in his own way, which was probably to hide himself in a corner of the Qantas lounge and immerse himself in work until Marianna's flight arrived.

After waving the black sedan on its way to the airport, the party of three walked back to the reception desk, looking for Chris and Miriam. The much-loved guest opened his wallet, estimating how much The Pensione might charge for a police investigation's worth of hot beverages and a bottle of whisky.

'We're leaving now. Thanks for looking after us. D'you want me to pay now or can you send me an invoice?'

The hotel manager waved his hands. 'Nonsense. I wouldn't hear of it, Mr Diamond. I wish you well. Again, we're all extremely sorry. I don't know what else to say.'

The grateful musician smiled, his eyes scanning the semi-circle of sullen staff who had scrambled to see them depart. What a horrendous few hours they had all endured. Cynically, he wondered how long it might take them to slip back into normality, compared to the journey now ahead of the victim's family and friends.

'Thanks very much for your help, guys. I'm sorry to screw up your day.'

Miriam giggled at the quirky comment, receiving a steely glare from her boss.

'It's fine, Chris,' Jeff came to the woman's defence. 'It's my fault. Things didn't go according to plan for anyone today.'

The widower returned to the others, who were waiting by the revolving door. He chose to go through the side exit to avoid reliving the encounter with his wife's killer. The same doorman lurched towards him, endeavouring to reach the handle before his hero had to push it himself. The songwriter held out his right hand to the stunned valet, who shook it gingerly.

'Thanks for your help this morning. What's your name?'

'Fruchtmann, sir,' he replied in a formal, Germanic accent. 'Karl.'

'Well, thanks, Karl,' the superstar repeated, his warped mind amused by the stereotypical stiffness. 'You did well, mate.'

The Diamonds' manager directed them to a black Holden Statesman with heavily tinted windows, which was waiting for them on the far side of the hooped driveway. Kierney climbed into the back, and Jeff almost slid in beside her. Thinking better of it, he sat in the front passenger seat instead, alongside the good-natured Irishman, ready for the familiar journey across the city. He had no doubt they would be spending a lot of time behind darkened glass in the next few weeks.

'Is our luggage on board?' he asked, somewhat panicked by a rare sensible thought.

'Yes, mate. It is,' Gerry nodded, sighing at the forlorn image of a world-changing billionaire in floods of tears.

Said billionaire's daughter unfastened her safety belt and sat forward on the edge of the leather seat, putting her hand on her dad's right shoulder. 'You don't have to worry about all that stuff now, Papá,' her kind voice told him. 'I know what you're thinking... That Mamá used to take care of all the organising... Were you?'

Her father sniffed. 'Yes, I was. Your telepathic powers are working well.'

Weekends always started early in Sydney on sunny days, with commuter traffic already clogging the city's roads as the Statesman cruised over the Harbour Bridge. They had been driving for about fifteen minutes when Jeff's mobile buzzed in his back pocket. Leaning sideways on the rigid leather seat, he reached for it with his left hand.

'DI Bob,' he coughed, recognising the number he had entered into the directory not so long ago.

'Yes, Jeff. How are you?'

'We're OK, thanks. Driving to Gerry's parents' place for some downtime. What can I do you for?'

'A word of warning, if I might?' the inspector ventured, chuckling.

'Sure. Sounds ominous.'

'Well, yes. It'd be best to make some sort of announcement sooner rather than later. Our media office is beginning to take quite a few calls, so it won't be long before the story gets a life of its own.'

'Yep. I hear you,' the songwriter acknowledged. 'We've been talking about it too. Bart Dyson's gone to the airport. Should we come back into the city?'

'Might be a good idea,' Fisher agreed. 'We can set something up here fairly easily, if you like.'

Jeff inhaled through his nostrils, fending off another bout of lightheaded panic. 'Hold on a second, please. I need to speak to my advisers.'

Gerry grinned, relieved that his friend hadn't lost his sense of humour. 'Turn around?' he asked, checking his door mirror and preparing to change lanes.

'Yeah. Sorry, mate. Back to Surry Hills police station,' he confirmed, reading from the business card in his hand. 'Goulburn Street. Press conference. Is that alright, Kizzy?'

'S'pose so,' the teenager sounded resigned. 'Better get it over and done with.'

'That's what I think too,' her father agreed, lifting the handset back up to his mouth. 'OK, Bob. Thanks for the offer. We're on our way back in. Probably twenty minutes or so. I'll ring Big D. He wants to be part of it.'

BREAKING NEWS

Information had begun to travel orders of magnitude faster with the steady proliferation of mobile telephones, the two venture capitalists conceded. By the time the unidentifiable black Holden arrived at the police station, a huge crowd had gathered. There were trucks loaded with antennæ from every television channel, and operators with handheld cameras and microphones milled around, waiting for the signal to take up their positions.

This type of attention-seeking scene was the Diamond family's staple diet, but today they hadn't come to launch a new project or to commemorate their latest sporting triumph. Jeff and Gerry sandwiched Kierney between them as they scrambled through the crowd and up the steps into the building. The threesome was ushered through a bustling hallway filled with blue shirts and into an auditorium permanently configured for media events. Bart Dyson was already there and span round on his heels when he heard the others arrive.

'Thanks for coming,' the detective inspector shook their hands again. 'As you can see, we ought to proceed as soon as possible. We've prepared a statement from our side.'

Fisher handed the two tall men a typewritten sheet of paper that the widower took first and skimmed over. Satisfied on the surface, he passed it to his loyal manager, who walked away to examine it with more critical eyes. When Gerry had finished, he passed it to Bart, nodding in approval to his client. To complete the round, after his father-in-law had digested its contents, Jeff requested Kierney also be allowed to read it. A bizarre chain of command, to say the least; all executed without a word, almost as if they were preparing to declare which city had won the right to host the next FIFA World Cup.

'It's amazing how they make these things sound so dry and empty,' the youngster lamented, once the celebrities broke away from the super-efficient police media team. 'I suppose they're relying on our presence to give it colour.'

Jeff chuckled at her innate scepticism. He constantly heard himself in her words. How much was inbred, he wondered, and how much had she absorbed over the years? Perhaps they oughtn't to have been quite so forthright with their offspring. In situations such as this, the emperor was laid stark naked in his gorgeous daughter's eyes.

'You're spot on,' he frowned. 'Tears sell, baby. Primetime news tonight.'

The superstar felt sick, thinking of what he might say in front of all those clicking and flashing cameras, and to all the microphones which would soon be banked up along the table. He didn't want to stage-manage the event by agreeing each person's set lines. This wasn't the Oscars after all.

Unsworn staff at the district station brought out jugs of water, placing them at intervals across a long table on a raised platform at the far end of the room. They were eager to discover why the Sydney-born rock music idol had commandeered their press room. Five seats were lined up behind the table, with another two banks of eight chairs on each side of the main floor, stretching back at least ten rows. What a monstrous circumstance, Jeff cursed. Performing to an audience again. His family was just one gigantic fairground attraction from start to finish.

Dyson and Diamond fell over each other in a light-hearted tussle not to sit in the centre chair, each believing the other deserved it more, although "deserved" was hardly the most appropriate word.

Kierney sat with her father on one side and her grandfather on the other, with her pseudo-Uncle Gerry on the end. DI Fisher sat next to Jeff, with a high-ranking Australian Federal Police media specialist standing to attention on the other flank. Looking first to his left and then his right, the widower wondered when the cake-cutting ceremony was scheduled to take place.

The doors were opened on the orders of a swashbuckling, self-important desk sergeant, allowing the hordes to rush in. Watching them jostle as close to the front as possible, the scene reminded the performer of the awful concert in Chicago which led to the other female fatalities in which he had played a part. Miss Irony wasted no time in donning her athletics spikes and dancing anew on his heart. Any positive karma the world-changer had held in reserve instantly poured out over the floor and was lost.

Bob Fisher called the proceedings to order, thanking everyone for their silence and asking the assembly to show some respect for the family who had been kind enough to attend in person. Jeff listened to the inspector's prepared statement, which was greeted with gasps of astonishment and cries of anguish from all over the room. He refused to look up, with no desire to make eye contact with anyone at this earth-shattering moment. The AFP representative also spoke, though in much more generic terms about the ensuing investigation and the fact that a suspect was already in police custody.

It was then the widower's turn to speak, prompted by the senior officer. The hall fell quiet, save for the odd squeak of a camera tripod being adjusted. As he had done on countless previous occasions, the renowned public figure somehow found the right words to thank the police and the hotel staff for helping them through the morning's difficult events. He played into their political hands and requested the media afford his family and friends space to come to terms with the loss of this most beautiful of women. As his voice cracked and tears began to flow, Kierney placed her hand on his wrist in the same way Lynn would have done.

This simple act of kindness was the last straw for the emotional man. He gestured to his father-in-law to carry on before standing up and striding towards the door. The star's business manager left his seat and followed hot on his client's heels, finding him in the corridor, bent over a rubbish bin. Gerry put his arm on his friend's shoulder, and both stood crying for a while.

'Jesus Christ,' Jeff murmured after a long pause. 'What a fucking spectacle! Let's get out of here as soon as we can.'

The executive waited with his long-time buddy, leaning against the wall and straining to hear the questions still being fired at the spokespeople. The same answers must have been proffered five or ten times over, as was always the case when precious little factual information existed with which to feed the starving press.

'Come on. It's not fair to leave Kiz and Big D in there alone,' the celebrity said out of the blue, slapping the wall's hard surface with an open palm. 'I have to go back in. You can stay out here if you like, mate, but I can't leave them to those lions and hyenas.'

Gerry nodded, and the pair filed back around the side of the room to take their seats. As expected, the journalists clamoured to ask the bereaved husband more questions, most of which were skilfully deflected by the AFP media man. Kierney delivered an eloquent off-the-cuff tribute to her mother which made Jeff very proud, and it relaxed him a little to hear her so much in control. She had inherited her supreme composure from Lynn and not from him.

The session was brought to a close, and those on the top table were ferried under escort out into the open air, emerging in the staff car park. Sunlight blinded them, and the midday heat was rising from the melting bitumen.

'Well, I'm glad that's over,' Bart Dyson said to the others, breathing in deeply through his nostrils and out again open-mouthed. 'What an awful ordeal.'

'Are you sure you won't come back with us, Grandpa?' the youngster asked. 'Celia wouldn't mind, would she, Gerry?'

'Definitely not,' the stars' manager confirmed. 'You'd be very welcome, sir. I could take you back to collect Mrs Dyson when her flight gets in. It's no trouble, honestly.'

Bart and Jeff exchanged glances, and the big man relented. The black Statesman ferried them all back through the city and over the Harbour Bridge for the third time that day. Each struggled to speak about anything other than Lynn's murder, with the conversation always ending up back in the present. After a while, they retreated into themselves, and a strained quietude descended over the rest of the trip.

Gerry pulled the car up to the front of the Blake residence, his mother having opened the door wide before the wheels stopped turning. Theirs was not a driveway one could creep up on. The four exhausted passengers received welcoming hugs from the stoic lady, who burst into floods of tears as soon as she saw them.

'Kierney, darling,' she gushed. 'You poor thing. Your poor mamá. How positively dreadful.'

'Thanks, Celia,' the brave teenager said, tears pricking at her eyes too. 'We don't know what to say anymore. We've been over it so many times already. I'm sorry, but I don't know what to say.'

'Don't worry, Kizzo,' her father consoled her, putting his hand on the girl's shoulder and walking her into the house. 'It doesn't matter what we say or don't say. Just be yourself while you're here 'cause tomorrow the circus starts all over again.'

'That's right,' her grandfather agreed. 'Well put, Jeff. And thank you, Celia. I'm a bit of a gate-crasher. Hope you don't mind.'

'Don't be silly,' the lady of the house admonished the all-Australian hero. 'It's lovely to see you again, Bart. And Marianna too, when she arrives. I am so, so sorry you've lost your lovely daughter. We all loved her so much.'

'Hear, hear,' her son agreed. 'Never a truer word spoken.'

Big D smiled to hear such generous words used to describe Lynn, who had been all but adopted by the Blakes a long time ago. They were an upright and genuine family, accepted as his in-laws by now. Gerry's parents had watched the Diamond children grow up, as he and his wife had done, and he couldn't help noticing how close a bond there existed between Kierney and their host.

'You're very kind, all of you,' Bart said. 'Is your husband home?'

Celia shook her head. 'Not yet, no. I haven't got the gumption to ring him and tell him the news. I suppose I should, before he hears it on the radio in the car on the way home.'

'I'll do it, Mum,' Gerry piped up. 'I'd like to.'

Surprised by the junior partner's uncommon willingness to take responsibility for family matters, the woman smiled and gave him a tacit go-ahead. The group moved through into the drawing room, where each found a couch and sat down, issuing a collective sigh at being able to relax at last.

'I'll fetch some tea and coffee,' Celia announced, pleased to help these wretches in their hour of need.

Jeff hadn't spoken since arriving at the Blake residence, now cloaked in his old leather jacket despite the heat. Kierney scrutinised his expressions with interest in an effort to fathom what might be going through his head. He sat with his elbows on his knees, looking downwards at his black jet-stone ring, which he had twisted over his knuckles and was now being flipped over and over in his hands.

'Papá,' the eighteen-year-old called over, 'are you OK?'

'Will you come out for a walk with me, please, angel?' he replied, lifting his tired eyes.

'Yes, definitely. I'd love to,' Kierney agreed, happy to spend some time alone with her remaining parent.

Father and daughter left the others and walked out through the French windows, towards the pool and the tennis court where they had spent many a happy hour as visitors to this capacious and friendly home.

Jeff pulled two chairs into a shady spot under one of the huge oak trees. 'Jesus, *pequeñita*! What the hell are we going to do?'

'Only three diamonds now,' his gipsy girl nodded, her gaze alighting on the ring with which her dad continued to play. '*No se, Papá.*'

'D'you remember the expression we often use about us: "*Nuestra vida singular*"?' he asked, gratified to hear her answer him in Spanish.

'*Sí.* Of course I remember. It's gone. *Es ist weg?*'

'*Ja! Sicher,*' her father laughed at the *à propos* choice of language. '*¡Muy buen!*'

Kierney smiled but returned to their previous topic straightaway. She knew how much her parents meant to each other and how their love had only grown stronger over the years. She couldn't begin to understand what it must feel like to have something so special ripped away.

'It's different for Jet and me,' she acknowledged. 'You brought us up to be *weg* eventually, so that's what we're working on. But for you, it's going to be a massive pit of emptiness.'

Jeff wept as he heard his darkest fear put into words. The teenager stood up and moved her chair closer, leaning her head on his shaking arm.

'We'll stick together, Papá,' she murmured. 'We need to ring Jet soon. Once the news gets out, he'll hear it when he's shaving or something. That'd be awful. He'll want to be on the first plane out of Heathrow.'

The duo looked up, distracted by the jangling sound of silver cutlery on fine bone china. Celia was bringing a small tray of drinks for them, along with Jeff's favourite biscuits. They imagined her rushing out to buy them especially for the sad occasion as soon as she heard they were on their way.

'Here you are!' she called out, as if nothing unusual was in train. 'I didn't know how long you'd be.'

The very proper gentlewoman set the tray down on the grass in front of their feet and smiled at the sorry duo, so alike in every way. 'Are you alright? Is there anything I can do?'

'No, thanks, Celia,' Jeff forced a smile. 'Unless you know how to turn back time?'

'Oh, darlings, I wish I did. I really wish we could. You must feel so bereft.'

The widower stared at the ground, his vision as blurred as his thoughts. The situation's true gravity, with a small "g" this time, was finally sinking in, now the pressure to respond to questions and to adhere to due process had been discharged.

'Yeah,' the Blakes' extra son affirmed. 'You were spot-on when you told me I was "lost" last time we had such a conversation in this garden, and now you're right on the money again with "bereft". It's shit, Celia. Really shit.'

Kierney looked up and saw the sadness in the elderly woman's eyes, unable to think of anything to counteract her father's raw emotions.

'I'll leave you to it, dears,' the dignified lady said, wiping away tears from behind her glasses with a dainty handkerchief. 'I'll make some sandwiches soon. I'll send Gerry out to tell you when they're ready.'

The rest of the afternoon and evening dragged on through morose rounds of cups of tea, snacks and alcoholic beverages. Gerald had come straight home on receiving his son's call, after which the Diamonds' business manager drove Bart to collect Marianna from the airport.

Not long afterwards, their hosts' elder daughter, Jacinta, had rung to say that she would be leaving the twins with her husband and coming over the following morning. Tamilla, Gerry's younger sister, was overseas with her family, making the most of the last year before school terms would dictate when they took their holidays.

At six-thirty, while Celia prepared dinner for a dejected bunch of guests who weren't at all hungry, Jeff, Kierney and the Dysons gathered in the family's study to telephone Jet in Cambridge. It was half-past seven on a cold Friday morning, and the cricketer had recently returned from a run through frosty streets.

'Son, are your flatmates around?' his father asked.

'Still sparko, I expect,' came his typically casual response, having no inkling as to the significance of this question.

'Well, I don't want you to be alone after this phone call, mate. Kizzy's here with me, and Grandma and Grandpa are also on the line.'

The lad listened to a chorus of subdued hellos, realising something must be amiss. 'Oh, yeah? What's up, guys? Why are you all ringing me? It's not my birthday.'

Jeff scoffed, these words catapulting him back to the harrowing incident that had coincided with his own fourteenth birthday. 'No, mate. Far from it.'

Kierney took the reins from her father, and this time he didn't object. 'OK, Jetto... There's been an absolute disaster today,' she began, her eyes filling with tears. 'Mamá was shot dead in a Sydney hotel.'

There followed another long pause from the other side of the planet. The nineteen-year-old had heard his sister perfectly, and everything was now beginning to make sense. So this was why his whole family had rung first thing in the morning.

'Bloody hell,' he exhaled. 'No way. When?'

'About nine-forty-five this morning,' Jeff explained, knowing the lad was more like his grandfather than his father when it came to showing emotion. 'I'm sorry to break it to you over the phone, but you needed to know from us before it hits the news over there.'

The young man fell silent again, and they could hear the sound of heavier breathing all the way from Cambridgeshire.

'Jet, it's Grandma,' Marianna took a turn. 'Are you alright?'

'Yes. It's... Jeez. I don't know. Yes, thanks, Grandma,' he replied, ever polite and with a definite English accent. 'I'm shocked, I suppose. I can't believe it. We only spoke yesterday when Kiz rang about her driving licence. What happened?'

'Jesus, mate,' his dad blurted out. 'It was supposed to've been me. That's who the arsehole was hoping to get, not your beautiful, precious mamá. I was parking the car at the hotel after we'd flown to Sydney. Before I could get inside with the bags, your mum took a call that was meant for me. And then she was shot at point-blank range, they reckon, sitting in the lobby and talking on the courtesy phone.'

'Whoa. Not very courteous,' the sportsman quipped, before biting his tongue. 'Sorry. That was a stupid thing to say.'

The songwriter chuckled. 'No, it's not. Say exactly what you want to say. That's what we've all agreed here. There's no right and wrong way to behave today. We need you here, mate. Can you fly over?'

'For God's sake, Dad, yes!' Jet responded, the pitch of his voice raised and anxious. 'Of course I will. I need to be with you too. I'm sorry. I just can't believe it.'

The young man's faraway family could tell he was crying, and Kierney reached out towards the telephone instinctively, hating the sound of her brother so upset.

'Jet, we need each other so much,' she echoed. 'Please come as soon as you can. Mamá's gone, bro'. It's just terrible.'

'Does this mean we have to go to her funeral?' he asked, even more shaken. 'How the hell do I go to my own mum's funeral?'

His father groaned. 'Yeah, mate. I hear ya. I've been thinking about that too. We did a press conference this arvo. That was bad enough. People asking questions we've got no answers for. It was bloody awful, let me tell you.'

'Would you like us to book you a ticket, son?' Bart's voice was strong and direct. 'And can you ask someone to drive you to Heathrow?'

'No, Grandpa. I'll be fine. I'll go by bus. It's much easier. There are buses to the airport from here. It's a bloody long journey though. A long way to think morbid thoughts.'

'Can someone go with you, dear,' Marianna butted in.

Jeff shook his head. 'Mate, do whatever you want to do. Have you got enough money to pay for the ticket?'

'Yeah. Should have, thanks. I've got money left over from buying the bike.'

'A bike? What sort of bike?' the Olympian couldn't help himself, curious as to why he hadn't been told his grandson was into cycling.

'A motorbike, Grandpa,' Jet answered, knowing it would disappoint the veteran. 'It's to help me get to cricket faster.'

Jeff and Kierney grinned at each other, their eyebrows raising in unison. The confident young man was ready to stand up to anyone these days, and he did it in a way that seldom put people offside.

'Right. I see,' Bart answered. 'That's good then. I look forward to hearing about it when the formalities are over.'

'Hey, Jetto?' his father asked, about to sign off.

'Yes, Dad.'

'Fly safe, OK? Let me know what time you're arriving, and we'll pick you up.'

'Oh, wait! Am I coming to Melbourne or Sydney?'

'Melbourne!' sang a chorus of replies.

'OK, OK!' he laughed. 'Stupid question, I know.'

His dad sighed. 'It's not a stupid question at all. We're going to be up here quite a bit in the coming weeks. Sorting things out, *et cetera*. But come to Melbourne anyway. Cheers, mate. See you soon. *Te amo, Jetto.*'

'I love you guys too. See you tomorrow.'

Between them, the callers must have pressed every single button on Gerald's complicated office telephone until they were sure the call had cut off. The songwriter sat with his head in his hands, thankful that their news had been imparted with comparatively little additional pain.

Celia called them all to the table, and her husband fulfilled his favourite duty, that of fixing everyone a strong *apéritif*. All bar one were on their best behaviour over dinner, recounting pieces of mindless trivia and half-heartedly discussing world events.

Jeff proceeded to drink a great deal during the meal however, becoming quite hysterical at the spiralling sense of pointlessness which now consumed him. Kierney rescued everyone by removing her father from the table, and the matching pair once more found themselves outdoors in the sticky summer evening air.

Gerry followed them to the swimming pool at his mother's request, concerned for the young woman's welfare. The Blakes still remembered how dependent this dark-hearted musician had been on his superstar girlfriend in the early years, and there were already dangerous signs of this unhealthy trait returning. He rounded the corner just in time to see his friend lash out at an imaginary opponent, yelling at the top of his lungs.

'Mate!' the successful accountant shouted, grabbing the musician's arm. 'Take it easy.'

Jeff reeled back, his expression thunderous. 'Take it easy? Why?'

'Because we're worried about you and what you might do,' Kierney answered on behalf of everyone. 'Papá, we love you. We hate seeing you hurt so much. Really we do.'

The widower sighed, sitting down and wiping blades of dewy grass cuttings off his shoes. 'Thanks, angel. I know you do. I'm sorry. I just don't care right at this moment. Not about me, I mean.'

'Come in and watch some TV or something,' the teenager suggested. 'We need to take our minds off what happened today. Let's watch a video.'

Jeff heaved himself to his feet, which were sore and tired from carrying his ten-tonne weight around all day. The trio walked back into the house, where Celia was about to make yet more hot drinks. They caught her in an act of defiance, wagging an irate finger at her husband's suggestion of a round of liqueurs.

Blake Senior pouted at his wife, making their distinguished guests laugh. They had discussed the older man's medical problems over dinner, much to his embarrassment, during which both Dysons had declared their support for his wife's stance on the matter.

'Coffee would be lovely, Celia. Thank you,' Marianna requested. 'Can I help?'

'No, no. Please stay where you are,' their host insisted. 'It's very kind of you to offer. Your daughter had your lovely manners.'

The two mature ladies stared at each other for a few seconds, both pondering the other's thoughts on Celia's comment.

'She did,' Jeff interrupted, having sobered up in the fresh air. 'I apologise, everyone, if I got too offensive earlier. It won't happen again.'

'We're going to find a film on TV,' Kierney announced before anyone had a chance to respond to her father's apology, 'if you want to join us. We thought it might help distract us before bedtime.'

The diners agreed this was an excellent idea, filing into the drawing room. "The Firm", starring Gene Hackman and Tom Cruise, was showing on one of the commercial channels, and they all settled down to watch it whether they had seen it before or not. Its plot was absorbing enough to give their beleaguered minds a rest.

The Diamonds cuddled into each other, sharing a cigarette as they frequently did of an evening. Her gipsy presence went some way towards substituting for his invisible elastic connection to Lynn, which now completely eluded the rock star. During a bathroom break, his nerves had jangled the whole time his daughter was gone, and it had taken a few minutes for his heart rate to return to normal upon her return.

Unable to concentrate on the film, Jeff used the quiet time to run over the many tasks which now lay ahead of him. Lynn and he had often discussed their wishes in the event either of them passed away without warning, never once expecting to have to enact their plans. He wondered how his beautiful best friend would be faring now if the gunman had succeeded in killing his original target. For a fleeting moment, he gave thanks that she wasn't destined to go through what he was about to endure, yet the charitable feeling was short-lived.

Anticipating another acrimonious flare-up, the bereaved man tilted Kierney into an upright position and slunk out of the room. Celia found him not long afterwards, leaning on the swimming pool railings and smoking. He had borrowed the family's kitchen jotter to list the many looming and unpalatable duties, but the sight of them stretching most of the way down the page was too much to bear at this late hour.

'Just let it all out,' the mother figure crooned, rubbing his back as if he were a baby needing to burp. 'It's going to take a long time.'

'Yeah. That's what I'm afraid of,' Jeff replied, taking a deep breath in an effort not to fly off the handle at this latest invasion of privacy.

'What are you up to?' the kindly woman asked, peering at the pad in the lamplight.

'Nothing much. Just trying to make up for the sudden disorganisation in our family.'

'Oh, we can help you with all that, dear. You're bound to be all over the place.'

'I don't want your help with all this,' he snapped. 'No offence, but I just want my wife back and for everything to be as it was yesterday.'

Celia stood firm next to him and helped herself from the cigarette packet balanced on top of the pool fence, recognising the wayward boy she had come to know all that time ago. She hadn't smoked for several years, but today was no ordinary day. It was gone ten o'clock at night, and the humid air held no trace of a breeze.

After a while, the peacemaker apologised again and thanked her for her company. He wasn't the only one plunged into misery on the eve of a summer weekend, even though he wished she would go back into the house and leave him alone.

'I do have a request, please,' Jeff said after several minutes of silence.

'Oh? What's that, darling?'

'Could you put the Dysons in the room Lynn and I were going to sleep in, if that's OK?'

His host understood. The forever couple had shared so many happy nights in this house: times when Gerry's sisters had almost caught them out with their habit of bursting into rooms without knocking; or the odd occasion when all four Diamonds had slept as a family in the antique four-poster bed, from when the children were babies to not so long ago. The idea of climbing into the same bed after today's catastrophe must be insupportable.

'Yes, of course. I didn't think. I assumed you and Kierney would sleep where you normally sleep. Sorry, dear.'

'Thanks. No worries. I'll just sleep on the sofa down here. I'm going to be up watching TV and sorting out whatever needs to get done tomorrow. I don't want to burden Gerry or Bart with shovelling the rubble after this bloody bomb I caused.'

Celia objected in her antiquated way. 'Shhh... No, no, no. Stop thinking that way. Not while you're under my roof, you won't sleep on the couch. You need your sleep, dear. I can give you one of Gerald's sleeping pills.'

'Christ,' the forty-three-year-old adolescent moaned. 'No, thanks. It's been ages since I took one of those evil buggers. They totally screw me up. I'd prefer to take my chances downstairs. I slept well last night, before...'

'I'll get one out for you,' the lady of the house persisted. 'You can take it or not, depending on how you feel.'

The desolate man waved an indifferent hand at his friend's well-meaning mother. 'OK, cheers. Whatever you want.'

Celia walked away, refusing to allow herself to be hurt by a man who had spent the last twenty years encouraging the world's population to live in harmony. Tomorrow was bound to be another difficult day.

Jeff returned to the poolside table to resume his planning. 'Where are you, angel?' he asked out loud. 'Can you hear me?'

His ears were battered by stillness, interrupted only by possums in season, hissing and screeching from the copse beyond the stables. The lonely soul forced himself to picture his dream girl at last night's dinner in Port Melbourne, celebrating their younger child's independence day. Lynn had been wearing a short, white denim skirt and a light green top, with her long, golden hair clipped back off her face to protect it from the salty wind. In fact, he remembered remarking to mother and daughter that they looked like photographic negatives of each other, with Kierney cloaked in her customary dark hues.

The love of his life had not been worried by growing older. At least, she had never voiced any such fears. She was far less vain than her husband in this respect, and the children loved to tease their dad for his regular complaints about ageing. The tennis champion had no reason to worry, of course... She was as irresistible to him at forty years old as she had been on the day they reunited after her time in America.

The songwriter next tried to replay their wedding day, starting with the heady excitement of the rehearsal, then seeing the bride arrive by his side to speak their vows. Their energy had turned into red-hot passion after the ceremony and had finally petered out in the balcony's sublime serenity at the end of the day, after they decided to abandon their hotel room for the familiarity of their own apartment. What a magnificent day that was! It surpassed every possible hope and dream he had ever dared.

His mind wandered next to Jet's birth, when Lynn's waters had broken while he was on a flight home from Los Angeles. He had flown in right at the last minute, scared he would miss the most important show of his life. The father-to-be had arrived at the maternity ward so wound-up that the expectant couple had disappeared to make love in the shower while in the throes of labour.

He had no trouble recalling the moment when they first heard the cry of their healthy baby son, looking into his wife's eyes and seeing her joy at giving him the child he had craved. And then there were the nervous first few days, confined to their apartment and making parenthood up as they went along.

Jeff's chest tightened around his heart when he reflected on quite the longest few weeks in Jet's eighth year, and how they had argued about his wife's insistence on sending their boy away for an entire summer to the cricket programme that her father had organised. In their twenty-three years together, this had been their single fundamental disagreement, and what a disagreement it had grown into…

It was also the one and only time they had used the word "divorce" throughout their marriage, the memory of which had continued to haunt them long after the rift had been filled in and paved over. Never again, they had vowed, would they let themselves drift so far apart on an issue before taking action to resolve it.

The songs that had been given life at this painful time were still among the couple's favourites, their lyrical sincerity and the subtleties of both musicians' arrangements resulting in lasting products of a crucial phase in their life singular.

'D'you remember how much we wanted to make up?' the melancholy singer sent into the night sky. 'Remember getting together that night in Germany? Jesus! I wanted you like never before. Please tell me you remember that night, angel.'

Again, the air remained tranquil and noncommittal. Jeff cursed the loneliness which had seized his soul. Perhaps Celia's sleeping pill wasn't such a bad idea after all. At least it offered an escape for a few hours before he would need to deal with tomorrow's macabre but necessary chores.

'Hey, Papá!' came Kierney's relieved voice from the doorway. 'I thought you'd been gone a long time to still be in the loo.'

Jeff turned to see his daughter's smiling face. He pulled the chair next to his out from under the table and patted it, inviting her to sit with him.

'What are you doing?' she asked, seeing his scrawly handwriting on the pad in front of him.

Her father scoffed. 'Not a lot, as it turns out. Has the film finished?'

'No, but I've seen it before. I'd rather be with you. What's this?'

'I came out to start a list of everything we need to do tomorrow and once we're home,' her dad sighed, feeling emotional again on hearing her kind words, ''cause my mind wouldn't focus on the movie. Then when that didn't help either, I made myself remember stuff from the past. Happy memories, y'know... Forcing myself to think about all the fantastic images I have of...'

The widower broke down, lifting a heavy right arm behind his compassionate child and bringing it to rest on her shoulders.

'Of Mamá,' she finished his sentence, resisting against his mass to look into his eyes. 'Say it, Papá. Fantastic images of Mamá. You're allowed to speak her name, and you're allowed to cry at the same time. It'd be weird if you didn't. Wrong, even. Wouldn't it?'

Jeff listened to the eighteen-year-old sage's words and nodded, sniffing back the tears. 'Yep. It would,' he agreed. 'Fantastic images of your mamá. Of Lynn, my beautiful best friend and sex goddess. Is that better?'

Kierney hugged him. '*Sí. Muy bien.* Much better.'

Her dad managed a smile. 'Listen... When you were born, *hija mía*, it was like you already knew us,' he reminded his daughter. 'Your eyes followed every sound and every move we made. You and I were connected from that first time I held you, and your mamá knew it too. She gave me you and your brother, and that's the most wonderful thing. I have to remember that.'

'And Mamá was the best mother in the world for us. We must remember that too. I'm going to work on some really nice words to say at her funeral.'

Jeff pressed his lips hard against her cheek, his thumb brushing tears away. 'We all shall, *pequeñita*. Everyone loved your mamá. We'll need to give everyone a time limit, or it'll be the longest funeral in history.'

A girlish smile spread across the young woman's face, and she turned to repay the kiss on her father's unshaven jaw. The pair sat in the freshening air for a long while, reminiscing with other shared memories: the trips they took to Africa when Kierney was still in primary school; the days they had spent volunteering at Childlight and The Fellowship centres; and also the many holidays they had enjoyed in unusual places, where as a family they had learnt about different cultures and customs.

'You two've given us such a meaningful life,' Kierney stated. 'I know it was deliberate, so it shouldn't be a surprise to any of us, but just how meaningful I'm not sure you really take credit for.'

Her father smiled. '*Muchas gracias.* That's great to hear. It certainly was all done on purpose, and there were times when we met with resistance, didn't we? It would've been very easy... and it was tempting occasionally... just to say, "Fuck it! Let's go to Disneyworld instead." But we stuck to our principles mostly.'

'We did go to Disneyworld though! Was that a capitulation holiday, or did you plan to take us there? I loved it!'

'No, we planned that one. Sometimes parents need to have fun too. It wasn't all about you, y'know!'

The dark-haired duo gave each other a few playful shoves, relishing the lightness of humour after such an exasperating day. Kierney was glad to see her beloved papá smiling again, especially knowing the turmoil he was sure to go through in the coming weeks and months.

They walked back into the house to find everyone else ready to retire for the night. Celia was in the middle of urging the Dysons to make themselves at home, insisting she had nothing specific to do the following morning, so could be at their disposal. Tomorrow was Saturday, meaning it would not be possible to complete many items on their checklist.

'Fuck,' the short-tempered star muttered under his breath. 'I didn't think of that. What the hell are we going to do over the weekend with all this hanging over us?'

'Sleep on it, mate,' Gerry replied, unable to offer anything more useful. 'Let's get some rest and we can regroup tomorrow. Sleep in late, have a slow breakfast... Whatever.'

Bart Dyson fixed the petulant artist with a stare, also aware of his volatile history. 'I'll be up early, Jeff. Let's you and I go for a run or a long walk and we can talk things through. Celia told us you were making a list of things that need doing. We can make a start on sorting all that out together in the morning.'

'And, darling, try to relax a bit,' Marianna encouraged, standing up from one of the leather couches and walking over to her fractious son-in-law. 'Think of all the happy times you two had together. How much you loved each other... Hopefully, you'll manage to get some sleep so you can face tomorrow more optimistically.'

'Thanks, but don't count on it,' the cynic shrugged. 'You too.'

The elegant woman frowned. 'I know it's going to be so hard for you. We're all here to help you and the children, Jeff.'

'Thanks, Grandma,' Kierney piped up. 'We were just swapping some funny memories outside. We were laughing about going to Disneyworld a few years ago.'

Celia, wise to the youngster's methods, averted another awkward reaction by giving Marianna a quick tour of the kitchen in case the newcomers needed anything. The Dysons followed Gerald and his wife upstairs, wishing everyone a comfortable night.

Once the elders were out of sight, Gerry sat back down on the couch next to his shell-shocked friend and put his arm around him. 'I don't think I actually said this earlier, mate, but I'm really sorry for your loss.'

'Cheers,' Jeff responded, unused to such touchy-feely behaviour from the affable accountant.

'Those words sound so clichéd and overused,' his friend continued, 'but I can't think of anything else. I know how much you loved her. She was your world, I know that. And I can't begin to know how that feels.'

The widower began to cry again and held his hand out towards his daughter, who was perched on the edge of the cushion opposite the two men. She walked over and crouched down in front of her father, taking his hands in hers. All three comforted each other for a while, before Jeff broke the silence.

'Thanks, you guys. You're both amazing. I couldn't do this without you, or your mum, Gerry. She's fantastic too. Get out of here and get to bed. Go and ring Fiona and have phone sex.'

His manager sniggered. 'I don't think so, mate. Not tonight. Even I wouldn't stoop so low.'

'For fuck's sake, why not?' Jeff disputed, unabashed as the tears streamed down his face. 'If you love this woman, go for it. I know I would, if the shoe were on the other foot. Take every chance you get to make each other feel good because one day it might all be gone.'

Kierney cuddled into her dad. 'That's a lovely thing to say.'

Nodding, Gerry blanched. 'It is, but can I ask you something, mate?'

'Sure. Anything.'

'Did you two part on good terms?'

The superstar's rampant paranoia made him see red, suspicious that ugly rumours were already being spread. 'Christ. Yes, we effing well did. Why are you asking? Was there something on the news?'

'No, mate. We haven't seen any news. It's just that when I spoke to Fiona earlier, she said she hoped there wasn't anything you wished you'd said to or heard from Lynn that could never be spoken or heard now,' Gerry explained, crying his own tears for a long-time buddy in crisis. 'It's just such a bloody frightening thought, that's all.'

Squeezing his mate's arm, Jeff apologised. 'No, mate. There was never anything left unsaid between Lynn and me. We knew exactly where we stood with each other. Every damned day,' he answered, turning to his daughter to make sure she heard these words too. 'Last night, we had dinner with this one here, to celebrate her getting her licence, before going home and having the hottest, most exciting sex you can imagine two old folks getting up to once both their kids are legally allowed to drive. That's how it always was with us, don't you worry.'

'Good show,' Gerry bleated. 'Perhaps I will have phone sex in that case.'

'Cool! Can I listen?'

'Papá!' Kierney yelped. 'That's disgusting. Please! I'm just a child.'

'Yeah, right,' the doting father laughed, kissing her forehead. 'Can I have a sound bite of that, please, for when you next tell me to stop treating you like a kid?'

The teenager huffed. 'Damn! Not fair. I walked into that one.'

'You did rather,' the family's manager smiled. 'I'm off upstairs now. I'll see you in the morning for your run with Big D if I wake up early enough. Otherwise, I'll see you at brekkie.'

The exhausted widower stood up to embrace his trusty right-hand man. 'Thanks for all your help today. You're an amazing bloke to have in my corner, you know that?'

'You too, mate. And I'm very sorry, again.'

With Gerry's departure, the dark-haired Diamonds found themselves alone in the large salon. The television had been switched off, and all but two table lamps were out. Jeff walked over to one and extinguished it too, before flicking the television on again.

'Are you going to bed?' he asked his daughter.

'Are you?'

'Nah. I'm staying down here to watch some more mindless crap. You go on up though. You must be completely knackered.'

The teenager paused for a moment. She remembered again how her mother described the reliance her father placed on her company whenever his mind was troubled. How could she leave him on his own tonight? She wasn't sure if she wanted to be alone either, if she were honest.

'No, Papá. Is it alright if I stay here with you?'

Jeff watched the young woman remove her shoes and belt and set them on the floor at the base of the couch opposite him. He was overcome with gratitude for her thoughtfulness, knowing full well she would be tapping in to his wavelength.

'I'd love you to stay here,' he replied, cycling through the channels for something light-hearted and diverting to watch. '*Gracias, pequeñita.*'

As the programmes flashed by, the identical pairs of dark-brown eyes fixed on a view of The Pensione Hotel's façade spliced alongside Detective Inspector Fisher's familiar face. Jeff's fevered fingers pressed the channel search button in reverse until they found it again.

'D'you mind?'

'No,' Kierney replied with some trepidation.

They watched footage of their press conference and some more of Bob Fisher back at The Pensione, presumably filmed later that afternoon. The show's producers had unearthed a recent photograph of Lynn from their media library, giving both bereaved relatives a reality check. The report was mercifully short and factual, the presenters resisting the temptation to provide their own commentary.

Once the segment finished, Jeff muted the television's volume and turned to the glassy-eyed gipsy girl. 'Oh, well,' he sighed. 'If you see it on the news, it must be true.'

The teenager nodded.

'Fuck!' her father shouted at the top of his voice.

He threw the remote control with some force onto the leather seat cushion. It bounced off the couch and clattered onto varnished floorboards, causing the latch at the back to open and spill its batteries over the floor.

'Why, Kizzo?' he ranted, on his feet and pacing around the room, watching his daughter scamper after the rolling batteries and replace them into the unit. 'Why did he have to shoot her? Why didn't he wait five minutes and get me?'

'I don't know,' Kierney shouted back. 'But if he'd got you, the rest of us would be just as sad, especially Mamá. I wish that fucking bastard had stayed at home today. Or didn't even exist.'

Sobbing, the pair embraced, standing in the dim light of the drawing room. They stared into each other's eyes.

'I'm sorry, angel,' Jeff said. 'I don't want you to be sad any more than I want to be sad. That was a shitty thing for me to say. You lost your mamá today, and I lost my *regala*.'

'I'm sorry for your loss. It doesn't make it better, does it? But I mean it.'

'Yeah. Thanks, baby,' her dad nodded, resting his forehead on hers. 'And I'm sorry for your loss too. Sit down. Let's watch something else.'

Calm restored for the time being, the pair roamed across the television stations again until they found an innocuous wildlife documentary. Just as they were settling back down, Celia appeared in the doorway in her dressing gown, clutching a pile of blankets.

'Is everything alright, dears? We heard some noise.'

'Yeah. Sorry about that,' Jeff responded, standing up again. 'I got angry and chucked the remote onto the couch, but it fell off and hit the floor. Sorry to disturb you. Please go back to bed. We're good.'

The older woman was relieved that nothing more sinister had occurred, holding the blankets out to Jeff at full stretch as if frightened he might attack her. 'I brought these down for you, in case you get cold.'

'Thank you,' Kierney's sweet voice interjected. 'That's very kind of you. Goodnight.'

'Are you going to bed soon, darling?' Celia asked the ashen-faced teenager.

'No, I'm staying here with Papá. It's OK. These couches are really comfy. It's fine.'

Their host frowned. 'If you insist, darling.'

'Yes,' Kierney insisted. 'Sleep well. See you in the morning.'

Jeff watched his friend's mother leave the room, feeling guilty and confused. Why wouldn't it seem logical for family members to stick together at such a time? Were their hosts' fears reasonable? Did his past and long-forgotten indiscretions present such a danger to his loyal seraph? His world had been turned upside down, and the ability to recalibrate it now eluded him like never before. All he knew for sure was that he was grateful for everyone's latitude while he flailed in this whirlpool of grief.

'You should go upstairs if you want to, *pequeñita*,' he offered again. 'Or later. Whenever.'

'No. I want to be with you. I need us to be together. I feel so sick.'

The relieved man held his arms out towards her. 'Come and sit here for a while. We can keep each other company until either of us wants to go to sleep. Let's find some late-night drama to pretend we're enjoying.'

Now after eleven o'clock, it wasn't long before Kierney began to yawn regularly in her dad's right ear. They had found a black and white movie to watch from its halfway point, and they struggled to make sense of the story, having missed vital pieces of the plot. Yawning again, the teenager sat upright and stretched her long legs out in front of her.

'I'm sleepy now. Do you mind if I stretch out over there?'

Her father followed her gaze to the couch not three metres from where they were sitting, a huge gulf opening up in between. He knew he had no right to stop her. Kierney was not Lynn, and neither should he try to imagine she was.

'Go ahead,' he agreed, with only a trace of regret in his voice. 'Sleep well. Have good dreams of Mamá.'

'Thanks. You too, I hope. Leave the TV on though.'

Jeff stretched out on the leather sofa and watched his daughter do the same. Like her mother and brother, she never had any trouble falling asleep, soon leaving him on his own with the movie and his overactive mind. He pictured Jet on the flight from London to Melbourne, in transit via Changi Airport, and wondered whether he was sleeping too. How he looked forward to having both teenagers with him, to help support each other through the horrific days ahead.

Searching for some more pleasant memories, the proud father ventured back to the day their little girl was born, and the loving way in which their son had interacted with his new baby sister. The Diamond clan had been so happy from the very beginning, all the way to the telephone conversation they had shared only the night before, with the handset being passed around the windswept dinner table.

Poor Jetto... He was closer to his mother than Kierney was, although their allegiances had begun to switch with approaching adulthood. The sportsman had sought out his father's wisdom as maturity shifted its focus from brawn to brain. His sister's feminine side was emerging too, developing more than a passing interest in fashion and style. And in men, her father smiled.

Jet had always been independent. Both children were, but in distinct ways. Jeff remembered his own father's memorial parade, an event his beautiful best friend had organised through the streets of Fairfield and Canley Vale, ending up at his less than modest childhood home. The young boy had insisted on marching alone, refusing to hold hands with either parent. A photograph had been sent anonymously to the stars' management company which showed Lynn bending down to talk to her son, who was biting his top lip in an effort not to cry. This picture had become one of the young parents' most prized and priceless possessions.

The lonely songwriter sighed. What would happen to these prized and priceless possessions now? How was he supposed to live surrounded by their collection of personal *mementi*? As Kierney had rightly pointed out, she and Jet were raised to leave, whereas Jeff was not and neither was Lynn. Or so he had thought.

Tears rolled down the widower's cheeks once again. He stared at the ceiling, with the television volume turned down low, and pondered his wife's final contemplations at the moment the bullet hit her skull. Did she have time to register any pain before her resplendent light was snuffed out? How many words were exchanged with the mystery caller before she suspected something was wrong? Did she realise she was dying? Had she thought of him and the kids and wished she could stay with them?

So many questions for which he would never find answers...

Never more than now did the philosopher cherish the extra vow Lynn and he had made in private on their wedding night; the commitment they honoured always to make love as if it were the last time they would ever be together. Last night had been no exception, and his imagination re-enacted their impassioned undulations from start to finish. He recalled how his lover had felt in his arms, how they had spoken of their devotion in so many ways, and how they managed to mix laughter with sensuousness in perfect measure.

Sensing sleep overtaking him, Jeff shook himself awake again, unwilling to succumb and risk the prospect of a nightmare. He shuddered to think of the inevitable quagmire of the next few days. They needed to transport Lynn's body back to Melbourne and find a place for it to reside before the funeral. Gerry had their wills locked in a safe deposit box at his bank, along with a batch of letters to each other and to the children; messages the couple had recorded for posterity in case anyone should shoot either of them in the head. They had both written three notes every year since nineteen-eighty, inspired after John Lennon's murder, amassing quite a collection by now.

This, Jeff mused, would be an interesting exercise indeed. It even gave him a faint glimmer of optimism, lying here in the dark. Seeing how the language altered over the years, especially those written to Jet and Kierney as they grew up and gained a greater awareness of life's important subjects, would be a fascinating way to remember their missing family member.

Writing these letters had been one of the young mum's more unusual ideas. They had imagined together how dreadful it would be if either star were assassinated like the acclaimed Beatles songwriter. And now the unthinkable had eventuated, her husband foresaw how these special glimpses into their loved one's soul would bond them together in this watershed of sadness.

There would be no surprises in Lynn's will, not even as far as the generations above and below were concerned. The Diamonds had ensured all financial matters were discussed openly, so there could be no indefensible accusations at a later date. The most painful of surprises would be those which dragged on into the future, such as the gradual arrival of post and straightening out their diaries: his engagements to postpone and hers to cancel. What to do with the numerous projects the tireless worker had in train, and all the albums that were works-in-progress for other artists? Her unfinished workload would require honouring somehow, and its sheer enormity made Jeff's head spin.

Eventually, the exhausted man fell asleep. As he drifted off, he steered himself back to the recent twentieth wedding anniversary and to the promise of a new song Lynn had written for him as the title track of the upcoming "King of Diamonds, King of Hearts" tribute film.

He must have done something very right to deserve a screenplay from his wife as an anniversary gift, even if she hadn't managed to finish it on time. And the fact that so many formidable stars of the screen had jumped at the chance of starring in the movie was testament to how much she was respected by their showbusiness colleagues. Its imminent release promised to be a bittersweet moment indeed.

AND THEN THERE WERE THREE

Some four hours later, the squawking of cockatoos at sunrise woke Jeff with a start. His back ached from sleeping at a crooked angle on the Blakes' couch. It took him a few seconds to remember exactly why he was not lying next to Lynn in a comfortable bed, and his eyes opened to the sight of Kierney curled up in the fœtal position on the sofa opposite.

The father let out a bloodcurdling moan, levering himself upright. The vulgar noise woke the young woman straightaway, and she went through a similar emotional nose-dive as soon as she realised where she was.

'Oh, Papá,' she cried, walking over to sit closer, hugging him as his head hung down. '*Te amo. Te amo.*'

'Hey, gorgeous. *Te amo* too. Sorry to wake you like that.'

The pair sat sobbing in each other's arms again. The wall-clock told them it was only five-twenty in the morning, with the rest of the household still sound asleep.

'Let's make some tea,' Kierney proposed, standing up and grabbing her dad's hand.

Reluctantly, he rose to his feet, and they walked arm-in-arm to the kitchen. 'Did you sleep OK?'

'Yes, thanks. Did you?'

'Must have. I thought happy thoughts after you nodded off, and it must've worked. Took me a while to figure out where I was just now though. Bloody oath, that was revolting, waking up like that.'

'Yeah, I know,' Kierney groaned. 'Me too. What a horrible feeling. I felt really sick as soon as I remembered yesterday.'

Jeff hugged his daughter close. 'So did I. I'm so glad you're here.'

The sun was already heating up the morning, and the early-birds took their tea out to the pool so they could smoke. The father's mobile rang in his trouser pocket, causing their nerves to spring to attention. It was Jet.

'Hey, mate. How're you going?'

'Dad! Thank God you're awake,' came his son's voice, sounding worried and upset. 'I've just landed in Singapore and I need to talk to you. I'm going crazy. It's taking so long to get there.'

'Sure. More than halfway, mate, but talk away,' the empathetic man invited, hearing the young man stifling his sobs. 'Where are you?'

'In a random corridor,' Jet recovered. 'It's OK. No-one can hear me. My battery's low, so can't talk for long.'

'Well, nothing's changed here since we last spoke, more's the pity,' the widower lamented, the pain in the lad's tone causing him to shiver. 'What time d'you take off again?'

'Not 'til seven-thirty Sing-time. I've got nearly five hours to spend in the airport. What the fuck am I going to do?'

'Go into town and see a movie,' his father suggested. 'You'll remember your way around, won't you? Take the bus to Orchard Road, to that huge cinema by the Scotts Road intersection. They're twenty-four-hour there, I'm sure. Don't lose your passport though.'

Jet sighed. 'Thanks, Dad. That's an awesome idea. I shall. Is Kiz there?'

'Yeah. Hold on.'

Kierney took hold of the handset. 'Hey, bro'. Are you OK?'

'Shit, actually,' her brother replied, laughing in relief. 'What about you?'

'*Mismo, mismo,*' she confirmed with one of their made-up childhood phrases. 'We're going to try to get to Tullamarine at the same time as you, so hang around if you arrive first.'

'OK,' Jet answered. 'Thanks for cheering me up. I'd better go 'cause this phone's cactus. Need to buy a spare battery.'

'Bye, Jetto. Fly safely. We're looking forward to seeing you. Papá's waving,' Kierney said before pressing the red "End call" button and putting the telephone down on the table.

'That's a good arrangement you lied about just now,' her dad grinned. 'We'd better book some flights, or he'll be there before us.'

The young woman chuckled. 'That's what I thought as I was saying it. Otherwise, he should've met us here after all.'

'Come on...' Jeff invited, standing up. 'Let's go for a walk.'

Still without shoes and socks, the dismal duo walked over the dewy lawn and along the path leading to the tennis court. The hems of their trousers grew wetter and wetter, but neither cared. Reinvigorating their circulation and breathing in the fresh, damp air helped lighten their mood in preparation for the morning's onslaught.

Half an hour later, Celia appeared on the veranda, laughing at the dark rings creeping up their legs. 'Look at your pants!' she called out. 'What on Earth are you doing?'

'Morning,' Jeff waved as they climbed the sculpted steps from the lawn.

The Diamonds made their way to the table by the pool and shared another cup of tea with their host, who seemed a little more refreshed than the promenading pair. Red-rimmed eyes betrayed a recent descent into sorrow on her part too.

'How are you feeling this morning?' the kindly woman asked, looking from one to the other.

'Pretty low,' Kierney admitted. 'Jet rang. He's in Singapore, changing planes. I can't wait for us all to be together.'

Not quite all of us, her father rued. He said nothing, merely staring into space.

'And what about you, dear?' Gerry's mother turned to the widower. 'Did you manage to get some sleep?'

'Yep, thanks. Some. Sorry, but I'm not in the mood to answer questions at the moment. Please forgive me.'

Celia squeezed his hand. 'That's alright. I understand.'

The French doors swung open, and the large frame of Bart Dyson stepped out onto the deck. He was dressed in sports gear, ready for some exercise.

'Good morning, all,' his voice was less booming than normal. 'How are we?'

Jeff raised a half-hearted hand. 'Morning, sir.'

'Hi, Grandpa,' his granddaughter responded with a bright smile, standing up to give the athlete a kiss. 'How are you?'

'Ah... Could be better, Kierney. You too, I expect.'

The teenager nodded, as did their host. They were all putting on brave faces for each other; a necessary strategy under the circumstances.

'Would you like some tea?' Celia asked. 'Or are you heading off for a run now?'

'Depends if anyone else is coming with me,' Bart responded, focussing on his son-in-law and granddaughter, who were still clad in yesterday's clothes. 'I'll need a map if not. Anyone up for it?'

'Sorry, Grandpa. I haven't got any other clothes with me,' Kierney replied. 'Otherwise I would.'

'I see. No. Of course. Jeff?'

The younger man considered the proposition. He and Lynn had packed running gear for their weekend away, but he couldn't face the prospect of opening the suitcases which presumably still sat in the hallway where he had left them. He didn't wish to see anything to remind him of Lynn. However, a run with his father-in-law was an opportunity to score much-needed brownie points, therefore foolish to pass up. He was going to need all the assistance he could get from his wife's parents over the next few months.

'OK, sir,' Jeff resigned, standing up and shaking his wet trouser legs. 'I'll give it a go. At least these'll have a chance to dry out that way. Give me a few minutes to change.'

Kierney and Celia looked at their favourite tall, dark, handsome stranger with a shared maternal pride. In truth, he was doing better than either of them expected. They understood the significance of what the two important men were about to do for each other, but preferred to keep their thoughts to themselves.

'Would everyone please stop staring at me,' Jeff protested. 'I know what you're thinking, and I'm thinking the same thing. But hey, life goes on. Unfortunately.'

Kierney gasped as she fought to hold back tears. Her father rested a hand on her shoulder and kissed the top of her head before disappearing inside in search of the couple's abandoned baggage.

Bart sat down with a deep sigh. 'Jeff always expresses the things we others don't. Have you noticed that?'

Celia nodded. 'Yes. Poor thing. We're all feeling particularly tender this morning, I imagine. How's Marianna?'

'Not too good,' the Olympian affirmed. 'She asked me to leave her alone for a while.'

Kierney pushed her chair back from the table. 'Sorry. Do you mind if I leave you too? I'm going for a shower.'

The motherly woman brushed the girl's arm as she passed by. 'Are you alright, darling?'

'Yes, thanks. I just want to go home, to be perfectly honest.'

Bart and Celia gave the reserved youngster sympathetic smiles. On the way to her bedroom, the broody teenager found her dad in the hall, crouched down next to an open suitcase. He turned around when he heard the swishing of wet jeans coming towards him.

'Shit. This is so damned hard,' he confessed through gritted teeth. 'You OK?'

'Yes. Do you want some help?' she asked, kneeling down beside him. 'What are you looking for?'

Jeff put his arm round his daughter's shoulders. 'I forgot,' he sniffed.

Smiling, the teenager pulled out some blue shorts she recognised, and then a pair of sports socks, holding them up to her dad's face like the Holy Grail. Batting them out of her hands in jest, he found his running shoes and a T-shirt.

'That's all I need,' he said, reaching over to close the case.

'Papá?'

'Hey! What's wrong?'

'May I borrow a pair of Mamá's undies and a top, please?' she asked tentatively. 'Do you mind? If it's too painful for you, I won't, but I didn't bring a change, and it'd make me feel closer to her.'

Sobs erupted from Jeff's mouth as his well-mannered young lady dissolved into tears, sitting down on the floor beside her. 'No, baby. I don't mind at all. Go for it. It's a lovely thought. It'll probably be good for us both.'

Kierney headed upstairs to the bedroom which had been reserved for her, where she was sure Celia would have provided a towel. The widower changed in the downstairs cloakroom, his mind flying back to his teenage years, when he would freshen up in here after a secret midnight romp with one of Gerry's sisters. The memory turned his stomach.

'I'm sorry, angel,' he said to his wife's spirit, staring into the mirror at the guilt on his reflection's face. 'I hate myself for still thinking about those days. I love you. That was just playtime. By the time you and I came to this house together, we were already a *bona fide* couple. You know that, don't you? Let no man put asunder, and all that. Fucking hell, Lynn. When are you coming back? We need you here.'

Bart sprang out of his chair as soon as his running partner reappeared at the French windows, longing to blow the previous day's cobwebs away. He was still a lithe, strong man, and Celia contrasted this with her own husband's largely self-inflicted health issues.

'You need to talk to Gerald about staying in condition.'

'Yeah. That's what we were originally coming here to do,' Jeff reminded her, 'wasn't it?'

The North Shore housewife nodded. 'Yes. That it was. Don't let me hold you back, gentlemen. Take advantage of the cool breeze.'

The empathetic celebrity squeezed her shoulder. 'We shall. See you soon.'

After a few quick stretches, the pair jogged off towards the tennis court, round behind the stables, out via the back lane and onto the narrow track which ran behind the Blakes' property. It was a well-worn route for the New South Wales native; one he and Gerry had taken ever since they were teenagers.

'I have difficulty remembering the Blakes aren't actually your parents,' the sixty-three-year-old opened, setting a steady pace. 'You all know each other so well.'

The boy from Canley Vale smirked. 'Ah, yeah? Me too, sometimes. You've never seen where I grew up, have you? Not quite as nice as this.'

Bart chuckled. 'No. I'm sorry. I didn't mean to sound condescending.'

'That's fine. I'm way beyond caring about all that.'

'So what are your plans for today?'

'Well, most pressingly, Kiz and I need to leave pretty soon. Jet'll be home before us if not. We've got to be there to meet him,' the singer's voice sounded eerily robotic, unnerving the Olympian. 'Maybe you and I can fly up again to accompany Lynn back to Melbourne after the post-mortem.'

Bart stopped in his tracks, his face turning a shade of beetroot.

'Jeez! Are you OK, sir?' the younger man asked, seeing his father-in-law bury his head in his hands.

Walking back, Jeff tapped him on the shoulder. 'I'm sorry. I didn't mean to startle you.'

By the time the kind gesture had been delivered, the athlete had already pulled himself together and set off again at a cracking lick. His partner scrambled to keep up with him, smiling to himself at the futility of such manly games.

'You're showing admirable fortitude,' Bart praised the musician once he caught up. 'I expected you to be in a bad way today.'

'Christ! I am in a bad way,' Jeff countered. 'What about you? It's only that I had a few lucid moments last night. It was Kizzy who reminded me we had to be back in Melbourne by late afternoon because we don't want Jet arriving to an empty apartment.'

'That sounds like the best plan then. My car's at the airport, so we'll drop you guys back. Will Gerry be coming down too?'

'Don't know. That's up to him. I don't want him saddled with all our shit. He does enough of that already. He should really stay here with his folks for a bit longer, but he's got a hot, new girlfriend whom I expect he's keen to get back to.'

Bart let slip a disapproving smile. 'As you said earlier, life goes on. Isn't he too old to be having hot, new girlfriends?'

Jeff turned to face his conservative father-in-law, letting out a wry chuckle. 'No comment! Gerry'll be one of those sleazy old blokes who always have a trophy on their arm. Although, having said that, he does seem to be showing signs of slowing down these days, particularly after meeting this latest woman.'

'Each to their own. What about you? Did you and the children want to come out to Benloch while we sort everything out?'

The widower considered their options. 'Probably not, if you don't mind. Being in the city's going to be easier, I reckon.'

'The city or Mount Eliza? Won't you go back to the house?'

'Nope,' Jeff asserted. 'I'm not going back there. That's one of the better decisions I made last night. Escondido's lost its appeal for me already. That was *our* house.'

'What about Jet and Kierney though?' Bart asked, his expression still critical. 'It's their home too. They might want you there.'

The tactful world-changer glanced sideways at his father-in-law, who was matching him stride for stride. 'If you don't mind, sir,' he repeated, 'that's something for me and the kids to work out. Some things'll never be the same again, and for me that's non-negotiable.'

'Fair enough,' Big D acquiesced. 'You're right. It's none of my business.'

The skilled negotiator changed the subject, not wishing to put the big man off side. 'One thing you and I need to agree on, sir, and with Marianna too, is where we take Lynn before the funeral. I don't want any of this horrendous lying-in-state crap. Do you?'

Bart let out an involuntary groan. 'Absolutely not. My God, no.'

'Cool,' the widower smiled, feeling nauseated all of a sudden. 'That'd be horrific. The funeral's going to be bad enough.'

It was the forty-three-year-old's turn to stop, and he leant into a hedge on the side of the road, heaving on an empty stomach. Two cars went past at speed, causing both men to throw themselves deeper into the dense gorse.

'Jeez! New South Wales is turning into a dangerous state. I hope I'm not chucking up next time. Nearly got lucky then.'

'That's enough,' Bart urged, concerned that grief was mounting. 'There's no need for those kind of thoughts. Let's run back to the house and have some food. You'd better show me the way.'

The two men sprinted back through the main gates of the Blake residence, their shoes scrunching on the gravel drive. Celia opened the front door on cue, but Jeff signalled their intention to carry on round to the rear to cool down. They watched the impressive, green portal close again.

Reaching the pool, they found Gerry and his father sitting at the large outdoor table, drinking coffee and smoking, with Marianna and Celia inside preparing breakfast. The scene resembled a cosy family Christmas, which rendered the showman bilious all over again.

'Where's Kierney?' he asked the ladies as he made his way through the house to change.

'I don't know, dear,' Celia replied. 'Isn't she by the pool with the men?'

'Nope,' Jeff barked, looping back outdoors.

The alarmed father tore down the steps beside the swimming pool and headed towards the paddock. Why had he left his daughter on her own this morning? Christ! He could be so selfish sometimes. Perhaps she wasn't as self-sufficient as he gave her credit for.

'Kizzo!' he yelled as he approached the stables. '¿Estás aquí, pequeñita?'

'Sí, Papá. Aquí, inside.'

Following her voice, Jeff rounded the corner and spied his gorgeous gipsy girl sitting on top of the closed lower half of a stable door, leaning against the wooden jamb. Her hair was tied in a ponytail, and his heart skipped a beat when he recognised one of Lynn's T-shirts. The youngster was clutching her mobile in amongst a grab of tissues, and her eyes were pink and puffy.

'Nice run?' she asked. 'Where did you go?'

The songwriter leant over the stable door and stared at the chestnut thoroughbred munching away on its feed. His pulse rate was still high, prolonged by the panic that had set in when he couldn't locate his precious child.

'Am I glad to see you! I had visions of you hiding in a cupboard, rocking back and forth. My mind's really playing tricks on me.'

Kierney's eyes widened. 'Oh, no! I'm sorry, Papá. My phone's been going crazy this morning, and I didn't want to talk to my friends in front of Grandma and the Blakes. I came down here because I needed some privacy.'

'*Bueno*. Who's been ringing?'

'Ah, school-friends mainly, and Dylan. It's all out in the open. Natalie said the news is just twenty-four-seven on Mamá at the moment. The TV channels are running old interviews and concerts. We won't be able to turn the television on at all when we get back to Melbourne.'

This was exactly the sort of grim intelligence the famous man was anticipating, but it hit him hard nonetheless. He needed to contact Cathy Lane again and ask her to staff the office over the weekend to answer calls; another bad dream waiting in the wings.

'I bet there's a crowd outside the apartment,' he bemoaned. 'Christ! It's going to be an absolute blast going in and out of the building for the next few days. We'll have to go everywhere by car. Shit, Kizzy... My phone'll have been going off too, I expect. I didn't check it yet this morning. Although most people are probably too scared to ring me.'

Kierney smiled. 'Probably. Everyone asks me how you are. I just say you're devastated, which you are. Dylan wants to come over, but I've asked him to leave it for a few days.'

The songwriter sighed. 'Thanks, *pequeñita*. I don't mind if he wants to come over. He's welcome whenever. It'll be nice for you and Jet to have someone else to talk to. Let's not become hermits over this. Mamá wouldn't want that.'

'No. That's true. What about you though? You need someone to talk to as well.'

'Oh, I've got someone to talk to,' Jeff lamented, pointing to the black ring inset with its four diamonds, 'but she ain't givin' me too much back just now. She's mighty pissed-off about something.'

Before either had a chance to process the widower's latest weird statement, the teenager's telephone rang again. She pressed the red button, and the ringtone stopped.

'Take it,' her dad counselled.

'No. That was Isabelle. I really don't want to explain everything all over again. I'll SMS her to get the info' from Nat.'

Jeff approved of his junior technocrat's course of action. Cellular technology had taken hold of the nineties. He was reminded of Bob Fisher's comment from the previous day and acknowledged the phenomenon had come about largely as a result of his company's investments. He watched his daughter's fingers skip over the keypad, forming words with fluent number combinations.

Lynn's timing was poor, her husband concluded. To think what she would miss over the next few years... So many of their projects were beginning to bear fruit after years of incubation. She would never have the satisfaction of watching people's lives change for the better.

The sombre pair sauntered back up to the house. The smell of a grilled breakfast wafted from the barbecue, where Gerry and Bart were cooking and chatting to the others.

'Are you hungry, mate?' his old friend called out, once the Diamonds came into view.

'Should be,' Jeff answered. 'Do I have enough time to shower?'

Kierney joined her grandmother, leaning in for a cuddle. It was enthusiastically given, and the unbalanced Ace of Diamonds was comforted to see everyone together and supporting each other. Disappearing inside to the bathroom, he felt especially protective towards his children right at this moment. He locked eyes with those of his mirror image, attempting to make contact with his departed lover.

'Angel, can you hear me?' he begged, eyes closing as grief surged again. 'I miss you so much.'

Warm water from the shower mixed with the many tears he shed. Jeff wished he didn't feel quite so alone while surrounded by people who cared about him. Wretchedness was an emotion he thought he had outgrown years ago. Yet here he was, feeling lost and lonely, exactly like before. He was hungry though, which he took as a positive sign. Bart Dyson was a wise man when it came to physio-psychology and the beneficial effects of exercise on mood.

Unable to face rifling through Lynn's belongings for a second time, the grieving husband dressed in yesterday's clothes, which he had draped over the heater when he changed for his run. The legs of his trousers were stiff below the knees and creased from the dewy moisture, but were presentable enough for their flight back to Melbourne.

By the time the celebrity returned to the veranda, breakfast was being served onto large, white plates. He helped himself to orange juice, which was cold and tart on his freshly-brushed teeth. He watched Kierney tucking into her meal and relaxed a little. Turning to the man of the house, he started to say what had been on his mind since before he had gone to sleep.

'Gerald...'

'Yes, Jeff?'

'As we said last night, part of the reason for Lynn's and my trip up here was to encourage you to give up the booze and the ciggies. Until yesterday happened, at least... I was thinking about it more overnight, in the context of this travesty. Lynn and I had talked at length about it the day before too, and I said then that giving these things away should be your choice.'

The retired accountant issued a forlorn smile to the man he considered a second son. He didn't understand why the acclaimed musician was bringing this topic up now, concluding he simply sought to unseat the other excruciating subject matter that occupied everyone's minds.

'That's true,' he nodded. 'It is my choice, but we don't have to talk about this now.'

Jeff continued, all eyes directed his way. 'No, but we should,' he sighed. 'I think you have to ask yourself some questions, such as, "What do I value most?" Is it your ability to enjoy life to the full or the pain you'd save your family?'

Celia and Marianna both inhaled at the plainness of the younger man's words but let him continue regardless. Few people understood the human condition better than Jeff Diamond, and he had been proven right on so many other occasions.

'Never has this question been more pertinent to me, and the answer so acute in my mind, as now.'

Bart Dyson set his knife and fork down onto his plate and took a gulp of fruit juice. 'I agree, Jeff,' he nodded, staring at his son-in-law, 'but there are also all the points in between too.'

The widower shrugged, beginning to cry for the umpteenth time this morning. 'I have to let Lynn go, because we always agreed we wouldn't spend our life avoiding the death threats. We knew the risks we were taking, and here we are, facing the consequences of not hiding away. It was a choice we made as a couple, and later as a family, so I can hardly sit here and preach moderation and conservatism, can I?'

Marianna looked her daughter's mystery man in the eye, and he watched a tear roll down her cheek too.

'Whether Lynn died yesterday or in another forty or fifty years' time,' the influential celebrity continued, 'our grief'd be exactly the same. So it's what you do with all these bonus years that'll count, Gerald. Does that make sense?'

There were subservient nods all round. Kierney left her seat and walked over to her dad, placing her hands on his shoulders to massage his aching muscles. At first he recoiled, wishing they were Lynn's hands instead, before steeling himself to accept the very best alternative on offer.

Jeff reached up with his left hand and took hold of his daughter's. 'Thanks, gorgeous,' he whispered. 'I love you.'

A subdued ringtone from the other end of the table caused all heads to turn towards Jeff's mobile. Marianna picked it up gingerly, and it was passed down the table, still ringing and vibrating, as if it were a firework about to explode. Its owner checked the screen in case it was a call he wasn't willing to take. It was their office manager in Melbourne.

'Cath, hi,' he spoke into the mouthpiece, relieved he wouldn't need to endure another awkward condolence conversation in front of his audience. 'How did you go yesterday? Is everyone OK?'

'Oh, Jeff, we're not OK at all,' Cathy wept into the telephone. 'I didn't know if you'd answer. Thanks.'

'No worries,' the sympathetic man replied with a half-smile. 'You're on my very short "Yes" list. I'm screening, baby! Waiting for that all-important call from Lynn saying, "Surprise! Had you going there for a while, didn't I?"'

This caustic remark caught those around the table by surprise, and six jaws dropped together at the possibility, be it delusional desire or simply the intellectual's deadpan sense of humour.

Seeing the effect he was having on his friends and family, Jeff excused himself from the table and headed back into the house. Now wasn't the time to be cracking jokes, although his mind was so twisted that he could hardly tell the bizarre from the serious anymore.

'Sorry, Cath,' the songwriter said, once he had sat down in the kitchen with his checklist. 'I had to escape from the circle of concern I'm surrounded by up here. How're you going over there?'

'We're all here today,' the Stonebridge Music marketing guru replied. 'Couldn't stay away. Everyone sends their love, Jeff. And to Jet and Kierney. How're they doing?'

'Ah, y'know... It's just a shithouse situation for all of us. No-one knows whether to laugh or cry at the pure pointlessness of it all. I even went for a run with Big D this morning, which was a good idea, even though I didn't think so at the time. Jet's flying home as we speak, and Kizzy's wearing Lynn's clothes, which is strangely comforting. So, in answer to your question, I guess you could say we're bearing up.'

Cathy calmed down on receiving his well-articulated account of their wellbeing, or lack thereof. Her boss heard her take a deep breath as if she were about to say something he wasn't going to like.

'Jeff, the Federal Police have been on the phone,' she said. 'I didn't speak to them. Diana took the call, and apparently New South Wales Police has been told to hand the case over, given your profile. And so on and so forth... They want to meet with you as soon as possible. When are you coming back?'

The joker cackled. 'Never! We're never coming back. What's the fucking point, eh?'

'You're not serious, are you?'

'Yes and no,' Jeff responded, backing off a little. 'Apologies. I'm in a fucked-up mood this morning. Just ignore me. Hysteria's setting in, I think. Haven't had a cigarette for a few hours though, which is a feat in itself.'

Cathy relaxed. 'Good. That's a relief. I was scared for a minute there.'

'All good. We'll get through this. Y'know... Shit! She's fucking dead, Cath. Completely, irretrievably, irreversibly dead. So I don't know why the AFP are so desperate to talk to me. They can't do anything to help us, can they?'

'Except put the murderer away. His picture's all over the television and the papers. He looks so innocuous.'

'You're not wrong,' the widower sighed, his mind threatening to overreact to the word "murder" being used in connection with his wife. 'I thought he was some sort of delivery guy. It's weird, but I don't bear any malice towards him at the moment. I ought to, and expect I shall in the future, but the way I feel now, it doesn't make any bloody difference to me whether he's banged up or free. I couldn't give a fuck about anything except finding some way of winding back time.'

'Oh, Jeff, that'd be so wonderful,' Cathy agreed. 'I was wishing the same all day yesterday. Hoping it was all a bad dream; that we'd wake up this morning, and life'd be back to normal.'

The musician chuckled. 'Ah, so it's not just me then... I'm sure my family now thinks I'm totally off my trolley, but that's fine. Anyway... You can tell the AFP I'll meet them anytime from Monday onwards. Can I ring you back from the telephone here 'cause my battery's nearly flat? I need to charge it before we fly back. Lynn's parents are here, so I'll ask them if they need any flights booked. Call you back in a few minutes, alright?'

'Sure. I'll be waiting.'

'Cheers. Please tell everybody how grateful I am for their help today, and for their good wishes. And no-one's to come into the office tomorrow if they don't have to. Bare minimum coverage only.'

'Yes, OK. Bye for now, Jeff.'

The forty-three-year-old rose to his full height and stretched his arms high in the air. His shoulders and neck had stiffened up with the stress of having to focus his tired mind. Where were his cigarettes? And his telephone charger? Exhaling noisily at the thought of having to go into that damned suitcase again, he knew there was no alternative. He wandered along the hallway to the downstairs cloakroom, which had become his temporary home.

Taking a deep breath and half-expecting to have developed some new luggage phobia, the songwriter raised the lid and fished around for the mains adaptor. He came across the small jewellery case Lynn used for travelling and hugged it to his chest, visualising the familiar items it contained, most of which he had given her over the years.

Was it his imagination or were the tattoos on his chest itching? Get a grip, he chastised himself, rubbing the "JL" symbol on his left pectoral muscle through his shirt. It was more likely to be the effect of wearing a day-old shirt. Ludicrous notion or not, it was uplifting to think there might be some sort of connection still to be had with his beautiful best friend.

Jeff located the telephone charger, two new packets of cigarettes and a clean shirt and then closed the case again as quickly as possible. 'Right... Let's see if it's dirty clothes or the touch of an angel, shall we?' he smiled into the mirror, undoing the buttons. 'Maybe I should start wearing your jocks too.'

The inverse image of his tattoos, obscured by thick, greying chest hair, transported the lonely man back to the day he and his dream girl smeared their fingers all over the glass in the en-suite bathroom of his Melbourne penthouse, designing a symbol to represent their relationship from that point forward. This had been the very first day of their life singular, he recalled, before which had stretched more than two years of forced separation. Now they had been separated again with no grand reunion to sustain them.

'What've we got now, Regala? What's going to happen to us?'

Feeling nothing from his tattoos this time, the philosopher shook his head and gazed blankly at his own reflection. His mobile rang again while connected to the power socket next to the mirror. Madalena.

'Fuck,' he hissed, furious at being delivered from much happier times.

Accepting the call, Jeff summoned another shot of civility. '*Lena, olá.*'

'*¡Chico!* I can't fuckin' believe it,' his sister's raw accent clanged out of the tiny speaker, through his ear and into the inner reaches of his brain. 'Is it true? You OK?'

'Yes and no,' he answered. 'Yes, it's true, and no, I'm not OK. How're you going?'

'You still in Sydney?'

The globetrotter steeled himself, his eyes stinging. He couldn't face dealing with the spirited woman today. Was this an occasion which justified a lie?

'Yeah, but I'm about to fly home,' he replied with a half-truth. 'Jet's coming in from the UK, and we have to be there to meet him.'

Madalena was crying. Jeff had never known her to cry, and it affected him more than he expected.

'*Chico*, I'm sorry,' she whined into the telephone. 'You must o' been so shocked. What 'appened? Did you see it?'

The forty-three-year-old leant on the bathroom wall, tears once more streaming down his face. 'No, Lena. I didn't see it happen. I was parking the car. Parking the fucking car. Howzat, eh? I was playing with a bloody toy Merc', and now she's dead.'

'Can I come down to Melbourne?' Madalena begged, scarcely even listening to her brother's responses. 'Can I come and stay with you?'

'*Sí. Cierto.* But listen, *hermana mía*,' Jeff pulled himself together. 'Come to Melbourne whenever you like. I can't talk now. I'll ring you *mañana*, OK?'

'Hey, hold on...' his older sibling implored. '*Te amo, chico.* I wanna help you.'

'Thanks, Lena. *Gracias muchas.* I'm going to need a shitload of help. I love you too. *Adiós.*'

The beleaguered star terminated the call and dropped the telephone onto the marble vanity. Nothing like a crisis to bring out the best in people... So his sister finally got around to telling him she loved him, the day after he became a widower. Be grateful, he told himself. Don't make things any worse than they already are.

Jeff slammed the cloakroom door to vent his frustration and walked back towards the steady drone of chatter he could hear coming from the kitchen. Marianna and Celia were deep in conversation like long-lost friends, exchanging information about grandchildren and the various good causes with which they were involved. Bart and the Blake menfolk were watching a televised golf tournament, and Kierney occupied herself with a magazine at the breakfast bar.

Jeff put his arms round the youngster's strong shoulders and kissed the back of her head. 'How're you going, you gorgeous thing? We need to get our travel organised.'

'Hmm... Where've you been? You were gone for ages.'

'Sorry,' he replied, kissing her again. 'Auntie Lena rang just now, but I couldn't talk to her. She invited herself down, so look out!'

Kierney pulled a face. 'Yikes! That's good, I think.'

Her dad turned to address the others. 'Right... Guys, I'm about to ask Cath to arrange us some flights back to Melbourne. Who wants to take advantage of this very generous offer?'

The entire complement put up their hands, even Celia and Gerald, making the billionaire laugh.

'OK! Didn't realise I was quite that generous!'

Marianna raised her hand. 'Actually, Bart and I are staying 'til this evening. We're going to do a few things in the city this afternoon.'

Noting that it was already gone eleven o'clock, Jeff collected everyone else's requirements and lifted the cordless telephone sitting next to Kierney, requesting that Cathy book his daughter and himself on the first flight feasible to catch without breaking the law on the way, then another for the Dysons and his intrepid manager in the early evening.

They heard the front door open down the hall, and Gerry's elder sister let herself in, already in floods of tears. Jacinta ran straight into the superstar's arms when she saw him, despite her mother's protestations.

'Jesus Christ,' he groaned, prising the wailing woman away from his neck. 'Is this what my life's going to be like for the next few weeks? Jac, how are Ray and the kids?'

'They're fine, Jeff. Fine, thank you,' the eldest of the Blake progeny replied, wiping her eyes and greeting everyone else. 'I'm sorry. I was composed all the way in the car, but as soon as I saw you, I went to pieces.'

'We noticed,' Gerald scolded, standing up to give his daughter a welcoming kiss. 'These fine folk are leaving in a few moments, so get all your histrionics out of the way now. Have you spoken to your sister?'

'Yes. Three times already. Jeff, Kierney, I don't know how you're coping so well. You look remarkably composed.'

Kierney glanced at her father, and they both shrugged. 'Composed on the outside maybe,' she answered. 'It's just the horrible "What now?" feeling. That's been my overwhelming thought over the last hour or so, like we're in some kind of limbo.'

'Purgatory, more like,' Jeff agreed, standing with his hand on Kierney's shoulder.

HOME IS WHERE THE HEART WAS

While waiting in a private room in the airline lounge, Jeff checked all twenty-three voicemail messages which had arrived on his mobile since the news broke. Scanning down the log of missed calls, he was amazed at the array of people who had been given his number in the three years since taking delivery of his first reliable device. He listened to each message, wrote down the details of those he needed to call back and then deleted the lot.

After the fifth or sixth recording, he turned to his daughter with a smirk. 'I think the world's been issued a script. All these messages are exactly the same. "Oh, my God! What terrible news. How are you? Don't worry about ringing back. Best wishes," insert name as appropriate.'

Kierney smiled in resignation. 'This is just the start too. Is there anyone you want me to ring back?'

'Thanks. Anna maybe,' her dad suggested. 'We'll do it together when we get to the apartment. I just want to focus on getting home now.'

The flight back to Melbourne was not quite the nightmare the Diamonds had feared. Sitting in the Airbus' front row, it was as if an aeroplane full of eyes were drilling into the backs of their heads. The ground staff were considerate in allocating the famous pair the most invisible seats and had sent security staff to accompany them from the Qantas lounge to their departure gate.

Jeff insisted Kierney slide into the window seat, and she was happy to accept and hide from the world for an hour. The businessmen sitting on the other side of the aisle pretended not to recognise the unmistakable passengers across the way, only stealing the occasional glance while meals were being served or when the watchful flight attendants were diverted elsewhere.

'At least no-one can ring us,' the sad celebrity thought aloud, as he poured himself a pathetic-sized glass of tepid Victoria Bitter. 'I can foresee a whole bunch of small mercies to be grateful for over the next few days, can't you?'

His daughter sighed. 'Yeah. S'pose so. How are you feeling?'

'Same as you, I reckon. Can I tell you a secret?' he whispered, leaning in and staring out of the window at the clouds.

'Yes, please. Is it a nice secret?'

'Hope so. I'm beginning to be able to feel her with me.'

'Mamá? Really?' the teenager gaped, her eyes shining with spontaneous tears.

Sympathy, Jeff wondered, or pity? 'Yep,' he confirmed, rubbing his chest again. 'I keep feeling a weird stinging sensation around this tattoo. I'm probably going nuts, but I like it.'

The teenager sniffed and wiped her eyes, unsure what to make of this odd notion. 'That's lovely. I hope you're right. You deserve it.'

Kissing Kierney's cheek, the widower thanked her for her encouragement before settling back into his seat and closing his eyes. *Pick a year*, he suggested to his rampant mind.

It chose 1986. Yes, that was a good year. Famine relief mania was finally calming down, both children were doing well at school, and he and Lynn had been married for an assiduous but heavenly decade.

The opening of their musical, "The Black Sheep", had been a worldwide triumph, and neither Diamond superstar had toured for twelve months. Yet to say they hadn't been busy as a result would have been a gross misrepresentation. The young mother had thrown all her spare energies into the first finals year for The Good School with pleasing results.

Towards the end of this same year, the rocker-turned-philanthropist appeared on stage in New York with Tex Fletcher and Steve Christie at a Moonshine gig for a three-way rendition of a song he had written and all three had recorded individually, using it to kick off a worldwide mental health campaign. The Diamonds had never in a million years imagined the level of success that one collective appearance might achieve in raising both awareness and those all-important funds to pay for clinics across the world through royalties alone.

Above all, the megastar remembered, this could well have been the year when his family had spent the fewest nights apart since the generous sabbatical he had afforded himself while the children were tiny. The final few weeks of 1985 had seen him slump into a profound, post-euphoric depression, fuelled by criticism their charities had received and the problems which had beset the aid efforts in Africa. These trials were cured by his beautiful best friend's ministries, using her unique brand of compassionate and revitalising therapy.

'Are you asleep, Papá?' Kierney asked, interrupting his daydream.

'Yes,' Jeff murmured without opening his eyes. 'Are you?'

The young woman giggled. Her dad always responded in the same vein, and his skilful timing still caught her unawares every time.

'Can we talk about what's going to happen?' she asked with trepidation in her voice. 'I mean once the funeral's over and things need to get back to normal.'

The doleful father opened his eyes and crossed his long legs, his right shin pressing affectionately against his daughter's calf. He took a breath and shrugged.

'"Back to normal" is an interesting concept to define. What will normal look like, I wonder?'

'Yeah,' Kierney agreed. 'That's kind of my point. What do you want normal to look like? Have you thought about it?'

'No. Not really,' the widower lied through his teeth. 'If you mean do I still want you to go to Sydney Uni', the answer's yes, if you want to. Or no, if you don't want to. It's up to you, *pequeñita*. You can defer a year or whatever. We're not ready to make those sorts of choices yet, are we? Nothing's going to make sense for a while for any of us.'

'OK, thanks. But that's not what I'm getting at,' Kierney pressed. 'I mean what's going to happen to *you*?'

Jeff already knew what she meant. The downside of being open with one's children was having then to put one's money where one's mouth was. Over the years, the tight-knit family had discussed every potential scenario they might encounter, and now they were slap-bang in the middle of one. He had been expecting this question.

'Jeez, Kiz. I don't know,' he owned up. 'Way too early to say. We've got a lot of talking to do once the three of us are together. We made some promises to each other that'll be bloody hard to keep, so let's not rush into anything.'

Kierney felt a certain respite slide through her, cooling her soul. A door had been left open, for which she was glad.

'Thanks, wise, old man,' she whispered, nudging her dad's shoulder. 'I'm so scared.'

'Jesus Christ,' the songwriter whispered, biting his lip and inhaling. 'You're not the only one. It's easy to make decisions based on hypotheticals, but not always so easy to see them through. Nothing's going to happen that we don't all fully support, OK?'

'*Bueno.* How long do you think Jet'll stay home for?'

'That's up to him too. He's probably sitting in exactly the same situation as us, asking himself the same questions.'

'On his own,' Kierney rued. 'Poor Jetto.'

'Indeed. We'll hang around in the lounge once we get there. I'll text him to let him know where we are. That way, we can meet up as soon as he lands.'

The young woman nodded, picking up the newspaper she had been reading. Her papá breathed a sigh of relief at having been let off the hook for now. His eighteen-year-old alter-ego was determined to keep him honest, and he rejoiced at the maturity she had shown so far. It gave him some hope that the next few months might not be quite as bleak as they had seemed when first looming large on the family's horizon.

The droning of the engines changed pitch, and the aircraft's nose dipped forward on its descent into Tullamarine Airport. Hit by a sudden pang of longing, Jeff's mind was thrown back to the first long-haul flight the couple had shared, marking the start of their year in London as superstar students. How excited they had been to be together and away from home! This milestone was now twenty-one years old; more years ago than his dream girl had been alive at that time, and with the scabs still fresh on their matching tattoos.

The reformed tearaway remembered an uncomfortable conversation the young lovers had shared about belonging to the Mile High Club, and then how he had completed Lynn's silent induction in the dimmed cabin a few hours before landing at Heathrow.

It occurred to him that he now felt nothing when his mind turned to sex, and he wondered how long this void would last. The same side-effect had been visited on him when the sixteen-year-old schoolgirl first announced her departure to the USA, as if the man in him had initiated strike action. He was far less troubled by this physical response now than then. In fact, it was much better than the alternative. If only his heart could adopt the same ambivalence...

'Landing,' Kierney muttered, eyebrows raised at the aeroplane's steady reduction in altitude. 'Life's in slow motion.'

Her fellow passenger smiled at the powerful and accurate image, squeezing the young woman's arm. 'Hang on in there.'

The senior flight attendant appeared at their side, requesting the airline's VIPs to be ready as soon as the seatbelt sign was switched off. The crew had received a directive to make sure the Diamonds disembarked and made their way through the secure zone before any other passengers had the chance to pursue them. Jeff acknowledged the glum woman.

Father and daughter whiled away the hour and a half between their arrival in Melbourne and Jet's, squirrelled away in another small office within the Qantas lounge. It was too early to ring Anna in London, but the widower responded to a few of the messages he had picked up earlier on. His script was also alarmingly similar for each reply, and his reaction to people's kind words became somewhat anaesthetised by the repetition.

Jeff caught his daughter gazing at him during a conversation with Gerry's executive assistant and dealt her a playful wink which moved her to tears. Seeing her vulnerability so plainly displayed, he switched his telephone off.

'Jeez. I'm sorry, baby,' the musician said, after terminating the call. 'I didn't mean to upset you. You OK?'

'Yes. I guess so.'

The pair sat together in silence, hypnotised by the clock's unswerving tempo until inaction gave way to yet more grief.

'Fancy a game of poker?' her dad suggested, spotting a pack of cards on a bookcase behind them.

'OK,' Kierney replied with scant enthusiasm.

They played for an hour, therapeutic for both. There was no rush to return all these calls, Jeff realised. More had arrived while they were in the air, and no doubt more still would bank up until he next switched the telephone back on. A member of staff knocked on the door to let them know Jet's flight was landing half an hour ahead of schedule, which was welcome news.

When the time came, the two Diamonds were escorted air-side to wait in yet another claustrophobic echo-chamber close to the arrival gate.

'My heart's thumping,' Jeff confided in his daughter. 'I want Jet to feel like he can behave exactly how he wants. I'm sure he's going to give us the Bart Dyson stiff upper lip act.'

Kierney nodded. 'Probably, but I know I'm going to do a Jacinta as soon as I see him, so that might tip him over the edge.'

Jeff laughed, remembering the quivering mess who had hung around his neck a few hours earlier. He stood up and stretched his back, peering through a tiny window giving out onto a roadway under the long line of aerobridges.

'Yeah. So shall I, *pequeñita*. Guaranteed.'

'Will you stop walking round in circles, please?' the young woman requested, watching her impatient father pacing. 'It's making me dizzy.'

Several minutes later, they heard the sound of voices outside the room. Through a narrow pane of glass to one side of the door, the room darkened noticeably with the arrival of Ryan "Jet" Diamond's substantial frame, flanked by the same security staff. He was dressed smartly, as usual, but unshaven and dishevelled.

'Mate,' Jeff greeted his son, hugging both children close. 'We're so glad to see you. Long flight.'

As predicted, all three dissolved into tears, standing together without speaking for several minutes. They exchanged kisses and wiped each other's faces while an outpouring of pent-up emotion overtook the exhausted traveller.

'I don't know what to say to you, Dad. I've been wanting to say something meaningful for the last twenty hours and couldn't come up with anything except "What the fuck?"'

His sister laughed. 'That's pretty meaningful, considering.'

Out of the corner of his eye, the grieving husband saw the uniformed men were still loitering outside the door, trying their best not to invade the family's privacy. 'Let's get out of here, shall we? Where's your luggage, mate? Are they bringing it here?'

'It's already here,' the lad replied, pointing through the slim window beside the door. 'I didn't pack very carefully. It's just in that bag over there.'

'*Bueno*,' Jeff put an arm around his son. 'Who cares? It's so bloody good to have you both here, let me tell you.'

They pulled the door open, and their protectors snapped to attention. The empathetic celebrity couldn't wait to be back in their apartment and no longer setting other people on edge merely by existing.

'We're ready to go,' he announced. 'My daughter's car's in the short-term car park. We can give you the keys or we can all just walk there. I don't care either way, as long as we don't have to stop.'

The two guards went into a huddle, leaving the family to stare at each other for a few more eternal moments. The widower watched his children exchanging secret messages which he guessed he wasn't meant to see, and it warmed his heart. He remembered the indifference with which his own sister and he had interacted when their parents passed away.

The siblings had scarcely exchanged two words over their mother's demise, yet had managed to open up a little when their dad later succumbed to lung cancer. They had been downright hostile, truth be told! Anticipating Jet and Kierney embarking on this most painful of life's tribulations, Jeff was comforted that at least they had each other; and such an easy relationship it was too.

One of the bodyguards beckoned for their famous clients to follow, and the troops fell in to a strange sort of drill formation to navigate the airport jungle. Father and son swapped telepathic observations, unable to stop grinning at how seriously the burly minders were taking their special operation. Jet broke away to the right as a test, only to be swooped on within a couple of seconds and brought back into line with a deftness that would make a sheepdog proud.

Kierney shot her brother a scolding glare, and Jeff was taken aback at how like her mother she was. In their own ways, each was embarking on a new journey, stepping up to fill parts of a gaping hole in their family structure. Eyes front and docile, the five conscripts and their overloaded luggage trolley moved through the terminal building, past the carousels and out into the open air.

People scattered around the celebrities, reeling in shock and with momentary pained expressions as they recognised the revered Melburnians who had dominated the news in the last twenty-four hours. As soon as anyone showed the slightest inclination to approach the Diamonds, one of the uniformed border collies would bite the offending bottom, figuratively speaking, causing him or her to retreat to a safe distance.

'I hope I can remember where the car is,' the pretty teenager piped up from between her towering menfolk. 'Level Two, but I don't know which row it's in.'

'Didn't you write it on the ticket?' Jet chided.

'No. I was hardly in an organised frame of mind when I got here,' the young woman retorted. 'I don't even know if I locked it, so it might not even be here anymore.'

Jeff rolled his eyes. 'Ease up, mate. It'll be here.'

It was. The compact silver Golf was waiting patiently in Row P. No sooner had its owner been permitted to play with it unchaperoned, than she had abandoned it and disappeared.

Kierney held her key-ring out towards the others. 'Please would one of you drive? I can't remember how.'

'Bullshit!' her father smiled, accepting the keys. 'I'll drive. It's OK, baby. No pressure on any of us over the next few days. That's the rule, alright?'

'*Gracias, Papá.*'

They piled their luggage into the hatchback's small boot and thanked the security staff, who were relieved to have completed their mission without incident. Jeff slid the seat backwards to its limit and checked the rear-view mirror while he adjusted it, watching his daughter shrink again in the back seat to the toddler she once was. Jet, on the other hand, overflowed the passenger area to his left.

'Have you grown or have cars got smaller?' he teased, hitting his son on the arm.

The cricketer shrugged. 'Both probably.'

The rock star reached his left hand backwards to collect the ticket from Kierney's hand. 'Has anyone got any cash?' he asked, pulling the handbrake on again and flicking the gear lever into neutral. 'We'll need about thirty bucks.'

Between them, they rustled together a combination of notes and headed towards the exit, hoping they could pay up and leave unnoticed. The woman behind the counter obliged by only uttering a short scream before discretion kicked in. She avoided eye contact altogether, simply handing over their change and raising the barrier.

'Bloody hell!' Jet exclaimed. 'Is this what it's been like for you since it happened?'

The dark-haired pair answered in the affirmative, and the lad sighed. Their father took his hand off the steering wheel, threaded his fingers along his son's shoulders and squeezed his neck.

'Yeah. And every man and his dog's leaving messages on our mobiles,' he replied. 'And the funny part is they're all the same message.'

The traveller chuckled. 'You can't say "every man and his dog" in the UK anymore.'

'Why not?' his sister asked.

'Because it's discriminatory. You can't leave out any minority these days. You have to say "Every person and his or her domestic pet."'

Kierney giggled. 'That's funny. Can't be species-ist. How quaint.'

'Hey... Where are we going?' the recent arrival asked, noticing his father drive past the freeway entrance. 'Are Grandpa and Grandma still in Sydney?'

'Yes. They're flying back tonight,' the young woman answered.

'Cool. So when's Mum being brought down to Melbourne?'

'Early next week, I'm guessing. After the post-mortem. Depends how quickly they get everything done.' Jeff replied, watching his son stiffen in the seat beside him.

'Why?' the lad asked with some aggression. 'Isn't it obvious how she died?'

'It's a formality son, they have to do a full-on PM whenever there are suspicious circumstances. I heard from Cath this morning that the New South Wales police have been told to transfer the case to AFP, so they'll most likely have to do everything twice now.'

Kierney huffed. 'That's ridiculous. Don't they trust each other?'

'With the number of botched cases you hear about, they're right not to trust each other,' Jet countered. 'But surely they won't find anything unexpected? What could they discover? That Mum was terminally ill and she would've died yesterday morning anyway, so it might not have been the bullet that killed her?'

'Mate!' the widower shouted. 'For Christ's sake! That's enough of that. Who gave you permission to dick around with your mum's memory like that?'

The startled student felt guilty to have provoked such wrath in his father. Perhaps he had become too accustomed to being his own man since he left Australia.

'Sorry, Dad,' he said, with genuine apprehension in his eyes. 'There wasn't anything wrong with Mum, was there?'

'No,' breathed the older man, steadying his raw nerves again. 'Its' all good. Sorry to snap at you. It's just that she shouldn't be dead, regardless of what killed her. She should still be here with us, and I'm bloody sick of talking about it.'

The siblings sat in silence as their father cried his way down Sydney Road. Jet offered to take the wheel, but the driver declined. They reached the north-eastern corner of the city's grid within twenty minutes, pulled into their apartment building's basement car park and parked next to Lynn's blue Maserati, in which the couple had driven up from their coastal hideaway only a few days ago. Locking the doors of Kierney's silver pride and joy, Jeff leant heavily on his wife's car and placed a yearning hand on its roof.

The young woman accepted the keys from her dad's outstretched hand and hugged him. 'Come upstairs, Papá. Mamá'd want us to have some tea, so let's do it.'

Between them, the trio loaded their bags into the lift and soon found themselves on the top floor. They had arrived home undetected by any neighbours, and all three breathed a sigh of relief when the doors slid closed.

'I'll make the drinks,' Jet volunteered, heading into the north kitchen. 'It's nice to be home. Nothing's changed, which is good.'

'Didn't you come here at all over the holidays?' Jeff asked, heaving their suitcases out of the way.

'Nope.'

The songwriter shoved his son sideways. 'Not even to get laid? What's going on? You're slipping.'

'Papá!' Kierney cried out. 'Let's not talk about that now either.'

The young sportsman gave the former playboy a half-hearted push, and they embraced again. It felt healthy, being together to face the world. They sat on the balcony drinking tea and smoking. Jeff updated both children on an earlier conversation with Cathy and relayed the information he had since received about Lynn's body being available for transport to Melbourne on Monday. Bart Dyson had also left a message to say he and Marianna had decided to stay the extra nights to accompany it down, so there was no need for him to make a return trip to Sydney.

'What d'you think, guys? Should I go up again and fly down with her?'

'No,' Jet answered. 'G and G can take care of it. There doesn't seem much point in you going too. Unless you want to.'

'I don't want to,' the widower admitted, rubbing his chest, 'but is it the right thing to do?'

Kierney's eyes met similar forlorn expressions on both stubbly faces. 'We need to decide what we're going to say at the funeral.'

'Hmm... That and a whole host of other things we have to decide in the next few days,' Jeff agreed. 'I need to go to the bank on Monday and get all the paperwork out of our safe deposit box. Gerry's office has the key, so I or we'll have to run the gauntlet in there, with all those wailing women. Jesus!'

'I can go,' his daughter offered. 'Is that where the letters are too?'

Seeing their father nod, Jet grimaced. 'Shit! Of course. All those letters. That's going to be an ordeal.'

'I'm looking forward to it,' his sister countered, forcing some brightness on the two long-faced men. 'It'll be lovely to read Mamá's words to us from when we were little and to see how things changed as we got older. I think it'll make us feel better.'

Jeff put his head in his hands. His position was somewhere between the two teenagers'. He agreed with Kierney that it would be fascinating to follow Lynn's train of thought along their family timeline, therein discovering her hopes for them. On the other hand however, he shared Jet's view that the exercise was likely to be an emotional rollercoaster. This dread, on the kids' behalf, concerned only the letters she had written as a mother. A far greater terror was the damage the envelopes marked with his name might inflict on his own fragile sanity.

'So how do we want to do this?' Jet asked. 'Bring them back here?'

'Yeah,' the man of the house affirmed. 'I think so. Gerry's flying back tonight, so what I'd like to do is organise a session with the solicitor to fast-track the reading of the will. We all know what's in it, in terms of assets and liabilities anyway. We have to be prepared to answer all sorts of probity questions about the will, so I want to make sure there are independent witnesses. Then, if you don't mind, I'll ask him to come back with us.'

Kierney sat up straighter. 'But why does Gerry have to be here while we read the letters?' she asked. 'They don't form part of the will, do they?'

'No,' Jeff answered, exhaling deeply. 'To be honest, what I'm worried about is my reaction. I'd just like Gerry to be here in case.'

'In case of what?' his son probed, seeing a wild look in the great man's eyes.

'In case I go crazy. I don't trust myself. I might as well tell you now.'

The youngsters stared at each other. They had a fair idea what this statement meant, long aware of their father's suicidal predisposition and no doubt both contemplating the drastic actions of a desperate man.

'Papá, what did you say on the plane?' his daughter reminded him. 'Nothing's going to happen that we don't all support?'

His son nodded in agreement. 'I'd prefer just the three of us here when we read the letters. We can take care of each other perfectly well.'

Jeff raised his hands in front of his face, wishing he shared their confidence. 'Alright,' he agreed. 'If you're sure you're OK with that? And as long as you understand the risks.'

Kierney stood up and put her arms around her dad's shoulders. He had managed to maintain control at the Blakes' but was obviously on a knife-edge in his own home. His guard was down now, she figured. How would her mum have set his mind at rest?

'Have you ever really gone crazy?' she asked, kissing his mop of dark waves.

'Sure have. When I was a teenager I did. Regularly. Destroying stuff, fighting with anyone who got in my way, irrational decisions. You name it...'

The slender gipsy glanced over at her brother, willing him to join in. 'And how long has it been since you were a teenager?'

Jet cackled. 'Bloody ages!'

'OK, funny man... Thanks for that,' their dad smiled, leaning his head backwards into his daughter's embrace. 'You guys are fantastic. I guess you're right. You've convinced me, *sorta-kinda*. I hope I can keep it together, for your sakes.'

His son changed the subject. 'What are we going to do for dinner? I'm getting hungry for something that doesn't come in a rectangular container with foil over it.'

'So takeaway's out then?' Kierney chuckled.

'Not necessarily,' the blond cricketer backpedalled. 'That statement was a tad rash on my part. I'll get the menus.'

Sliding the balcony door closed behind him, Jet strode across the lounge room floorboards and on through to the office. While fetching the family's stock of takeaway leaflets out of a filing cabinet, he took a moment to scan the room, imagining his absent mother sitting at the desk where she had worked for countless hours while he was growing up, either talking on the telephone or writing letters and e-mails, sorting out their life with minute precision.

This short diversion educed a fresh dose of empathy for his dad's situation, sensing anger and emptiness welling up inside too. Tears gathered in the corners of his eyes, and he sat down in his mum's chair, swinging from side to side as he checked out the photographs on her desk.

On the way back to the others, Jet stuck his head into his parents' bedroom. It looked tidy but recently occupied, complete with piles of clean clothes on the bed, ready to be taken back to Escondido, the family's idyllic seaside *hacienda*. He wondered what the next few days had in store for them. There had been many nights when his dad had slept in this bed alone, but tonight would be quite a different story. Even a carefree, sports-mad adolescent possessed sufficient sensitivity to understand this.

'Dad, I'm really sorry,' he said, depositing the menus onto the table on which his father was leaning. 'I still don't really know what to say, but I'd hate to be you right at this moment. I want to help in any way I can.'

The widower replied, raising his head and looking the huge hulk in the eye. 'Son, I know you do. Thanks heaps. Are you alright?'

'I went into your room,' the lad admitted, wondering if he had done the wrong thing. 'And I was in the office, sitting on Mum's chair. It's only just beginning to sink in, I guess. It's real now. When I was on the plane, it felt like I was coming home to someone else's life.'

Father and son cried together, renewing and strengthening their bond in the same way father and daughter had done the day before. Kierney left the pair alone and retreated to her own room for some space to reflect on what was to come.

After five minutes flat on her back and full of regret, she got to her feet again. *That's what Mamá would've done...*

The caring youngster went into one of the empty bedrooms to check if the bed was made up and the bathroom was clean. She then opened her parents' suitcases and, armful after armful, transferred her father's clothing and toiletries into the spare room.

Removing his alarm clock from the bedside table in the master suite, her gaze fell on one of her papá's favourite photographs. It had been taken long before she was born by her late Uncle Sandy. The lovers, both still teenagers at the time, radiated happiness and looked so relaxed in each other's company. Soul-mates, as they always described themselves; each other's very best friend.

Kierney was hit by the same guilt that had affected her brother moments earlier, needing to turn away and suppress her grief. Lynn was not the only one of their grandparents' children to die too soon: Sandy had succumbed to an AIDS-related illness several years ago, but his death was almost glossed over owing to his parents' lack of comprehension and tolerance.

Similar to many of their peers in nineteen-seventies Australia, the Dysons perceived homosexuality as a poor choice of lifestyle, and that those who indulged in such dangerous habits were obliged to accept the consequences. Poor Grandma and Grandpa, the nineteen-nineties Australian rued. Now they must also rationalise their elder daughter's murder. How terrible.

Lastly, she grabbed a selection of other items from Jeff's wardrobe and chest of drawers, rearranging everything in his new quarters. She brought a guitar from the study and a wad of notepaper in case he was inspired to write a lyric or two during the night. The television remote control was working, and she sat for a few minutes transfixed by a news programme which was, as she should have expected, conducting its own post-mortem on her mother's passing.

'We've decided on Thai,' Jet called out from the hallway, clutching two bottles of beer. 'What do you want to drink?'

'Nothing, thanks. Thai's fine. Are you going to collect it or will they deliver?'

'They deliver. I'll meet them downstairs.'

Kierney signalled to her brother to follow her into the kitchen. 'Hey... I have to tell you something.'

'What?'

'Papá says he can feel Mamá with him because his tattoo's itching.'

Jet raised his eyebrows, processing the young woman's statement in disbelief. 'Are you serious? Isn't that a bit weird?'

'He's hurting, bro',' Kierney reminded him. 'You've seen how he is. He was much more "up" when we were at Celia's, but it must be so hard not to completely dissolve. It's like he doesn't have to put on an act anymore, but he needs to 'cause of us and Gerry and Cathy, *et cetera*.'

The self-assured sportsman nodded. 'Yeah. Sure. I get that. But Mum communicating via his tatt'? You've got to agree it's highly unlikely, bordering on totally impossible.'

'I know, but what harm can it do?'

'None,' he replied with a smile, pointing to one of the kitchen chairs. 'As long as he doesn't start saying, "Don't sit there. Mamá's finishing her ghostly brekkie."'

His sister slapped him hard on the chest. 'Don't be a bastard, Jetto. He's not mad. He's just sad.'

'We're all effing sad,' Jet defended himself, 'but we're not pretending Mum's talking to us out of our arses or whatever.'

Kierney rolled her eyes, grunting her frustration. 'Well, perhaps we should try it,' she whined, unable to stop herself from breaking out in a grin at the silly image. 'I'd certainly like to feel closer to Mamá right this minute. Wouldn't you?'

'What's going on in here?' Jeff asked, appearing in the doorway while his children were arguing. 'Where's my beer?'

Jet handed a stubby to his father. 'Kizzy's up for Thai as well. Did you choose something?'

Jeff took a large gulp from the bottle and smacked his lips theatrically. He could tell by the shift from their hushed conversation to a sheepish exchange of wide, welcoming smiles that his children were scheming behind his back. Tipping the bottle to his lips for a second time, he bowed and scraped as they filed past him. So much for not putting on an act!

'Mmm... That's good,' he said. 'Let's get a combination of dishes and we can pick from each. That way, I'll escape with eating not much at all 'cause you won't be able to tell who's had what.'

'Right! Sly but stupid,' Jet responded. 'Don't you know it's a bad idea to divulge your tactics in advance?'

The songwriter shrugged, deferring to his son's superior intellect. Kierney's mobile rang on the kitchen table. She checked the name on the screen and lifted it up to show the others.

'Suzanne,' she read, looking up at her father, who had by now pinned his fully grown son up against the wall and was attempting to pour beer down his neck. 'I forgot I even had her number. The same problem you have.'

Jeff released the collar of Jet's polo shirt from his strong grip and held his hand out for the telephone. 'Let me take it,' he growled. 'She shouldn't be ringing you. That's not fair. Suze, hi. It's Jeff.'

There was an extended pause as their father's old friend gathered her thoughts after the very person she was trying to avoid had hijacked her call. The teenagers stared at him, wise to the discomfiture he had effected. After a while, a smile spread across his lined face as his ear was sprayed with a discharge of excuses.

'Apologies, Suzie-Anna. I didn't mean to shock you,' he said. 'I just didn't think it was right for you to call Kizzy when you really wanted to know about me. Yeah, I know. And thanks. We're bearing up. Well, put it this way: they're bearing up, and I'm seeking inspiration. What're you doing tomorrow morning? Can I come and walk your dogs?'

The Diamond children stood powerless against their father's impulsiveness. An outing so soon? Without Lynn's steadying authority, they caught a glimpse of "the old Jeff", the character often portrayed by a woman whose vision for a brighter future drove her to tolerate his dark past. Unpredictable, impetuous and occasionally plain irrational, the challenge of keeping tabs on this bohemian maverick while grief took its course was beginning to dawn on them.

'Six o'clock then? Cool. See you tomorrow morning. And don't treat me with kid gloves, please. It only makes me worse. If you think I'm being an arsehole, just tell me so. Great. *Adiós.*'

The songwriter ended the call and placed his daughter's mobile onto the kitchen table. Turning back, he found the youngsters frozen to the spot.

'What's up? You look as if you've been struck by lightning,' he chuckled. 'You can move now.'

Jet sniggered in a mixture of fear and frustration. 'You're giving us the creeps. Can we go with you tomorrow morning? Are you sure you're OK to go out?'

The bemused man put a hand on each child's shoulder. 'Hey! You're not s'posed to worry about me. I'm the dad. I'm supposed to worry about you.'

'Oh, for God's sake, Papá! How can we not worry about you?' Kierney whined. 'One minute you say you can't trust yourself, and the next you're arranging to drive thirty kilometres and back on your own. We *are* worried about you.'

The backlash took Jeff by surprise. 'OK. I'm grateful, guys, but it'll be fine. Let's order dinner. If you really don't want me to go on my own, you're welcome to come too, but I'm sure you'd both far rather stay in bed. I'm not going to sleep well anyway. You know that.'

'As long as you promise us you'll come back at a certain time,' his daughter shrugged. 'And charge your phone fully.'

Her brother gasped, turning away. Kierney also felt tears burst from her eyes as she listened to herself citing the same phrases their mother used on both teenagers with monotonous regularity. Seeing the level of anxiety he was inflicting, the widower relented.

'Alright. I get where you're coming from. Look... Let's not stress ourselves out over this. I'll ring Suzanne back and cancel. We're not ready, are we?'

Kierney shook her head. 'No. I'm sorry, Papá. I'm not, anyway.'

Jet reached the cordless telephone off the kitchen wall and dialled the restaurant. He placed their order before passing the handset straight to his father. The contrite man scrolled through the various stored numbers.

'Steve, it's Jeff. How're you going?' their obedient, loving father asked in response to a male voice the children could just about hear. 'Is Suzanne there, please?'

Another few mindless pieces of information were shared with his friend's husband before the star managed to speak to her again. 'Suzie, I'm going to postpone my visit tomorrow morning, if that's OK. The kids and I've discussed it, and we're not ready for me to go galloping across the countryside just yet. I'll give you a ring next week sometime. Yeah. Of course there'll be a funeral. You don't have to be religious to have a funeral. Don't know yet. Lynn didn't fly down with us. She's staying a few extra nights in Sydney. You know how she loves the nightlife up there.'

Although the great man's crazy talk scared the youngsters a little, they were reassured he had their best interests at heart. They listened to him with smiles on their faces, watching him rub his chest every now and again, as if something were irritating his skin.

'Hey... Gotta go,' Jeff interrupted the chatterbox at the other end. 'I'll ring as soon as I know anything worth telling you. OK. Thanks. Shall do. Have a good evening.'

The repentant father gave his children a coy grin and sloped off towards the cloakroom while Jet gave his sister a fortifying hug. They were all facing into a problematic period. He was keen to look after their dad's female carbon copy, since he anticipated she would bear the brunt of the classic Jeff Diamond introversion.

'It's all good. We're the parents now. Role reversal. We've waited a long time to get our revenge.'

Kierney sniffed. 'Well, I wish I was enjoying it.'

'Kizzy, what happened to our cases?' their dad asked on his return to the kitchen. 'They're not still in the car, are they?'

'No. I unpacked your stuff in the spare bedroom,' she answered. 'I didn't think you'd want to sleep in your room tonight.'

The bereaved man closed his eyes and let out a long, slow breath, holding his arms out towards his daughter. '*Gracias, pequeñita.* That was a very considerate thing to do. You're the best, both of you. You're so right. It would be good to have a neutral place to crash. I anticipated that place to be the lounge, but who knows? I might make it to bed.'

'The TV works in there. I've tested it,' Kierney added, relishing being hugged so tightly, 'and if you need anything from the other room that I didn't think of, just ask me, and I'll get it. You'll be more comfortable than on the couch.'

That night, Jeff sent the children to bed at midnight after watching them both struggle to keep their eyes open. His son had been granted a second wind due to his misaligned body-clock, but Kierney was washed out. Jet had sat on the end of his sister's bed for an hour, talking everything through and keeping each other company, before kissing her goodnight and leaving for his own childhood bedroom.

Back in the spacious living area, alone for the first time all day, their father's reality resumed with a malicious kick. Gazing around the room, all he could see were memories; happy memories admittedly, but none real enough to console a grieving lover.

'So, angel...' he cast into the air. 'Are you joining me in the spare room tonight?'

The songwriter cried in the silence for a long time before reaching for the television's remote control from the coffee table. Selecting a random channel, he sat fixated on the screen, half watching and half pondering the days to come. He recognised the pattern only too well: keeping things together with a mixture of humour and activity during the day, and then plunging into despair and loneliness at night.

'I thought you saved me from all this shit, *mon amie*. Turned your back for five minutes, and here I am, right where I started. Fuck, Lynn. What happened to our perfect patch of paradise? Where the hell are you?'

At least the children seemed robust, especially now they were reunited. There was no talk of chucking everything in from them. Jeff couldn't understand why, but he was glad nevertheless. His life was no longer worth living, but theirs were, which was right and good. This resilience was precisely what the family had strived for over the years.

'We made strong kids, angel,' he said to his beautiful best friend. 'Strong, mature, adaptable kids. That's your fault. You made them this way. Loving, caring and full of life. I love you for that, even if you did leave me.'

Jeff cursed the bitterness he was now feeling towards his gorgeous wife. He knew she didn't deserve such rancour and that he was only stooping so low in a desperate attempt to deflect the mounting guilt, already spooning molten blame over his own soul for having allowed its mate to be killed. This was no freak traffic accident. By all accounts, it had been a carefully arranged assassination, flawed only through its execution against the wrong half of their partnership.

Jesus Christ! How he wished the gunman had shot him instead. Lynn would have been heartbroken, he was sure, but she was built like the children. She could rise above any amount of pain. Kierney would have felt the loss of her father acutely however, and this knowledge warned him off voicing this opinion in front of them. Swapping places with his wife now was the second best thing that could happen, short of seeing her walk into the room as he awoke from this terrible dream.

'Pick a year,' he requested of Lynn's spirit. 'Tell me which year I can go back to for inspiration.'

The rock star approached the piano, his eyes alighting on a portrait taken at the end of 1992. This episode in their life singular had become known as the "Irish Christmas". He had been working on the Northern Ireland Peace Talks, and the Diamonds were invited to visit the ancestral home of Kierney's school-friend, the "violin vamp", as he had nicknamed the young exhibitionist musician, on account of her predilection for performing in black leather. Piraea and her sister Olympia had a Singaporean mother and a Northern Irish father, a combination which had given the festive season an unusual cultural twist that the Australians had lapped up.

The peacemaker and his hot-headed adolescent son had rented motorcycles and raced off into the hills of County Donegal to escape the household's overbearing female influence. They spent two dank and freezing nights in a wooden shack with a log fire, during which the worldly parent had answered every question his son could think of on the subjects of sex, drugs and rock'n'roll.

The bond which developed as a result of this "rite of passage" trip blew the whole family away. Lynn had been overcome with love the evening the pair returned to the house, soaking, bedraggled and covered in mud. The change in Jet was remarkable, leading her to praise the doting dad for taking their gorgeous boy away and bringing back a good man.

The reunited couple made love that night in a nineteenth century, wood-panelled room, on a four-poster bed surrounded by scented candles and red velvet. His lover had long referred to him as a benevolent king, yet this was the first time he felt remotely eligible for the crown.

Back in the desolate here and now, the songwriter sat at the piano. He had been unable to lift the lid when they first arrived home, now placing tentative fingers on the keys. Still he couldn't bring himself to press down on them and make music. His eyes settled on a batch of scribbled lyrics and chords in Kierney's handwriting, and Jeff scanned the sheets as a diversion.

The telephone rang on the table behind him while he read, making the forty-three-year-old jump. Who dared to call after eleven o'clock? Could it be? *Don't even go there*, he chastised himself.

'Hello?' he said, picking up before the sound woke the children.

It wasn't.

'Mate, it's me,' Gerry's voice sounded pained. 'Sorry to ring so late.'

'No worries. What's up?'

'I just wanted to see how you were going. Are the kids around?'

'Cheers. They're in bed. They're bloody knackered, as am I.'

'Fancy some company? I'm worried sick about you.'

Jeff smiled at the uncharacteristic charity. 'Sure. That'd be great. I'll bake a cake.'

'Fuck, mate! It's good you can joke, but...'

'But I give you the creeps,' Blake & Partners' most important client finished his friend's sentence. 'Yeah, I know. I'm doing it to the kids too. Sorry. Come on over.'

'Right you are. See you in fifteen,' the affable man declared before hanging up.

Good, old Gerry, Jeff mused. The pressure was off again. His thoughts turned to a bottle of Talisker single malt which Cathy's team had given him for Christmas, and he went to fetch it and two glasses from the drinks cabinet. On his way back, he diverted to the kitchen to check if there was ice in the freezer. Of course there was. Even after her demise, his guardian angel still saw to his every need.

Pouring himself a large tumbler of whisky, Jeff lingered outside the master bedroom, daring himself to go in. How kind it was of his baby girl to relocate him. Old anxieties made him turn around and walk into the spare room instead, flicking on the light and surveying his new home.

His alarm clock sat on the bedside table, alongside a photograph he didn't recall seeing before. He picked it up to examine it more closely, trying to figure out where the family had been at the time. Jet looked about twelve, and therefore Kierney ten or eleven, and the Fabulous Foursome stood on a spectacular white, sandy beach.

Muy buen, the songwriter sighed, now able to place exactly where the picture had been taken. 'You little fox, Kizzo,' he laughed aloud. 'Very funny.'

Slumping down onto the bed and placing the brass frame on the sheet beside him, the widower almost choked on an amber mouthful when spontaneous tears made him catch his breath. This memory emanated from the holiday they enjoyed in Antigua after he and Lynn had released a racy video clip for a single called "Cruel Game". It had been a brave move on his daughter's part, but his warped mind applauded the ironic point she was making.

When the entry-phone rang in the hallway, the nocturnal householder buzzed his visitor up and waited by the lift for him to arrive, still clutching his whisky.

'Bastard! You started without me,' Gerry jeered.

Jeff showed him through to the lounge room and filled a second glass. As they sat down and stared at each other, he wondered if he looked as wrecked as his long-time friend did. The bawdy Irishman had been a guest here for over twenty years, yet tonight's atmosphere was foreign to both of them.

'So how are you?' the older man asked. 'You don't look as bad as I thought.'

'Yeah? Well, that's good, I s'pose. Mate, I'm not sure how I am, to be honest. I have no clue how people are meant to feel in this situation. I definitely don't feel totally in touch with myself, if you know what I mean. Like I've taken some sort of teleportation potion.'

Gerry settled into the sumptuous leather couch and shook his head. 'Eh, what?'

'Yep. That about sums it up! I'm in this weird, transcendental state where I'm looking down on myself living this alternate life that I don't want a fuckin' bar of, waiting for my real life to kick back in again.'

The businessman frowned. 'I have no idea what that means.'

Raising his glass, Jeff laughed. 'Not surprised, mate. Neither do I.'

'Can I do anything? Either as your manager or as your friend?'

'Cheers, mate. This is a great start. I was freaking out about how I'd get through the night, so your call came at the perfect time.'

'Oh, OK,' Gerry dared. 'That's good. I was even a tad nervous coming up in the lift, you know. I'm really at a loss as to how to behave around you.'

'Well, don't be,' the philosopher reassured him. 'Just go with the flow. None of us is an expert in dealing with bereavement. That's what I've agreed with the kids anyway: just be ourselves, and let ourselves be ourselves.'

Gerry exhaled, gripping his arthritic left knee and rubbing it out of habit. 'I heard from Big D earlier. They completed the post-mortem today, so he's waiting for them to say when the body can be released.'

Christ almighty, the widower cringed. Having encouraged his mate to speak freely, this was the absolute last thing he wanted to hear.

'Yeah,' he croaked, fighting the urge to lash out. 'She's being taken to a funeral director's place in Bentleigh somewhere. He gave me the address. I have to take the kids over there.'

'Jesus, Mary and Joseph,' the visitor whispered, reaching for the bottle of single malt. 'Poor things. I forgot they haven't seen her. Do you want some more?'

'Fuck, yes! There are four more bottles in the cupboard out there. Lynn stocked up for the occasion obviously.'

'Hey, mate, please... Enough with the sick jokes already. I miss her too, you realise? Not as much as you, granted, but...'

Both men sat in silence for a while, holding their heads in their hands. Jeff put his glass down on the coffee table and wiped his eyes. The combination of grief, alcohol and exhaustion was bringing out the worst in him.

'I'm really sorry. D'you know if we can get access to the safe deposit box first thing on Monday? I'd like to get hold of the letters Lynn wrote to us. We need to read her will too, I guess. Can you arrange that for Monday afternoon or Tuesday morning, please, mate?'

Gerry nodded. 'Yes. Right-oh. Shit, mate. What a God-awful few days we've got ahead of us. Who do you want there, by the way? For the will-reading?'

'You, the Dysons, me and the kids. Anyone else?'

'How many legals?'

'Legals?' the songwriter echoed. 'Only one. We're not going to hear anything we don't already know about.'

His manager frowned. 'Can you be sure?'

Jeff frowned in abject displeasure, the effects of the whisky blurring his judgement by now. 'Yes. Absolutely fucking certain.'

'Fine, but I'll ask the Dysons if they want to bring their solicitor anyway, mainly as a courtesy,' his manager persisted. 'To cover off on the probity stuff, you know... You don't want anything coming back on you later.'

'Sure. Whatever. I just want it over with. Nothing's going to change as a result.'

Gerry nodded. 'True enough.'

'Where's *Cairdeas* at the moment?' the rock star changed the subject, referring to the executive's luxurious ocean-going cruiser.

'Airlie Beach. Why?'

''Cause it's Sunday tomorrow, and I've no idea what to do to keep the kids entertained,' the tired father admitted. 'I thought if she were local, we might take her out somewhere.'

'Nice idea, but sorry, mate. What about renting one? I'd be up for that. I'm not doing anything tomorrow, and it's supposed to be over thirty degrees. I'll look into it in the morning.'

'Cool, thanks. I'll see what they want to do when they get up,' Jeff decided. 'I'm keen for them not to feel obliged to hang around me, but it's too soon to go out, I think. We're still clinging to each other like limpets at the moment.'

'As it should be, mate,' Gerry responded with a smile. 'As it should be. I wouldn't expect anything less. You were always a close family.'

'We're still a close family,' the widower corrected his old friend. 'Just somewhat fractured right now. How's things with Fiona? Will she join us tomorrow?'

Clutching his empty tumbler, the executive took a deep breath. 'I asked her to marry me.'

'Did you? Fuck! Good on ya, you sly dog. How come you waited 'til now to tell me?'

'Mainly because she turned me down,' the party boy chuckled. 'She said I was reacting to your situation and to ask her again in a month's time if I still felt the same way.'

The grieving husband stood up and stretched, grinning at his mate's forthright tone. 'And I take it by your reaction that you agree with her.'

'Yes. I was a tad hurt initially. Bruised ego more than anything. But the more I think about it, the more right she is.'

'Well, congratulations anyway,' Jeff gave his old friend's shoulder a half-hearted slap. 'I'm sure everything's still moving in the right direction.'

The pair's idle banter came to an abrupt halt, both distracted by Kierney's appearance in the lounge room doorway, barefoot and with her hair gathered back into an untidy ponytail. She received a welcoming smile from her dad and raised eyebrows from their regular guest.

'Oh, hi, Gerry. I didn't know you were here,' the polite teenager said. 'I heard talking and wondered what was going on.'

'Come on in, angel,' Jeff held out his hand. 'Sorry to wake you.'

Passing in front of their business manager, the young woman gave him a peck on the cheek and took a seat next to her father. She was dressed only in a long T-shirt, and the visitor tried not to stare at even longer, slender legs which announced that she had moved beyond girlhood. His mate's shadow was transforming into a beautiful woman, with dark, sultry looks and the personality to match.

'How are you, Kizzy?' her pseudo-uncle asked.

'Alright, I suppose, thank you. Stuck.'

'Stuck,' Jeff repeated. 'I agree. Damned good word, *pequeñita*. Gez and I were just wondering how we might spend Sunday, seeing as we're going to be stuck all day with nothing to do.'

The young woman gazed from one miserable face to the other and groaned. 'I don't know. Another day hanging around here's going to drive us all crazy. How about going for a drive somewhere?'

'Yes. Could do, but we were actually thinking of renting a boat,' Gerry offered. 'It's going to be very hot tomorrow. We could go for a swim.'

'And get eaten by sharks,' Jeff threw in.

The older man grimaced. 'Shit, mate. You're really coming up with some weird stuff tonight.'

'He is,' Kierney agreed, giggling. 'We've already warned him.'

'You can talk! Leaving that photo by my new bed...' Jeff teased his daughter, kissing her temple.

The teenager winced. 'Oh, yeah. So you got it then?'

'Oh, I got it,' her dad nodded, raising his whisky tumbler, 'and I thank you for it.'

Perplexed, Gerry watched as his friend stood up and made his way to a filing cabinet behind the piano. Delving into the back of the second drawer, he pulled out a plastic envelope and brought it over to the coffee table. The contents of this envelope were never in dispute.

'Mate, can I be assured of your confidentiality while I invite my child to smoke with us?'

Business manager looked from father to daughter in a momentary dilemma. If she was old enough for him to fantasise about the length of her legs, she was probably old enough to share a spliff. The Diamonds had never been observers of age-related mores when it came to their rock-star lifestyle, so he could hardly expect them to start now.

'Of course. My lips are sealed.'

Kierney was speechless. She had confided in her dad that she and her boyfriend had smoked pot once or twice, and he had been patient and honest with her about the potential side-effects and the dangers of being caught as a public figure. Now she was being offered some in the company of their oldest friend.

'Thanks, Papá,' her voice was full of sincerity. 'But I'll go back to bed if you'd prefer.'

'No, gorgeous. I'd love you to stick around. Would you please make us some coffee? Hot and sweet, just like you.'

'For Christ's sake, mate!' Gerry exclaimed. 'She's your daughter. You can't say things like that to your daughter.'

'Blake-san,' the superstar taunted, wagging a finger in the air, 'I can say whatever I like to my daughter. She's my flesh and blood, and I love her. Some water too, please, *pequeñita?*'

By the time the youngster returned with three steaming mugs of coffee and three glasses of water, three joints had been rolled and were now sitting on the table in front of the men. Her father had disappeared, which made Kierney a little worried.

'Do you think he's alright?' she asked their guest. 'I mean, do you think he might snap?'

Gerry frowned. 'God knows. We're dealing with a complex beast full of conflicting emotions. Your dad's always been a wild one, Kizzy. I can't predict what he's going to do. I don't think he can either, half the time.'

'And without Mamá steering him, it's as if he's swerving all over the place, out of control. It's like we're continually having to stop him falling over the edge of the cliff.'

'Exactly right, my dear,' Gerry affirmed, seeing the man in question return.

Jeff offered his daughter an ordinary cigarette, took one for himself and skimmed his packet along the edge of the coffee table to his mate. Kierney chose some background music, and the trio sat listening to the soothing sounds of classical piano while sipping the hot coffee.

After their cigarettes had been stubbed out, the musician leant forwards, passing one of the joints to Gerry and handing the second to his dark-haired gipsy girl. 'Drink some water first,' he advised. 'It'll hit the spot faster.'

'Should we wake Jet up?' Kierney asked, feeling guilty that her brother wasn't here to share this special time with their father. 'He'll be annoyed he missed this.'

'There'll be other times.'

Gerry lit his roll-up and inhaled, leaning over to light the young lady's for her. The father looked on, inquisitive for her response. He lit his own in the usual, nonchalant manner, the muscles around his heart contracting painfully. The novice took a tentative drag on the joint and swallowed the smoke down. Having seen her dad do the same with cigarettes a thousand times, she leant back into the couch in anticipation of the slow burn.

Jeff relaxed too, never once taking his eyes off his daughter. For the first time in two days, he didn't feel sick and tired of life. The threesome sat listening to the ebb and flow of the tranquil sonata and allowed the drug to take hold of their senses.

'Jeez, this is nice, mate,' the older man crooned, stretching out on the sofa. 'Where'd you get it from?'

'Ah, y'know… I'll get back to you on that one. It's been in there for ages actually,' Jeff confessed. 'I wondered if it might be stale, but you're right, it's pretty good. What d'ya reckon, Kiz?'

The young woman smiled, closing her eyes. '*Te amo, Papá.*'

'*Te amo* too,' the veteran told her, grabbing hold of her knee and squeezing fondly. 'Let it ride, huh?'

Kierney sighed. 'Very mellow. It's already given me a really good idea for a song for you.'

Her father opened one eye and smiled. 'Oh, yeah?'

'Yes. It's going to be called "Walk Me Through The Rain" and it's going to be about this moment.'

Gerry sniffed in the background. 'You two are way too close.'

'Fuck off, Gezza,' Jeff objected, sliding down onto the floor in front of the teenager's elongated body. 'That sounds great, gorgeous. I look forward to hearing it.'

'Thanks for all the songs about me growing up,' she added. 'Did I ever say that before?'

'I'm sure you did. You didn't leave me after all, so my fears were ungrounded.'

'I won't leave you,' Kierney promised, crying. 'I'll never leave you. Damn Mamá for leaving us!'

Breathing out as his chest tightened again, the widower shook her leg. 'Hey, that's not fair. Take that back, please. Mamá didn't want to leave us.'

'Do you want me to go?' Gerry asked, conscious enough through his stupor to comprehend the torment in the matching pair's stand-off.

'No, mate. This'll pass. We have to get this shit out in the open. Kiz, it's no-one here's fault that Mamá died. Not even my fault, although I'm not at the point where I believe it yet. That arsehole, dwarf Spaniard killed her.

'He could've backed off, knowing it wasn't me in his sights, but he fired the gun anyway. Mamá didn't leave us. He took her from us. She didn't want to go, *pequeñita*. You know that really. She loves us so much.'

'Arsehole, dwarf spaniel?' Kierney dragged out a timeworn family play-on-words, laughing and crying at the same time.

'Yeah. A spaniel,' her father nodded, also moved to tears. 'A fucking spaniel killed your mamá. I always hated those dogs. Now I know why.'

'I'm sorry, Papá,' the teenager murmured, stroking his shirt and the tattoo underneath, 'and I'm sorry, Mamá.'

Jeff hung on to the young woman's right hand and sensed his mind purging itself of all the pent-up bitterness that had been haunting him. He heaved himself to his feet and crossed to the piano to pick out a construct of minor chords, singing random phrases as they entered his brain.

'No more birthdays, no more holidays, no more nothing at all... D'you know Kiley's writing something for Mamá's funeral?' he announced, twisting round to the others. 'She asked me if I minded.'

'And *do* you mind?' Gerry asked, chuckling at the strange lyrics that were generated from the star's altering psyche.

'No, I don't fucking mind,' the sad songwriter snapped, tears streaming down his face. 'It's fantastic. We should organise a bloody great memorial service, as big as our wedding, where everyone can play a part. I want to celebrate the life of Lynn Dyson Diamond so fuckin' hard that no-one'll ever forget her.'

Kierney jumped up, eager to calm the orator down. 'Papá, shhh. Jet'll wake up, and I haven't got enough weed left to share with him.'

Gerry laughed. 'I'm sure there's plenty more where this came from. It's fine, Kizzy. That young bloke sleeps through anything, doesn't he? He won't wake up.'

'Will you play "Walk Me Through The Rain", please?' Jeff encouraged the budding songstress. 'Is it happy or sad?'

'Don't know yet. Bit of both. It's about honesty and sharing and being stronger together.'

The protective man kissed his daughter's shoulder as she sat next to him on the piano stool. 'Sounds perfect. How're you feeling?'

'Amazing, thanks. Not stuck anymore. I'm flying around my life. What about you, Uncle Gerry?'

The older of the two men cackled, lying back on the couch and kicking off his shoes. 'Hey! You haven't called me Uncle Gerry for yonks. I'm fine, Miss D. Just fine, thanks. I wish I had one of you.'

Jeff grinned, raising his eyebrows. 'Ah, yeah? You do have one of her, if you remember. You just never talk to her.'

'Don't say that,' Kierney whined. 'That's not fair, Papá. It's different.'

'Yeah, Papá,' Gerry echoed, too stoned to be offended. 'Jenna's different. She's not really my daughter. Not like you two.'

'No, but she could've been,' his friend reminded him. 'It's not too late to change it. You could have a wife *and* a child soon, if you play your cards right.'

Kierney slithered off the stool and dropped down onto the floor beside the baby grand, remembering in the nick of time to pull her T-shirt down in male company.

'You alright down there?' her dad chuckled.

'*Sí, gracias.* It's really nice. I'm just enjoying myself before tomorrow forces us back to Horribleville again.'

'Well, don't enjoy yourself too much,' her father cautioned. 'It wouldn't be appropriate, and there are always some things the memory doesn't block.'

The sultry teenager pulled a face. 'Papá, that's disgusting. Is it true though?'

'Who knows? I'm making it up. I'm your father. I've been doing it for years.'

'Can I stay here tonight, mate?' Gerry asked, pouring two more whiskies. 'Sorry! Should've asked earlier, but you know me...'

'Course you can, mate. Except that I'm in your room. You'll have to search around for a bed, but just crash anywhere.'

'Papá?' a dreamy voice drifted upwards.

'*Sí.* You still with us?'

The teenager giggled. 'Did you ever do this with Mamá?'

The lost soul smiled at his daughter as she lay stretched out on the floor, unruly locks splayed around her head and arms spread wide at each side. 'Yeah. We did, baby,' he replied. 'Not often, but we did. We were always quiet about it though, in case you guys woke up. She didn't want you to know.'

'Why not?'

'Neither of us wanted you to know, I should say. Not when you were younger anyway. We wanted you to make up your own minds about this stuff. It's one thing to give you information, but seeing it happen right in front of your gorgeous, naïve eyes may have been too tempting too early.'

The young woman nodded. 'Oh, OK. Makes sense. Thanks. I'm glad you did this with Mamá too. That makes me feel a bit better.'

'Does Jet smoke?' Gerry asked. 'I always imagined Cambridge to be above that sort of thing, but I guess it can't be.'

'Don't know,' the loyal sibling answered. 'We haven't talked about it. I'm sure he has, but he's very careful with his diet and training. He doesn't smoke half as many ciggies as I do, for example. Does he, Papá?'

Jeff shrugged. 'I don't watch you these days. Black sheep versus white sheep. We're the sinners, they're the saints.'

'Only the good die young,' Kierney sang, referring to the Billy Joel hit from the late nineteen-seventies.

Gerry stifled a laugh when he heard his friend sigh. The statement was as painful as it was accurate. The songwriter rose to his feet and found "The Stranger" in the apartment's CD collection, starting it playing at the upbeat track. The young woman's jiggling hands and feet made him smile, tapping on the floor in time with the music.

The effects of the cannabis were beginning to level off, and Jeff's face contorted into a theatrical yawn. 'We should try and get some sleep, I s'pose. D'you think the boat thing's a good idea?'

'Yes,' his daughter answered. 'I do.'

'And you, mate?'

'Yes, sir. What time is it now?'

'After two. No rush in the morning. Just whenever.'

The dark-haired nymph rolled herself up to a sitting position using her strong abdominals in graceful but exaggerated control, before balancing on gravity-defying feet. 'Ooh,' she giggled. 'I'm all wobbly. What have you done to me, Daddy?'

'Stop that!' Jeff tapped her arm. 'Go to bed. There's a good girl.'

The teenager gave her father an affectionate punch, and the pair stood with their arms wound around each other for a while, hanging on tight. Gerry voiced another pathetic objection as he struggled to his feet too, causing them to break apart and settle for a goodnight kiss.

'Come along, Uncle Gerry. Let me show you to your accommodation,' Kierney invited, flirtatiously taking his arm.

'Careful,' came her dad's light-hearted warning.

The older man twisted round, responding with a naughty grin for which the parent in his wayward client had no taste. Left to himself for the second time on this very long evening, the lonely man sat back down at the piano and played with a spray of desperate lyrics that swarmed into his mind.

LIFE GOES ON

Feeling guilty for including his daughter in his very adult pursuits, Jeff raised his eyes to the ceiling once more and spoke to Lynn's ghost. 'Hey, I'm sorry, angel. I know that was wrong, but she's old enough to make her own decisions now. I wish you were here. Jesus Christ! I really wish you were here. Let me know if you can hear me.'

Nothing happened. The lonely man folded his arms on top of the piano, leant his forehead down and wept. How long was this mess going to take to resolve itself? He knew he had to stick it out for the sake of the children and for his in-laws, and also for all the millions of fans who would want to see him rise above and be strong. But to what end?

An oppressive silence had descended on the apartment. The songwriter stared at the plastic bag of cannabis leaves still sitting on the coffee table, next to his lighter and the empty mugs. The scene reminded him of the many nights during his early career when his parties would carry on long after the rest of the guests went home or had passed out. He didn't want to take this selfish, destructive path again. He sealed the bag and returned it to the filing cabinet drawer where it belonged.

On his way to his new billet, Jeff hovered outside the doorway of the master bedroom he and his dream girl had shared for their whole life singular. His heart raced when he contemplated going in, and a wild inharmonious frenzy assaulted his ears as if urging him to back off. Was Lynn expecting him in there? What if she were somehow waiting for him? And what if she were not?

Too soon, the grieving husband decided, turning and heading for the door on the other side of the corridor. He stretched out on the bedclothes, removed his watch and lay staring at the ceiling. Dazed and a little numbed by the combination of drugs he had consumed, he twisted his wedding ring and forced himself to remember an assortment of sensuous nights he and Lynn had spent in this apartment in recent months.

The couple had been using their city pied-à-terre much more regularly since Jet moved overseas and Merak and Janey were long gone, busy chasing rabbits and seagulls in higher pastures; and these days, even more frequently now, their little girl chose to spend her free time in the inner suburbs with her friends. Taking advantage of this rare and precious downtime, they had spoiled themselves with trips to the theatre or hidden blues clubs, enjoying the convenience of a leisurely homeward stroll through Chinatown instead of an hour's drive through speed-restricted streets to reach their house.

Marooned in unfamiliar surroundings, rage surged inside the lonely man as his thoughts turned back to Kierney's resentment of her mother's departure. He hoped it was the weed coercing these extreme emotions and that she harboured no hard feelings towards their missing family member.

If anyone was enamoured with being alive, it was his gorgeous wife. She cherished every single second with her brood, through good times and bad. After a regimented childhood fashioned for making herself into a champion, the adult Lynn Dyson had led her life in total dedication to others, especially to her reprobate lover and their children.

The closeness the Diamonds had enjoyed, both as a couple and as a family, was the envy of friends and associates far and wide. Jeff smiled, picturing his uninhibited daughter spread out on the floor in her nightdress. Gerry was not alone in considering his relationship with Kierney as too intimate for a father and daughter, yet he had spent endless hours analysing it and still found nothing wrong.

He had never forgotten the look of pleasure on the young mother's face when she and the three-year-old had sung "My Father's Girl" at his birthday party. Lynn knew exactly what it had meant for him to bring up a miniature version of himself, for Jet had always been a miniature version of his mum.

The widower pressed the back of his head into the pillow in an effort to release the tension gathered in his neck. This time, he twisted the ring on the middle finger of his right hand; their four diamonds. Although he couldn't see too clearly in the darkened room, holding it up at a certain angle to the light filtering through the window was enough to give life to the quartet of gems. He kissed the symbolic stones as more tears flowed from his eyes.

Try as he might, the songwriter's mind refused to visualise Lynn naked in the bedroom across the hall. He could see her face, her enticing smile and her golden hair, but couldn't picture her making love to him. Reaching down to his genitals, nothing registered there either. Peculiarly, the lack of sensation was reassuring. Perhaps only due to the combination of grief and illicit substances, the old urges would likely return in a few days or weeks. But for now it was entirely the right response to losing the love of his life.

Sailing out of sight tomorrow was as good an idea as any, he thought. Jet would approve, having arrived out of the British winter; a welcome chance to swim and fish in the calm waters of Port Phillip Bay, out of mobile range and away from prying eyes.

Jeff hadn't seen or heard a news bulletin all day, having no trouble imagining the endless speculation fed by various all-knowing commentators to a public impatient for information.

Once their loved one's funeral was arranged, the widower decided, he and the children would hold another press conference to show the world they were doing OK and sticking together. He would then ask his publicity office to request a media blackout to afford Jet and Kierney space to figure out how best to get through the next few months.

It was four-thirty in the morning before Jeff closed his eyes and fell asleep, and shortly after nine when his son knocked on the door with a hot drink.

'Hey, Dad,' the young man said, putting the mug down on the bedside table. 'Coffee, if you want it.'

The nineteen-year-old stared at his dormant father, still fully clothed and with a growing beard that emphasised the angles of his face as he lay with his right arm resting across his stomach. Was it his imagination, or was the star's body already thinner? His eyes were ringed with dark circles too. The middle-aged poster boy had grown old overnight. In fact, the lad rued, were it not for the rise and fall of his chest, one could be forgiven for thinking he too was a corpse.

The older man stirred at the sound of his son's deep voice and opened his eyes. The same sense of shock engulfed him this morning, slightly less intense compared to yesterday's violent awakening to which his daughter had been subjected. He swore under his breath and groaned as he returned to full consciousness.

'Cheers, mate,' he said, coughing stale air from his lungs. 'Good man. Did you sleep?'

'Yeah. Not too bad, thanks,' Jet replied, perching on the edge of the bed. 'You?'

'Eventually. Gerry's here, by the way. Is Kiz up?'

'Gerry? When did he get here?'

'After you'd gone to bed. He rang and asked if I wanted company, so I said yes.'

The youngster laughed. 'That explains the spoils of debauchery in the kitchen. I wondered how you'd managed to consume so much on your own.'

The musician cast his mind back to their late-night session and grinned. 'Ah, yeah. I owe you a party. Kizzy woke up, and we all had a smoke. She wanted to wake you, but I overruled her because of your "you-lag".'

'A smoke smoke?' Jet asked.

Jeff shrugged. 'Smoke smoke? As opposed to what smoke? Is that some dodgy Cambridge code?'

'Shit!' the young man cursed. 'I didn't think that'd ever happen. Damn! I hope it wasn't a one-off.'

His dad sniffed, feeling irresponsible. 'Ought to be. Moment of weakness on my part. Anyway... We hatched a plan to rent a boat today and go out on the bay, seeing as it's Sunday and everything's closed.'

Jet nodded. 'Cool. That was going to be my next question. I can't face being holed up here all day. Sounds like a cunning plan, my Lord Slackbladder. I'm going for a shower.'

Swinging his legs off the bed and planting his stockinged feet on the carpet, Jeff smiled at the comic's dogged attempts to cheer him up. The room pitched back and forth before righting itself well enough to allow him to stand up.

'Very well, Baldrick. Let's do it then. Let's get the others up and the show on the road.'

'I'm stoked that you're somewhat positive, Dad. I was wondering what sort of person you'd be this morning.'

'And what sort of person am I?' the widower quipped, walking out of the bedroom with a hand on his son's broad shoulder.

'Not quite as black as you were last night,' the young man answered with considerable resignation. 'Just grey today, I think.'

At eight o'clock on Monday morning, the Diamond family ceremoniously switched on their mobiles, which had been equally ceremoniously switched off twenty-four hours earlier before their seafaring diversion. All three breathing apprehensive sighs, they listened to the bright series of emitted beeps and buzzes and watched the handsets skate around the kitchen workbench while the messages banked up.

'Bloody hell,' Jeff moaned. 'Who the fuck are these all from?'

'We should listen to each other's,' the nineteen-year-old suggested. 'That way, we can keep some level of detachment and just write them down.'

'That's actually a great idea,' his sister agreed. 'Papá, what do you think?'

The father shook his head, picking up his telephone. 'No way. I can't do that to you, guys. Whoever picked this phone'd be drawing a very short straw.'

All three disappeared to different parts of the apartment to collect their respective condolences. Jeff sat on the balcony with a cigarette, a coffee and his lengthening to-do list. His most recent message was from Bart Dyson, giving him their estimated arrival time at the funeral directors', in case he wanted to meet them there. The despondent man added another line to the checklist without hesitation. It was macabre, but he couldn't wait to be close to Lynn's body again, even though he firmly believed her soul to be elsewhere by now.

Gerry had called before Big D, having arranged a solicitor's appointment for the next day to read the will, which he was collecting this morning along with the contents of the celebrities' safe deposit box. This item was already noted, as was a time allocation for reading the collection of letters. He and his offspring had made a plan, while floating off the Sorrento shoreline, to order their absentee's favourite Indian meal and read her annual dedications as they ate.

All three remaining Diamonds managed to adopt a lighter mood, thanks to the previous day's escapism, with only the occasional sudden memory triggering bouts of distress. Much to Gerry's chagrin, they had consumed no proscribed substances all day. Returning home after eleven o'clock, they had each vanished straight to bed, knocked out by the bracing, salty air.

However, the quicksand of loss was swallowing them again this morning. Jet switched on the SBS international news programmes, a habit the children had developed while very young to polish their language skills. They watched in silence, listening to each country's opinions of the calamitous headline. At first, their father had asked for the television to be turned off, but the youngsters insisted they wanted to hear the world's points of view.

'It makes it real,' Kierney pleaded. 'And it shows Mamá mattered to everyone. While we're here, shut away from everything, it's nice to know people are thinking of us.'

In a bizarre replay of the lead-up to their wedding, Jeff found himself talking to all three of Lynn's bridesmaids in quick succession. Both his sister and sister-in-law had booked flights to Melbourne, but only one was anxious to know how she could help. Anna was heading straight to Benloch to spend time with her bereaved parents, whereas his ragged sister required collecting from the airport on Tuesday night.

And Michelle was on her way to the apartment right now. The confused songwriter agreed to every proposed plan, having relinquished all control over the next few days. Kierney answered the door to her mother's childhood friend, who rushed towards them with arms outstretched and sobbing noisily.

'Oh, my God! Look at you! You look so tired,' the distraught woman cried, wiping her tears off the perplexed man's cheek after kissing him over and over. 'Are you sleeping?'

'Yeah,' he assured her. 'Enough for now. Cheers.'

'I want to help, Jeff. Tell me what needs doing. Lynn and you have always been so good to us. I want to help take the pressure off you guys.'

'Thanks heaps, Mish,' the celebrity replied, addressing their visitor by the nickname his wife always used, which made them cry even more.

He scanned down the growing task list while Kierney handed round steaming mugs of coffee. The funeral needed a location, flowers, a celebrant and some sort of seating layout, and then he needed to choose somewhere for the family and close friends to gather afterwards.

He had made a tentative arrangement with Bart and Marianna to use the function room at Dyson Administration. Yet, as the time passed, he became less and less keen on this idea, particularly now all three of Lynn's bridesmaids were homing in on him. The prospect of watching a coffin being carried along the same aisle they had walked down as newlyweds was too grotesquely ironic even for him.

'What are you like at arranging funerals?' the impudent star asked. 'That'd be the biggest-ticket item you could help with. I hate to ask you though.'

'Leave it to me,' the tearful woman agreed, squeezing his forearm. 'I'll give Marianna a ring and ask her and Anna if they can come up with an alternative. I'm with you. It'd be too upsetting to have it at Admin. Can I ask if you want cameras?'

Jeff inhaled, taking hold of his daughter's hand to steady his nerves. 'We spoke about this yesterday,' he explained. 'We'd like to keep the funeral simple and then have a grand-scale memorial service in a few weeks' time. That's where we'll have all available cameras. We want everyone to celebrate Lynn's life in a blinding show of defiance.'

'Oh, that'd be lovely,' the overwhelmed woman murmured.

'Yeah. Maybe,' he shuddered. 'Jesus Christ! According to Cath's latest message, the TV companies are pushing me hard to televise the funeral as well, but we don't want to do it. The Premier offered us a state funeral, no less, and I was expecting Bart to insist I accept. I was gobsmacked when he said they'd rather something simple too.

'Shit, Mish, it's going to be bloody horrendous, no matter the scale. Everyone needs to be able to express themselves honestly, not worrying about what they do or don't want broadcast on the evening news.'

Jet and Kierney both nodded.

'I think we should say yes to coverage of people arriving and leaving, but not the service itself,' the younger man suggested. 'It's private to us. Dad's right. The memorial service is where we'll let it all hang out.'

The redhead tittered. 'I love how close you guys are. What about the house? Do you want me to go there and get anything for you?'

The trio looked at each other and shrugged, grateful that someone among them was thinking straight.

'Oh, yes. Please could I go with Michelle?' Kierney asked. 'I know you don't want to go, Papá, but there are some things there I need. Is that OK?'

'Sure, *pequeñita*,' he nodded. 'There are some things there I need too. That'd be great, if you wouldn't mind going with Kizzy, Mish. And use Cath to arrange the details of the funeral. Don't do it all yourself. She and the team really want to help too, so I'll ring them today to ask them to liaise with you. Thanks for doing this. It's amazing of you. I'm incredibly selfish, but I just can't face all that logistical shit. I'm useless at organising things at the best of times. You know that...'

'Stop!' the lawyer shouted, reaching up on tiptoe and kissing the widower on the cheek. 'It's perfectly fine, Jeff. It's the least I can do. What are you doing for the rest of the day? Did you want me to go and get you some lunch?'

'Jesus, no!' the man of the house exclaimed, nudging the flame-haired woman away. 'Next you'll be volunteering to take a piss for us. Michelle, we're all good. We just need to stay on our feet and get on with stuff. There's enough here for us to make you lunch, isn't there, kids?'

Kierney nodded. 'I think so. We're going to see Mamá's body when it arrives. Grandma and Grandpa are flying down with it soon.'

'It?' Jet snapped.

His sister bit her lip. 'Sorry, Papá,' she whispered, tears in her eyes. 'I mean her.'

Jeff put his arm around his daughter's shoulders, her regret ringing in his ears. 'It's alright, angel. It's beginning to feel like an "it" to me too, to tell you the truth. D'you want to come with us, Mish?'

'Oh, can I? Would I be intruding? Please say if I am.'

'No,' the musician insisted. 'Come with us. Is that cool, you two?'

The youngsters didn't mind at all. Anything to take the pressure off. Their dad's current frame of mind was easy to deal with, but they didn't expect it to last. Having someone else on hand to help with any demonic episodes could prove invaluable. The coming evening promised to be tough, so a little light relief during the day with their mum's mate would bolster their combined resolve.

'Can we go in your car, please?' Jeff asked the former Collins Street solicitor, recalling the image of his son squashed into the passenger seat of Kierney's hatchback. 'It's just that we've only got small cars here at the moment.'

'No worries. It's a pig-sty, by the way, courtesy of my little darlings. But hey, Kizzo! I heard you passed your test!'

'I did,' Kierney smiled, having forgotten all about it.

'Congrats! Independence at last.'

'Thank you. Yes,' the young woman responded, glancing sideways at her father. 'It sort of lost its impact though, didn't it?'

'You're not wrong there. No sweat. You'll get plenty of time to gloat soon.'

'Ask Auntie Michelle if you can drive the Mercedes,' Jet quipped. 'Alan'll never find out.'

'Shhh,' his mum's friend warned, sensing neither Jeff nor Kierney appreciated this latest line. 'I'll drive us all there and drop you back afterwards. That's perfectly fine.'

The grieving husband nodded to the helpful woman, for more reasons than one. His children's voice of reason was no longer here to prod their young consciences, and he lacked the inclination to step up and fill the role. Lynn was so much better at discipline than he was.

Michelle turned into the funeral directors' car park, and they all jumped down from the car and checked the area for any unwanted attention. No-one had spoken for the last few kilometres, all worried about seeing Lynn and how they might react. Jeff put an arm around each child and hugged them tightly. He then did the same to Michelle.

'Here's what we're going to do,' his voice sounded authoritative, belying the molten jelly swirling in his stomach. 'If you're OK with it, I'll go in first with these guys. You can go in after that, Mish, either on your own, or with me or the Dysons. Whomever, it doesn't matter.'

His voice trailed off, searching his children's eyes for any unvoiced and unmet requests but seeing none. Both stood in silence with vacant expressions which likely reflected his own. They walked towards the door and were met by a middle-aged man in a dark suit who held out his hand.

'Good afternoon, Mr Diamond. I'm William Forbes. Please come inside.'

The celebrity shook William's hand and introduced the others in turn. It was a force of habit, the futility of which hit him hard. Lynn's parents had already been shown in and were on their way back to the parlour's front office, looking sombre and tired.

Jet broke away from the others and made straight for his grandfather, hugging him close. Bart gave the teenager's back a resounding slap, and Marianna reached over to put a hand on the young man's shoulder too. It was as if gestures compensated for the missing link between grandparents and grandson, and its apparent simplicity gnawed at Jeff's heart.

The Olympian stepped forward to shake his son-in-law's hand, and the pale grandmother gave everyone enthusiastic hugs.

'Oh, Michelle,' the elegant lady sighed. 'What a horrible place to see you after so long! How are you all?'

'We're well, thanks, Marianna,' the ginger-haired woman kissed the grieving mother. 'How about you?'

Jeff walked away with Bart, Jet and William, leaving the ladies to console each other. He explained their wishes for the funeral and received earnest nods all round. Lynn's father agreed that the ballroom at Admin was less than ideal for the service and offered it again for the memorial concert. He was pleased to find the afflicted showman sufficiently well-adjusted to be making plans already.

'Thanks, sir,' the seasoned performer responded, 'but I'm thinking somewhere outdoors at the moment. That way, everybody can share in it much more easily. We'll see... That's not why we're here today, so I'll get back to you in the next few days. You ready, guys?'

The colour drained out of Jet's face at the call-to-arms, causing his dad to take pity on him. This timid reaction was out of character, and he could tell the cricketer was trying so hard to act like a grown-up in front of his mighty giant of a grandfather.

Summoning Kierney over, Jeff turned his son away from Big D and ushered both children toward the door where William was waiting. 'D'you want to go in on your own?' he asked under his breath, feeling the lad's hand grab his. 'Whatever you want, mate.'

'With you,' Jet whispered. 'Can I?'

The compassionate rock star didn't give Bart a chance to overrule, standing between the big man and his grandchildren. Forbes put his hand on the door handle, inviting the Diamonds in. His son was shaking, leaning against his arm, so he put a supportive hand on his back and gripped the teenager's left shoulder.

'Relax, mate. This isn't a test. It's a training session for the funeral. You can do this as many times or for as long as you need to. Or not at all. Your call, both of you.'

'I want to see her,' his daughter insisted. 'I need to, I think, even though it's going to be really awful.'

Sensing old shadows circling in his head for the first time in many years, the star's heart plummeted once more. He was pleased to have the door opened for him on this occasion, and the trio turned to each other in relief to find themselves in some sort of antechamber instead of coming face-to-face with the bloodcurdling sight they had prepared for.

They entered the small room, with its dark crimson wallpaper and carpet of the same colour. It put the self-styled bohemian in mind of an old, Parisien strip club, and it was at once both disgusting and humorous to consider his sophisticated and relatively untouched wife ending up in a place that reminded him of a brothel.

Being in this halfway zone which separated the living from the dead was more than a little disturbing, especially when considering the distress this process was causing his son.

Jet had calmed down a little, now flushed and sweating. 'Dad, I feel sick,' he declared, holding his head in his hands and breathing deeply.

'Take your time,' William advised, having seen every possible human reaction during his time in the undertaking business. 'I'll leave you now. When you're ready, just go on in. And if you need me, I'm only through this door.'

A sticky stillness hung in the air, and Jeff felt obliged to break the silence. 'How're you going, guys?'

'Is Mum really in there?' the young man asked, sounding unsure of himself. 'This is so wrong. So bloody gross. I can't believe there's a dead person in there. I'm not sure I can go in.'

The forty-three-year-old sat down on the seat beside his son, who was still hunched forwards to combat his laboured breathing. He rested a steadying hand on Jet's back.

'You don't have to go in, but you do need to go in,' the compassionate father told him, more firmly than he wanted to. 'You'll feel better for having seen her. Believe me, it helps make sense of everything. I didn't have time to think about it. That's why it's worse for you two.'

'What does she look like?' his daughter hazarded.

'Not too bad,' he encouraged, as much to counteract his own trepidation. 'She's got a small hole in her forehead, and there's a lot of blood on her back, but otherwise she looks normal... You'll recognise her. Every time they move her, her facial expression changes a bit...

'That's what freaked me out the most when I saw my dad after he died. And I don't know what's happened to Mamá since I last saw her... in the post-mortem, y'know... so I'm just as scared as you are. D'you want me to go in first?'

Jet perked up at this idea but soon had second thoughts. 'No,' he concluded. 'That wouldn't be fair on you. If you can do it, we can do it.'

'I'll go first,' his sister said, already waiting at the next door.

'Good man,' Jeff slapped the teenager's shoulder once more for luck. 'Thanks, Kizzy. Let's go then. No time like the present.'

The tall, blond athlete leant to his left and bumped shoulders with his dad's. It brought them both close to tears, but they stood up together and laughed with as macho an attitude as either could manufacture. The father walked towards Kierney, who pressed down on the handle a little too readily for his liking.

'Jeez, *pequeñita*! You're much braver than I am.'

Kierney stepped into the room, more curious than her brother. She had never seen a dead person before, unsure what to expect or how she might react. Through an apprehensive haze, she became aware of her father speaking.

'Lynn, look who's here,' he said to his wife's inert form.

The room was larger than they had expected, with blackout curtains covering the windows and more of the same blood-red wallpaper. A shiny pine coffin sat on a table in the centre, surrounded by a few scattered chairs. The lid was propped up against the wall behind.

Momentarily, he caught the old images forming in his mind's eye, and the almost forgotten feelings of panic rushed through him. Fighting them off like in days gone by, he followed, sensing his son right behind him.

Sweeping her eyes around the room, the young woman eventually found the courage to look over to the far side. She shivered as she registered her mother lying so still.

Jeff tracked her every move, taking hold of her arm as her step faltered. *'No te preocupes.* I've got you.'

The sight of his children's pained endurance was unbearable. It was difficult enough to handle his own tattered emotions, without the deep responsibility he now felt for their grief as well. He smiled, gesturing that they should move a little closer and speak to the mother who had loved them so much.

Kierney clenched and released her fists a few times to strengthen her resolve, thankful for the conditioning she and her brother had received in handling difficult situations. Conversing with an unresponsive human body was about as difficult as it got, she figured, and even though she was anxious to please her dad, this was hardly a scenario they had covered in role-play.

'Hi, Mamá,' she began. 'I love you so much. This is terrible. I can't believe you'll never talk to me again.'

Crying softly, the teenager leant on the edge of the coffin and reached for Lynn's left hand, dragging her fingers across the three special rings she wore. Jeff picked up on yet another uncanny likeness, and it gave him hope. He bit his lip and turned away as mother and daughter held their private conference.

'I'm so sorry to lose you. And that Papá and Jet have lost you too, and you've lost us. It's so horrible. You're the best mamá ever, but I hope you already know that.'

Jet gasped and lurched for one of the chairs. 'Oh, my God. This is repulsive.'

The widower turned around, not knowing which child to stick with. 'Yeah. Know what you mean,' the widower whispered, holding his hand out for his son's. 'Give it a go, mate. Hey, angel. Jet's here too. We want to talk to you for a while.'

Leaning over the casket across from Kierney, the men steeled themselves for seeing Lynn's face, a chill seeming to rise from its occupant. Several tell-tale signs told her husband that other people's hands had been all over her, and nausea welled up to his throat. Readied for her final public appearance, the beauty no longer wore her suit jacket, and her long hair was bunched up behind her head in an unfamiliar style.

'Bloody gross. It doesn't look like Mum at all,' Jet groaned, his stomach churning like a washing machine too.

'No,' his dad agreed, tears streaming down his face. 'Jeez, angel... They've been messing about with you. Hope you're not really here to go through this. I can't feel you anymore. Give us a clue where you are, please?'

The younger man turned away, unable to cope with the monstrous situation. He moved one of the chairs further away, sat down and watched his father and sister both crying and stroking Lynn's face.

While neither child was looking, Jeff tried to ply the inanimate features into something resembling a smile. It was an experiment of the most hideous and gruesome nature, but it appeared to be working.

'Mate, come over here, please. Speak to Mum for a while with Kiz. Tell her what you want to say to her.'

Jet heaved himself to his feet and approached the coffin once more, tentative but with renewed energy. He reached a trembling hand out until his fingers could brush her cheek, its desiccated surface causing him to recoil in shock. His dad's eyes insisted he try again, and so, taking a deep breath, he touched her hand instead.

'Hello, Mum,' the teenager began, crying like his father. 'I miss you so much. I can't think of you as not here anymore. How come her face has changed?'

The kind man forced a smile. 'Shhh! Don't tell her. Just talk.'

'I love you, Mum,' the young man continued. 'I hope you're in a good place now, and that you know we miss you and wish you could come back.'

The widower walked over to the window, peeled back the shade and looked out at a plain brick wall. The more he listened to the teenagers speaking through their tears, the worse his own grief and anger grew.

After a minute or two, he returned to place his hands on their shoulders. Jeff stared at his lover's expressionless face, drinking in her infinite beauty. Kierney's slender frame drooped against his torso like an inflatable Santa whose supply of compressed air had been turned off.

This cultivated and worldly woman was still so young. He often forgot this fact, since she had been his trusted adviser for so long.

'Come on, *mes amies. On y va.* Let's say our goodbyes to this physical incarnation of Sleeping Beauty and concentrate on whatever each of us wants her to be now. Elvis has left the building.'

Jet gave a nervous chuckle. 'Sorry. Thanks, Dad.'

Kierney approached the coffin for a final farewell. 'Mamá, we'll see you later in the week. I love you so much. You look peaceful, so that's good at least.'

Her tall chaperones stood behind her, and Jeff put a hand on the back of each child's neck.

'I love you too, Mum,' her brother added.

Jeff squeezed both children's shoulders to signal his appreciation. 'Thanks, guys. That was great. Regala, I love you too and I'll continue this conversation later. Rest well.'

Lowering his hands, the songwriter invited the children to leave the room in front of him. They walked back into the curious anteroom, and he closed the door on their lifeless family member, not wishing to prolong the anguish any further.

The nineteen-year-old lunged for another chair, which creaked under the strain of his colossal weight in motion. 'Ugh,' he groaned. 'What a god-awful experience that was. I felt like we should be saying a prayer or something.'

Kierney nodded. 'You're right, it was horrible. I'm glad I saw her though. I didn't want to miss the opportunity, despite the fact it doesn't change anything. Are you OK, Papá?'

Jeff propped his exhausted body against the wall and listened to his offspring expressing themselves freely while confined in this safe space. He was relieved that all four Diamonds had been in the room together for the last time before their loved one's official farewell.

'Did you change how Mum's face looked?' the cricketer jumped in.

The widower nodded. 'Yep. All good, thanks, Kizzy. Yes, I did. I wanted you to see someone you recognised.'

'Oh. Thanks. How did it feel?'

'Creepy as fuck, but it was well worth it. The whole thing was easier afterwards.'

Kierney grimaced. 'Ew, gross. Shall we go? Michelle was going to come in now, wasn't she?'

Despondent, the languid widower levered his frame away from the wall's support, following the youngsters into the office to confront the enquiring faces of the Dysons and their daughter's friend. No-one said a word, and it was left to William to direct the uncomfortable sketch.

'Mr and Mrs Dyson and Mrs Hadley, would you like me to show you in now?'

Marianna rose from her chair, casting a magnanimous invitation to Michelle. For her part, the redhead was fixated on the handsome man and his children, preoccupied by their uncharacteristic solemnity.

'Jeff, do you mind?'

The statuesque celebrity raised his left hand towards his wife's oldest friend. 'Sure, Mish. Give her my best.'

'Thank you,' Lynn's mother replied on the lawyer's behalf, embarrassed that she hadn't shown the great man a similar courtesy.

Once the ladies were out of sight and with Bart stepping outside to take a call, the bereaved husband asked the undertaker to go over the funeral plans. The date was set for the coming Friday, with a scheduled time of two o'clock in the afternoon. The nearest crematorium had been booked for family and close friends only.

He noted that Friday was only a week after Lynn's death, but it mattered little when the event took place. Between them, they discussed who should say what while William took notes.

Jet shuffled in his chair. Sensing some disquiet, the funeral director excused himself and left through a door at the back of the reception area on some made-up errand. A career spent mastering the art of tactfulness, the rock star assumed, he probably followed the same process with every set of sorry clients.

'This is beginning to sound like yet another school production,' the young man complained. 'I'm sorry, but does it have to be so formal?'

'What don't you like about it?' Kierney asked. 'We have to do something formal. What could we do instead?'

'Kizzy's right, Jetto,' their dad agreed, wiping tears from his eyes. 'And it's not only us we have to consider either. Grandma and Grandpa have a say in this too, and they've obviously told Mr Forbes and Michelle they want these things. We can't just let Mum drift away, can we?'

'No, I know,' the undergraduate acknowledged, 'but it's as if we're trying to make it into something religious when we don't believe in God. It's like your music. Are we playing God here too?'

'Hey!' his sister scolded. 'Don't make this into Papá's problem. These are everyone else's wishes, not his.'

Jeff pacified his irate miniature. 'Hold your horses, angel, and I hear you, mate. Totally. I'm perversely stoked to see some anger in you. It means you care. And if that's what you think, how would you do it differently?'

'Oh, I don't know,' Jet sounded flat. 'If it's only me who doesn't like it, keep it the way it is. I just think Mum'd prefer it to be more casual, and we can save all the pomp and circumstance for the memorial service, which really will be like a hellish school production.'

The troubled father stood up and began to pace around the office. His heart was racing, making him dizzy. After all the years he had spent arbitrating between political parties and warring factions on a global scale, negotiating with his own family was by far the hardest. Just as in the tense rounds of peace talks, there was so much at stake for each party, and no-one wanted to be seen to concede to the other. However, one key factor was different for the famous middleman this time: it was impossible to mediate his own wife's funeral arrangements with an objective outlook.

He was in no doubt that he had earned the final say on the format and content of Friday's proceedings. More than twenty years of unwavering devotion had granted him this right, but he also knew how much the event would mean to the generations above and below.

What gave him the power of veto over the woman who had brought his gorgeous wife into the world? Or over their son, who had hung off his mother's every word and done everything the Dyson family had expected of him?

'Are you alright, Papá?' Kierney asked.

'Yes and no. The walls are closing in on me,' he responded, leaning against the back of her chair. 'I can't do this now. I need a ciggie. Shall we go outside for a few minutes?'

The three remaining Diamonds stood in the car park while the dark-haired pair shared a cigarette in Pareto proportions. Meanwhile, Jet kicked the kerb repeatedly, more impatient with his own unease than at his dad's delay tactics.

'Son, what's worrying you? Are you scared of how you'll react at the funeral? Or of what Big D'll think?'

Jet shook his head. 'No. Not really. It isn't either of those things. It's just that I can't see how reading our prepared lines out loud can give Mum a decent send-off when she's already gone.'

Surprised by the lad's perspective, the irate forty-three-year-old struggled to think of a response worthy of a supportive parent. Hearing himself saying the same thing at the same age, he thumped the spare tyre on the back of Michelle's four-wheel drive, and the car rocked a little.

'You'll set the alarm off,' Kierney warned.

'Correct, mate. She has already gone,' the older man affirmed, as demoralised as his son. 'But this piece of amateur dramatics we're planning is as much for us to say the things we want people to hear about how we loved her. That's what funerals are for, I reckon. We can say whatever we like to your mamá whenever or wherever we like. She's just as likely to hear us here in the bloody undertaker's car park as she is at her own funeral.'

The gipsy girl looked from one man to the other with tears in her eyes. 'For God's sake, come on, guys,' she implored. 'I'm just as pissed off as you are, but we have to do it. It's only going to last an hour, and it'll be really horrible watching the coffin disappear through those doors. But then it'll be over, and we can concentrate on something else.'

Kierney lurched forwards and hugged her father, bursting into tears and bashing his chest with manic fists.

'Let it out, baby,' Jeff said, cupping his hand behind the mass of dark waves and feeling moisture soaking into his shirt. 'We've got a long way to go. Let's not fight with each other, huh?'

Jet conceded, coming over to stand behind his sister, sandwiching her between himself and their dad. 'I guess the amount of grief we express is relative to how much we love her, don't you think?'

'Undoubtedly,' the wise man agreed, kissing his son's bowed forehead. 'Let's get back inside and finish off. Are we keeping it the way it is?'

The sportsman's eyes flashed with sudden inspiration. 'How about arranging the seating in a more informal pattern, like in a circle around the coffin, instead of in rows?'

'Oh, yeah. That's a great idea,' his sister chimed in. 'That'd be more friendly. Can we, Papá?'

'Why not?' Jeff replied, opening the door and ushering his children in before him.

The Dysons and Michelle were back in the open area, looking almost as anxious as the Diamonds. William stood at his desk and indicated for everyone to sit down together.

'The format for the funeral's fine by us,' the widower spoke, 'except we'd like to arrange the chairs in a less formal way. In semi-circles or something.'

Conscious of all eyes directed his way, the peacemaker prepared to stand his ground. Jet and Kierney must be his highest priority now. They were saying goodbye to their mother at a most precarious point in their young lives. This he understood only too well.

Marianna spoke up. 'Yes, I think that'd be lovely. Would semi-circles work, Mr Forbes?'

'I'll give the crematorium a ring, Mrs Dyson,' the undertaker replied. 'Most of the chapels there have fixed rows of pews, but I'll find out if they can be replaced with chairs for you.'

The arrangements were committed in writing, and Jeff's credit card was flexed. Funeral directing was a lucrative business. How many grieving families would have the stamina to haggle for a discount? He ought to have delegated this job to Gerry after all...

Back in the car park, the Dysons whisked themselves away without delay, leaving the Diamonds and their kind driver to breathe a sigh of relief.

'Can I ask you a strange question?' Michelle asked, unlocking the car. 'Did you really think that was Lynn in there?'

The youngsters gasped and turned away, not sure how to respond. Their father's gloomy features focussed on the serious woman, and for a moment, they feared he might launch forth with a tirade of abuse.

'She used to be,' he sighed, wrenching the passenger door open. 'But not now, in my opinion.'

'When my mother died,' the solicitor continued, 'I still felt something when I looked into her face. But with Lynn, I didn't feel anything.'

Jeff shrugged. 'Everyone's different, I s'pose. The fact that there's a human body in there that used to contain the most beautiful woman in the world is kind of meaningless for me. I just feel fuckin' angry that some bastard took her from us without warning.'

'Me too,' his son agreed. 'And why? That's what I want to know. I can't wait for the funeral to be over so we can start finding out why he did it.'

The celebrity breathed in and out several times, sensing he was about to throw up. His son's words brought their new reality home like a slap in the face. The funeral was only the beginning. He ran behind the Mercedes and crouched over a flowerbed to vomit.

Kierney came to his aid, but he pushed her away. 'I'm OK,' he barked. 'You guys get in.'

The young woman did as she was told, crying quietly to herself. Her brother invited her to cuddle in on the rear seat. Michelle stole a glance at the Diamond progeny in the back of her car and remembered them as bright and energetic toddlers, not so long ago. Now they were motherless, a teenaged fate they shared with her and their father.

'I'm so sorry for you two,' she said, twisting round. 'This is very hard, isn't it? You'll feel better soon.'

After two or three minutes, the front passenger door opened to admit the queasy heartthrob. He was still breathing heavily, and his face had taken on a greenish-white hue. The driver lifted the armrest on top of the centre console to retrieve a bottle of water, offering it to him. Accepting it with thanks, he took several large gulps and offered it around with an impish grin.

'That's better. So! Where would you like me to take you?' their patient friend asked, pulling a face and shaking her head. 'You can keep that one! Back to the apartment?'

Her commander-in-chief wilted as if his fuel tank had been syphoned dry. 'We're supposed to pick up those bloody letters. There's probably a message from Gerry. Sorry, Mish. Are you in a hurry?'

'No. Check your phone. I'll do whatever you need me to do.'

Jeff had indeed missed a call from his manager. The package was ready for collection or delivery; he was only to give the word. Dialling the number for Blake & Partners' corner office, he heard the call being answered on the first ring.

'Yep. Thanks, mate,' the superstar replied to the Irishman's enquiry. 'We're OK. We've been arranging the effing funeral. It's shithouse actually. We just want it done and dusted. Yes, please, mate. We can swing by and collect them in half an hour or so. D'you fancy a beer? Good. See you in thirty. Cheers. *Adiós.*'

Jeff cut the line and swivelled round to Michelle and the children, who were awaiting their next instructions. He smiled at Kierney.

'I'm sorry I sent you away, *pequeñita*. I didn't want you to have to deal with me chucking up. That's not your job.'

The teenager shrugged. 'It can be my job if I want it to be.'

Good on her, the headstrong man thought. His gorgeous gipsy girl wasn't about to take his poor behaviour lying down, and neither was her brother. Another sign that he and Lynn had built robust offspring. He reached his right hand backwards and squeezed his daughter's knee, receiving a playful rap on the knuckles in return. Message received and understood.

'So where are we going?' Michelle reminded him.

'Back to the CBD. Sorry, Mish,' Jeff replied. 'My head's spinning, but that's no excuse. Just yell at me if I ignore you.'

The confident redhead rocked the handsome man's right thigh to inject a little lightness into the vehicle. He shot her a stern glare, cautioning her not to flirt with him. He was definitely not in the mood for such frivolous body contact. Michelle's guilty eyes fixed back on the road.

'I'm going to have a quick beer with Gerry,' the father announced to the quiet pair behind him. 'You're more than welcome to come with us, but we all probably need a bit of time to ourselves before the next episode of "The Crying Game" tonight.'

Jet nodded with a reluctant smile. 'Yeah. Good call.'

'OK,' Kierney agreed too. 'Michelle, when are you free to go to Escondido?'

'Tomorrow morning, after school drop-off? Half past nine or thereabouts.'

'Thanks. Perfect. We'll make a list of stuff to bring back.'

The car's occupants fell silent again as it drove along Dandenong Road towards St Kilda. The mourners each stared out of their nearest window, watching half-empty trams trundle alongside them and processing the days ahead: funeral outfits to be decided upon; how to pass the time between now and Friday; and what was to happen after Friday? So much uncertainty, and so many hours to think about it.

'Dad?' Jet broke the silence.

'Jetto,' the musician answered, turning round to pay attention after his earlier rudeness.

'What's going to happen to Mum's rings?'

The older man sighed. 'Nothing. Why?'

'Don't you want to keep them?' the sportsman sounded surprised. 'Otherwise they'll just melt down and be gone.'

Jeff rested his head against the passenger window. He was exhausted and fed-up to the back teeth with the endless stream of decisions, but this was a sound observation from his son.

'Good point, mate. I told you I can't think of anything sensible at the moment. We should retrieve them. She only put the extra ones on for our lunch gig. Y'know... Special occasions, and all that. I'll ask our friend the undertaker. Jesus! Thanks heaps for reminding me.'

The teenagers were satisfied with their father's positive response. With Kierney still leaning on the blond colossus, Jeff saw the pair nudge each other out of the corner of his eye.

'I'll ring William later,' Michelle offered. 'I've got to call him anyway. Maybe they take jewellery off beforehand anyway, I'm not sure. I'll remember to ask.'

Catching his breath, the widower was hit with a sudden change of heart. 'Thanks, but actually... Can you ask them to leave the eternity ring where it is, Mish, please?'

A muted shriek burst from the driver's mouth as she grappled with the horror of such an exclusive and expensive piece of jewellery liquefying into what would remain of her best friend. Embarrassed, she managed to suppress the urge to ask her passenger if he had gone stark, raving mad, realising she was obliged to accept his wishes.

'Are you sure?' she asked instead.

Jeff eyed the children with an illicit chuckle, lifting his brows ever so slightly. 'Yes, I'm sure. Unless you guys have any objections? The wedding and engagement rings: they were transitory, to cover what's become a shorter than expected, yet always finite period of time. Till death do us part, as they say. But eternity is, well...'

The songwriter blinked as tears formed again in his eyes. Kierney reached forward and put a hand on his shoulder.

'Eternity is "Together, Forever, Wherever",' she finished his sentence. 'I think that's a perfect idea.'

Michelle nodded, annoyed at her own material greed. While the philanthropist was explaining his rationale, her covetous mind had gone as far as to contemplate keeping the stunning two-tone gold, diamond- and ruby-encrusted masterpiece for herself, trusting she would remember never to wear it in the Diamonds' company.

Come to that, how much longer would she be part of the famous family's circle anyway, now their friend-in-common had departed? Lynn's eternity ring was by far the most exquisite piece of jewellery she had ever set eyes on.

'Okey dokey,' she sang out. 'Wedding and engagement ring it is. That's fine, guys. Leave it with me.'

'Thanks heaps,' the bereft man responded.

The expression on the solicitor's face told him everything he needed to know, and he resisted the temptation to reassure her that she would be offered the opportunity to pick over the spoils of his wife's possessions in the fullness of time. Acknowledging the magpie gene with which many women were born, he chose instead to give a silent vote of gratitude that his dream girl had missed out on it.

'Will the coffin be open on Friday?' Kierney's innocent voice floated from behind his right ear.

'Jesus. No, I don't think so,' Jeff answered with a deep groan. 'D'you want it open or closed?'

'Closed,' Jet interjected from the same direction.

Kierney nodded. 'Oh, yeah. Definitely closed, if we can.'

'Cool. Me too,' their dad smiled, turning to Michelle. 'Got that, boss?'

Their chauffeuse laughed. 'Loud and clear!'

The luxurious Mercedes four-wheel drive pulled up in Flinders Lane, outside the rear entrance of 333 Collins Street, to let Jeff Diamond jump out. His son was quick to run round and take his place in the front seat, and they all watched the instantly-recognisable icon disappear into the building unimpeded.

Jeff managed to avoid making eye contact with most people in the lift up to Blake & Partners' offices. Those who insisted on passing on their sympathies were met with a wave and a brusque thank-you, for he was in no mood to prolong any conversations with strangers.

He slammed the heel of his left hand against the glass to open the swing door into the reception area, causing the pretty young things at the counter to jump out of their skins. He waved an apology and marched straight through into Gerry's suite.

'Marcia, g'day,' he said to the Irishman's mature-aged executive assistant. 'How're you going?'

'Oh, Jeff. I'm fine, thank you,' the startled woman replied, moved to tears. 'And how are you?'

The firm's biggest client answered with a sardonic smile. 'Wonderful, thanks. Just wonderful. Can I go in, please?'

'Yes. He's expecting you. Keep your chin up.'

Rolling his eyes, Jeff marched into the grand office and straight into his manager's waiting embrace. They slapped each other on the back, as if the physical contact made everything better.

'Keep my chin up?' the celebrity laughed and cried at the same time. 'What the fuck does that mean anyway?'

'Did she say that to you? Shit! I thought those expressions were long gone. I'll have to send her on some cool-speak training. Take a load off, mate.'

The rock star collapsed his tall frame into a chair next to the desk, opposite his talented business manager. He spied a collection of small envelopes in a clear plastic wallet sitting to one side, along with a document with a wax seal. Lynn's Last Will and Testament, he concluded with a shudder.

'Is that it?' the widower asked, pointing to the folder. 'The sum total of my wife's remaining intellectual property?'

Gerry sighed. 'I guess it is. Bullshit, isn't it? I'm getting angrier and angrier as the hours go by,' he confessed, receiving a mute shrug from the visitor in return. 'I just can't fathom what's happened. I'm sick to death of hearing about it on the radio and TV, and everywhere I go, people want to talk to me about her. You must be so fucked off, mate.'

'You might very well say that,' Jeff laughed bitterly, pinching a line from one of the pair's favourite television dramas. 'I couldn't possibly comment.'

'Indeed. Lager, Sir Francis?' the affable accountant suggested, grinning and swivelling round to retrieve two beers from his secret executive refrigerator. 'Your chin is up, old boy. Well done.'

The celebrity accepted the bottle with a grateful nod, twisting its top off. He flicked the metal disc cheekily at his manager, who caught it and diverted it into the bin underneath his desk.

'To funerals,' Jeff toasted. 'What a godforsaken macabre and stressful morning we've had.'

'How are the kids? I thought Sunday was bloody good for all of us, didn't you?'

'Yeah. Absolutely. Jetto's on his angry curve too, and Kizzy drifts in and out. They're both sensible and grown-up one minute, then back to being little kids the next. You should've seen how tightly Jet gripped my hand when we walked into that coffin room.'

'Coffin room?' Gerry repeated with a grimace. 'Christ! That's too revolting for words. Did you see Lynn again too?'

'Yep. It was fuckin' revolting, mate. The autopsy'd disfigured her, and they'd bunched her hair up behind her head like a bloody schoolteacher. It didn't look like Lynn at all.'

'Perhaps that's a good thing. Like it helps you let go?'

'Yeah, maybe. But it's almost as if we're burning the wrong person.'

His manager gasped. 'Fuck that!' he exclaimed. 'I don't know what's worse: burial or cremation. Rotting or burning?'

'Mate, do you have to?' Jeff scoffed, knowing he was in no position to castigate anyone for poor taste. 'Doesn't matter either way, if you ask me. There's nothing left of Lynn in that body. She's long gone. But how're *you* going? I know how much you loved her. I'm not completely blind, Gez.'

Gerry swung his chair ninety degrees clockwise and stared out of the window. The celebrity could see his eyes were shining with unshed tears.

'Jeez, forget about me. How are you?' the executive asked, collecting his thoughts. 'The truth.'

'Truth?' his friend mocked. 'I'm fucked off, as you say. Utterly fucked off, not to put too fine a point on it. I'm short-tempered with everyone, my attention span rivals that of a goldfish, and I just want my old life back.'

The frustrated world-changer stood up and let out a reverberating roar, kicking the solid, mahogany desk five or six times for petulant effect.

And I'd like my old wife back too, his warped brain taunted.

A twinge of pain gripped his chest at that precise moment, again on the site of his "JL" tattoo. He rubbed the spot and replaced the ire with a wry smile.

'Whatever... Lynn's lying on a beach somewhere, in a bikini, waiting for me. She can't believe the fuss everyone's making, and it's about time we opened her letters and found out what she's been trying to tell us.'

'Oh, you don't know how much I want to believe you,' Gerry replied, resplendent on his black, leather throne. 'Sounds like a bloody nice place to be right now.'

'Yeah. Better than here, that's for sure. Well, I believe me at any rate.'

'Good on you, you delusional bastard!'

'So what time are we reading the will tomorrow?' his client checked, picking up the folder of envelopes. 'Here?'

'No. At the solicitors' upstairs at ten. The Dysons aren't bringing a lawyer.'

Jeff glared at the man across the table, transported back to the time he had sat in this man's former, much less grandiose office, in the same building over twenty years ago, where he had ranted and raved about the fact that Bart had summoned his daughter's unsuitable suitor to Dyson Administration to inform him that his dubious past was under investigation. Those old wounds had taken a long time to heal, or perhaps they hadn't ever completely healed.

'How good of them,' the widower murmured. 'Let's hope Lynn's left everything to the Polish Jewish murderers' sports society.'

Gerry laughed aloud. 'Watch it, mate. Let it go.'

The celebrity raised his hand. 'Yeah, yeah, yeah. I know.'

'So what are you going to do with those?' the older man asked, pointing at the paperwork tucked under the songwriter's right arm.

'We're going to order takeaway from Lynn's favourite curry house, drink a bottle of the oldest wine we can find and read all this. And cry a lot, I expect.'

'Will you be OK? Should I be worried about you?'

'No, mate,' Jeff reassured him. 'That's what the kids've told me to say anyway, and they're right. I'm sticking around for them. They're my Number One priority. Lynn'll just have to be patient on that beach until I'm confident they're on their feet and happy.'

'Bloody hell, you idiot,' Gerry cursed. 'You need to watch yourself. I'll see you tomorrow morning.'

The visitor gripped his manager's hand. 'Thanks for caring, mate. I know you're hurting too, and I know what you're saying. I'll keep my chin up.'

The successful company man opened the door and watched his old friend disappear into the lift lobby. Once at ground level and outside, Jeff walked at a brisk pace through town, criss-crossing the grid pattern of roads between Collins Street and his apartment, choosing the narrow laneways wherever possible. Closing his mind to the pointing, whispering and shouting as best he could, he arrived back at his building within ten minutes. He stepped into the lift, and tapped in the code for the penthouse floor .

'Anyone here?' he shouted when the doors slid open.

His jet-lagged son appeared in the doorway to the lounge room, where he had been dozing in front of the television. Kierney also came running from her bedroom, her hair untidy as if she had woken from deep slumber.

'Did you get them?' she asked, excited. 'Did you walk back?'

'Yes and yes,' Jeff laughed, peeling his shirt off his sweating back. 'It's hot out there.'

'What time are we going to open them?' her brother chipped in.

'Hey! Jesus, guys... Why are you so impatient?'

'Because we're stuck,' his gipsy girl moaned, stamping her foot like a toddler.

The siblings followed their dad through from the hallway and watched him deposit the folder of letters on top of the piano. He turned round, still bare-chested, and hugged them both.

'You guys are awesome,' he said. 'You're really helping me. I love you so much.'

LOVE LETTERS

Jeff removed the cork from a second bottle of aged Rioja and poured three large glasses. The Indian meal had been as delicious as usual, and all three were stuffed to bursting point. They had taken turns to describe their fondest memories of their departed fourth Diamond, many making them cry but every one raising a smile. Inside, they each knew how important tonight's process was for accelerating their healing, and agreed that it felt good to be reminded of these special, shared remembrances.

'Can we start?' the impetuous sportsman asked, looking over at the documents on the piano.

With an assenting flick of his eyebrows, the widower watched his son spring off the cushion and cover the six metres or so between couch and baby grand. Kierney cleared some space on the coffee table in front of them and the folder was placed in the middle like an offering to the gods.

'Open it,' Jet urged his father.

'Christ, mate. Hang on,' the sad man sighed. 'I don't share your high level of enthusiasm for this exercise. I'm glad you're both so keen, but I'm scared shitless.'

'But why, Papá?' his daughter asked in surprise. 'Mamá won't have written anything to you that you don't want to hear.'

'No, I know, but it's going to make me miss her even more than I do already. I just don't know if I can cope. That's why.'

The siblings gazed at each other, dumbfounded that they had overlooked this obvious reaction.

'We're sticking together, remember?' the younger man assured. 'We'll help you cope. We coped through dinner, with all those stories. Isn't that pretty much the same?'

'Yes and no,' their father nodded, seeing both teenagers roll their eyes. 'These letters are going to be so personal though; from one heart to the other. Stuff that means something specific to each of us. Don't underestimate the effect they're going to have on you. Just picture *la mamá* writing them, thinking of this exact situation and how we were all going to feel without her. That's how I was feeling when I wrote mine anyway.'

'What's going to happen with the letters you wrote to Mamá?' Kierney asked. 'Are you going to open them?'

Jeff leant back on the couch, tears rolling down his cheeks before the activity had even begun. 'Jeez, I don't know,' he sniffed. 'I haven't even thought about them. Probably just leave them untouched. You can read them later.'

'Later?' his son echoed. 'Jesus, Dad. Don't talk about that now.'

'Sorry,' their dad replied, sitting forward and regrouping for the task at hand. 'You're right. Let's get these sorted into date order, shall we?'

Unzipping the edge of the clear, plastic folder, he tipped its contents onto the coffee table. The envelopes varied in size and colour but were all marked similarly, with a name and a year. All three pairs of hands reached into the pile and began to distribute the letters by tossing them on the floor at each recipient's feet until the only ones remaining on the table were those addressed in Jeff's handwriting.

The grief-stricken husband groaned, looking at them. 'What a waste of emotional energy they turned out to be.'

'You don't mean that,' Kierney wagged her finger. 'I bet you loved writing them.'

Jeff went to clip the top of his daughter's head with his hand, and she ducked just in time. 'Right again, smart-arse,' he agreed. 'And there's nothing in there that would've come as a surprise to your mum anyway.'

'So is that why you're not keen on opening yours?' Jet teased. 'You want to hear something different but you don't expect to?'

'Yeah. In a way, I guess so. I don't want to be disappointed, so I'd rather just imagine what's in them.'

'OK. So we're opening them chronologically? Is that what we agreed?' the nineteen-year-old checked, sorting his pile by year.

'Yes,' Kierney nodded. 'Unless you want to go back in time? That wouldn't make sense.'

The children had more envelopes than their father. He was envious of their full hands, continually rubbing his pectoral muscle. Jet glanced over at his sister, willing her to notice their dad's absent-minded actions.

'You guys better start,' Jeff suggested, 'or we'll be here 'til Friday.'

The lad sniggered, pointing to his dad's busy fingers. 'Does your tattoo really itch? Or are you just doing that in the hope it will?'

The older man moved his hand away from his chest and looked from son to daughter as if to say, "So you told him about that?" Kierney blushed, remembering the golden nugget had been given to her as a secret on the flight back from Sydney.

He smiled and winked, which only made the young woman more uncomfortable. 'I don't know, mate,' he replied. 'Bit of both.'

'Hope for the best but expect the worst,' Kierney dared, impersonating her lookalike and thereby lightening the mood. 'Who cares, eh, Papá?'

Jeff emptied his glass of wine after a brief toast, and his dutiful son refilled it while Kierney lit her father a cigarette. This was shaping up to be a tough few hours.

'Go on, one of you,' the widower urged. 'Start opening. The suspense is overwhelming.'

His dark-haired gipsy girl lifted the envelope marked "1980", as did her brother.

'You must have one for 'eighty,' the cricketer said, ''cause that's when it all started.'

Jeff did have a letter for this inaugural year. He picked it up gingerly, and they counted down together from five. On "Open", they all tore into their first envelope, laughing before falling silent as the words Lynn had written began to come to life.

Each letter started the same way, telling its recipient that this was the year when an amateur assassin had gunned down John Lennon. She told her precious family members how much she loved them and that she hoped her words would not see the light of day for a very long time.

'Fifteen years, Mum,' Jet said out loud. 'I wonder if that's sooner or later than she was imagining when she had the idea?'

Neither of the others responded; the very thought sending shivers down their spines. They read on about how happy they had been, interspersed with examples of special occasions which had stuck in Lynn's memory.

For Jet, it was the introduction he had given the newborn Kierney to their extended family, all gathered around her bed in the maternity ward. And for her little girl, it was the fact that she had connected with her father so deeply from Day One that it was clear she would turn out to be the last missing link in his life.

And for Jeff, it was a thank-you for the magical journey on which he had taken his chosen partner up until this point, with the promise of so much more to come. The grateful husband read the cluster of paragraphs time after time, his heart bleeding as he superimposed his dream girl's voice and face over the words on the page.

> "To my beautiful black stallion,
>
> I don't know the circumstances that cause you to be reading this letter. I only hope it helps to ease the pain. This idea we had when John Lennon died to write each other letters felt like a good one at the time, but now I'm putting pen to paper, I wonder if they will have the desired effect, should we ever need them.
>
> I know that neither of us will ever take each other's love for granted. It is my greatest honour and privilege to be your wife and to accept your

unswerving loyalty and your unending love. You are my best friend, my all-consuming lover and my intellectual inspiration.

Jeff, I wish I could find words to express the depth and breadth of my love for you. It started the day we met, sitting in the theatre when I leant back against your arm and you didn't move it, and I dearly hope it will never end. We have enjoyed a perfect love affair the like of which cannot be matched, in my opinion. You share the best and worst moments of my life and have always provided the sanctuary and security of friendship.

I take comfort in knowing you will continue to prepare Jet and Kierney for their adult lives. They both possess your strength of character and sense of what is right. You are as close to a saint as it comes. So many good things have happened and will happen by your insight and dedication. I treasure the poem you wrote after our family was complete, because I know the joy that parenthood has brought to both of us.

I also know that, should you leave this world before me, I would not wish to carry on. You are my life, and without you and the kids it's worthless. I hope, if the tables are turned, that you find some way of overcoming the emptiness. Just remember what we have and that we made the most of every day we were together.

To say any more would be superfluous. I love you. I will always love you. If there is another place, please, please find me.

Yours forever,

Lynn xxxx"

'*Muchas gracias, mi amor,*' Jeff mouthed. 'I love you too. And I *will* find you.'

The only sounds in the room were the rustling of paper and the sniffing back of tears. Without a word, they each reached for the next letter in the pile, which for all three was marked "1981". The frantic tearing of envelopes didn't happen a second time. In its place, they set about the solemn task of reading the following year's heartfelt summaries, deep in their own thoughts.

Jeff's next message reminded him of the visit the young family had made to his father in prison, shortly before the frail man had died, and how this one short meeting had changed both men. He hadn't had occasion to think about this significant episode for many years, and Lynn's words gave him a warm glow of pride. He *had* been a good father in spite of the dreadful role model. He was still a good father.

That January, the young mother had written specifically to request her husband spend more time with Jet. She insisted that, should she no longer be around, the blond side of the family would need as much guidance as the dark-haired side. It had been a good observation which they had discussed *ad nauseam* at the time, and now utterly appropriate to have it brought to his attention.

'Mum says I have to make sure the blond-haired one gets as much attention as the dark-haired one,' Jeff blurted out, looking up at his son.

'What? Did she forget our names?' Kierney forced a laugh. 'Was she drunk when she wrote these?'

'Maybe she used a ghost writer,' her brother quipped.

'I doubt it,' Jeff smiled. 'What do yours say?'

The eighteen-year-old read a passage from her next letter. '"Dear Kierney, you are almost three and you are already older than your brother. Slow down, please. You don't have to grow up in such a hurry."'

She paused for a moment to contain her emotions before continuing. 'This is my favourite part. She says, "You always make your papá so very happy. Treat him gently if I'm not here anymore because he will be extremely sad."'

The young woman broke down, hiding her face in the letter. Jeff slid onto the floor in front of her, consoling her through his own tears.

'You are extremely sad, aren't you, Papá?' she sobbed. 'It's not fair. This really isn't fair.'

'Come on,' the empathetic man cajoled, rubbing her back. 'We're all extremely sad. But it's good that we're getting it all out. She was damned clever, your mamá. What does yours say, Jetto?'

The cricketer cleared his throat, glad to do his bit. 'Mine's all about going to school and learning. Mum says it's important to try to learn how to learn, so you keep wanting more knowledge. I have to become a Philomath just like you, Dad.

'Mine goes, "Dad knows the difference between knowledge and wisdom, and one day you should ask him to explain it to you. That's the difference between ordinary people and great leaders. Most people concentrate on what, where and when, but Dad understands how and why. That's what you need to do too."'

'I guess she never reckoned on both of you dying at the same time,' his sister ventured, feeling a little better, '"cause these letters all talk as if we'll be left as a three. What if we'd been orphaned? There isn't any mention of that.'

'Does it matter?' Jet asked. 'We would be reading both sets of letters in that case. Are we allowed to know what's in yours to us, Dad?'

The widower shook his head. 'No.'

Not yet, each was thinking. The children opened their next letter, for 1982. Jeff didn't have one with this label.

'Why not?' his son wondered. 'Did nothing happen to change anything that year?'

'That was the idea,' the songwriter confirmed. 'Mamá was very organised. She had photocopies of every one, and when we sat down each year to update them, she'd make an assessment as to whether anything had changed from the last time. I was never that organised, as you can see...'

Both children chuckled at the large collection of remaining letters. Their dad stood up, watching his offspring opening their third envelope. He was confused as to why he didn't have one too. He had expected Lynn to write about the amazing European summer holiday they had taken and how it had brought them so super-close. He left the room to make some coffee, unable to justify his wife's apparent oversight of this momentous time in their life singular.

He stood smoking next to the boiling kettle, still rubbing his chest. No, Jeff decided. There must be a letter for him from this year. Leaving his cigarette burning on the edge of the sink, he ran back into the room. Much to the children's surprise, he delved into the pile of his own offerings and scattered them feverishly.

'Yes!' the triumphant man whispered, brandishing the missing envelope. 'I knew there must be one for 'eighty-two. We had that fantastic trip through France and Italy. You two probably don't even remember.'

Full of relief, the forty-three-year-old took his letter back into the kitchen and opened it while the coffee was brewing, smoking the last centimetre of his cigarette. When finished, he held the envelope over his tattoo and breathed deeply several times before taking the single piece of paper out.

'I knew you wouldn't let me down, angel,' he said into the air. 'I knew you'd have something to say about that holiday. I love you so much, and thank you for suggesting this letter-writing thing. Just so you know, it's one of your greatest ideas.'

Lynn's message was simple but perfect. It was written for the most part in French, of course, and told of how she had come to understand far more about who her mystery man really was. She suggested that in a former life he might have been a European prince with unfinished business, and the reader saw no reason to reject this theory.

His beautiful best friend also described how "immeasurably adored" she had felt when he had crept back into their hotel bed after having been allowed out to play with his "pot-smoking, cognac-swilling, philosophical fraternity". Here was the subject he had been so desperate to hear from his wife's perspective, for that memorable night still burned white-hot in his soul.

'Very true,' the songwriter agreed with his absent wife in French from the kitchen in 1996, the recollection as vivid now as it ever had been. 'It felt like you had given me my absolute freedom that night, angel. I loved you more than ever before.'

Kierney entered the kitchen, wondering why her father was taking so long to make coffee. She found him sitting on the tiles in front of the sink, with his head leaning back against the cupboard door and his eyes squeezed shut as if trying to sharpen the mental image. Tears glistened on his cheeks, offset by a slight smile on his face.

'*Papá, estás OK?*' she enquired, resting a tentative hand on his shoulder. 'Come back in with us. We want to share this with you.'

'My gorgeous girl-child,' Jeff answered, reaching upwards to make contact. 'Pull me up. You guys need to read this one. It's the best.'

'*Excelente*,' the youngster replied, yanking her dad up from the floor with all her strength, like she used to as a five- or six-year-old. 'You've put on weight.'

Jeff sprang to his feet, causing Kierney to tip backwards with the force she had exerted in trying to help him stand up. 'Crap,' he denied, embracing her willowy frame. '*Je t'adore, pequeñita.*'

They carried the three mugs of coffee into the lounge room to find Jet weeping over his pile of letters. The father sat on the couch next to him this time, weaving an arm behind his shoulders. No doubt about it, Lynn was a smart woman. This exercise was not only helping them leech the grief out of their systems, but it was also bringing them closer together at the time when they most needed each other.

'What're you thinking, mate?'

'How lucky we are, I suppose. Although it's hard to feel lucky when your mum's just died, but she loved us so much. You both do, and I want to say thanks for having devoted so much of your life to us.'

Kierney nodded. 'Me too. The dark-haired one agrees.'

Her dad chuckled, raising his coffee mug. 'Cheers, from both of us to both of you. You're very welcome. It was always our intent to bring you up with a strong set of values, and it's worked in spades. You understand what's necessary for a successful life. You can't go wrong, guys. And this forced backtracking through happy times is an important lesson for me... no, for us... in building resilience.

'I've gotta tell ya... This afternoon, driving back from that bloody funeral parlour, I was ready to chuck it all away.'

'We figured as much,' his gipsy girl affirmed.

'Sorry,' the father offered with a half-smile. 'But doing this together and reading all these inspiring words, it makes me want to carry on. Listen to this...'

Jeff unfolded Lynn's original letter, along with the one he had shoved in his shirt pocket a few minutes ago. Scanning down to the sentences he wanted to share, he recited clearly and with due passion from the lines his dream girl had penned when their children were still tiny.

'"Please, please find me," she says,' he told them, intoxicated with relief. 'D'you know what this means?'

Jet and Kierney both looked on in expectant silence.

'It means that Mamá wrote this long, long before we made our "Together, Forever, Wherever" pact. She asked me to follow her because she had become as dependent on me as I am on her. This is such amazing vindication, and it makes me feel strong again.'

The bereaved man's audience could scarcely believe he was the same person in whose company they had been throughout the last few days. He was vibrant and forward-facing again. They were happy for him and yet also scared that his improved mood might be short-lived. However for now, it was encouraging to see the transformation in his body language and the change in the pitch of his voice, and there was life in his tired eyes again.

Jeff continued. 'And she wouldn't have written it just to give me strength. She meant it, 'cause she knows I would've automatically suspected she did it to boost my morale.'

'That's awesome,' Kierney told him, holding out her hand. 'So this was worth it for you too then, after all. I'm rapt about that.'

Back in their original places, the trio searched for the letters written at the start of 1984. Jet had been seven-and-a-half, and his sister about to turn six. Their dad didn't have a letter for this year, which was perfectly fine. He remained on a high from the previous message, conceding that any significant events taking place during this latest twelve-month period were predominately for the children's benefit. It was also the time when his beautiful best friend had coerced him back on the road after the death of two fans at a Chicago gig, of which she would have seen no value in reminding him.

Watching the others, Jeff guessed the following year's letter to him would contain Lynn's analysis of their toughest period, and he became apprehensive again. In an effort to stop Gravity from wrestling away his newfound positive viewpoint, he sat back to savour Jet and Kierney reading their latest epistles.

'Mine's all about what winning means,' the ambitious sportsman explained. 'It's a bit weird to read this from before the big argument over me. It makes me curious to read next year's, to see how Mum's attitude changed.'

Jeff exhaled, his heart rate on the rise. His son was exhibiting exactly the maturity he had hoped for, and yet it still unnerved him to think Lynn's next instalment might push him away.

'It's up to us,' he replied. 'We need to interpret her words carefully. Try to remember how things were back then. I'm not looking forward to reading about 'eighty-four for precisely that reason. It depends whether you think we treated you fairly, and I'm happy to talk about it now, with the benefit of hindsight. I'm quite prepared to admit I did the wrong thing if you or Mum can convince me I did.'

Kierney felt awkward. She had been too young to understand her parents' one huge difference of opinion, and she didn't want to take sides and risk opening old wounds again. She remembered how their mini world had rocked on its axis for a week or so, understanding the rift was serious even at the tender age of five.

'We're not up to 'eighty-four yet, are we?' she asked, to diffuse the situation a little. 'Mine's all about "Laura's Light" and making sure I get the same opportunities as a girl as I would've had as a boy. It's a really simple lesson in appreciating diversity, written for a five-year-old. Do you want me to read it?'

Kierney looked up at her brother and father after reading most of the letter, they were mesmerised by the insights simplified for their young but inquisitive recipient. Both nodded, and the older man wiped a lone tear from the corner of his right eye.

'Go on, angel,' he invited his daughter. 'How does it end?'
Kierney sat up straight and resumed reading.

> '"When you're at school, it's important that you listen to what the teachers have to say, but don't be afraid to ask all your questions. Without asking questions, we will never learn the answers. You could be waiting a long time for someone to tell you something if they don't know you want to know."'

'Especially Mrs Stavrakakis,' Jet interjected, grinning at his sister. 'She was hilarious! She should never have been a teacher, that woman.'

'Oh, yes! I can hardly remember her. I wonder what happened to her,' Kierney laughed, before switching to a haughty voice. '"Miss Diamond, if you have one more thing to say about my lesson, I shall have to ask you to visit the Principal."'

Their dad raised his hands in front of his face as if to say he denied all knowledge of having run interference on this occasion. 'Who knows?' he defended himself and the woman in question. 'She wasn't a bad teacher, but just not for kids with enquiring minds. She had no time for people who thought broadly. It interrupted her train of thought. I'm sure she got a job at another primary school. Well, Kizzo... You didn't need Mamá's letter because you did come home and tell me, and we did something about it.'

'String-puller,' her brother sneered. 'So that year, I was in training to be a king and you were in training to be a pain in the bum.'

Jeff flicked out a quick left-hook and caught his son on the side of the head as he leant forward to pick up his next letter. 'Careful, Your Highness,' he teased. 'You were a right royal pain in the bum from time to time also.'

Kierney giggled. 'I have to go to the loo. There's no 1984 for me, so you guys go ahead.'

The men reached into their piles of envelopes and pulled out the next one. They both became nervous as they watched their sister disappear, taking her natural break at a most deliberate and effective moment.

'Shit, mate,' the older man muttered. 'What d'you think? Did Mum really forgive me?'

'Of course she did. Sounds like you didn't forgive yourself, more like.'

'Bloody hell,' his father conceded, hearing these words with gratitude and humility. 'You might be right.'

Jeff looked at his watch. Midnight was fast approaching, and there were still eleven years to go. They were destined for a long, long ride on this particular rollercoaster. He tore open the envelope and unfolded two sheets of paper. Two sheets! Lynn did have a lot to say about 1984...

The nervous man heard Jet breathe a sigh of relief, raising his eyes to see a wide smile on the lad's face. With a kindly smirk, the teenager gathered the paper close to his chest to indicate its confidentiality. Jeff focussed back on his own letter, which opened with a quote from a hit song he had written towards the end of this difficult period: "Love is not victory".

Yet another outpouring of emotion was imminent, Jeff could tell. He could hear his gorgeous wife crying while he read her words. This schism had knocked the couple for six. On top of this, the Dyson family had discovered Sandy was HIV positive and had contracted the AIDS virus.

The cricketer gave his dad a thumbs-up sign, twisting his wrist first one way and then the other, inviting a vote as to where on the scale he should stop. Seeing Jeff shake his head, he understood to wait a while longer. He raised his eyebrows to his sister, who had slipped back into the room unnoticed and remained uncommonly silent while figuring out what she had missed.

The remorseful husband turned back to his letter.

> "Every day you find new ways to inspire me. Even when you don't achieve the outcome you're looking for, you carry on fighting for what you believe in. That's the mark of a true leader and a great, great man. The love I have for you has found a new level over the last few months, and even more so in the last few days.'
>
> 'My beautiful black stallion, I always called you. Now I'm adding "noble" and "benevolent" to the list, which puts me in mind more of a lion than a horse. You don't see many pantomime lions, but I'd like to apply, if I may. If you're reading this letter - which breaks my heart - please know that I realise you still have a lot left to do with your life. Take whatever time you need, but be assured that I'll still be waiting for you. If there is another life, I want to spend it with you."

After drinking in "All my love, Lynn," Jeff folded the sheets of paper in half again and let forth an almighty roar, as befitting a noble and benevolent lion. Kierney moved next to her father on the couch and hugged him tightly as he sobbed.

'Are these tears of happiness? Please tell me they are.'

Jeff motioned to his son to join them, and the three sat silently for a few moments. 'Happiness, sadness, regret, pride, loss, gain... All of the above,' he replied after a while, ticking a column of imaginary boxes in the air.

'*Excelente*,' his romantic daughter decided. 'That's what love is: all of the above.'

Jeff kissed her hard on the side of her head. 'Abso-fucking-lutely,' he laughed. 'The people you guys end up with better understand that too. Christ! If you kids are a tenth as happy as Lynn made me, you'll have a fantastic life. Read this, if you want, while I make room for more wine. Then I want to hear yours, Jetto, if I may.'

'Abso-fucking-lutely,' the young buck mimicked his father, slapping him on the thigh as he rose to his feet.

Kierney shuffled closer to her brother, and they both read a summary of their parents' hardest year from a mother's viewpoint. Jet gave a self-satisfied sniff and pointed to the sentence which claimed he had saved the day, and his sister stuck her tongue out.

'So that's how "The Boy Who Would Be King" all started,' a tired Jet murmured. 'Amazing, isn't it? Do you think we're going to have relationships like theirs?'

'It's cool to think so,' Kierney answered, wiping tears from her eyes. 'It still looks as if the plan stays in place though, doesn't it?'

Jet grunted. 'Let's not think about it just yet.'

On his way back from the cloakroom, Jeff stopped outside the master bedroom again. How could Lynn have resisted the temptation to make reference to the pantomime lion in all these years?

He laughed, allowing himself to lean on the doorframe and steal a glimpse inside at their bed. It had been less than a week since they had last slept in this room, yet his brain still refused to reconstruct those memories. These last few days had dragged like a lead weight.

'Angel, are you in here?' he asked. 'Where are you?'

Jeff inhaled and switched the light on. Simultaneously, his heartbeat raced with alarm, and dizziness disoriented him. Walking in and around to his wife's side of the bed, where everything was as she had left it, he saw evidence of where Kierney had removed his possessions on their first night home. Lynn's remained untouched, and rightly so.

He dropped down onto the quilt and picked up a wristwatch his dream girl had deposited on her bedside table. It was an ordinary, everyday timepiece bearing no significance for their relationship. He opened the top drawer and placed the watch inside, sliding it shut straightaway. He was not yet ready to trawl through her private zones, if ever he would be.

There was a photograph of him and the children staring back into the room, taken only a few weeks ago by Marianna on their twentieth wedding anniversary. Kierney was in the middle between the two tall men, and she looked innocent and well protected.

'I failed to protect you, angel,' Jeff said, starting to cry again. 'I'm sorry. I wasn't there when I should've been, and now we're apart when we shouldn't be. Thanks for all your letters to me and the kids. You are a genius of the highest order. It's a fantastic way to celebrate our family. Are you going to tell me where you are, or do I have to work it out?'

Overcome, he tipped forward and slammed his elbows into his knees, twisting the black jet-stone ring on his right middle finger. Longing for a sign that his words were being heard, he willed his tattoo to itch again.

Nothing happened.

'Well, thanks anyway, angel. I'd better get back to the rest of your letters. Maybe there'll be some more clues. I love you, *mon amie*.'

Jeff's chest tightened as he walked around the end of the bed and headed towards the door. Looking back towards the couple's pillows, his left pectoral muscle twitched twice involuntarily. He reached to unbutton his shirt, sticking his fingers inside and rubbing the hairy skin over their inked insignia.

'Was that you or me?' he joked. 'Either you're trying to drive me crazy, or I'm doing it to myself.'

Switching the light off, Jeff tapped the doorframe a couple of times on his way out, mimicking the old Jewish custom. There it was again; two distinct muscle spasms. Shaking his head at his wild imagination, he re-joined the children in the lounge room.

His wine glass had been refilled. 'Cheers, guys.'

'Cheers, Papá. Did you go in the bedroom?'

'Maybe. Were you spying on me?'

Kierney shrugged but declined to answer. Jet coughed and waved his "1984" letter under his father's nose. The great man took it from him and started to read. The boy's mother had begun by thanking him for making her see sense, and telling him he needed to carry on being open and determined about what he wanted to do.

She also told him how ambitious his grandfather was for him to be a successful cricketer, and that the seven-year-old would have exciting opportunities to play for Australia if he trained hard and learnt as much as he could about the sport.

Lynn went on to describe how much the boy's father wanted him to make up his own mind, an idea she applauded in general. She wrote about how disappointed she had been when her parents disregarded her wishes and sent her to the United States for two years after she had first met the man of her dreams. She went on to explain that the boy's dad had accepted their fate and waited for her to return; the moral of her story being that if one wanted something badly enough, it was worth either striving for or waiting for.

Jeff let out a sarcastic laugh and shook his head. 'Son, this is good stuff, don't get me wrong,' he said, seeing the lad was spoiling for a feisty reaction, 'but you know the real issue was total immersion. There's nothing in this life worth a hundred percent of your energy. That's too narrow-minded, don't you think?'

'But this was written for a young bloke,' the grown-up sportsman objected. 'I didn't even know what narrow-minded meant back then. All I knew was you two were fighting over whether I went to cricket camp for the school holidays or not. I didn't want to go for the whole time, but I wanted to go for some time. So I guess, yes, total immersion wasn't what I wanted.'

Kierney was annoyed by the raised voices. 'Come on, guys! Why are you arguing about this now? You're not seven anymore, bro', and we're not totally immersed in anything. You won, Papá. Why does it still rancour you so much?'

The world-changer pressed his backside into the corner of the couch and stared his daughter down. 'Fuck knows,' he admitted. 'It just does. It wasn't right at the time and it's not right now. And reading about it just brings it all back. I'm sorry. Let's forget it.'

The angry father checked his watch. It was almost tomorrow.

'Yeah. That's what I was thinking,' Jet said, slapping a hand down on his dad's knee with a loud crack. 'There are still eleven more years to go. Do we want to keep going?'

'We have to,' his sister replied. 'Or do you need a break? What's happening tomorrow?'

Jeff groaned. 'Tomorrow? Tuesday. Back to reality.'

'Curry for breakfast?' the younger man quipped, fired up from their last discussion. 'Boxing gloves on the balcony?'

'Jet, shut up,' Kierney scolded. 'You need to get laid.'

'I do!' he laughed, stretching to his full height and twisting his back. 'We all do.'

'Speak for yourself,' their dad chided. 'Let's call it a night then. We've got the will-reading in the morning, but we can resume afterwards, if that suits you guys.'

'Papá, are you OK?' Kierney asked, seeing a wistful expression returning to her dad's face.

'Yeah. I'll be fine. I'll stay here and watch TV for a while.'

'Will you sleep in your old room?'

'Don't know,' the widower answered, accepting a hug from his daughter and reciprocating with a tender kiss on her forehead. 'Don't think so. But don't worry about me. I'm a crazy, mixed-up kid, that's all. I'll survive.'

Jet slapped his father on the back. 'Thanks for tonight, Dad. I hope it wasn't too agonising for you. And I'm sorry for picking a fight.'

'It's fine, mate. You're well within your rights. It was your life we were messing with.'

The trio said their goodnights, and the teenagers disappeared to their rooms in the southern half of the apartment. The lonely husband cleared away the débris from the coffee table, checking each envelope for anything they might have missed before throwing them out. Back in the lounge room, he re-read his letters in reverse sequence, finishing again with the request for him to follow his dream girl into the next life.

'Nothing'd give me greater pleasure, angel,' he told her, massaging his tattoo again. 'But you already know that.'

An old French film was showing on SBS. The couple had seen it before, many years ago, and the polyglot settled down to watch again with a hot cup of coffee and a cigarette. His thoughts turned to the marijuana in the filing cabinet but decided against it. He would save it for after the funeral, when he planned to invite both children to share a "smoke smoke" with him, as Jet had put it.

The proud father wondered when his son might consider it appropriate to return to university. He didn't want him to miss too much of the new term, but it was up to him how long he stayed. And for Christ's sake, he would miss the obnoxious bastard when he left!

He and Lynn had hatched a plan for the busy star to spend a few weeks of the short British summer with Jet on his new home turf, riding motorbikes and watching him play cricket for Warwickshire. The Indians were touring in England this northern-hemisphere season, promising tight contests that would be great to experience together. He decided not to broach the subject until the severity of his children's grief had diminished.

Stretching out along the length of the three-seater leather couch, Jeff's thoughts again drifted to his dream girl's overarching message through her letters. Her desire for him to find her in an afterlife had surprised him with its intensity and insistence, but it also warmed his heart incredibly. After all these years assuming it was he who depended on her, their need for each other now appeared much more equal than he had ever dared to believe.

In the public eye, Jeff was undoubtedly the dominant force in their partnership, even in recent times, when the children were growing up and Lynn had been freer to travel. However, the celebrity husband had never felt as if he called the shots. He had always been the one who was eager to be home while on the road and who missed her angelic touch throughout the long nights in hotels of all descriptions, resorting to sex over the telephone night after night. Yet he knew Lynn had been equally delighted with their regular reunions, so why did it amaze him to discover her words of absolute devotion?

Jet's vehement reply about all three Diamonds needing to get laid was also playing on the widower's mind. Despite longing to have his lover nearby, bereavement had altogether extinguished his rampant sexual urges, while his son was champing at the bit, at nineteen years of age and approaching the prime of his testosterone-producing life. For the couple who were now both in their forties, seldom had a day gone by when they hadn't enjoyed pleasures of the flesh at least once. Yet Friday's tragedy had left the world's greatest lover dead below the waist.

Jeff smiled to himself. 'That'd disappoint you, wouldn't it, angel?' he whispered. 'If I managed to find you and then couldn't get it up? You'd tell me to get back whence I came.'

Still, for now he didn't care. The former sexual mercenary was secretly content that his libido was in defiant shutdown. There were more important things to sort out first, before he turned his mind to what to do with his body over the months ahead.

The next day, the widower was woken by both children begging him to come for a run. He was grateful for their enthusiasm to gee him up and out of the all too familiar doldrums. Six hours' sleep was not to be discounted though, and he was feeling far better than he had on recent mornings. Obediently, he changed into sports gear, and they headed through the city to the Botanic Gardens and the running track they had frequented for as long as the children could remember.

The Diamonds attracted an extreme amount of attention, especially when Jeff forced the youngsters to slow down at the top of Anderson's Hill on their third lap. On the whole, the depleted family was met with silent, sympathetic gazes rather than comments and whispers. Lynn's funeral had been announced in yesterday's papers, and the news coverage was beginning to subside in advance of Friday's private ceremony. The threesome remained stoic, giving only the odd wave.

'I forgot last night that I'm supposed to go to Escondido with Michelle this morning,' Kierney reminded the others. 'I need to ask her if we can change it to tomorrow instead.'

Safely back in the apartment, with the morning's visit to the solicitor for the reading of the will and the afternoon with their individual piles of letters stretching ahead of them, a melancholy ambiance permeated the expansive space. Their mum's school-friend had been happy to postpone their trip to Mount Eliza, and the family sat in the lounge room, munching on cereal and drinking coffee, with the paperwork on the low table drawing vacant stares all round.

'So what happens at this will-reading?' Jet asked. 'Do we have to do anything?'

His father shook his head. 'Don't think so. I know as much about this as you do though. Just turn up and listen to what your mum wants done with all her assets and liabilities.'

'Are we her assets or her liabilities?' the Cambridge student quipped.

Jeff laughed, pleased to hear some levity. 'I expect you have entries on both sides of the balance sheet.'

Kierney giggled. 'You know what Mamá wanted, don't you?'

'Yep. Unless she changed hers without telling me, but I doubt it.'

The Diamonds arrived at the Collins Street law firm, smartly dressed and fifteen minutes early. Gerry was already present, as Lynn's appointed Executor, followed in shortly afterwards by the Dysons. They were all shown into a large office with a commanding view over the south of the city and the bay.

The accountant sat next to his old friend, patting him on the back. 'How are you doing?' he muttered, before the proceedings got underway.

'Ah, y'know... Same as before really. It's taking us bloody ages to get through these letters, but it's a worthwhile process. Extremely therapeutic in an excruciating way. What about you?'

'Better than you, I expect. Shit though, to be honest. I still can't believe she's gone.'

Jet and Kierney sat side-by-side behind their father, flanked by their grandparents. The lawyer introduced himself and set about opening the sealed envelope which had been extracted from the same safe deposit box as their letters.

The contents of Lynn's will had not been amended since the family last discussed its contents. Jet soon became bored with listening to the monotonous details, remembering his father telling them a long time ago that he had spent the entire duration of his grandmother's funeral fantasising about girls, so much so that when it came time to leave he was too embarrassed to stand up.

Now, with Bart to his left and Marianna only two seats to his right, the red-blooded teenager didn't wish to succumb to a similar discomfort. To keep his mind from wandering, he stared out of the window at the blue-green ocean in the distance and imagined himself back in the freezing Cambridge winter.

For Jeff's part, no naughty thoughts were touring his head this time. Instead, he took a few moments to consider just how wealthy the foursome had become, and how utterly useless such wealth was when it came down to what was important.

The soul-mates hadn't maintained many separate financial investments, meaning most of "their money" would simply convert into "his money" to spend, redirect or bequeath as he saw fit. The thought sickened him; another stark dose of reality in his lonely fate.

However, he was pleased the Dysons heard their daughter had left a substantial sum to the Australian Institute of Sport and to Melbourne Academy. There were endowments to be set up for new scholarships, one for Anna and Brandon's cancer research work and a significant chunk of change for the continuation of The Good School programme. Lynn had also targeted Childlight and The Fellowship to receive lump sums, but it was to be left up to Jeff and the children as to how this money might be utilised.

'Thanks, angel,' her husband murmured, loud enough for her parents to hear.

Their departed loved one had not been too definitive about personal effects, most of which would transfer to the youngsters. Her Maserati was to go to Jet, which the boy already knew, and various items of jewellery were earmarked for her long-time friend, Michelle.

Jeff breathed a huge sigh of relief when the solicitor informed them that all required information had been passed on. As expected, his wife had not made any specific wishes for her funeral or any other ceremony, merely stating that whatever her husband and children sought to do would be perfect.

With the formalities over, Gerry left the room to call down to his executive assistant, and the Dysons moved to sit next to the grieving billionaire while morning tea was served.

'Jeff,' the Olympian began. 'We're concerned about you. Are you alright?'

'Thanks,' the bereaved man replied, looking around to see if the children were within earshot. 'I'm OK. We're doing as well as can be expected, between us.'

His mother-in-law began to cry. 'Oh, darling, we miss her so much. I can't imagine what you're going through. You must let us know if you want us to look after Jet and Kierney if it all gets too much over the next few days.'

Irritated by his own frustration, Jeff's first response was anger. He hoped to have conquered this weakness long ago, but evidently he had only suppressed it. He knew Marianna meant well, but her comments made him seethe.

'We need to stick together,' he did his best to remain cordial. 'Next week'll be different. I don't expect them to stay around the apartment forever. I'd rather they got out and started seeing their mates again, but it might be good if we could come to Benloch after Friday's over. At the weekend, if that's OK?'

'Definitely,' Bart nodded. 'That's what we'd hoped. What about your sister? Is she coming down for the funeral?'

The songwriter issued a deep sigh. 'Yeah. Tonight. I'd forgotten all about that. Oh, Jesus! I'm forgetting everything at the moment. I haven't got my sexy social secretary telling me what my diary looks like anymore.'

The elegant Melbourne stateswoman rested a manicured hand on her son-in-law's forearm and watched tears roll down his cheeks for the first time this morning. This was a difficult ordeal for them all, and like Celia, she admired the celebrity's public stoicism and his devotion to the children.

And now the poor dears had their excitable relative to deal with too. Lynn had often recounted stories to her mother about Madalena's antics and how tiring it was for Jeff to handle her. His older sister had been like a third child on many occasions, and a problem child at that.

'Well, Madalena's welcome too, dear,' Marianna insisted.

'Kierney tells me you're still not comfortable going back the house,' her husband took over. 'Is there anything you want me to do over there?'

'No, thanks, sir,' the determined man gritted his teeth. 'Kizzy's going down tomorrow with Michelle. I'll ask her to bring back a few things. I doubt if I'll go there again.'

'At all?' Marianna sounded surprised. 'You'll feel differently in a week or so, I'm sure.'

'Maybe,' Jeff shrugged, unconvinced.

Gerry appeared behind his friend, putting both hands on his shoulders and waiting for an appropriate break in conversation. 'Excuse me, good people. Would you like some lunch?' he asked the glum gathering. 'We could arrange it in my office if you'd rather not go to a restaurant.'

'Yes,' Bart nodded. 'That's a good idea. Kind of you.'

'Sure. Whatever,' the morose star agreed, turning to check on the teenagers. 'These guys'll need something to eat.'

The famous family thanked the law firm's staff and headed back down in the lift to Blake & Partners in the same building. While Gerry's receptionist organised the lunch order, Jeff and the children took some time to collect their messages.

Cathy Lane, a few floors below at Stonebridge Music, the celebrities' management and publishing house, had dropped up a list of people who hoped to attend Lynn's funeral, the names reading like a "Who's Who" of contemporary public life.

The forever couple's business manager scanned the list over Jeff's shoulder and whistled. 'Jesus, Mary and Joseph! This is shaping up as a major event. Cath said they've already replied to most of these, saying the service is limited to family only. She also said it looks as though next Saturday arvo's favourite for the memorial service. How does that sound? They've got a chamber orchestra concert at seven-thirty, so we'll have to commit to being cleaned up and out by seven.'

His client sighed, drumming the table with nervous fingers. 'I don't care when, mate. The only request I'd make is that we do it soon, so Jet can get back to uni'. It's not doing him any good hanging around here.'

'Sure thing,' Gerry agreed. 'Is Kierney still going to Sydney?'

Jeff groaned. 'Don't know yet. I've left it up to her. Oh, and mate, would you do me a favour, please?'

'Of course,' the older man nodded, squeezing his friend's shoulder. 'What's that?'

'Could you take Jet out tonight? He's as horny as hell, and I get the impression he doesn't want to go out with people he knows.'

The businessman guffawed. 'You're asking me to get your son hooked up? I really need to revisit my job description!'

Jeff wasn't in the mood for humour however, and Gerry regretted his comment. He pulled a chair up close and straddled it, attempting to empathise with the widower's plight and how keen he was to protect his offspring.

'Sorry, mate. No worries. I'll take him to a club tonight. Does he know?'

'Cheers, Gez. I haven't asked him, but I'm pretty sure he'd be up for it. It's like I'm revisiting my past, watching him fight with all that tension.'

'What about you? Could you do with some anonymous fun?'

The handsome superstar stood up, pushing his chair away behind him. The Irishman reeled back, startled by the sudden movement.

'Are you kidding? No! There's nothing I'd like less. Let's change the subject.'

'Fair enough,' Gerry agreed, backing off. 'I'll wait to hear from one of you. Lunch'll be ready, I expect.'

Jeff let out a bitter laugh. 'Jesus Christ. I can't eat anything. I need to get out of here. Friday can't come quick enough for me, perverse as that may sound.'

His manager put his hand on the grieving man's shoulder as they walked back to the Boardroom where Lynn's parents were waiting. Jeff left him to chat with them while he went in search of the children. He let himself into a spare office where Jet sat at a computer and Kierney was on the telephone.

'Lunch is here, guys. Everything OK?'

'Yes, thanks,' his son replied. 'Nothing much going on. Just a whole lot of people saying how sorry they are.'

Jeff smiled, beckoning to the strapping blond to step outside the room. 'You too, eh? Listen, mate. I'd feel better if you went out tonight. Gerry's happy to take you somewhere for some female company, if you want.'

Jet gaped at his father, not knowing what to say. 'Wow. Thanks,' he responded after a long pause. 'It's an ace idea, but are you sure you don't mind?'

'I insist,' Jeff chuckled, dealing the lad a playful blow to the stomach with the back of his clenched fist. 'I can just about remember being your age.'

Kierney appeared in the doorway, her telephone conversation over, and latched straight onto her father's waist. 'What are you guys laughing about? What've I missed?'

'Nothing, gorgeous. Come and eat.'

'Papá?' the young woman began, as they walked towards the Boardroom's open doors.

'Yeah?'

'Do you mind if Dylan comes to the apartment tonight? Just to hang out?'

Jet shot his father a furtive glance, which was met with a "keep quiet" nod.

'Why not?' Jeff replied. 'It'll be good for you. D'you think we'll have the rest of the letters polished off by then?'

'God, I hope so,' his son sighed, sitting down at the table with his grandparents. 'I'm famished. Thank you for lunch, Gerry.'

HAPPY MEMORIES

As soon as lunch was over, Jeff ushered the children out of Gerry's office, and within fifteen minutes they were back home in the apartment, preparing for another marathon session with Lynn's letters. Jet had arranged to meet Gerry at ten o'clock, which had seen the older man blanch at the thought of starting a night out so late. The rock star was amused to see his mate was finally acting his age.

'OK!' the lad proclaimed, putting his empty coffee mug on the floor beside his feet. 'Let's get back to 1985. Isn't that where we were up to?'

All three Diamonds had a letter for a year dominated by two major events, one instigated as a deliberate antidote for the other. The Ethiopian famine relief campaign, kicked-off at the end of the previous November, had gathered momentum at an unprecedented rate, largely driven by the rock star's charismatic and fervent appeals and the whole family's tireless efforts to raise the profile of ordinary people in dire straits.

The benefit concerts had been an enormous undertaking initiated by musicians and film stars all over the world. Lynn and Jeff had driven the movement hard during the first half of the year until there were over thirty simultaneous events planned in all corners of the globe for the second Saturday in July.

Caught up in fundraising fever, the generosity of celebrities and public alike held no bounds, and the most serious problem soon became the charities' and non-government organisations' inability to spend the money. The Diamonds found themselves fighting criticism in the media and corruption behind the scenes, while continuing to fly around the world almost constantly to keep the awareness campaigns and the aid distribution efforts on track.

This concert series had seen Jet and Kierney's performing débuts on the world stage. Lynn wrote of how proud she had been to see them adding their voices to the cause and helping to prevent children from starving and dying in Africa.

Her words went on to remind them of the fantastic holiday the family had taken in Kenya in September, driving its contrast home: how important it was to appreciate the diversity of life's opportunities while understanding their obligations to consider the less fortunate from their position of good fortune.

Jeff's letter from the same period had a quite different tone however. Towards the end of the year, after their safari under the stars, he had returned to the long-running talks aimed at stamping out civil war in North Africa. His car had been ambushed outside Addis Ababa by guerrillas and chased until it hit a rock on the side of the road and rolled over. The driver sustained serious injuries, but as luck would have it, the famous passenger was left with only a few cuts and bruises, finding himself negotiating with the six-strong band of militants for his own freedom and that of his driver.

Out of contact from everyone for four days, Lynn's letter described the eternity which dragged on and on while those back in Australia waited for news. Was her husband still alive? Would she ever see him again? Would she have to bring up their children on her own and keep his memory alive for them? She wrote of the efforts made back home to maintain media silence, fending off reporters and working with their management company to draft regular statements, having no idea what had become of her beautiful black stallion.

Jeff stood up and opened the sliding doors to the balcony, as if the fresh air and long-distance vista would help diffuse the anguish in his lover's words. Back in the present, the widower counted Lynn had been gone for four days too, yet those who remained were in no doubt whatsoever that she wasn't coming back.

To know or not to know? Which was worse? Not knowing was better, the distraught man decided, because one could always hope. He remembered as if it were yesterday the first telephone call he had made upon securing his and the driver's release, and how he could almost touch the love oozing out of the receiver when his dream girl told him how worried she had been and how overjoyed she was that he was unharmed.

The letter then spelt out the agony the couple had endured for another two weeks after his freedom had been granted, longing to be together after their ordeal. They had both agreed that the high-profile peacemaker coming home straight after his release, instead of attending the talks as planned, would have sent completely the wrong message. Lynn praised her husband's unselfishness and dedication and conveyed her pride in telling astounded friends and family that the hostage hero would not be returning home until his job was done.

Kierney watched her father smiling as he read these pages, leaning against the open door. She could see his lips moving but had no idea what he was saying. She tapped her brother on the knee, her eyes inviting him to look at their dad.

'He seems OK,' Jet ventured. 'Don't you think? Better than yesterday anyway. More relaxed.'

The last two paragraphs of Lynn's letter thanked the ingenious lyricist for his enthusiasm and creativity in putting together the musical "The Black Sheep", based on the classic novel *"La Rabouilleuse"* by Honoré de Balzac. She described how excited the twenty-two-year-old Kiley Jones was to be involved with this project. The two best-respected Australian female musicians had been collaborating on the orchestration while their chief librettist was overseas.

Also mentioned was the moment when, at the dress rehearsal which the star had flown home to attend, the curtain fell at the end of Act One to a deafening silence. Lynn remembered exchanging glances with Kiley as they watched the face of the project's chief architect express every single emotion during the long *Finalé*, before jumping to his feet and understating to the assembled company that the result was "pretty good".

Being reminded of this moment made the songwriter laugh out loud. His daughter sprang to her feet, excited to hear such a positive response.

'What are you laughing at?' she implored, craning over his shoulder.

Jeff pointed to a paragraph halfway down the page. Kierney leant her head on his arm while reading, and the closeness felt unusually warm. Together, they scanned the final few lines which described Lynn's feelings about having been married for ten years. She had written this particular letter at Benloch on the afternoon of New Year's Day, after the couple had escaped from the rest of the family and headed to the seclusion of Coldwater Creek.

'That's a great memory,' the dreamy youngster said. 'It's awesome that you two were so open about sex. And how good your sex life...'

She faltered, knowing she had started a sentence she didn't want to finish.

'...was,' her dad completed it for her. 'Don't be scared to tell it how it is, *pequeñita*. It's not as if the fact hasn't crossed my mind.'

Kierney nodded, biting her lip to stop herself from crying again. 'I'm sorry. It must be so painful, and our awkwardness can only make it worse.'

'Forget it,' the father urged. 'The truth is we did have the best sex life, and we always intended for you two to understand that sex is a vital part of life, not to be hidden away behind closed doors. Well, figuratively speaking, that is...'

The teenager gave a shy giggle while the wise man carried on.

'And now you know what it's like first-hand, if you pardon the expression, there's definitely no point keeping it a secret anymore.'

Jet sniggered in the background. 'I know all about it first-hand,' he agreed, joining them by the windows and flexing the fingers of his left hand a few times as if limbering up. '*Malheureusement.*'

'Sorry, mate,' the empath slapped his son on the back. 'I can imagine. We'll make sure your show gets back on the road a-s-a-p.'

The young man shrugged. 'I'm only joking.'

The teenagers were ready to move on to the next envelopes, so Jeff returned with them to the couch, and they each opened the letters marked "1986". This was another year of mixed memories. Lynn's younger brother Richard, or Sandy as he was known in the family, had succumbed to the AIDS virus after a three-year struggle with his failing immune system and experimental drug treatments, not to mention the stigma surrounding HIV during this era of fear-mongering.

Jet and Kierney's letters focussed more on the need for them to open their hearts and minds to people's suffering, rather than blaming different lifestyles and behaviours. At ten and nearly nine years of age respectively, the brother and sister were given some sage advice on appreciating the positives about all people and compelled them to ignore any prejudices they might notice in others. Their mother thanked them for helping her to recover after their uncle's funeral, reminding them of the song "Hold Me High", which their dad had penned for them to sing to her.

Jeff's annual summary was three pages in length this time. Lynn had written several long, rambling, straight-from-the-heart paragraphs on the support he had given them all through Sandy's last months and after his death. She mentioned that she hoped her family would look after him well, should he ever have to read these words.

"I only hope you're not left on your own again. I couldn't bear to think, after all the years building the happy home you always wanted, that a freak accident might take all three of us away from you. That's my worst fear. I hope Jet and Kierney are with you right now, as you read this letter. They love you, and I know how much you love them."

'They are here, angel,' Jeff answered aloud, rubbing his tattoo and hoping Lynn could hear him. 'We're together, and it's saving my soul. You're so damned right.'

The compassionate wife recalled the deep depression into which her husband had slipped as a result of the lack of progress in solving the African poverty and famine problems. The rate of change was so slow, and he had become increasingly pessimistic as the year progressed, to the point when he ceased travelling and even stopped fighting his critics.

As he read each page, the world-changer cast his mind back to the endless patience his beautiful best friend had shown while he plunged the depths of his dark side. She had slowly but surely pressured him into action, using the children to entice him out of bed each day. It had worked time and again, as indeed it had this morning, and the protracted episode resulted in an updated edition of Doctor Friedman's Post-Traumatic Stress Disorder Treatment Guide, based yet again on her walking, talking and ever-recovering case study.

Jeff read his dream girl's closing words like a crackly recording of one of his favourite songs. During their tenth year of marriage, he had provided a journalist from a women's magazine with an off-the-cuff quote which had winged its way around the world's press like wildfire when asked how the couple had managed to stay committed to one another for ten years in a world where celebrity relationships were becoming shorter and shorter. "My grass is green enough, thanks" was written in bold, green lettering and underlined twice above the familiar signature.

Filled with longing, the desolate lover folded his latest gift and exhaled heavily. 'Someone stole my grass, angel. It's being green somewhere else now. Can you tell me where?'

Kierney appeared beside her dad with a cup of coffee and a packet of cigarettes. He accepted them in exchange for a kiss, and the three Diamonds took a break on the balcony, accompanied by their next missives. This was turning into another arduous afternoon, mostly because Jeff's letters were much longer than the children's, leaving them with no option but to hang on his reactions.

'Well, things should speed up now,' Jeff remarked. 'After this, I don't have one 'til 'eighty-nine.'

'Seoul Olympics,' Jet mused, opening his latest envelope. 'No. That's next year. What happened in 'eighty-seven?'

'"Generation Share",' the father replied, seeing the title Lynn had written at the top of his. 'Was that really 'eighty-seven? Jeez! Nearly ten years ago now. That's right. It was just before you went to MA, mate.'

'Mamá loved those video clips,' Kierney remembered. 'She used to play them in the office all the time. She told me once that she loved them because they showed we were old enough to all do the same thing together.'

'Yep,' Jeff confirmed. 'That was important to her. Y'know, your mamá changed so much over the years. Sometimes I forget just how much. When we first met, I don't think she'd ever seriously thought about being a mum. Then she morphed into this awesome teacher, and motherhood became her whole life. She didn't want to be Lynn Dyson superstar sex-nymph sportswoman anymore. As soon as you guys came along, all she wanted to do was grow you up. She wasn't satisfied with that either, to be honest, so she started to grow everyone else up too.'

'So she did,' Jet declared, flicking both hands out as if to say *"fait accompli"*. 'Did *you* always want to have kids?'

'No. Absolutely not,' their father answered. 'In fact I was so determined to avoid fatherhood that I became totally paranoid about using condoms. Long before the whole AIDS thing.'

'Especially after Auntie Lena had an abortion,' Kierney supposed.

'Yeah,' Jeff agreed. 'That certainly contributed. She had two actually. Well, two that I know of. Maybe more than two... It was bloody awful. Terminating a child's life.

What a decision to have to make, huh? But those babies' lives would've been pure hell with her as a mother. I was so dead-set against bringing someone into the world to have a life like mine.'

'So how did Mum change your mind?' Jet asked, sporting a broad grin. 'I'm very glad you did, by the way.'

Their dad chuckled. 'She didn't. We both changed our minds independently, but neither of us knew for a while. In Mamá's case, she just grew up herself, I think. Her biology changed and turned her into a parent-in-waiting.

'But the trigger for me was seeing my own potential finally being realised. It sounds bloody pretentious, I know, but it wasn't like that. I knew Lynn and I had so much to give, and how better to pass yourselves on than by producing the next generation?'

'Hence "Generation Share",' Kierney declared with pride. '*We're* Generation Share, Jetto. Shall we find the tape?'

Jeff shook his head, not sure he wanted to watch it so soon. 'Shit, baby. I have no idea where it'd be.'

'I know where it is,' Kierney piped up. 'It's in the office.'

'Why did you only have two kids?' her brother asked. 'You should've had a whole army.'

Jeff turned to answer the lad's question, seeing the young woman skip out of the room. 'We talked about having more children a thousand times. And we nearly did a few times, but something always stopped us. Two was always what we'd wanted; just to replace ourselves. Having more would've been greedy. Didn't want to be accused of over-populating.'

'Over-populating? By whom?' Jet laughed. 'Uncle Junior's got three. Is he over-populating?'

'You said "an army". Three's not exactly an army!'

Kierney ran back into the room with a video cassette and inserted it into the player under the television. 'I'm glad there are two of us,' she chipped in. 'I definitely wouldn't have wanted to be an only child, and a family of four's just perfect. I'm glad you guys made that decision, Papá. Should we read the letters first or watch the video first?'

The widower shrugged. 'I'm not sure I can, to be honest, but you go ahead. I'll have a ciggie and check my phone.'

'Oh, please, Papá,' Kierney beseeched him. 'It's so good. You've already got Mamá's face in your mind all the time. It'll only be on screen for a few seconds.'

'My letter tells me to watch it again,' Jet piped up from the couch. 'Yours probably does too.'

Jeff raised his hands. 'Alright, already. I'll watch it, but I reserve the right to close my eyes when I want to, OK?'

The children nodded, and Kierney pressed the "Play" button. The joyous sight of a ten-year-old boy with curly, blond hair cycling away from school and off on an intercontinental journey brought back happy memories for them all. Kierney's part in the video was very short, but she remembered the hype it had caused and loved the themes of inclusion and tolerance the song preached.

Trying his hardest not to be captivated by the clip, the director slid down onto the sofa and put his arm around his son. 'You were amazing. This is a great video.'

Jet leant against his father's side, reliving the good times they had spent making daily flights between cities and piecing each scene together. He had learnt a lot about filmmaking on this trip, his father insisting he be included in all the production discussions.

'Thanks for sticking it out,' the nineteen-year-old murmured, as the final few seconds of Lynn tucking the weary traveller into bed played.

'That's where some of the words for "The Boy Who Would Be King" originally came from,' Jeff thought aloud, tears welling up again. 'I forgot about that. Y'know, those lyrics about travelling and bringing back stuff from all over? They came from making that video.'

'Well, I'm flattered to be the inspiration for all those great songs,' Jet said, puffing his chest out.

The next set of envelopes were labelled "1989", and only the men had a letter. Jeff had a fair idea of their main topic. As their son's thirteenth birthday approached, Lynn had suggested his dad organise a *bar mitzvah*. The half-Jew had always spoken fondly of the peculiar celebration his paternal grandmother had arranged for him, and hearing about it had led his wife to believe their son might also find significance in recognising this first step towards manhood. The father remembered being enchanted by the idea, seeing it as the perfect way to cement their bond.

'What's yours about?' Kierney asked her brother, coming back into the room with some biscuits and drinks.

'My Bathurst *bar mitzvah*,' the younger man laughed, using the phrase they had coined in those days. 'Sex education, Jeff Diamond style.'

The instructor in question smirked, reading the same on his page. Lynn wrote about worries expressed by their neighbour, who was also the mother of Jet's best friend, when she had reported her husband's account of the weekend.

'What was Mum's verdict?' the songwriter asked. 'What's her advice?'

The sports-mad teenager had tears in his eyes. 'Shit, this one's hard going,' he sniffed. 'I'm not sure I should let you read it. I can hear her saying the words too. Sometimes I forget what you went through when you were a boy.'

'Whoa, son. I'm sorry,' Jeff sighed. 'This shouldn't be about me. This is between you and your mum.'

'Please may I see it?' Kierney asked.

'I expect you'll get something similar in your next one,' Jet ventured. 'But yeah, if you like. I've got shivers running up my spine and all the way down my arms.'

Their father groaned and put his head in his hands, creasing the single sheet of paper in half. His letter was full of deep, insightful observations and memories bittersweet now their author would no longer share their special occasions. Her theme was "It is only through suffering that we truly grow", and he too heard his wife's voice reciting lines that reminded him of many deliberations, unravelling the conundrum of raising happy children, and in the process having to inflict hardship on them to foster a genuine appreciation of their fortunate start in life.

The bereaved husband knew Lynn had become philosophical about the two long years her parents had forced her to spend away from him, particularly when their children reached the same age. In fact, the steadfast Australian champion had ended up more philosophical than her impetuous life partner, a rare occurrence indeed!

While a new decade dawned on the unstoppable Dyson and Diamond families, the superstar parents had agreed that simply observing tough times did not count as a true test of one's ability to empathise with or challenge the status quo.

And now, in the second half of the same decade, sitting back and watching Kierney read over her brother's shoulder, both wiping their eyes in silent contemplation, Jeff felt uncomfortable and utterly responsible for their current pain.

Gulping the lump down in his throat, the intellectual turned back to the second theme. The couple had created a screenplay that year entitled "When You're Gone", which foreshadowed recent events in far too freakish a manner. They should never have embarked upon it, in hindsight, since it had evidently tempted providence. The film idea had originally been inspired by the many dangerous trips the peacemaker had made to Africa, Northern Ireland and other troubled corners of the globe, and thus the screenplay evolved as if Lynn were the surviving partner.

His beautiful best friend had composed the very words which filled his head now, line after auguring line. It was as if they had predicted his demise, and somehow the short, Spanish gunman had appropriated a copy of the script for the basis of his assassination plot.

Could this possibly be true? *No*, the widower chastised himself. *Get a grip*. The draft remained under lock and key in one of the couple's other safe deposit boxes, the artists having consigned it to the "Too dark" basket the following year.

An old anthem roiled the musician's wounded brain, its volume dominating his concentration. His co-writer had put "The Sun Won't Shine" forward as a candidate for the film's soundtrack, which made him cry even harder. As the plot unfolded, the story had seen the deceased character no longer able to feel anything, even though he longed to. However, here in reality, this curse appeared to have been handed down to the character left alive.

'Fucking hell, Lynn,' he shouted, sobbing. 'This wasn't supposed to happen. It was bloody fiction. A stupid idea right from the start, and we knew it, didn't we? Now we're stuck in this godforsaken half-life.'

Kierney and Jet both rushed to their father's aid, dropping down onto the floor in front of him.

'What's the matter?' his concerned daughter pleaded. 'What are you talking about? What was a stupid idea?'

The forty-three-year-old looked from one child to another, debating whether it was worth burdening them with this latest memory. The song continued to ring loud in his ears, taunting him to the point of distraction. Was Lynn doing this to punish him or was he punishing himself? Taking a deep breath, he sat back on the couch and closed his eyes in a vain attempt to block the music.

'Sorry, guys. A visit to the dark side.'

'I thought we were already on the dark side,' his son lamented, feeling powerless.

Jeff nodded, still without looking up. 'Mamá and I wrote a script in 'eighty-nine, 'ninety that we shelved because it was way, way too morbid. We decided it'd be tempting fate to finish it, but it now appears fate was tempted in any event. She reminds me of how we argued about how it should end. She says, "If you're reading this letter, you must know how it ends."'

'So it was about one of you dying,' Kierney voiced her assumption. 'And do you know how it ends?'

'No. Not yet,' came a cryptic reply which unnerved all three.

'Ugh. Wish I'd never asked. We need a break,' the young woman declared, slapping a cushion off the couch in resignation. 'How about we ring for pizza?'

'No,' her father objected. 'Pizza's not what we need. Empty food, as Mamá'd say. It's what we want but not what we need. Ain't that the truth?'

Both teenagers nodded, their mouths widening into reluctant smiles. It was unlike their dad to uphold the value of healthy eating, especially in times of stress, but they realised he was now obliged to cover all parental angles.

'There's probably some steaks in the freezer,' Jeff continued. 'I don't have a letter for 'ninety-two, so you guys open yours, and I'll get the barbie going. There's bound to be salad left over from Thursday lunchtime. Might not be too fresh, but it'll do.'

Kierney caught her breath again and fought back tears. Last Thursday, she remembered, was the last time she had shared lunch with her mother, only hours before taking her driving test. How the world had changed since then... Hugging her dad, she leant down to select her next envelope and signalled to her brother to do the same.

In the kitchen, the superstar made himself useful by preparing a healthy dinner. His thoughts turned to the old adage "Life imitates art", and he felt the hairs rise on the back of his neck again. Could art be a medium through which one could transcend parallel worlds? Was this where Lynn was hiding, and how might he be able to reach her? In the greenest of all Green Rooms, waiting to go on stage in front of her new audience?

Jeff dismissed the outlandish notion as the ramblings of a desperate man, focussing instead on the searing hot barbecue. 'Did you put that song in my head, angel?' he whispered. 'Can you hear us? I wish I knew. I want you to know how horribly cathartic this process is.'

What had happened during 1990 that had failed to make it a year of letter-writing significance? "Feel The Heat" was the most significant output from the turn of the decade, a romantic comedy made deliberately to counteract all the heavy lifting they had been doing for Africa and at the various peace negotiations which consumed so much of their physical and emotional energy. On top of this, Jet had written and starred in his first movie, for which Kierney had scored a big hit with the theme song.

It was also the year when the humble songwriter had made the comment to a television interviewer in the UK that he could release a cheesy version of "Waltzing Matilda" and it would still have gone platinum. True enough, the Diamond family perfected the Midas touch during the early 'nineties, but the downside of such universal acclaim was a spate of security threats. Lynn employed bodyguards for the children for the first time, supplementing their drivers who were recruited from a range of former defence force personnel and policemen.

Waiting for the juicy sirloins to brown, Jeff stood on the balcony and stared through the heat haze rising over Melbourne's northern suburbs. What a price they had eventually paid for their success... He could easily comprehend the jealousy felt by certain others towards the Diamonds' lifestyle and the financial rewards that made it possible. Yet it had always frustrated him that these bitter, envious defamers rarely took the time to understand how hard the couple worked and how many hours they spent apart, easy pickings for fans while on aeroplanes or holed up in lonely hotel rooms for hours on end, talking trivia with total strangers night after night instead of being wrapped in each other's arms in front of the television at Escondido.

'There are always at least two sides to every story,' he yelled into the air. 'Don't you know that, you fucking, spic arsehole? What pissed you off enough to want to shoot us dead? Why didn't you talk to me? Why did you have to kill the most beautiful woman who ever lived? Why couldn't you've taken me instead?'

The lonely man kicked the wall so hard that his shoe left a dark imprint on the pale render. He felt no less angry now than he had in his traumatised teens, but somehow the years had taught him how to control it much better. He didn't want to take his fury out on the kids; they were going through enough as it was. Maybe he should see if they fancied a game of squash this evening. Yes. This was a good idea. Anything to give them a break from sadness.

Scratching his tattoo again, the grieving husband rolled his left shoulder to see if the piercing irritation would abate. He was learning to read the signs. This delicious sensation happened whenever he did something sensible, whereas the loud music and the all-consuming, obsessive thoughts drew his attention as soon as he began to lose control.

'OK! I get it, Lynn,' he laughed, flipping three medium-rare steaks onto a waiting plate. 'I'm starting to understand this new language of ours. Hey! D'you remember we had this same meal before we slept together for the first time? Remember that? I do. Damned fine!'

Australia's richest butler served dinner to his two teenagers. They ate from their knees in front of the television, the peaceful interlude welcomed by everyone. Kierney checked her mobile to find a new influx of missed calls.

'Mmm... Smells great,' Jet said, grabbing some cutlery and shaking a generous helping of tomato sauce onto his food. 'Thanks for doing this, Dad. It is much better than pizza.'

Jeff poured three glasses of Shiraz as the perfect accompaniment. 'Are you guys alright? I mean after that last revelation?'

'Ah, yeah. Guess so. I get the feeling there'll be more revelations as the days go by,' his son smiled.

'We're more worried about you,' Kierney added. 'I hate to hear you so desperate.'

Jeff pointed from one teenager to the other. 'I've had an idea... Because you guys are so awesome and we've been through a lot over the last few days, I thought we might take a break this evening and play squash. It'll be fun.'

Jet's eyes lit up. 'Yay, very cool! Are you sure you're up for it?'

The father nodded, turning his gaze to their third *amigo*. 'Well, Ms squash champion... Whadd'ya reckon?'

His gorgeous gipsy girl began to cry again, her shoulders so heavy they caused her to slouch in her chair as she picked at her food. 'It is a good idea, Papá,' she agreed, 'but we really need to finish the letters. If we keep stopping, this process'll carry on way too long.'

'So you think we should keep going 'til we're up-to-date?'

'Yes,' Kierney nodded. 'Don't you, Jetto?'

'I agree we need to get through all the letters, but I'd also appreciate some light relief,' her brother replied.

'Make a bloody decision, mate,' Jeff laughed. 'We're the power of three now. There needs to be a casting vote, so fence-sitting's not an option.'

'Fair enough,' the sportsman acknowledged. 'I'm with Kiz then. I'd rather finish the letters and play squash tomorrow.'

'Good man,' Jeff cajoled, shaking his shoulder vigorously. 'OK, Kizzo?'

'Yes. Thanks, guys.'

'Done! The people hath spake. Democracy in action. Letters it is. What time's Dylan arriving?'

'Not 'til eight-thirty,' his daughter replied. 'Do you think we can knock the rest off by then?'

Another hour went by, the trio's emotional pendula swinging from side to side as their missing loved one's words sparked happy memories or emphasised her absence. On the other side of the room, Jet gasped, overcome. Kierney looked up to see her brother put his head in his hands and begin to sob. If he too was reading from 1992's letter, she had a fair idea what he was thinking.

'Mate, it's OK,' the bereaved husband said, moving to sit beside his son again. 'We all have to live our own life now. When you two meet whomever you want to spend the rest of your life with, you'll hopefully feel the same way as we did. For now, just enjoy yourself. Fuck knows, I did at your age!'

Kierney watched the two most significant men in her life exchange secret messages and felt her mother's loss more acutely than she had up until this point. The shock of Lynn's untimely death was wearing off, and with the threat of life establishing its new "normal", it was clear the family was destined to struggle for a long time to fill the void she left.

Jeff picked up his son's letter for 1993. They were on the home stretch, bringing them ever closer to the present day.

'Open this, mate, please,' he urged. 'I have to meet Auntie Lena at the airport soon, so we need to have all this finished and get moving. She wouldn't understand all this joined-up stuff.'

Chuckling feebly at the analogy, the young man took the envelope from his father and tore its seal. Kierney did the same with hers. Their mother had written to congratulate her children again on their sporting achievements and artistic performances and for being able to engage in these time-consuming extracurricular pursuits without impacting their schoolwork.

She told them both of the difficulty she had faced at their age with fitting in training, music and homework, and not to mention a romance with a certain RMIT student which her parents sought to curtail, fearing she wouldn't reach her potential with this additional distraction.

"Patience makes you stronger," Lynn wrote, advising the ambitious pair to analyse each situation before making those priority decisions. She expressed regret about not taking the time to understand their dad's childhood traumas well enough before she agreed to go along with her parents' request, saying that it might not have stopped her from obeying them but she would have drawn the line at a complete embargo on their contact.

'Mum still really hurt about those two years you spent apart, didn't she?' Jet said to his father, who was deep in contemplation from the contents of his own letter.

'Why? What's she saying?' the tearful man asked, looking up.

'Just about balancing the things in my life and understanding everyone's situation before prioritising,' he explained. 'Have you got that too, sis'?'

'Yes. Word-for-word.'

Jeff took a few moments to consider this assertion and how he should supplement their mother's good counsel. With the benefit of hindsight and many years of married bliss, the painful memories of their two-year hiatus had dulled somewhat.

'I think it was the right choice in the end,' the father admitted, 'even though it was effin' torture at the time. I'm guessing she's saying she wished she knew more about me at that stage, but I'm not sure it would've been a good thing, in all honesty. It worked out though, didn't it? And much as it pains me to say so, it actually did us good to grow up a bit before we got together properly.

'My advice would be just to try and take a long-term view, even if you don't have much of an clue about what the future holds. My problem back then was not being able to trust the future to deliver me something better than the present. I was petrified of losing what I had, in case I could never get it back.'

Both teenagers appeared spellbound by this idea, with their whole lives ahead of them and unable to envisage being in a similar situation. Neither was in a hurry to prioritise a relationship in his or her life, satisfied with their stable family environment and a set of good friends each.

Kierney wondered if their mum's death might change their outlook on life. If her father's research with Sarah Friedman proved true, a loving, nurturing childhood built sufficient resilience to weather the storms of adulthood in most cases. However, she and Jet were only on the cusp of majority, so what might this huge disruption have in store for them?

'I'm scared for the future,' the young woman blurted out.

Her compassionate father responded without hesitation, having expected this statement at any moment. 'I bet you are, *pequeñita*. Me too, on your behalves. It's shit timing, losing Mamá now, but I promise you I'll work so hard to keep you above the line.'

'I know you will, Papá. And we're in so much better shape than you were when your mamá died. But I know you only want to be with your *regala*.'

'That's not true, *pequeñita*. At least not for now. You guys are my Number One priority. Please believe me. I'm not going anywhere 'til I'm certain you're OK. We'll just keep talking, all four of us. Whatever happens, you'll be fine. You have my word.'

'Dad, what's in your letter?' Jet demanded his father move on. 'Wasn't this "Ostrich year"?'

'Thanks, mate,' he replied, grateful for the lad's decision to take the heat out of the conversation. 'You *will* be OK, you two, 'cause you know how to help each other.

And yes, mate. "Ostrich year" is right. "Little girl no longer little girl year." It was agony.'

The corner of Kierney's mouth turned downwards only half in jest. 'I'm sorry, Papá.'

'Don't be,' he objected. 'It's exactly what should happen. Your rite of passage. I wouldn't have been much of a father if I'd let you go without a second thought. Like the discussion we had about marrying Youssouf Elhadji just the other day... Mamá said to me on the way home that I'd love to have him as a son-in-law, which I absolutely would.

'But my control-freaky, hyper-protective nature used to put me in a tailspin at the very thought of you being handled by someone much stronger than you. I know how strong-willed I was when it came to getting sex, and it made me sick thinking of you in a situation you couldn't get out of. Don't you think so, Jetto?'

Kierney joined her father on his couch and hugged him close.

'Yeah,' the young buck nodded. 'It's certainly good for a bloke to have a sister. I know I think of it every now and again, and I guess it must help subconsciously to stop me going too far.'

'Good stuff,' the father praised his son. 'And the other thing Mamá and I completed in 'ninety-three, at long bloody last, was "The Boy Who Would Be King". In the end, the timing was perfect, to coincide with your high school graduation.

'Can't get more different than those two reactions to you guys growing up, can you? Casting one out into the wild and clutching on to the other like a bloody Klingon. And here, she's pushing me to make sure you get to UNICEF, Kizzo. I promise I'll do that too, angel.'

'Angel me or angel Mamá?'

'Angels both of you,' he confirmed, emphasising the plural. 'Sorry, do you need me to be more specific?'

'No,' she laughed. 'Unless you want an answer.'

'Oh, I'm getting answers, by the way,' the widower interjected in a quieter voice, waiting for his children's reactions.

'From me or from Mamá?' Kierney asked again.

'Both of you angels,' he responded, rubbing his tattoo.

The cricketer rolled his eyes and sneered. 'Bloody Nora! What are you on about? Have you completely lost the plot, old man? The world's first talking tatt'?'

The philosopher shrugged, and with lightning reflexes, picked up a shoe that happened to be sitting on the floor next to him. He flung it at his son, hitting him squarely on the chin. Jet sprang out of his chair, and the two men began to wrestle each other in the tight space between the couch and the coffee table.

'Hey!' Kierney squealed, leaping clear of the cushions. 'For God's sake, you idiots! Boys will be boys. I'm going to make some tea.'

'Tea?' both men shouted in unison, dissolving into a fit of giggles.

'Just bring beer,' Jeff commanded with an ostentatious wave. 'We don't want tea.'

'Argh!' the exasperated young woman groaned. 'We've only got one letter to go. Please can we get on and finish them?'

The two men called a halt to their antics, as if the wind had been knocked out of their sails. Both sighed at the frustrated female spoiling their fun for all the right reasons.

'You're right, Kizzy. I'm sorry,' the widower agreed, reaching out for her hand. 'I hear ya. We're sick of this too. We're only letting off steam. You make some tea, and we'll make an effort to be sensible for a while longer. Do we have a deal?'

Kierney nodded, prising herself out of her father's tight grip. She disappeared into the kitchen, and the two wired blokes sat staring at each other, still breathing heavily and determined to remain positive. *One letter to go*, Jeff thought. This would bring them pretty much up-to-date; to just before last Friday, when paradise was lost.

'Jesus, mate,' he said to the blond colossus, who sat gazing out of the window across the balcony and beyond. 'We're going to be reading stuff Mum wrote only a few weeks ago. It's going to be really tough.'

'Like this hasn't been tough?'

His dad nodded. 'I mean about stuff we were going to be doing soon, and things we've only just finished. Christ Almighty... That's way too close for comfort.'

'Yeah. Are you sure you're going to be OK here with Auntie Lena when I'm out with Gerry? Why don't you come with us?'

'I can't, mate. It'd be a nightmare for all of us. I'd be lousy company.'

'So? Who cares?' the lad challenged. 'You have a good case.'

'Cheers. I know, but I won't come. I don't want to saddle Kiz and Dylan with entertaining Lena. And besides, your mum's not a week dead,' the grieving man went on, his heart aching. 'I can hardly be seen in a nightclub before my wife's funeral, can I?'

'Neither should I then,' the teenager countered with remorse.

'Mate, it's fine for you,' Jeff persisted. 'You need to get out even though you're officially in mourning. Look at you! You're like a caged lion. I don't have that sense of urgency anymore.'

'Thank God for that, huh?' his son joked. 'But what'll you do? Just watch TV?'

'Jesus, "Thank God for that" is right!' his father smiled. 'I've got a heap of correspondence to deal with. I'm going to create one e-mail and send it to everyone. "Dear insert name, blah blah blah... Piss off and leave me alone. JMD."'

Kierney returned to the lounge room and sat the tray on the coffee table, which looked decidedly barren now that the pile of letters their father had written had been bagged up again, rather like a mantelpiece on the thirteenth day of Christmas.

Silence soon descended, while the remaining three of Diamonds opened their final letter.

'"May I borrow your daughter?"' the eighteen-year-old read out. 'Did Mamá really ask you that?'

'Yep,' Jeff chuckled. 'She did indeed. After you'd finished your exams. She wanted to take you for a weekend away, to take you clothes shopping and pamper you a bit. Y'know... Woman to woman.'

'She calls me a "woman of the world",' Kierney wept. 'She tells me I'm ready to take on anybody and anything, but I really don't feel like it.'

The handsome middle-aged superstar sympathised with the forlorn child who was trying so hard to fill her mother's shoes. She had been poised at the exit door of the in-between zone for so long, and now it appeared her ticket had been temporarily invalidated.

'You are,' he assured. 'You will be, *pequeñita*. Just not right now. You'll come through this. Be patient with the way you feel. Mamá's very proud of you. It was only a few weeks ago when she wrote this. I caught her writing them at Benloch, by the pool. She told me she was describing the "Building Bridges" sessions.'

The young woman nodded. 'Yes, that's right. She says she loved that she and I were in the same video clip and the way we interacted. It was so much fun to do. What's yours about, Jetto?'

'Uni', mostly. Wasim Akram and Mark Taylor, and the benefits of keeping my mouth shut.'

'Interesting,' Jeff smiled. 'She didn't want you to keep your mouth shut. She wanted you to challenge for the captaincy.'

'Yeah. She says that later on. I have to promise her I'll go for it. I shall, Mum.'

Kierney's mouth opened to say something, but her papá's stern glare stopped her. He didn't want her to tease her brother about communicating with a dead person like the gregarious joker had tried with his father. She looked down at the page in her hand, ashamed.

The most recent offering bearing his name was too much for the lonely man to bear. He had had quite enough for the day, dissolving into floods of tears upon catching the opening line. The song she had given him for their twentieth wedding anniversary had been entitled "These Perfect Years", and its theme had flowed on into her letter. It opened by telling him that as each year went by, it became harder and harder to write as if she were no longer part of his life. "It's like we've always been together," she told him. "I can't conceive of life without you."

Jeff couldn't even reply, neither in a whisper nor in silent, unspoken words. His heart felt as if it were splitting in two. "Would I even be me if I didn't have you?" Lynn had written. Her rhetorical question personified, he now knew precisely what this meant and detested it. What could he do to counteract the sense of nothingness which engulfed him? He issued a heartfelt prayer to die right here and now, before taking it back as images of the children stampeded through his mind.

There you go again, the philosopher mused. His wise ghost was cleverly polluting his faulty thought-processes to break the pattern. So comprehensively disoriented was the despairing powerhouse of popular culture that he was unable even to convey how enamoured he was with her sentiments.

'Papá, are you OK? What did Mamá write this time?'

Still rendered mute, her father simply shook his head and closed his eyes. Both children put their arms around him and waited for him to cry out this latest batch of gloom.

'I'll ring Dylan and ask him not to come round,' Kierney said. 'We don't need to see each other yet. I want you to feel better.'

Jeff shook his head again. 'No,' he objected, finding his tongue after a valiant struggle. 'You guys've got to have some relief from this shit. The emotional volatility I'm projecting is exhausting for us all. I'll be alright. I'll get on with replying to the e-mails piling up, *et cetera*. It'll be a good anaesthetic, mindlessly churning out the same glib responses. I need to fetch Lena from the airport soon anyway.'

'Oh, Christ!' Jet exclaimed. 'She'll keep you busy at least, whether you like it or not.'

His dad chuckled. 'Cheers. Don't remind me.'

Reading on through Lynn's last note, the widower began to feel better. Since his wife had been liberated from daily motherly duties and was spending more time either in the city or on the road, she had afforded herself ample opportunity to work on her own projects. She had informed him last year of her intention to make a movie to celebrate their twentieth anniversary, and that she had secured some of his greatest friends to star in it; actors whom he most admired. The intrigued husband had failed to coax her into giving away any details about the script, no matter how hard he had tried to woo her with his persuasive powers.

However, it was apparent from her account that the filmmaker had had second thoughts when it came to writing this letter with the remote possibility of it being opened before the movie's release date. There was no guarantee a grief-stricken Jeff Diamond would even see the movie, should she die before it was out. She was not prepared to take the chance on him never knowing how much she still loved him at the start of her fifth decade.

> *'As you know, I wanted to make a film about you as the world's greatest lover. I know I'm not as qualified as some to judge, but I am utterly convinced I have the best. Or had the best, if you're actually reading this. Jeff, you know the meaning of love and how to combine it with sex to create an intoxicating*

cocktail of feelings. I only hope I managed to learn enough from you to give you such a satisfying love life in return.'

'You did,' her husband murmured. 'You gave me more than I could consume, angel. More than I ever thought possible.'

'And if, as you'll see in the movie, this level of happiness is unique to us, then even better. That's all that matters, isn't it? That we made each other happy. And you make me happier than I could ever imagine. Like you said in your song yesterday, through all those rough times we have always treated each other well and I always feel so completely loved.

'So if we haven't already, please see the film when it comes out. And dream about how nuestra vida singular might carry on. When you get a moment on your own, after reading this letter, please sit down with a glass of wine and watch our wedding video again. It's been ages since we've seen it, but if you're feeling abandoned and unloved, it will remind you of how much we loved each other then and ever after. Coming back from London knowing I was going to be your wife was the most amazing thing to look forward to. I still get butterflies in my stomach when I think about that time.

'Jeff, I love you so much. You gave me the most fantastic marriage, our two gorgeous children and so many life-changing adventures. Whatever has happened to mean you are reading these words, you should know that every second with you is a treasured memory for me. Hold on to the good memories you have, and they will see you through until we're next together.

'All my love, Lynn xxxx'

'*Gracias, Regala*,' Jeff whispered, massaging his chest. 'I love you too. Back at ya, baby. And rest assured, the letters I wrote to you say pretty much the same. I'm not sure I'm up to watching us walk down the aisle, or the new movie either, but I promise I'll give 'em a shot. Anyway, Lena's coming tonight, so interesting times ahead, eh?'

Kierney and Jet listened to the adoring tone of their father charming his lover as if she were sitting beside him on the couch. It was the right time for him to spend some time alone, if only to express these innermost feelings to his beautiful best friend.

'Which tape does Mum mean?' Jet asked. 'Not "King of Diamonds, King of Hearts"?'

'Yes and no. That too,' he confirmed, 'but she wants me to watch our wedding video tonight. It's way too soon, but she made me promise.'

'Oh, no...' his daughter warned. 'You can't do that when Auntie Lena's here. When'll you watch it?'

'In the middle of the night, I expect. All good, *pequeñita*. I'll read the letter again once you're all asleep, with a Scotch or three or four, and then put the wedding tape on. D'you know where it is? Not at Escondido, I hope.'

'There are copies in both places,' Kierney laughed. 'You know Mamá... Always organised. I'll find it in a minute. It's in the office along with the others.'

The entry-phone buzzer sounded, making them all jump. The eighteen-year-old became instantly nervous, looking from one man to the other like a startled rabbit.

She gulped. 'That'll be Dylan. I don't know if I'm ready to see him.'

'You should've thought of that earlier,' her dad chided. 'Go on... Answer it! Don't leave him standing outside. Or turn him away. Whatever you want, but you have to do something.'

His daughter disappeared to let her boyfriend into the building and up into the lift. She met him on the landing, and they kissed for the first time in a week.

'I'm sorry for your loss,' the visitor murmured, following Kierney into the lounge room and seeing father and son sitting there.

Jeff stood up, walked over to the wacky, eighteen-year-old musician and shook his hand. 'G'day, Dylan, mate. Thanks for coming over. You need to find a way to take Kizzy's mind off what's going on.'

'Oh, my God. I'm really sorry Lynn's passed away,' the awkward lad stuttered, before turning to his girlfriend's brother. 'I can't believe it. Everyone's gone completely insane out there. Have you been watching the TV?'

'Not much,' Jet replied, clambering to his feet to greet his former school-friend. 'We're trying to avoid it. It's a total mess, and we're bloody sick of it all.'

'Well said,' their father smiled. 'Anyway, get out of here, you guys. I don't want to see you for hours.'

Kierney gave her dad a bear-hug, and he kissed her forehead in return. She had tears in her eyes but was no longer afraid. The master communicator had helped break the ice, as always, and the couple disappeared to her bedroom, leaving father and son once more alone.

EXTRA GUEST

Jet arranged to hook up with Gerry earlier than originally planned, which suited the older man much better. It was already approaching nine o'clock, and the widower needed to summon the courage to leave the sanctity of their apartment and drive to the airport.

He had asked Madalena to meet him in the drop-off zone, to avoid being identified and mobbed in plain sight. His sister was notoriously hopeless at following instructions however, so the best he could hope for was that she would remember to switch on the mobile he had bought for her last year.

Jeff bundled up his collection of lifesaving letters and took them into the spare room for further comfort and safekeeping. Now well and truly redundant, what ought he to do with those he had written to her for the same purpose? He returned to the lounge room, where the folder still sat on the floor, having been tidied up after his frantic search for "1982". Picking up the remaining envelopes, his first thought was to throw them away, seeing their intended recipient would never open them.

No, he changed his mind. These artefacts were as much historical records unread as read, so he must keep them. The children may wish to read them after he was gone or even open them in a few months' time to balance things out. It was even possible that he might want to read them again once life was back on an even keel, although the likelihood appeared low at this point.

Who could estimate the unfathomable sum these pieces of memorabilia might raise at auction in the future? Their charities stood to benefit enormously from the almighty scrum into which the family's legions of fans would undoubtedly hunker down to own a love letter from Jeff Diamond to Lynn Dyson!

With a heavy heart, the rock star removed the envelopes addressed to his soulmate's extinct incarnation from the clear plastic folder and slipped them into a drawer in the office. This left only his to the children, destined to be restored to the safe deposit box whence they had been delivered. He would give them back to Gerry on

Friday for storage until they were next required. The passionate confessions addressed to his wife were left to languish among the family's voluminous collection of sheet music until their separate fate was decided.

His chest twitched twice. 'Hey! Welcome back, angel! Did I do something you like? I'm not quite a lost cause, but it's pretty damned close.'

His son now departed and his daughter having migrated to the southern half of the spacious apartment, Jeff felt the silence oppressing him. It was high time to escape, even if it was only to the airport.

With any luck, a plane'll miss the runway and land on the car, he fantasised, pulling on some shoes and grabbing his old leather jacket from the end of the bed. *That'd be a quick way to go.*

Instantly, his brain filled with the melancholic strains of "The Sun Won't Shine" once again, and he scolded himself for such suicidal thoughts. On the brighter side though, he was becoming quite adept at interpreting this new avenue of discourse.

Yelling goodbye to Kierney and receiving a cheery "Drive carefully!" in reply, the songwriter found himself downstairs in the basement car park, scanning the line of vehicles in the family's allotted spaces. He had only brought the keys to the Discovery down with him from the apartment, thereby denying himself the option of taking Lynn's Maserati. He felt strong enough to take the risk, but was also wary of being hit by a panic attack with his sister in the car and then not being able to drive home again. Besides, it wasn't smart to draw too much attention at the airport.

The Land Rover was by far the best option, with its elevated driving position. Jeff had asked the housekeepers at Escondido to bring it over during the day, in order that the family could move around together in comfort and somewhat undetected. The two-year-old Discovery was a utility vehicle more than anything, with little personal attachment; used for the transportation of schoolchildren with as diverse a schedule of pursuits as their parents.

He unlocked the driver's door and climbed in. The couple had made sure all their cars had windows tinted to the darkest legal grade, and he was thankful for the anonymity they afforded him as he skirted the top of the city, towards the freeway that snaked north to Tullamarine.

He wondered if Bart and Marianna were still in town or if they had traversed this very road earlier on their way back to the farm. They must be feeling fairly morose too. Tapping into Lynn's ingrained sense of duty, he resolved to make contact with the Dyson clan tomorrow. He shouldn't wallow in self-pity when so many others were also suffering around him.

The sullen driver circled the Arrivals terminal four times, unable to shed the lead weight which had taken up residence in the pit of his stomach. He waited for a sign from his feisty older sister. Madalena's flight had been delayed by storms in Sydney, yet she hadn't had the courtesy to let him know. Some things never changed, he rued.

At nine-forty, when he was beginning to think she had changed her mind about coming down, he spied a lanky woman dressed in jeans and with a long, black ponytail standing by the bus stop for the long-term car park. He swung the lumbering, four-wheeled elephant alongside the kerb and wound the passenger window down, tooting the horn.

The recent arrival cottoned on within a few seconds and squealed, picking up her compact cases and trotting over to the black vehicle in her ridiculous, impractical high heels.

'*Chico*, is that you?' she yelled through the open window. 'I didn't know what car you'd come in.'

'Get in, please,' her brother urged, jumping down from the driver's seat and running round to the back door to toss her bags inside before he was marked. 'Thanks for coming. It's nice to see you.'

The car sped away from the airport initially before swerving into a small service road beside the perimeter fence. Screeching to an abrupt stop beyond the line of streetlights, the driver took his seatbelt off again and leant over to kiss his sister, who immediately burst into tears.

'*Chico*, what the hell?' Madalena sobbed. 'How could someone shoot her? I've done nothin' but watch TV since it 'appened, and I can't fuckin' believe it. She was so beautiful, and you were so happy. It's not fair. It's not fuckin' fair, is it?'

Jeff chuckled as his sister unloaded, grateful for her exuberance and this uncharacteristic show of solidarity. 'Thanks, Lena,' he shook his head. 'No, it's not fucking fair at all. Two kids have no mother, and I'm just me again after twenty-three bloody amazing years. It's definitely not fucking fair.'

'You OK, but? You look OK. What ya been doin'?'

'Not much,' Jeff replied. 'Hiding from the world. Reading the will, which was a non-event.'

'Did you get ev'rythin'?'

'No,' Australia's third richest man couldn't help but laugh. 'And anyway, it's none of your business.'

'Did I get anythin'?' the insensitive woman asked again, as self-absorbed as ever.

'No,' he laughed again, this time more bitterly. '*Plus ça change...*'

Rain started to fall in heavy droplets on the steep windscreen, and the driver switched on the wipers. Why did his sister always make him want to scream? He pulled back onto the road and focussed on answering her previous question, determined to remain calm.

'For the last two days, we've been reading a bunch of letters Lynn wrote to us in the event she might die. We only finished them an hour ago.'

Madalena nodded, scarcely bothering to listen to the information her brother had taken the trouble to explain. Jeff sighed and concentrated on the road. He realised he should know better than to expect more after all this time.

'Where're the kids?'

'Jet's gone out for a drink with Gerry, and Kierney's boyfriend came to the apartment.'

'Kizzy's got a boyfriend?' the Sydneysider shrieked. 'Already?'

'What do you mean, already?' the father shot back. 'She's eighteen! And you met him before. Dylan. You saw him at Lynn's birthday party.'

The sudden visualisation of his wife's fortieth birthday celebration brought tears to the celebrity's eyes, but he blinked them back. He didn't want to cry in front of his sister before they had even made it home.

'She still goin' out with '*im*?' the clueless aunt cackled. 'He was "out there".'

'He *is* pretty "out there",' Jeff agreed, 'but so are you, and so's Kizzo. They're just having fun.'

'And sex,' Madalena chastised her brother, remembering how difficult it had been for him to come to terms with his innocent little girl playing with boys.

'Yep. Thanks for that,' he replied in mock frustration. 'I'm over all that now. I'm glad she's got someone to spend time with. Right now, I'm very jealous.'

'So what about Jet?' his sister continued the inquisition. 'He got a girlfriend?'

'One in every port. Like father, like son.'

'Ha! Hope he's bein' careful.'

The former playboy rolled his eyes and refused to be drawn into any further conversation on the topic of his children's sex lives. The four-wheel drive carved its way through the pelting rain towards the city for a few minutes before the next awkward question came.

'When's the funeral? And where?'

'Friday arvo,' her brother answered. 'At a crematorium. It's going to be bloody awful.'

'Crematorium?' Madalena parroted. 'Like Dad?'

'Yep. It's what Lynn wanted.'

The pair drove on in silence, soon drawing close to the CBD. The taller buildings of the inner suburbs, over which their penthouse surveyed, loomed like grey giants over the car, and their eerie benevolence comforted the widower in a strange way. It was almost as if the city he had made his own was bowing in respectful mourning for his loss.

'I'm hungry,' his skinny passenger moaned. 'Can we get somethin' to eat?'

Jeff sighed. 'Sure. What d'you want? We could order pizza.'

'What about Chinese?'

'Yeah. That's fine, but I don't want to get out of the car,' the driver came clean. 'You know how it is for me. Everyone knows what's happened, and they'll want to pass on their condolences. I just can't face it.'

'Oh, OK. I get it. All good. I'll go in and buy it. No problem,' Madalena's hand reached across towards the driver's seat, palm facing upwards.

'Haven't you got any money?' her brother asked, feigning incredulity but in reality not at all surprised. 'Jesus, Lena! You're keeping my mind off my situation by being your usual self, so thanks for that at least.'

'I didn't 'ave time to go to the ATM.'

'We booked the ticket two days ago,' Jeff teased. 'Plenty of time to find a cash machine. They're all over. It's not hard.'

Both knew this lesson in self-sufficiency was a waste of time. The car came to a standstill outside an unassuming Cantonese restaurant which the Diamond family had used many times over the years. The celebrity reached into his back pocket and pulled out his wallet. Madalena snatched the fifty-dollar note he offered and turned to let herself out.

'Y'wan' anything, *chico*?' he taunted the back of her head, relishing the cool air rushing in through the open door. 'No, thanks, Lena, but it was nice of you to ask.'

'Oh, yeah. Do you wan' anything?' the passenger turned round, her face bearing a shameful smile.

'*No, gracias.*'

Jeff watched his sister disappear into the restaurant and switched the radio to a news station. The model citizen, normally so well-attuned to current affairs, had lost touch with what had been happening in everyone else's world these last few days.

He listened to an interview with Prime Minister Paul Keating, who was being bombarded with thorny questions about the upcoming Federal election. Forcing his brain to focus on the content of the interview, he wondered whether he would ever regain his powers of concentration.

A debate about foreign policy followed, and the weary world-changer rested his tired head against the window and let the words wash over him. 'Stay out of my head for a few minutes, will you, angel, please?' he requested. 'I need to chill for a while. Just 'til Lena comes back.'

The vibration of the door opening on the other side of the car woke the driver from his half-sleep. Madalena made a big deal of climbing into what she termed a "truck", dumping a plastic bag of takeaway containers on the floormat. Her dutiful chauffeur turned the key in the ignition, and they drove back to the apartment in silence.

'Hey! Why aren't we going to your house?' the woman asked, once she realised they were circling the city block.

'It's easier to base ourselves here for the moment,' Jeff only half lied.

'Shit! I was gonna have a swim in the mornin'.'

Her brother let forth a stifled roar of frustration, slapping the steering wheel with the heels of both hands. 'Have you come for a holiday, Lena?'

'No, *chico*,' the woman replied, jolted out of her selfishness for a moment. 'Sorry.'

'Right,' he growled, calming down. 'Just remember that, please. The kids and I need you to know why you're here. Or I can drop you off at Hepburn Springs and pick you up next week. Either's fine by me.'

Kierney heard her father emerge from the lift with her auntie and ran to meet them, leaving Dylan behind in her bed. The widower was grateful for her unfailing support and watched the teenager expertly manœuvre their guest into a bedroom well away from his.

Lynn's request to "borrow" his daughter last year had been a fortuitous move, since the thoughtful methods he remembered his wife using to make their household run smoothly were now evident in their graceful girl, all with an apparent natural ease.

Taking advantage of a few moments' peace before the inevitable storm, Jeff reheated Madalena's Chinese food and served it onto a plate. It sat waiting for her in the lounge room in front of the television, alongside a stubbie of beer. The woman flopped down and picked up the meal without a word of thanks, scoffing her food down with her eyes trained on the screen.

Her brother poured himself a large glass of red wine and gave the rest of the bottle to his gipsy girl to take back to her waiting boyfriend. Beside the television sat a video cassette which hadn't been there earlier. She must have found the wedding movie, and his heartbeat missed a couple of beats while he steadied his nerves.

'What d'you want to do tomorrow?' the widower asked.

'What day is it?' Madalena asked back, her mouth full. 'Wensdy?'

'Yep. All day,' he quipped, wondering what difference this level of accuracy made to the visitor's activity preferences. 'Kizzy's going with Michelle to get some stuff from the house. I've got about three million phone calls to make in the morning and then I'm s'posed to meet with the police. But we could go out in the afternoon somewhere, if you like. I need to get out of this bloody mausoleum. D'you wanna play golf again? That was good for a few laughs last time.'

His sister shrugged. 'Yeah. OK. Just us?'

'Or with Jet. I don't know what his plans are tomorrow.'

'Where is 'e? Oh, yeah. Out with Gerry. He's a bit old to go drinking with your son.'

The younger sibling frowned. 'He's the same age as you, remember? The lad's not that interested in drinking anyway. He's just out to get his end away.'

'Gerry?'

'No. Jet, you idiot! He's an animal these days. Can't go for five minutes without a shag.'

'Just like you then,' the former prostitute cackled.

The tall, dark stranger shrugged. Not anymore, he thought. Those days were over. He left the room to fetch two more bottles of beer, handing one to his sister and taking a long gulp from the other. This next week was scoping out as painful on so many fronts.

Seeing the impressive star deep in thought, Madalena felt sorry for him. She hadn't seen him unhappy for many years, although she had no real clue what he did all day, making money hand over fist and travelling all over the world for no apparent reason.

She took advantage of complimentary ring-side seats at his gigs whenever his shows rolled across the border into New South Wales, and her friends pumped her for gossip that she could never deliver. Now however, even from her narrow viewpoint, she could see this amazing man, to whom she hardly related beyond flesh and blood, was damaged to the core.

'So what's it like for you? What ya feelin' like, after a few days since she died?'

Jeff stared straight into his sister's eyes; she who had never allowed herself to get close to anyone in her whole life. How might he explain the way he felt to someone like her?

'It's like my life's been stolen,' he said. 'One minute I'm the king and the next minute I'm nothing. One minute we're driving through the streets of Sydney, in the sunshine, anticipating a nice lunch and a fat cheque for Childlight, and the next I'm staring at my dream girl with a bullet in her head. And the sun's still shining as if it hasn't yet noticed she's gone.'

Madalena whistled. 'That's mad. I'm sorry, *chico*. Really I am. I just dunno what to say to you.'

'That's OK. Thanks. You don't have to say anything. We have no choice but to wade through this river of shit until we reach the other side.'

'Aw. That's funny,' the visitor smiled. 'At least you can still joke about things.'

'Yeah. Probably shouldn't though,' her brother sighed. 'The kids keep telling me to hold the black humour, but it's the only response I have sometimes.'

'You didn't get a chance to say goodbye,' Madalena mused. 'That's what people always say, isn't it? "I wish I 'ad the chance to say goodbye."'

'Bullshit,' the widower smiled ruefully. 'I'd far rather be saying hello. What good is goodbye to anyone? It shits me to think I was offered valet parking and turned it down. If you want to talk about regret, there's the big one. If I'd let someone else park the bloody car, Lynn'd still be alive today.'

'How would it?' his sister enquired. 'Wouldn't the bastard've shot you instead?'

'Yeah. But I'd be the one with less pain,' Jeff replied, putting his head in his hands. 'Lying there in a box waiting to be set on fire looks like a far better option from where I'm sitting.'

'Fuck that, *chico*!' the startled woman exclaimed. 'The kids are right. Don't say them things. I'm sure Lynn'd prefer to be alive.'

'I'm not sure she would actually,' the grieving husband replied, reflecting on the content of his letters.

'It just takes time to get over it. You'll be OK.'

'How would you know?' came her brother's retort, losing patience not only with his sister's lack of empathy but also with his inability to deal with it.

The reluctant host switched the television channel to avoid a news bulletin and handed the remote control to their visitor. Picking up her dinner plate and the empty beer bottles, he walked into the kitchen and stood over the sink, breathing deeply.

Don't let her get to you, he told himself. *She doesn't understand. It's not her fault.*

The telephone rang on the wall, and the celebrity lunged towards it, his mind playing its same old tricks. 'Hello?'

'Jeff, it's me,' came a familiar voice.

'Hey, mate. What's up? Everything OK?'

'Sure thing. Everything's fine,' Gerry answered. 'Your man's having a good time. He's quite the action hero in these parts, let me tell you. What about you? Do you want some company?'

'Cheers. Thanks a lot, mate. Madalena's here. It's a bundle of laughs.'

'Jesus!' Gerry exclaimed. 'That's right. Do you need some moral support? Where's Kierney?'

'Here, in bed,' Jeff chuckled, relaxing a little. 'She's getting fixed up too. Comes to something, doesn't it, when you're the old fart sitting in front of the TV with your spinster sister, and your kids are getting their rocks off all around you?'

The Diamonds' long-suffering manager guffawed at the other end of the line. 'That's bloody hilarious, mate. Glad you can see the funny side. Hey, do you mind if I leave Romeo Junior to it then? He doesn't need Uncle Gerry hanging around anymore. I feel like a child molester in this place.'

'Absolutely,' the rock star affirmed. 'Mission accomplished, mate. Thanks. Get back to Fiona. Why should you miss out? I'll be fine with Lena. I'm going to answer my long list of e-mails and leave her to it.'

Content that his son was having a good night, Jeff opened another bottle of Rioja and delivered a glass to his sister, before taking the rest and another glass into the office. He sat down at his desk and gazed across at his wife's, over which a canvas made from one of his late nineteen-seventies album covers bore down. Lynn had always loved this picture of him crouching barefoot on the sand, wearing blue jeans and a tatty, long-sleeved T-shirt.

'What d'you think, angel?' he asked into the air. 'Should I go back to the house? I really don't want to, but what's the difference between here and there? This place feels better 'cause it's enough like a hotel suite for me to pretend you shouldn't be here. That's my crazy rationale anyway.'

While his computer booted up, Jeff leafed through a few pieces of paper that had been lying around on his side of the office for a few weeks. He tried to remember the outstanding items waiting for his attention at Escondido. And for his stunning partner too. There would be a large number. He made a note to ask Kierney to bring everything back with her tomorrow.

'Shit. That's going to be a fun job,' he murmured, both to himself and to Lynn's ghost, which he hoped was keeping track of his every move. 'Sorry, Lord Mayor, my wife can't come and open the primary school fête because we scattered her last week.'

Unbeknown to the tired man, Jet had written a program to pop up a cartoon on his dad's screen, and the silly caption made him smile. The teenagers were trying very hard to cheer him up. Scrolling down the long list in his inbox, Jeff selected odd lines here and there which he thought might ease him into the mammoth task. Like his telephone and text messages, every e-mail seemed to echo the same sentiments. There weren't too many possible variations on this theme, regardless of their method of delivery.

An abundance of encouraging words lay in wait from good friends. There were others from business associates with whom he had shared no more than a single conversation, and still more from all points in between. He picked a few straightforward ones from people who wouldn't expect him to dress things up and began typing suitable responses, steering clear of the sarcasm and irony crowding his brain.

Several e-mails from Lynn's friends would require a great deal more thought, best left for another day, and those from relative strangers who were no more than a name to her handsome husband deserved to be ignored altogether.

'Why is it that everyone wants to get in on the act?' he threw into the ether. 'Who's Francesca Anderson? She hopes the kids and I are coping and offers any assistance she might be able to give. Thanks heaps, but who the hell are you? And Han Nguyen. Why's he writing to me, and how did he get my e-mail address? I don't want all these new friends to take your place, Lynn. I just want you back.'

A dull, tingling sensation gripped the doleful man's chest as he spoke. '*Merci, mon amie,*' he said with a tired smile. 'That feels so good. I knew you'd understand. Thanks for your support, angel. What can I do for you?'

Wiping his eyes, Jeff worked on down the never-ending list of messages. *Thank the Lord for copy and paste.* He soon became bored with the monotony of this nocturnal exercise, choosing instead to trawl back through old e-mails, laughing at some and crying at others.

After a while, he heard his name being called from the hallway. The churlish celebrity pushed his chair back and stepped out to find Madalena with her hands on her hips and pouting.

'Where'd ya go?'

'Answering messages. What's wrong?'

'Nothin'. I was waitin' for you,' his sister whined. 'When's Jet comin' 'ome?'

'I don't know. Tomorrow morning, I expect. It's pretty late. D'you want to stay up or go to sleep?'

The forty-seven-year-old was behaving like an overtired toddler, unwilling to go to bed in case she missed out on something and yet lacking the wherewithal to amuse herself. Her younger sibling remembered these compulsions all too well and gave in to a pang of sympathy.

Regardless, he wasn't in the mood for any of the normal entertaining antics he and Lynn used to rustle up when friends stayed over: singing, dancing, playing the piano or dragging out a board game. His mind flitted to the weed bagged up in his filing cabinet, but dismissed this too. Perhaps in a few days' time, once their annoying visitor had managed to assimilate into the environment a little better...

'I'll make coffee,' he announced. 'D'you know which is Kizzy's room?'

'No.'

Jeff laughed. 'Did you even think about it before you answered?'

'No,' Madalena shrugged. 'I don't wanna walk over there.'

'Fine,' the widower shook his head in exasperation, feeling the sarcasm boiling up within. 'It *is* a long way. Make yourself comfortable, and I'll serve you coffee forthwith.'

Leaving the dark-haired woman where she stood, the irritated man made his way down the hallway to Kierney's bedroom and knocked. 'Guys, I'm making coffee. D'you want some?'

Light footsteps padded towards the door, which opened to reveal his tousled daughter and her spindly-legged boyfriend both in a state of semi-undress. It was a lovely scene, and Jeff drank it in wantonly.

'Yes, please. Do you want me to make it?'

'No,' her dad smiled. 'You're too busy.'

'We're not busy!' the teenager objected, fighting her embarrassment as she turned to Dylan. 'Come on. Let's join Papá and Auntie Lena for a bit.'

Jeff left the two lovebirds to decide on their next move. It was encouraging that Kierney could adjust so quickly and carry on her normal pattern of life.

On his way back to the kitchen, he noticed a light coming from the master bedroom. Madalena was snooping around, and her brother felt the hairs on the back of his neck prickling.

'Lena, please don't come in here. This is *our* room. It's sacred just at the moment, if you don't mind.'

'What, *chico*? Why not?'

'Because I said so,' Jeff snapped. 'Please, Lena. Not even I can bring myself to be in here.'

'OK. Whatever... It's just a bedroom.'

'To you maybe, but it's my house, and I'd prefer it if you didn't go in here,' her brother lowered his voice, turning out the light and shepherding the busybody back down the hallway.

'It's a flat,' the petulant woman corrected.

The widower smouldered inside, feeling his jaws clenching. 'Yes, of course. My mistake. It's a flat, and I own it. You're our guest, and this "just a bedroom" is off-limits. Sorry, Lena, but that's just the way it has to be.'

Kierney and Dylan appeared outside the door, wondering why they could hear raised voices. Fully-clothed, the eclectic duo looked as if butter wouldn't melt in their mouths. The music student had a copy of a Janis Joplin biography under his arm, borrowed from his girlfriend's sparse apartment bookshelf.

'Dylan's going home.'

'Thanks for letting me come over,' the gangly teenager said, before his girlfriend's ultra-cool father could ask why. 'I hope Friday's not too bad. I forgot to say my parents send their best wishes.'

'Thanks, mate,' Jeff replied. 'And thanks for coming. You're welcome any time. Say thanks to your parents too, please.'

The man of the house placed a hand on his gaping sister's back and guided her into the kitchen, to allow the youngsters to say their goodbyes in private. He handed her the empty *cafetière* and pointed to a cupboard.

'Coffee's up there,' he said, switching on the kettle. 'And mugs are over there.'

'She's cute,' Madalena mused, trudging across the floor to where he was pointing.

'Yeah, I know. And so thoughtful too.'

The visitor chuckled. 'Not like me, you mean.'

'I didn't say that.'

'You don't 'af ta,' his sister replied, slapping his arm. 'I know I'm a selfish cow. I don't mean to be. I just am.'

Something to be proud of, her younger brother thought. He heard the lift bell sound, and Kierney trotted into the kitchen, quick to grab milk, sugar and some spoons and take them through to the lounge room.

'Please could we have some ice cream?' she asked, suddenly the kid again.

'Sure. If there is any.'

'There is,' she replied, holding up two different flavours. 'Auntie Lena, would you like some?'

'Yeah. Great,' Madalena nodded, pointing to the container in her niece's left hand. 'That one.'

The three dark-haired gipsies sat down and flicked through the channels to find a suitable midnight show. Kierney caught her father's attention and guided his gaze to the video cassette by the television set. Jeff shook his head, smiling. The teenager's eyes insisted, and his head remained stubbornly on message.

'Oh,' the young woman whined, flapping her feet against the base of the couch like a toddler.

'What's goin' on?' Madalena demanded to know.

Kierney kept quiet, but it was too late. Her dad glared in jest, and her eyes apologised.

'Go on then,' Jeff capitulated, waving a hand to the women. 'Put it on.'

'Yay! Thanks, Papá. Mamá asked him to watch the wedding movie tonight.'

Her aunt looked up in disbelief. 'What? How?'

'In a letter. Shall we start?'

Jeff groaned, putting both hands in front of his eyes. His daughter grabbed his long fingers and playfully tried to pull them away from his face. He resisted hard, and she gave up after a few failed attempts.

'*Por favor,* watch it, Papá,' she begged.

'OK. I'll watch it, *pequeñita,*' he gave a long sigh, 'but I warn you I'm gonna cry .'

'That doesn't matter. Me too. *Mucho, mucho.*'

A classical melody played over the title sequence, and the opening credits rolled. It had been at least ten years since the star had seen the footage of his own wedding, and a lump formed in his throat straightaway.

There followed edited highlights of the bridal party getting dressed upstairs, of the groom and best man sharing a joke before the others arrived, and of the orchestra rehearsing.

To signal the ceremony was about to commence, the camera panned upwards, above the stage, to a huge golden banner. Adorned with the "JL" symbol which was to become synonymous with their partnership and had long been tattooed on their bodies, the sight of it caused both father and daughter to gulp.

'Are you doing OK?' the youngster checked, seeing her dad's eyes shining in the stream of light from the television.

'No,' he nodded with a smile.

Kierney cuddled into his side like a five-year-old, across from Madalena, who sat bolt upright and full of concentration as the tape rolled. They watched Bart Dyson lead his elder daughter from the rear of the ballroom towards the celebrant, next to whom were two impeccably-groomed gentlemen waiting in their best suits and ties.

The film then switched to the bridesmaids, causing Jeff's sister to jump up with a start, surprised to see herself. '¡Ai! There's me!' she cried out. 'I look like... young.'

'We were all like... young!' her brother teased. 'Look at Anna. She was only nine. She's the one who's changed the most.'

'And I didn't even exist,' Kierney laughed.

'True. Although we were practising very hard, gorgeous,' Jeff nudged his daughter, knowing what she had recently been up to on the other side of the apartment.

The processional march finished, and the enchanted audience listened to the couple's vows being spoken for all to hear, both inside the great hall and outside on the street. The widower broke down unashamedly on seeing his golden-haired beauty for the first time in a long few days.

All three smiled at the sight of Celia Blake and Marianna Dyson both dabbing their eyes on opposite sides of the aisle, not to mention quite a number of men staring straight in front of them in an effort to remain steadfast and unaffected.

Kierney hugged her father even closer. 'Mamá looks so happy, doesn't she? She told me she felt like she was floating off the ground all day.'

'That's nice,' Jeff sniffed. 'It was a really fantastic day. Even better than I'd hoped for.'

Madalena was captivated by the replay of her first day as part of the Dysons' extended family. Her coffee mug nearly overbalanced in her lap when she saw herself sitting next to Michelle and Anna at the front while the happy couple exchanged rings and made their pledges.

'Jesus!' she exclaimed. 'Look 'ow many people's there! I can't remember so many people bein' there.'

'Haven't you seen this before?' Jeff asked. 'I didn't know that.'

The tape continued through the couple's individual and joint performances, the meal and the speeches, then on to more music. The camera had followed the couple around right up to the time they left, while their guests were dancing and chatting, and finished with a comical shot of Michelle collapsing into Gerry's arms.

The groom relived every minute in painful ecstasy, marvelling at how much of the day he could recall more-or-less verbatim. 'D'you know what the most remarkable thing was about that night?' he asked the two awestruck women, who both shook their heads. 'Everything was done and dusted before ten o'clock. We were already in our hotel room by then.'

'For your wedding night!' Madalena added in a tantalising tone.

'Indeed,' the world's greatest lover affirmed. 'We didn't stay in the hotel for long though. We decided to walk home and sit on the balcony here, just like the day had never happened. It was the perfect end to the perfect day.'

'But you came to brekkie,' the visitor argued, 'because you was angry that I was so late.'

Kierney's body shifted sideways as her father took in a long, slow breath and let it out again, in tune with his frustration as always. He was doing his best to rise above the sorrow by describing happy memories, yet Madalena seemed intent on trying his patience. The young woman knew her aunt wasn't being deliberately malicious, but the end result was the same.

'I wasn't angry,' Jeff responded. 'We had to get you back to the airport, or you'd have missed your flight.'

Kierney changed the subject. 'You and Mamá looked amazing. Did you like watching it again?'

'Yeah. *Sorta-kinda*. It was easier than I thought it'd be.'

'Probably because we're here,' the young woman surmised. 'You need to watch it again on your own, so you can really get into it. Hopefully, Mamá'll talk to you during it.'

The video came to an abrupt end and began rewinding itself noisily, leaving the trio staring at each other's long face.

Jeff squeezed his eighteen-year-old sage. 'Bed?' he suggested, watching both women yawn and stretch.

'And you?' Kierney asked. 'Are you going to bed?'

'No, not yet. I've got a few more e-mails to send. I'll see you in the morning. What time's Mish coming for you?'

'After she drops the kids at school. Have you done your list of things you need?'

'Yep. It's in the kitchen,' he nodded, 'but if you think of anything I've missed, just bring it.'

'I'll go with you,' Madalena suggested to her niece.

'No, Lena. Let Kiz and Michelle go on their own, please,' Jeff stepped in. 'It's going to be very tough to walk into the house after what's happened.'

The frustrated man didn't care to pass on to his daughter that her aunt only wanted to tag along so she could take a dip in the pool. Kierney kissed the adults goodnight and disappeared back to her bedroom. Their visitor decided to do the same, and the widower once more found himself alone, although this time somewhat relieved. His mind turned to his son, who was by now most likely in someone else's bed.

Jeff set the video to fast-forward, standing in front of the television. He stopped the tape at random, wondering what he would see when he pressed the button. It started at the part where he had played the piano while his brand new wife sang to their guests. Kierney was right. Lynn was chock-full of joy.

He rubbed his tattoo, hoping for some sort of sign of approval. 'D'you want me to watch it again on my own?' he asked his dream girl's spirit. 'I know what was in the letter, and that's what I was aiming for. But Kizzy made me, didn't you see?'

Still nothing. The bereaved husband sat down in the dark, lit a cigarette and started the tape playing over again, watching from start to finish without batting an eyelid. The tears came again, but so did the smiles and the occasional cynical snigger during the speeches. He saw himself dancing with his new mother-in-law, with his sister, and then again with his new wife.

'Is this better?' he checked, his heart leaping into his mouth on finally feeling his pectoral muscle itch again. 'I'm a slow learner. Sorry, angel.'

Jeff spread himself out across the couch and ran the whole reel through for a third time, fast-forwarding past the boring bits. His head began to clear at last, and his mood lightened a little. He could hear Lynn's voice in his head; the words weren't too distinct, but it was unmistakeably her voice. She loved him so much. They had enjoyed twenty years of pure heaven, and he felt grateful for having been granted this much time in paradise.

'So now you're my dream girl again,' he told his absent friend. 'I can feel you with me. Well, who knows? What does it matter if I'm going mad or if you're really here? It's a shitload better than feeling alone.'

After a while, the songwriter heard the lift doors open. His watch said two-fifty. Jet's huge frame filled the doorway, looking tired but relaxed.

'Hey! You're still up. You didn't stay up for me, did you?'

His dad raised his eyebrows. 'Nah! Why would I do that?'

'Cool,' the teenager laughed. 'That's OK then. What were you doing? Watching the wedding tape?'

Jeff nodded. 'Yep. We all watched it together once, then I've watched it twice more times on my own.'

The teenager chuckled at his father's reminder of an expression he had often used as a little boy. 'Oh, be quiet, old man,' he mocked. 'Were there cameras in your hotel room on your wedding night?'

'Excuse me? You're as crude as your auntie.'

Jet gave his dad a patronising tap on the head. 'Just checkin'.'

'Fuck off,' Jeff snapped, whipping his left arm back behind him in an attempt to deliver a swift tweak to his son's private parts. 'So, did you get what you wanted?'

The sportsman was too quick. 'Yes, thanks,' he replied, dodging out of the way.

'*Excelente*,' the proud father nodded. 'Gerry rang me to ask if it was OK to leave you there. Said he felt like a child molester. Where did you go?'

The young charmer smiled. 'Yeah. We ended up at Circa. He was about twenty years older than everyone else, even the bar staff. It didn't matter though. Some of those girls were so off their faces. They wouldn't have had a clue how old any of us was.'

'Go to bed, son,' the widower instructed, standing up and giving the fair-haired monster a manly hug. 'It's been another huge day, and tomorrow'll be a chance to regroup. I might take Lena to play golf, if you're interested. I've no bloody idea how to entertain her while she's here.'

'Is Kiz still going to Escondido? How is our delightful auntie, by the way?'

'Delightful as ever,' he sighed. 'Kizzy's off about nine-thirty, I think. Have you given her a list of the stuff you want?'

'No. I'll do it now. G'night, Dad.'

'Good man,' Jeff praised, dealing the lad an affectionate bump on the shoulder. 'I'm glad you had a good time. You deserve it. Thanks for sticking with us earlier.'

'No worries. Hope you can get some sleep.'

The father shrugged. Sleep wasn't on his mind. Despite being racked with exhaustion earlier in the day, for some unknown reason, he was now raring to go. Left to his own devices, he opened the drawer under the television and hunted for more footage of Lynn, every sense rendered voracious. A compilation of short clips from various birthday celebrations met the mark, along with a number of others with potential sidelined for future nights alone.

'*Excelente,*' he muttered under his breath. 'Let's watch this together, angel. Have you got *du vin rouge* up there where you are? D'you mind if I smoke?'

Feeling a strange sense of anticipation, Jeff delved into the filing cabinet behind the piano and rolled a generous reefer of sweet-smelling leaves. Lighting the joint in the dark, he settled down with his ghostly companion to chart a course through their children's special days.

Lynn was pleased with her black stallion, judging by the clarity in his head and a persistent irritation from his left pectoral muscle. Perhaps the worst was over, he dared to think.

Kierney found her father asleep on the couch the following morning, with the incriminating evidence strewn across the coffee table. It made her uncomfortable to think of him smoking on his own, but he looked at peace. She cleared up the mess and put on a fresh pot of coffee.

A few minutes later, Jeff became aware of muted activity around him. He opened his eyes to find his pretty daughter sitting on the floor next to his makeshift bed, sipping from a steaming mug.

'*Buenos días, Papá.* Sleep well?'

'*Sí, pequeñita,*' came a drowsy reply. 'You?'

'Coffee?' Kierney nodded, holding her dad's drink out in front of him.

'*Sí, gracias,*' he accepted. 'I watched a video of all your birthdays. I didn't even know it existed.'

'Did you? Which one?' the young woman asked, turning her gaze towards the television cabinet in surprise. 'From in there?'

'Yep. After I'd watched the wedding twice more, I looked for something else in the drawer, and there you were.'

'*¡Bueno!* I'll have to watch it,' Kierney smiled. 'I don't remember seeing it either. How old do we get to?'

'Oh, only young. Probably twelve and ten? You were cute as,' Jeff kissed his daughter's cheek with warmed lips.

'By the way, I finished "Walk Me Through The Rain" this morning,' the teenager said. 'Would you like to hear it?'

'Would I?' her papá echoed. 'You bet I would. In here?'

Kierney stood up and went to the piano. She had already placed the sheet music on the stand, and the majestic sound rang around the room, at a volume much less restrained than either musician had heard for a while.

'It's not really a keyboard song,' the young composer explained over the opening bars.

Her voice rang out with the first verse, subdued and a little nervous, but it didn't take long to strengthen to recital volume. Having homemade music in the house again was mollifying, and the impressed mentor clapped and whistled in approval at the end of her performance.

'That's fantastic. I love it,' he said, getting to his feet and hugging her close. 'Especially how you put "Endless Sky" in there... It's beautiful, and I don't feel I deserve it.'

'You *do* deserve it,' his daughter insisted. 'You absolutely deserve it. I also wrote this...'

Kierney began to play again, letting a faster, rhythmic beat transform their sombre mood. This second lyric disturbed the forty-three-year-old however, telling of suspicions that grow between a man and a woman. A few seconds of silence passed before he began to clap at this song's conclusion.

'Whoa! That's a very angry song, baby. Where did it come from?'

'Nowhere in particular. It's a combination of things.'

'Well, they're some nasty themes to be bringing out into the open,' the veteran songwriter went on. 'Dylan hasn't hurt you or forced you into anything, has he?'

'No!' the adamant youngster yelped. 'He hasn't. In fact, he was there while I was writing it.'

Jeff relaxed. His gorgeous gipsy girl was a complex being whose art-form regularly strayed into the unsavoury, but the timing of this song bothered him. He made a mental note to revisit the conversation later, to see if he could penetrate the heart and mind of his daughter of darkness and seek confidence that nothing sinister lurked therein.

However, his worries were cut short before either had a chance to change the subject, their attention diverted to the piercing sound of their guest's call welcoming in the new day. Madalena was ready for breakfast and was making sure everyone knew about it.

'*Buenos días*,' her brother sighed, walking towards the source of the din and giving her a peck on the cheek. 'Sleep OK?'

'Yeah. Hi, Kizzo.'

'*Buenos días,* Auntie Lena,' the youngster slipped off the piano stool to greet her with a kiss.

'We need to get some supplies in before any of us can have brekkie,' the reluctant host announced, heading for the refrigerator. 'Our cupboards are bare. Lena, would you mind going round the corner and getting some bread and milk, please?'

Madalena planted both feet on the tiled floor, dismay painted on her face. 'Why me?'

'I'll go, Papá,' Kierney offered.

'No,' Jeff waved a hand at the child who was always keen to diffuse any sort of conflict. 'I'll ask Jet to go.'

'Did 'e come 'ome yet? From 'is shag-fest?'

The dark-haired teenager burst out laughing. "Shag-fest" was not an expression she expected to hear from her aunt. Jeff laughed too, for the look on his daughter's face was priceless.

'Jesus, Lena,' he scolded with a grin. 'Who taught you that?'

'I dunno,' the uncultured woman shrugged. 'I'll go for the bread an' all if you want. Where's the shop?'

'Let's both go,' her niece resolved. 'You wake Jet up, Papá, and we can have brekkie all together before Michelle gets here.'

FUNERAL

'Cheers, mate. Looks great.'

The celebrity thanked the junior mechanic who had been given the task of returning the Land Rover, its black paint and chrome accessories polished and gleaming, ready for its owner's funeral. The embarrassed young man scarpered as soon as the cash was slapped into his outstretched hand, knowing full well whose car he had cleaned.

Stepping into the lift to return to the penthouse floor, the widower checked his appearance in the grey-tinted mirrors. He was a wreck, with a week's worth of beard on his chin, uncombed hair and wearing the same clothes for the third day running.

The rock star's reflection grimaced at what it saw. This rough-looking bloke would need to start early if he wanted to smarten up enough for today's big event. His mouth broke into a rueful smile as he stepped back into the apartment and into his temporary bedroom, remarking that nearly every piece of clothing Kierney had selected to bring back for him from Escondido was either black or dark blue. Apart from a few light-coloured shirts and some colourful underwear, the pile screamed "bereavement" at him.

It was ten o'clock, and the kids had already dragged him out for a run and fed him cereal like a baby, much to Madalena's amusement. They had walked through the Order of Service on the telephone the day before with Michelle, Bart, Junior and Gerry until they were all content with its structure, and the lonely man had gone to bed stone cold sober and with mixed emotions.

The same could not be said for his sister, who had somehow made her way to a seedy pub on Brunswick Street, after having been asked to make herself scarce. A taxi had deposited her back on the apartment building steps at around one o'clock in the morning, much to the family's annoyance at being woken up by the buzzing of the entry-phone.

'So how's the head this morning, Auntie Lena?' her nephew teased.

Jeff gave his son a half-hearted scowl to encourage him to take it easy. There was no point making anyone hot under the collar this morning. Kierney seemed particularly low after their earlier antics, so he moved his chair closer to hers and took her hand.

'You OK?' he asked. 'Your pilot light's gone out.'

The young woman smiled at the analogy and sat up straight, still gripping his fingers. 'I'm good,' she responded in a hushed voice. 'Today is a very sad day. I don't know what it's going to be like and I'm nervous for all of us.'

The morning was altogether too warm and inviting for a funeral. Jet took the ironing board out onto the balcony and began to iron both men's shirts while Kierney fussed around her auntie, as much to distract herself as to ensure she was kitted out appropriately.

Jeff left the rest of the family and shut himself in the bathroom in the master bedroom. He yearned to feel close to Lynn's spirit this morning, but it was nowhere to be found.

The tired celebrity had blunted two new razor blades in the process of cleaning up. After his shower, he reached for the electric shaver that his daughter had brought back from the house and ran it over his face as well, finishing by slapping on some after-shave.

Better, his reflection reported.

His eyes were not as bloodshot as their dull aching suggested, but the dark circles had not come off in the wash. The local heartthrob had planned to make time for a haircut yesterday, but as the hours passed by, he couldn't muster the fortitude to face the barber's awkward and inevitably intrusive chatter.

'Where is this crematorium?' Jet asked, leafing through the street directory. 'I don't think I've ever been to Keilor.'

Madalena shrugged. 'I never even 'eard of it.'

Hardly surprising, Jeff smiled to himself. His sister had reached the ripe, old age of forty-six without the need for a driving licence. She had attempted a few lessons over the years, with the promise of a car of her own, yet always gave up within a few weeks. She preferred to rack up a healthy taxi bill for her brother to pay off instead. The billionaire didn't mind. In truth, it was far safer for all concerned.

The foursome stood staring at each other in the hallway as they prepared to leave the apartment and head down to the car. The last funeral the Diamonds had attended as a family was for Lynn's maternal grandfather, now three years ago.

Jeff's heart caved in when he saw his sister as today's fourth Diamond, where his beautiful best friend had stood on that day. Father and son both wore dark suits, white shirts and black ties. The women were also in black dresses with their waves of long hair tied back.

'You two look so alike,' Jeff observed. 'Like mourners in a southern European village.'

Kierney caught her breath. 'Don't make me cry, please, Papá.'

'Sorry, Kizzo. Let's go.'

The two solemn ladies sat in the rear of the car. His offer to drive refused, the tall sportsman took his place in the passenger seat. The colourful street directory seemed surreal and incongruous spread out across his son's lap while the car's interior otherwise presented such a dour scene.

As agreed, there was no pack of paparazzi milling around the crematorium in the outer north-western suburb. Two independent cameramen whom Cathy had hired, also dressed in black, stood outside the doors in respectful silence, equipment not yet assembled.

The Diamond party got out of the car, full of sorrow and trepidation. No-one was on hand to greet them, so it was left to Jeff to provide the film crew with their instructions. Another cremation was in progress in the chapel of remembrance, so the others wandered around the gardens adopting a holding pattern.

There was still an hour to go before Lynn's service was due to commence, and they regretted arriving so early. They felt unsettled and anxious, especially their visitor from Sydney. As usual, it had taken Madalena a few days to settle down and to assume a few ordinary familial behaviours. She truly was the wild child who never grew up.

With the temperature hovering around thirty-three degrees Celsius, it wasn't long before the mourners headed for some shade. They had opted to forego lunch, a decision which the strapping university student also regretted.

'My stomach's going to rumble during the service,' he complained.

His dad smiled. 'Doesn't matter. Go and get something if you want. There's plenty of time.'

The younger man didn't need to be asked twice, hopping back into the four-wheel drive and disappearing in search of fast food. He passed Michelle and her husband at speed as the black Discovery slipped through the gates again, leaving confusion in its wake. The Hadleys drove around to the car park and spotted the guests of honour sheltering under an enormous oak.

'Morning, Jeff, Kierney,' the redhead said. 'How are you?'

The superstar kissed his wife's friend and shook Alan by the hand. 'Hey, guys. We're here. Thanks for coming, and for all your help. You remember Madalena?'

Michelle turned to her fellow bridesmaid and gave her a kiss on the cheek, swiftly examining her face and comparing wrinkles. Life had been kinder to the Victorian, as she had hoped and everyone else would have expected.

'I could've sworn I saw your car driving out just now,' the lawyer said.

'You did. It was Jet,' Kierney let on. 'He's hungry.'

Michelle smiled back. 'As usual.'

'Too right,' his father nodded, for once grateful for a superficial conversation. 'I'm glad you guys are early too. We can't go in yet. Some other poor bugger's on fire right now.'

Alan let go a belly laugh, only to receive a sharp jab in the ribs from his wife's elbow.

'For God's sake, you two!' Michelle raised her voice. 'You're as bad as each other. Don't talk about the deceased like that. Especially not Lynn.'

'Sorry,' the handsome celebrity responded. 'I can't take this seriously, Mish. I'm so over this whole long, drawn-out goodbye.'

'Me too,' his daughter agreed. 'And to think we've got to have the memorial service next.'

Her father groaned. 'Don't remind me. That's going to be a production and a half. Everyone wants to be seen there, watching us go to pieces every few minutes.'

Michelle reached her wallet out of her handbag, unzipping a small pocket and peering inside. 'I've got something for you, Jeff. The undertakers said all three had to be removed.'

The widower immediately guessed what she was referring to and broke into a cold sweat. The loose items of jewellery appeared in their long-time friend's fingers, glinting in the bright sunshine.

'Mamá's rings,' Kierney gasped, looking round at her auntie.

'You take them,' Jeff requested, watching his daughter turn very pale. 'D'you mind?'

The hesitant young woman held her hand out, palm upwards, and the three pieces of jewellery were dropped into it; first, the delicate gold band with its inner inscription of "JL 1.1.76", followed by the engagement ring, its matching pair of precious stones set close together. Lastly, the exquisite multi-colour eternity band, with its forty rubies surrounded by brilliant cut diamonds.

She closed her fist around the trio and felt them shaking against the muscles of her palm. Tears welled in her eyes on visualising her mother's elegant hand where the plain but treasured wedding band had been proud to ride on her long annular finger every single day.

'Put this on, Papá,' the romantic teenager suggested, holding the gold circle up towards his face. 'You should wear it now.'

'It's too small,' Jeff shook his head and turned away.

Kierney walked after him, leaving Michelle and Alan with a confused Madalena. 'Please, Papá,' she insisted. 'Put it on your little finger, so it's next to yours. Just for today.'

The grieving husband rested a hand on his daughter's shoulder, panic increasing while she waved the ring in front of his eyes. The teenager felt her father shiver as he held it up to read the engraving, tears running down his face.

'I think it's a good idea,' she whispered. 'It doesn't matter if it doesn't fit.'

Jeff exhaled, puffing out his cheeks to release some tension and lifting his left hand towards his glassy-eyed tormenter. 'Go on.'

'Awesome! *Gracias, Papá*,' she cried out, almost jumping for joy.

Together, both laughing as they wept, the matching pair twisted the narrow band onto his leftmost finger, as far as it would go. It became wedged on the second knuckle, which had swollen in the hot weather. The musician flexed his hand and admired the matching gold bands before pulling the smaller one straight off again.

'Papá, why?'

'Shhh, gorgeous,' her dad said, placing a patient finger on her lips and turning round to their friends. 'Mish, is there any sunscreen in your car?'

Realising what her dad intended to do, Kierney beamed with relief and darted over to the Hadleys' silver Mercedes. Alan reached into his pocket to deactivate the central locking, enabling the teenager to pull open the glove box and rummage around until she located a white plastic bottle.

She slammed the door and ran back to the others. Squeezing a small amount of the cool lotion onto her finger, she coated the ring and threaded it back onto her father's little finger. This time, and with a fair bit more coaxing, the simple band slipped over both knuckles until it was juxtaposed against Jeff's own wedding ring.

'Kiss them, Papá,' the ecstatic teenager smiled.

Jeff obliged, pulling a face at the taste of sunscreen on his lips and receiving an affectionate slap on the arm.

While this peculiar rite had been taking place, three cars carrying the extended Dyson family had arrived in a short, understated convoy. Anna and Brandon, who had flown in from London, were first to alight and greet the others, followed by Bart and Marianna, the Olympian's parents and finally Junior and his three teenagers.

To the widower's surprise, his brother-in-law's former wife, Julie, had also made the journey. He thought it considerate of her to park the ongoing acrimony for Lynn's sake, although her presence was bound to create an uncomfortable atmosphere.

The mood became increasingly sombre as more and more people arrived. Childhood friends and fellow musicians, Janice Stanski and Richard Kerr, had driven up from the city together, closely followed by Sir Bradley Morrison, who was Lynn's former musical director and the man who had made them all into child-stars.

Gerald and Celia Blake, accompanied by their two daughters, arrived a little flustered after their morning flight from Sydney had been delayed for several hours. Bart Dyson's sister and her children joined the growing throng, as did two branches of Marianna's family tree.

Kiley Jones and Guy Kahn represented the intermediate generation whose lives had been enriched by the Diamonds' active mentorships, along with Sue and Don Jenner, former neighbours and architects of the family's beautiful *hacienda* built high on a cliff above Port Phillip Bay.

Their son, Dawson, had been best friends with Jet since they were both in nappies, enjoying countless sleepovers and weekends away which had started out innocent and had gradually degraded as their independence grew. He had stolen out of class to provide his friend with moral support and was concerned when the sportsman didn't appear to be present.

Lastly, in the background and trying not to get in the relatives' way, were Cathy Lane and some of her loyal colleagues from the Diamonds' management and music publishing companies.

All heads turned as Jet drove the Land Rover at full pelt through the crematorium grounds, receiving black looks from his father and grandfather as he braked at the last minute and ratcheted up the handbrake in front of the assembly.

'Mate,' Jeff scolded. 'That was uncalled for. Stop showing off. Show some respect, will you?'

Each person took the trouble to greet the grieving family and exchange expressions of sympathy before finding their seats in the small chapel. As promised, there were no pews, and the rows of chairs had been arranged in two semi-circles around the platform onto which the coffin was to be placed.

'Where's Lynn?' Madalena asked her brother, twisting his wrist to check the time.

Jeff couldn't help but see the funny side of this tasteless comment, struggling to stifle a laugh. 'Late for her own funeral, you mean?' he replied, loud enough for the children to hear.

Kierney frowned and slapped his arm again. His wife would have done the same thing, the desolate man rued. The reunited school friends simply directed their eyes to the ground, sharing the poor joke.

Right on cue, Gerry Blake was at Jeff's side. He and Fiona had kindly offered to accompany the hearse from the funeral parlour. Now called upon to summon the significant men in Lynn's life to follow him out of the chapel and back into the bright sunshine, he left his weeping companion sitting next to the celebrity's nonplussed sister. With her grandfather, father, uncle and brother all gone, Kierney and Fiona joined the Dyson womenfolk, having to almost drag Madalena along with them.

Outside, the coffin had been lifted from the prophetic, black vehicle and was waiting on a trolley to be carried into the chapel. A sombre Adagio which Kiley Jones had written for the occasion wafted on a light breeze from the speaker system inside, adding further gravitas to the oppressive atmosphere.

The superstar's brain refused to believe his wife's body lay inside the pine container on such a bright, cloudless summer's day. He leant heavily on the side of the hearse, breaking down at the faint sound of strings playing to farewell the only woman he had ever loved. Jet stood next to him, looking round helplessly at his grandfather.

The undertakers put no pressure on the funeral party, and eventually Jeff straightened up, turning to indicate he was ready. The acute sense of astriction reminded him of the time when Lynn had waited patiently for him to pluck up the courage to enter his parents' bedroom in the old Canley Vale flat. How he had battled with his demons that day...

The tattoo on his chest gave a twinge of recognition, and the widower raised his eyes to the sky. 'I'm with you, angel,' he said, not caring who else could hear. 'Let's get this over with.'

As arranged on the telephone the previous day, the deceased's son and father led the procession into the chapel, followed by the coffin carried by eight strangers in dark suits, and tailed by her husband and brother.

Jeff watched Gerry slip into the building ahead of them, thankful that his friend had his new partner for company. The music became progressively louder the closer the casket came to the platform.

'True genius, Kiley Jones,' the songwriter murmured, searching for the couple's talented collaborator in the small congregation.

Her musical body of work was a compendium of emotional recipes, and this hurried composition had undoubtedly swept straight to the top of the list. While the pallbearers shuffled the coffin onto its plinth, the two musicians made eye contact and both burst into tears. Junior put his arm around his brother-in-law and steered him up the aisle towards their seats.

Michelle had placed a large photograph of Lynn as a teenaged tennis champion on one side of the podium and a recent Diamond family portrait on the opposite side. Jeff looked from one picture to the other, and then from one child to the other.

He leant over to kiss them one at a time. 'I love you. I'm so sorry you've lost her.'

Neither said anything in reply, each gripping one of their dad's hands. Beyond the coffin, the Diamonds could see the Dysons making a brave attempt to be strong as ever. The music finally faded, and the funeral celebrant began to speak.

The words were well-chosen and sensitive, but the widower heard none of them. His mind was awash with sounds and images from his past, swirling uncontrollably in a maelstrom of emotion. Closing his eyes, he whispered for Lynn to go peacefully to the new place and wait for him there. Kierney and Jet both sobbed all the more on hearing this request, and the celebrant paused to let their grief pour out.

Various guests took turns to make polite acknowledgements and issued expressions of sorrow in appropriate places. Yet as Jeff would later recount, for all he knew, the man at the podium could easily have been reciting from the owner's manual of his old Ford Fairlane or pledging allegiance to the American Constitution. Kierney leant against his right side and Gerry's heavy hand rested on his shoulder, while Jet did his best not to rely on anyone.

Bart Dyson rose to his feet to read a short message from the family. Junior and Anna followed, telling a selection of childhood tales before speaking more earnestly about the great leader Lynn had become as an adult.

Janice and Richard added to the stories from their times on the road with their good friend and fellow performer. Renewed bouts of sadness burst forth when a recording of one of their biggest hits started to play, always a favourite of the forever couple.

The pain in Jeff's heart and the drumming in his head were partly offset by a sharp but comforting sting in his chest as the track played on, to the extent that he could almost have sung along.

Next, Jet and Kierney stood up together on the celebrant's signal. They had prepared a duet for their mother, or more accurately, for both parents. The young man took his position at an electric keyboard, which his father hadn't even spied up until this point, to deliver a dark number called "Missing", which hit home perfectly in everyone's hearts.

The widower listened to lyrics that could only be Kierney's, set to a melody which could have been given life by either teenager. Their rendition under extreme duress was pitch-perfect, and he leant forward and dropped his head into his hands, unable to cry anymore.

Once his children had returned to their seats, by way of a few silent words over their mother's coffin, the bereaved superstar heaved himself off his chair. In the short time it took to reach centre-stage, the atmosphere became turgid with sympathetic expectation, and none felt the change more acutely than the man himself.

As always at such moments however, he found strength from somewhere deep inside. He stood tall and with a clear head in front of his wife's family and friends. This "autopilot mode" with which he had been blessed had never been more useful than now.

'Lynn Dyson Diamond,' the statuesque performer opened, his famous baritone resonant under the cathedral-style ceiling, right hand resting uneasily on the lid of the coffin. 'You were my world. You are still my world. The kids and I miss you so much, but I'm beginning to feel you with me all the time.'

He paused to allow his comments to sink in, greeted with polite gasps. 'You made everyone so happy, angel. Most of all me. You were a great teacher, the best mother and a lover without equal. There's no need for me to say anything else. You know how I feel. We'll give you a proper send-off next Saturday. For now, just know that Jet, Kierney and I love you *ad infinitum*. Safe journey, Regala.'

A respectful hush descended on the chapel, and Jeff's footsteps echoed as he walked back to his seat, every pace reverberating through his body and on into his aching head. His son stood to salute the poignant speech, and their right hands locked into each other in a very grown-up statement. Kierney put her arms around her papá, and they all sat down together without further ceremony.

People were crying all around as the sweeping Adagio resumed. The widower felt both of Gerry's hands on his shoulders this time.

'Well said, sir. Nicely done.'

After a few closing lines from the celebrant, the dreaded moment was upon them, a weighty silence descending once more on the gathering. To the strains of the slow movement from Marcello's Oboe Concerto in D Minor, recorded by Kiley's chamber ensemble two days earlier, the casket lurched forward on the rollers. Lynn's body made its final exit through the curtains covering the chapel's rear wall.

Save for the sound of stifled tears and the odd cough, the air was motionless while the ominous pine container inched eerily along until it disappeared.

Unable to watch his dream girl's departure, Jeff groaned deep and long once he knew the chamber's doors were shut and the curtains had drawn together. The body he had enjoyed so completely, from head to toe and from virginity to demise, had been sent away for good, soon to be reduced to almost nothing. Part of him had gone through with it, leaving him feeling fractured and hollow inside.

The celebrant paused for the family and friends to complete their private farewells and return to the present. As funerals go, it had been a good one; decent and understated. As everyone filed back into the unremitting February sun, Jeff made a point of thanking Michelle and Kiley for providing them with exactly the mood they had sought, as painful as it had been for them all.

'What happens now?' Jet asked his mother's school-friend, who was busy handing out printed directions to the restaurant where invited guests were booked in for a late lunch.

The ginger-haired lady turned to whisper in the young man's ear, and he bent over to meet her halfway. 'We have to arrange for your mum's ashes to be picked up in the next day or two. They'll want to give them to your dad, so best be on hand to help him.'

He nodded and scoured the scene for his sister. Spotting her talking with their cousins, he strolled over and pulled her to one side.

'These people have got to deliver Mum's ashes to us,' he continued the chain of whispers. 'No-one's mentioned this before, have they?'

Kierney winced, the thought nauseating her. 'Yuck. When? Do we have to drive home with them in the car?'

'No. Michelle said a couple of days,' Jet replied. 'That means we'll have to come back here. Gross as, isn't it?'

His sister put her hand over her mouth. 'Oh, God, bro'. Such a horrible thought. Let's go and ask. Where is he anyway?'

The two teenagers scanned the small groups of mourners either milling around in the car park or wandering through the rose gardens. Their father was nowhere to be seen. They searched the entire area, wondering who might have wandered off with him, yet everyone else was accounted for. Alarm bells started to ring. How could he have slipped away without one of them noticing?

'Have you seen Dad?' Jet asked Gerry, who looked up at the teenager's concerned tone.

'No, mate,' he replied, also casting his eyes around. 'Last time I saw him, he was talking to Kiley and Guy.'

The family's manager excused himself from his glamorous girlfriend and the Jenners, and he and Jet began to search for the widower-at-large. Kierney wandered off in the other direction. They met back in the middle, having drawn a series of blanks.

'Where's he gone, the bastard?' his manager moaned. 'And he complains about his bloody sister...'

'He's in the car,' Madalena told them offhandedly, her sharp ears picking up the indomitable executive's remark.

The youngsters thanked their aunt and ran over to the Land Rover. Sure enough, their dad sat in the driver's seat, listening to the radio with his head resting on the window and his eyes closed. Jet knocked on the bonnet, and the occupant's eyes opened. He wound down the glass.

'What are you doing in here?' Kierney asked, perturbed. 'We didn't know where you'd gone.'

Jeff smiled. 'Good. That was my plan.'

'Michelle told me you have to collect Mum's ashes tomorrow or the day after,' his son's voice caught. 'Did you know that?'

The sad man nodded. 'Yep. I need to get back to them. Better than leaving her in the car while we have lunch, eh? Get in, guys.'

'No, Papá,' Kierney objected. 'Please come with us. People'll be wondering where we are.'

'So let 'em wonder. Whose party is this?'

'Mum's,' Jet retorted, his patience with the day wearing thin too.

The great man flashed his dark eyes. 'Yeah. And she's in here with me.'

'Is she?' his son snapped, searching the interior of the car. 'Where? I can't see her. Come on, Dad. Please?'

The top edge of the car window rose steadily until it had sealed, and the sullen pair watched their father remove the key from the ignition and open the door. The handsome celebrity stepped down to the ground from the running-plate, dropping the car keys into his trouser pocket.

'You drive a hard bargain,' he told his son, putting his arms around both children.

Gerry held out his hands towards the Diamonds in exasperation when he found them walking back to the guests. 'Where have you been? The officials are looking for you.'

Jeff didn't respond, simply steering his offspring round to the back of the building, in the direction his manager indicated.

'It's revolting,' Kierney started, once they were out of earshot.

'What's revolting?' Jet asked.

'The thought of having to carry Mamá's ashes. I hope the box is well sealed.'

The widower chuckled. 'Yeah. They put some greaseproof paper and a rubber band around it, like when Helen used to make jam.'

His daughter made a face. 'You're not supposed to be joking about this, please.'

'You don't remember when we had Granddad's ashes in the plane, do you?'

Neither child did. They had been very young when Jeff's father passed away.

'We took them to New York,' Kierney replied. 'I don't really remember but I know the story.'

'I remember odd bits here and there,' her brother added. 'We went to Queens, by a river and threw them in.'

Jeff chuckled at his son's childish response. 'We didn't *throw* them in! We scattered them on the breeze.'

'Whatever,' Jet shrugged. 'What are we going to do with Mum's?'

The widower tensed up at the question he had been doing his best to avoid. 'Don't know yet. Nothing for the moment.'

To the grieving husband's relief, the sullen pair were satisfied with this answer. The crematorium's manager emerged from his office when he saw the famous trio approaching, eager to shake the star's hand.

'My condolences, Mr Diamond,' he said with an appropriate amount of dour humility. 'My name's James Price.'

'Thank you. Jeff, please. Can I call you James? These are our kids, Ryan and Kierney.'

'Yes, Jeff. That would be fine,' the man confirmed, accepting the children's hands in turn. 'Very nice to meet you all. Were you happy with the service?'

The celebrity sniffed. 'As far as one can be happy with a funeral service, yes, thanks.'

'That's good. And did Mrs Hadley speak to you about receiving your late wife's remains?'

'Yes again,' the widower sighed, despising the man's use of the word "late" but not wishing to enter into an argument at this point. 'What's the plan?'

'Righty-oh. If you wouldn't mind stepping into the office... There are some formalities first. Can I offer you some tea or coffee?'

Indubitably, the exhausted man's brain echoed. There were always formalities.

'No, thanks,' Jeff answered on behalf of them all. 'We're going to be feasting in a few minutes, perish the thought.'

The three Diamonds sat obediently in a small meeting room, its functional plainness only enhanced by a vase of fresh flowers in the centre of the table.

James soon returned, clutching a folder of paperwork with Lynn's name on the top. The grieving husband pondered on the number of files bearing her name all over the place. What would happen to all this information people were collecting about his beautiful best friend? He felt embittered and full of sadness, fighting to hold back tears once more.

'This form is for the release of your late wife's remains,' the manager explained in an impassive, clinical tone.

'My wife,' Jeff corrected him this time. 'As far as I'm concerned, Lynn's still my wife and these guys' mother.'

'Of course, sir. I'm sorry.'

The songwriter waved his hand to accept the man's kind apology and began to read over the form. One thing was abundantly clear: no matter who one was in this life, how successful one became or how much wealth one amassed, life's progress was always charted via an array of forms.

Even in death. He checked the information entered into each box, all the while thinking, "So what?" An administrative inaccuracy at this stage in Lynn's documented history would hardly make a whole heap of difference.

The official reached forward and pointed to the empty boxes at the bottom of the form. 'Please print, sign and date when you're ready, Jeff.'

'Mr Price, how do we know what you give us is actually our mum?' Jet asked.

The superstar turned and gave his son an appreciative nod, while Kierney blanched.

'We take the utmost care, sir,' James insisted. 'When the service is over, the chamber is thoroughly cleaned and the deceased's remains are encased immediately. You can rest assured that your mother is well taken care of.'

Jeff groaned. 'Which is more than I was able to do last week.'

Kierney hugged her father as she saw tears welling up in his eyes again. 'Papá, stop.'

Sighing, The Australian Elvis twisted the centre joint of the ballpoint pen and printed his full name in the box, authorising the release form with the signature he must have flashed out several million times during his long career.

'That it?' he asked, dropping the pen down onto the page as if it had become too hot to hold.

His evil twin dared to wonder if the nineteen-year-old cricketing legend sitting next to him might be waiting for the least tactless opportunity to slot in a quip about

The Ashes, when somewhat unexpectedly, he felt his chest twitch. The sick joke had not been lost on the boy's mother either.

'Yes. Thank you,' the crematorium's manager answered. 'Ms Dyson Diamond's remains will be available for collection from ten tomorrow morning, but there's no rush. Any day next week would be fine.'

S'pose not, the bereaved husband mused, suddenly queasy and lightheaded.

The next moment the widower was gone, snatching the door open and running towards the edge of the car park to vomit into the flowerbed against the fence. Kierney and Jet stood in the doorway to witness their father's extreme physical reaction, the young man glancing back at his sister.

'Could we ring you tomorrow?' the young woman turned back to James Price. 'I don't think our dad's up to dealing with this now. Sorry.'

James looked on unperturbed while the children debated whether to go to their father's aid, a benign smile giving nothing away. They met him in the doorway, his face as white as a sheet.

'It's OK, Dad. Let's go. All sorted.'

Jeff nodded his thanks and reached forward to shake Price's hand. Grasping his gorgeous daughter's arm as they walked back to the car park, the residue of bile and tar still stung the lining of his throat while the pressure of unshed tears banked up behind his eyes.

'You know it's mostly coffin in the ashes anyway,' he said, as much to convince himself.

'Logical,' Jet replied. 'It's still disgusting though, when you think about it, what's just happened to Mum. You know...'

Their dad sighed. 'Yeah. I do know.'

'Are you feeling any better?' Kierney asked, noticing some colour returning to her dad's cheeks and forehead.

'It's all relative, but yeah. I guess so,' he answered, hugging her tightly. 'You're fantastic, you two. Thanks for helping me out so much, and that song was perfect... If a little close to the bone.'

The car park's population had dwindled by the time the Diamonds reached it. Lynn's parents, along with Anna and Brandon, had waited to travel together, and Gerry and Fiona too, but most of the others had gone ahead to the restaurant. Including Madalena, it appeared.

'Bloody hell, guys. I don't want to go to lunch,' Jet moaned.

'Me neither,' his sister agreed. 'Why do people have a slap-up meal after a funeral? It's like we're going to celebrate something. Cheers! Long live Mamá!'

Jeff listened to the youngsters' conversation and couldn't help but concur. From the rear-view mirror, he could see his gorgeous gipsy girl was crying again, overcome with having to make light of the situation.

'I'm with you, guys,' he smiled. 'Where shall we go? Home?'

His daughter sighed. 'We can't, can we? Are you serious?'

'No, we can't,' the widower replied. 'But it's a nice thought. Let's go and chit-chat with everyone for a couple of hours and then we'll go home and get stoned.'

'Yes!' Jet hissed, making a fist and shaking it in victory. 'That's the best thing you've said for ages.'

Kierney remained serious though. 'Papá, I loved what you said in there, to Mamá. Everybody else talked *about* her, but you talked *to* her. It was fantastic.'

'Thanks, *pequeñita*. Glad you liked it. I just said what came into my head at the time. Your song's amazing too. You kept that one quiet. I hope you'll do it again next week.'

'We've got a better one for next week,' his daughter let on. 'It's less sad. Much better for a memorial service than a funeral.'

'Cool,' the songwriter accepted her word without dispute. 'I've got my work cut out to come up with something as good.'

'It's not a competition, you know,' the cricketer laughed.

The driver flashed a punch with his left fist and caught his son on the point of his elbow, an act that hurt them both more than it should have.

'Hey!' Jet yelped, before laughing when he saw his dad shaking the pain out of his tingling hand. 'Serves you right!'

'Where are we going?' the showman snapped to attention. 'Where's this bloody pub Michelle's got us going to against our better judgement?'

Jet studied the map, peering out of the window for road names. 'Are we on Keilor Road?'

'Yep. Think so.'

His son looked back at the street directory. 'Well, we're nearly there in that case,' he chuckled, pointing to their right about fifty metres. 'Hey, presto!'

'Lincolnshire Arms,' Kierney read the sign. 'It doesn't even look open.'

'That's probably why Michelle chose it,' their father remarked. 'Who cares? It'll be fine for what we need.'

The Diamonds recognised the out-of-place collection of prestige vehicles in the outer-suburban car park, and Jeff swung the heavy monster into a space next to Bart Dysons' Jaguar.

'What's Junior driving?' Jet asked, scanning along the row of cars.

'I don't think they're staying for lunch,' the widower remembered. 'He has to fly to Perth this afternoon for the Eagles' match tomorrow, and the kids were going back to Julie's. She's not very comfortable around us anymore either, which is hardly surprising.'

Obliged to play host at this most uncelebratory meal, the grieving celebrity requested his children sit with their grandparents over lunch. He found Madalena, judging it best to rescue his friends from her questionable social skills.

He needn't have worried however, since she was being unusually well-behaved and sat listening to the others talking about subjects to which she had no hope of relating.

'Where've you guys been?' she whispered.

Jeff picked a set of cutlery and a paper napkin out of the *faux* pale on the table and stretched it out over his lap. He leant back on a wobbly chair and sneaked a look across to make sure the kids were alright.

The black knight felt his chest twitch and exhaled through his nostrils. His beautiful best ghost was back, thank Christ. His frightening preoccupation that her funeral might signal the end of these sublime bites of communication was unfounded. Relief surged through his veins, and his head swam with a burst of uncontrollable emotion.

At a loss for words after the funeral service, Don Jenner held a bottle of red wine up to offer his friend a drink. Jeff nodded in gratitude, lifting his glass and watching as it filled with the deep, blood-coloured Cabernet Sauvignon. Before putting it to his lips, he cleared his throat and clinked another, empty glass with his fork to attract everyone's attention.

Every eye in the room fixed on him, including those belonging to the staff, to a one overawed by the gaggle of *glitterati* who had descended on their humble, rundown pub.

'I'd just like to say thanks to all of you for coming and being part of this awful day. I know we'd far rather have been doing other things, but I really appreciate you being here and everything you've done for me and the kids since last Friday. We have so many amazing friends and we value that very highly. I'd say I look forward to returning the favour, but I don't.'

The polite audience laughed at the great man's odd sense of humour.

'I'd especially like to thank Michelle and Cathy for organising today, and to Kiley for the unbelievable *Adagio* you heard as we came into the chapel earlier. Also to Kierney and Jet for the song written for their mamá, which I certainly hadn't heard before.'

The guests at the table all put down their glasses and clapped with tentative enthusiasm before Jeff continued. 'Lastly, I'd like to thank you on behalf of the most beautiful woman who ever lived, and who's sitting right here at this very moment, directing my every move...'

He patted the muscle covering his heart, to which Gerry responded by rolling his eyes and winding his finger in circles next to his right temple. The seasoned orator's hand directed an idle threat at his old mate, and everyone smiled in relief.

'Most of you know already that we're having a memorial service next Saturday afternoon, with a reception at the Hyatt afterwards. I hope you'll all be there. The concert's in the Sidney Myer Music Bowl, which'll be hard for many of us because of all the times we played there together, but we're extremely fortunate it was available to use at short notice.'

With everyone clapping again, Jeff cleared his throat, preparing to sign off. 'Lynn was such an important part of our lives... and that's a bloody understatement and a half... but you guys need to know you were all really important to her too. She had huge capacity to love, and you should know she loved everyone in this room very much. Thank you again for coming. Let's eat and drink and say nothing more about funerals, please.'

Nods and quiet mutterings of agreement were heard from around the table. Marianna Dyson then picked up her fork and tapped her tumbler of water to bring the table to order again.

'Ladies and gentlemen, I'm sure you'd like to join Bart and me in thanking Jeff for his kind words. And Lynn, if you can hear me, darling...' the dowager sniffed back the inevitable tears, which started everyone else off too. 'We know there's a long road ahead, but we wish Jeff, Jet and Kierney all the best as they resume normal life. Let's toast the wonderful Lynn.'

Glasses were raised high, and voices were united in chanting, 'The wonderful Lynn.'

The grieving son-in-law lifted his glass for a second time in response to the toast, and the staff took this as their cue to serve the meal without further delay. As requested, conversations remained light-hearted; stories of people's summer holidays were exchanged, along with tour dates from the various musicians around the table, and the many upcoming sporting fixtures.

After they had finished their main courses, the reluctant host tapped his sister on the shoulder. 'Ciggie?' he suggested.

Madalena nodded keenly, and the dark-haired pair left the table. No-one followed, which was another blessing. Outside in the late afternoon humidity, the disenchanted superstar leant on the wall and blew a long plume of smoke into the air.

'Jesus fucking Christ,' he moaned. 'What a day! How're you going? Sorry to leave you earlier. I had to escape for a while.'

'That's OK, *chico*. Kiley's nice. She's the violin player, isn't she? I seen her on your shows.'

'Yeah. That's right. Although she's too famous for our shows these days. She's way too expensive! We've been using Kizzy's friend, Piraea Loudon.'

'The Chinese one?'

'She's not Chinese,' the tired man corrected. 'She's half Irish and half Malay Singaporean.'

Madalena shrugged. 'Well, she looks Chinese.'

'Whatever. She's very talented.'

It hadn't taken long for the gloss to come off their discourse. Jeff lit two more cigarettes, enjoying the brief moment of solitude.

'Lena,' he began again, fixing his sister with a stare. 'I'd like you to go home tonight, if you don't mind.'

The woman became defensive. 'Why? What've I done?'

'Nothing,' her brother replied, walking towards her and putting a hand on her shoulder. 'I'd like to have some time alone with the kids. You can come down again next week if you want to go to the memorial. I'd love you to be there, but I just can't cope with us right now.'

'Has Lynn told you to get rid of me?' the bitter woman chided, repeating Gerry's prior gesture.

Jeff glowered. 'No. What are you talking about?'

'Well, you was 'appy to 'ave me 'ere yesterd'y and now you're not,' his sister said, giving his chest an impudent poke. 'Or do the kids want me to go?'

'No, they don't,' he confirmed. '*I'm* asking you to go, and then come back. It'll help us, and you can get back to normal for a few days.'

'But I like it 'ere,' Madalena protested. 'I'll be 'elpful, I promise. I'll do things around the flat. Cleanin' and washin' and stuff. Please, *chico*?'

Jeff looked into her pleading eyes and recognised himself from thirty years ago. His sister didn't have much of a life in Sydney. He had bought her a modest apartment and provided her with a regular allowance to keep her off the streets, but he knew she wasn't particularly fulfilled. He capitulated, unable to conquer the effects of his own deep-seated sense of injustice.

'Alright. Stay, if you like. But please try and think of the rest of us as well as yourself. And tonight, it'd be good if you can go to the pictures or something, so we can have the apartment to ourselves for a few hours after...'

'We're not allowed to say the "F-word",' Madalena interrupted, cackling. 'You said it yerself!'

Jeff smirked and raised his voice. 'You're correct. I did. Fucking funeral, eh?'

Before the woman could respond, Gerry came into view from around the corner, lighting up a cigarette of his own.

'Here you are,' he said, patting Madalena on the wrist. 'Are you looking after him, Mad Dog?'

'Mad Dog?' his client repeated. 'Since when've you called my sister a mad dog? And since when did you start smoking again?'

Gerry put his arm around the sultry Sydneysider's shoulders and kissed her cheek. 'Ah, you can blame your beautiful wife for this,' he answered, waving the cigarette around. 'And as for your sister...We have an understanding, don't we? A love-hate relationship.'

'Some musical Jac and Tammy know,' Madalena recalled an exchange from several years earlier. 'Man o' somethin'.'

'"Man of La Mancha"? Did they liken you to Dulcinea?'

His sister's expression turned vacant, the questions having become too hard.

Gerry came to her rescue. 'Indeed. "Hard-hearted harlot," I believe, is the phrase they used.'

'Cool! That's actually very good,' Jeff chuckled. 'Very accurate.'

'¡Ai!' Madalena screeched. 'How come everyone knows more than me?'

The handsome intellectual stubbed out his cigarette on the wall and tossed the butt into a nearby bin, his head cocked towards the door leading back into the pub. The others followed, as people always did.

'I'll play you the track when we get home.'

'Oh! So I'm allowed to come 'ome with ya now?' his sister teased.

'Yes. Jesus Christ! Forget I ever mentioned it. You win, Mad Dog. Let's go back in.'

When the smokers returned to their table, a bowl of sticky date pudding had been deposited in front of the host's vacated chair, ice cream melting fast. He picked the dessert up and sent it down the table towards his gluttonous son, who accepted a second serving eagerly. The bereaved star poured himself a cup of coffee and swigged down the last of his wine.

From the other end of the long table, Bart wandered across and loomed over his son-in-law's shoulder, extending his right hand. 'We're going to head off now.'

Jeff got to his feet again to embrace the upright Olympian, overtaken by a renewed flood of emotion. 'Thank you, sir,' he croaked. 'Thanks very much for your support, and for the fitting tribute you gave Lynn.'

Bart freed himself from the widower's grip, and the two men joined Marianna, Anna and Brandon at the other end of the table to complete their farewells.

'We'll see you sometime tomorrow, Jeff,' Lynn's mother stated, seeing how distressed he was, then transferring her attention to his children. 'And you two, I hope.'

Kierney nodded, hugging the tall couple. 'We'll be there, Grandma.'

Jet shook his grandpa's hand and reached his arms around Marianna. The occasion suddenly all too much for the young man, he began to cry in wild, unrestrained sobs.

The sympathetic father put an arm around the teenager's neck, pushing his head down towards his chest and unleashing a series of light punches to his chin and stomach. Long part of his paternal repertoire, it was a move guaranteed to make the lad want to fight back. It worked, the smile returning to his face.

Observing the poignant scene, Anna threw her arms around the brother-in-law whom she had idolised since she was in primary school. She knew how happy he had made her sister and could only guess how dejected he must be feeling now.

'Oh, Jeff, I hope you feel better soon. Come over tomorrow and relax with us, away from everything. It'll do you all good.'

'I know, Anns,' the forty-three-year-old sniffed. 'It will. We'll be there around lunchtime. I'm keen to hear how things are going over there in the lab' too.'

'Don't think about us right now,' Brandon advised the generous venture capitalist. 'We'll still be the same in a few months, whenever you're ready to come visit. Our door's always open. You're welcome anytime.'

'Cheers, mate,' the benefactor thanked the reserved Canadian. 'We'll see.'

The Dysons filed out of the hotel, obliging a few brave members of staff with autographs. They left in haste for the ring road and sped back to Benloch. Jeff gazed around, guessing everyone else was waiting for his next weighty pronouncement.

'You can all go now,' he joked, raising his hands in the air. 'Class dismissed.'

The remaining guests laughed, scrambling to their feet and gathering their belongings. One by one, they kissed and hugged the Diamonds in the car park, while Jeff inched towards the Land Rover, impatient to be on the road.

The sun hung low in the sky as they drove westwards back to the freeway, and the driver put on his sunglasses to cut the glare.

'You look great, Papá,' Kierney remarked. 'You're going to be OK. It went as well as expected today, didn't it?'

A tear trickled down from behind the dark lens covering her father's left eye. Back in the driving seat, at least for the time being, Jeff hid from the world and chose not to respond to his daughter's heartfelt comments. Beside him, his son leafed aimlessly through the street directory, and in the rear-view mirror, he glimpsed his sister falling asleep after a few too many drinks.

Kierney watched the scenery whizz backwards at a hundred kilometres per hour, or a good deal faster, truth be told. She pondered the future for their tight-knit family now the funeral was over.

Her brother would want to fly back to the UK soon, and she needed to decide whether to postpone her own degree course. Having already missed Orientation Week at Sydney University, she was seriously considering taking a year out to spend time with her beloved papá. Her education was important, for sure, but in the short term, his recovery was more so.

The pretty teenager knew the man she had adored all her life had no desire to be on his own anymore. Approaching his mid-forties, he was no longer the loner he had been in his teens. Could he really feel her mother with him? Was it possible for Lynn to communicate with him through his "JL" tattoo? Kierney doubted this very much, but if it made her father happier, then it was fine by her. It was reassuring to picture her parents still together on some level, even if this notion was a bit disturbing.

The young woman's mind turned back to her mother's ashes, soon to become their property. A shiver ran down her spine. What would her father decide to do with them? Was he planning to take them to Benloch to be scattered somewhere on the Dysons' farm? Or perhaps to Escondido and the bay off their private beach? Or would they occupy pride of place in their city penthouse, on the bookcase or in the pantry alongside the cereal and the tins of baked beans?

Gross, she thought. *Change the subject.* 'Papá?'

'*¿Sí, gorgeousita?*'

'I brought you a present from the house. It's in the console beside you, stuck on the lid. Please may I show it to you?'

'Sure. Is it dangerous?'

'No!' his daughter giggled. 'Why would it be dangerous?'

'I mean to look at while I'm driving.'

'Oh,' she said, undoing her seatbelt and crouching forward to open the box between the two front seats.

Peeling an object off the underside of the lid, Kierney reached over her dad's left arm to affix it to the centre of the steering wheel. The car's horn blasted, waking Jet and making both father and daughter jump out of their skins.

The people travelling in the lane to their left looked across in dismay at the sudden noise but were unable to see inside the vehicle, thanks to the darkened windows.

'Shit!' the embarrassed teenager exclaimed. 'Sorry, Papá. I didn't know it would be so sensitive.'

Jeff glanced down at the yellow, rectangular object which was now stuck to the Discovery's steering wheel. He recognised it as a fridge magnet that had lived on the edge of Lynn's computer monitor in the office. It showed a cartoon of a woman's smiling face, with red lipstick and a hairstyle reminiscent of a nineteen-fifties secretary. The caption read, "It's been lovely, but I have to scream now."

Hearing Jet snigger when he caught sight of the cartoon, their dad shook his head and grinned. '*Excelente*,' he said. 'That's perfect for today. What made you bring it?'

Kierney smiled. 'I saw it on Wednesday and remembered all the times when Mamá'd get off the phone after a really long call and go, "Argh!" like she always did. All sweetness and light on the phone, then turning into an angry monster after it was over. That's how we feel now, isn't it?'

'Too right!' her brother agreed.

Jeff nodded, thankful not only for the pleasant distraction but also for the fact that his clueless sister was sleeping through it all and therefore wouldn't require a line-by-line explanation of the family's special memories.

'Bloody oath, *pequeñita*,' he confirmed, frustrated fingers flicking the magnet's corner. 'So does this mean I can behave abominably tonight with my new "Get out of jail free" card?'

'Oh, no!' his son warned. 'Absolutely not.'

'OK, boss. Whatever you say.'

The songwriter turned the volume up on the compact disc playing in the car's music system and focussed back on the road. They drove the last ten kilometres without speaking, letting the West Coast rock tunes release some pressure from their solemn circumstance .

Madalena slept on. *Be grateful for small mercies*, he vowed again.

A LIFE TO REMEMBER

True to her word, Madalena left the apartment to see a movie at seven-thirty that evening, leaving Jeff and the children alone. The father had asked the teenagers to reprise their "F-word" ballad again for him, and they took advantage of the privacy to vent their grief yet again.

He followed this with a request for the more positive song Kierney had alluded to on the way home, which the pair rattled off without a moment's hesitation.

'That's really great,' the chart-topper told them, clapping and whistling as the piano strains faded. 'Perfect for next week. I'm under pressure now.'

'Why?' his son asked. 'Just use the one you gave Mum for your anniversary, "The Rest Will Be History". That's a fantastic song, and no-one's heard it yet. They'll think you wrote it 'specially for the event.'

'Maybe,' the musician shook his head, opening the top drawer of the filing cabinet. 'Haven't decided yet.'

The teenagers exchanged enthusiastic glances when they saw their dad's hands emerge clutching the hugely anticipated plastic bag.

'Why don't you know?' Kierney asked, her gaze fixed on the cannabis leaves which had made their way to the coffee table. 'Is this why you asked Auntie Lena to go out? So she didn't blab to anyone about us smoking?'

Her father winked. 'Bingo, *bambina mía*. Gerry can keep his mouth shut, but Lena... *Absoluement pas*.'

'So why don't you know about the song?' came the unanswered question a second time.

Jeff sighed. 'It's too cheerful, I think. I won't feel right. There's another one I'm working on that's more appropriate, but I'm going to have to get someone else to sing. I'm only going on stage to say a few words of thanks.'

Three cigarette papers were laid out on the coffee table, and the anxious man was busy spreading a layer of young leaves across the centre of each. His children were mesmerised, grateful to be included in something so private and illicit.

'Why not?' Kierney asked yet again. 'You wouldn't go to pieces. You've sung in an emotional state before, heaps of times. And people would understand anyway.'

'Mamá doesn't want me to sing,' he responded, rubbing his chest.

'Oh, for God's sake, Dad!' his son exclaimed. 'What's with all this talking tattoo rubbish? You can't really hear her, can you?'

His brain full of fond memories, the widower licked the side of each cigarette paper in turn and twisted them in his fingers. Lynn had always been aroused by this simple act, but she was no longer here to reap the benefit. And because she wasn't turned on, neither was he. He thought carefully about how he would reply to Jet's questions.

'Mate, of course I can't hear her. In terms of words, I mean. But I am convinced she's sending messages through here into my soul.'

The sportsman scoffed. 'You're insane.'

'Yeah. Most probably,' Jeff nodded, laying the three joints side-by-side on the coffee table.

Kierney objected. 'What the hell, Jetto? If it makes it easier to get through each day, what difference does it make?'

The nineteen-year-old shrugged, much more interested in what he was about to be offered. 'Are we going to light these or what?'

Jeff got to his feet and walked towards the kitchen.

'Oh,' Kierney jumped, as if snapped out of a dream. 'We need sweet coffee and water. Sorry, Papá. I'll do it.'

'No, baby. Sit down. You already do too much for us blokes. I'll do it. Put some music on instead.'

The siblings flipped through the apartment's limited CD collection, unable to find anything which took their fancy. Kierney disappeared to her bedroom and returned with one of their father's compilation albums, monster hits from the early years.

'He won't let you play that,' Jet sneered. 'It'll have to be something more bluesy or classical.'

The young woman ignored him and started the disc playing. They heard a loud groan from the kitchen, but no instruction to turn it off. Her brother stuck his nose into the bag of marijuana leaves, almost passing out with the strength of their scent.

Kierney laughed at the idiot. 'Told you so. It's good.'

Unaware of the friction between the pair, Jeff placed three mugs of steaming, sugary coffee on the table and sat down. The children knelt at his feet while he distributed the roll-ups, receiving pats on their heads for their dog-like obedience. Jet began to lick the end of his cigarette, making his dad laugh.

'You clowns! D'you know what that looks like, mate?' he teased.

Blushing, the youngster's mind followed his father's to precisely the same image, and the older man cuffed his scalp. Their third *amiga* didn't understand the connotation, and neither comedian was game enough to explain it. At least not until the drug had chased away a few more inhibitions...

Still the leader hung on to the lighter, watching his children almost salivating with expectation.

'Are we going to light the effing things?' the cricketer pleaded. 'Or do we just sit and gawk at them all night?'

'Drink your coffee first, and then we'll light them.'

'We have to have a mouthful of water when we take our first puff,' the knowledgeable novice informed her brother.

'Is that so? Have you had private tuition or something?'

'Yes, I have,' she nodded, seeing her dad's supportive smile.

'Right. Hey, I'm so glad Auntie Lena's not here,' the young man admitted. 'She wouldn't have been able to wait and savour the experience.'

'Can you?' Kierney giggled.

Jet shoved his sister hard enough that she rocked on her haunches. 'Shut up.'

'OK, *hijos míos*,' the Master of Ceremonies announced, flipping the lid off his lighter and slamming his empty mug down on to the coffee table's glass top. '*Vamanos*.'

The youngsters' joints were lit in sequence, and their dad watched both take a gulp from their glasses and wait for the smoke to wash through their mouths. He saw their eyes widen and then squint closed as the gentle heat hit their brains, rolling his shoulders as he imagined the sensation running into every grief-stricken crevice. The vicarious pleasure went some way to filling the gargantuan void, to his great relief.

Jeff lit his own and lived the experience for himself, all the while keeping an eye on his offspring. 'To Mamá,' he toasted, raising his water glass to eye level and taking another long drag. 'We love you, Lynn, and we wish you were here.'

'To Mamá,' the kids chanted in response. 'We love you and wish you were here.'

The 'seventies sounds of Jeff Diamond and his band filled the penthouse lounge room with a concert from a bygone era, and they all sang along *con gusto*. Within minutes, their moods had mellowed, indolence taking over; Kierney and her papá taking up a couch each and her brother lying flat out on the rug between the television and the coffee table.

'This is a great end to a shit day,' Jet announced, balancing a glass of water on his chest while taking deep breaths in and out. 'Don't you agree?'

'Mmm,' Kierney nodded. 'I love you guys. I really love you.'

Jeff flicked his shoes off and let them clatter onto the floorboards, chuckling half-heartedly. 'Ask me in half an hour.'

'If you love us?' his daughter joked.

'No,' he whined. 'I know I love you. I just don't know whether this is a great end to a shit day yet.'

Kierney shifted her weight so that she could see both men. 'When do you think we'll feel normal again?'

'What's normal?' the Cambridge undergraduate added.

'Happy again. You know, resolved.'

Jeff groaned. 'Change the subject, will you?'

Jet dissolved into a fit of giggles as his water glass slipped slowly off his chest. He caught it before it fell, amusing himself still further. While the others looked on in bewilderment, he rolled up to a sitting position, then fell forward onto his heels. Now laughing hard, he rocked back and forth to regain his balance.

'Hey!' he yelped, springing up and lunging for his father's stomach. 'Dad, get up. Let's play Trivial Pursuit or something.'

Jeff fended the brute off. 'Fuck off. Why?'

'Because you want to change the subject, and we're not capable of starting our own conversations without talking about Mum.'

'True enough,' the older man agreed, swinging his feet onto the floor. 'I'll get some beer.'

Kierney stretched out on the couch, enjoying her calm state of mind and slowly detaching from the sadness around her. The atmosphere had gone from fraught to comfortable, largely because the trio was so well in tune with one another. Jet was right. This evening would have been difficult if Madalena had stayed with them.

'I've had an idea,' Jeff declared, returning from the kitchen with three cold bottles.

The youngsters gaped expectantly, delighted with this apparent mood-swing.

'We're squillionaires and we're going to play Monopoly until we're broke,' he explained. 'But we can't just give it all away. We have to construct a whole series of bad business deals, and the first one to skint wins.'

Kierney moaned. 'I have no clue how to play Monopoly to get rich even...'

'Good,' her brother chuckled. 'You already have the advantage.'

'I'll help you, *pequeñita*,' the teacher reassured her, lifting slim legs encased in black leggings until he could sit down on the cushion underneath. 'Are you feeling better?'

'Yes, I am actually. Are you?'

Jeff squeezed her shimmering shins. 'Getting there, thanks. You don't need as much stimulation as I do.'

''Cause she's only got a small brain,' the blond teenager teased.

'At least mine's in my head, you bastard.'

Their father grinned. 'Now, now! Let's all stay friends.'

Jet set the board game up on the coffee table, and they began to play, laughing at the piles of fake cash lined up next to each player's feet. Jeff took his job as banker seriously, charging vast percentages of interest on an irregular but frequent basis.

'We'll be broke without having done a single deal at this rate,' his son complained. 'Come on, Dad. Give us a bloody break.'

'You're getting poorer though, aren't you? I'm gearing up to buy a small but corrupt island nation and then be required to procure Russian fighter jets on the black market. Planes that can't fly so I can claim a tax refund for my defence budget.'

'Papá, that's not fair. None of those things even exist on the Monopoly board,' his daughter whined. 'Don't make the rules up as you're going along.'

The empath put his hand on the young woman's head and ruffled her hair. 'We need another round,' he suggested, sensing their good humour already fading. 'You must've smoked yours too shallow, angel.'

'Yeah, cool. Can I roll them, please?' she volunteered, jumping up. 'I've never done it before. I don't know how much to put in.'

'Sure. Make mine a big one.'

'Mine too,' her brother chuckled. 'Join two papers together, like a cigar.'

'Hmm...' Jeff mused. 'A cigar'd be very nice, come to mention it. With another ancient bottle of wine later. The evening's getting better.'

The trio played, smoked, drank, laughed and cried their way through to midnight. They gave up on the reverse Monopoly once it was clear that no-one was likely to be bankrupted before dawn, yet both children had unwittingly learnt a fair amount about business. They had bonded further to boot, this latest surreptitious exercise from Professor Diamond's brand new master plan declared a success.

Shortly after pulling the cork on a dusty Pinot Noir and unwrapping a couple of stocky Cubans, the lift bell sounded to signify the return of Auntie Lena. The threesome stared at each other in mock horror before once again collapsing in uninhibited laughter.

'Good movie?' Jeff asked, unable to wipe the smirk off his face.

'Yeah,' Madalena replied. 'What the 'ell's been 'appenin' 'ere? You lot are stoned or pissed or both.'

Kierney giggled at the accusation. 'We are, and we lost heaps of funny money.'

'What funny money? Cigars too!' their guest exclaimed, seeing the empty metal tubes on the coffee table. 'Can I 'ave one?'

'Please?' Jet prompted his aunt, making his father laugh at the impudence thoroughly deserved.

'Mate, respect your elders,' he jeered. 'Please?'

The chivalrous sportsman rose to his feet. 'Auntie Lena, would you like me to get you a glass of wine and a cigar?'

'Jesus! You guys are off your bloody trolleys,' Madalena declared, annoyed at having missed the party. 'Yes, please.'

Their visitor remained on her best behaviour, within the bounds of her capability, for the next thirty minutes or so. Jeff began to count Kierney's yawns, the teenager struggling to stay awake after far more substance abuse than was good for her. It left him feeling particularly guilty.

'Kizzy, why don't you go to bed? You're knackered.'

The young woman crawled over to her father on all fours and put her head on his knee like an affectionate puppy. He stroked her hair fondly, and she began to cry again.

'Come on, baby. You're so tired. I'll come with you.'

Kierney lifted her eyes and saw her dad's smiling face. She nodded and stood up, reaching out for his hands. He grabbed hold, and she attempted to lever him out of the couch with a series of jerking movements.

'Goodnight, Auntie Lena,' she said, kissing the confused woman on the cheek through a cloud of cigar smoke. 'Goodnight, bro'.'

Jet waved to his sister from his position on the floor. 'Night, sis'. Sleep well.'

The widower accompanied his daughter back to her bedroom. He sat on her bed while she got ready, leafing through some of the manuscript paper next to her keyboard. Finding the song his thoughtful children had played at Lynn's funeral, he cried as he read the lyric and was reminded of their heartfelt performance. He leant his head against the wall and rested his eyes.

After a while, he felt the mattress dip when Kierney climbed onto the bed beside her father. His arms closed in around her like lobster pincers. Cuddling in against his warm body, the years melted away.

'Are you going to tell me a story?'

'Sure, *pequeñita*. Which story would you like?'

'The one about when I was born, if it's not too painful to tell.'

The showman sighed heavily. 'It is very painful to tell, but that's OK. That's just how life's going to be for a while.'

The youngest Diamond listened to soothing commentary about her arrival into the world, as told by the man who loved her the most. With the marijuana's mellowing effects wearing off, she found her thoughts drifting to her mamá and how tragic their situation was. She didn't let on, for fear of upsetting her papá, who was busy reconstructing precious moments for mutual benefit.

He described the time when he had been writing the songs for "Laura's Light" and "The Boy Who Would Be King" in parallel, telling her how different the couple's two gems had always been. Fascinated to hear about herself and her brother from another perspective, Kierney lost herself in the rich, nostalgic language.

'Are you asleep?' the storyteller asked, sensing the rhythm of her breathing change.

The teenager murmured and lifted her head.

'Get some sleep,' he urged. 'We'll head off to Benloch in the morning and blow the cobwebs away. Thanks heaps for your help today. I love you so much.'

His exhausted daughter climbed under the sheet after kissing him goodnight. 'I love you too, Papá,' she said, squeezing the two rings on his left hand. 'And you, Mamá. I hope you're OK.'

The lonely husband turned off the bedside lamp, closed the door and paced back towards the lounge room. On his way, he paused outside the master bedroom and peered in. There was no sensation in his chest to encourage him inside, so he chose to walk on by and find the others. Jet was attempting to give Madalena a piano lesson, the concoction of drugs having rendered him more patient than usual.

Jeff approached the piano stool and put a hand on each of their backs. 'Who's for more weed?' he asked. 'I didn't want Kizzy to have another one. Two's too many for her. I feel bad encouraging her.'

The lad turned his head while his pupil continued to thump out a simple tune. 'She's alright. I'm not going to have any more though either. I'm hitting the sack soon.'

'Very sensible, mate. You're a better man than I.'

'Can I ask you a question though, please?'

'Anything.'

'What are we going to do with Mum's ashes?' he ventured. 'Did you want me to pick them up on Monday? We don't want you to have to do it.'

Poor bloke, Jeff thought. This dilemma had obviously been playing on his mind for a while, not wanting to upset his sister. He clearly couldn't turn in without resolving it.

'Mate, I'm sorry. Don't stress about it. I'll probably ask Gerry to organise for them to be delivered here next week sometime. We can talk about where what's left of your mum's perfect body takes up residence this weekend, if you like. I have no idea where she belongs, so happy to hear your thoughts.'

'¡Ai!' Madalena whined. 'It's 'orrible to think there's bits of a dead person in a box in the 'ouse.'

'Thanks, Auntie Lena,' Jet said, his eyes widening. 'We don't need reminding.'

The peacemaker raised his hands. 'Enough. Pour some more wine, please, Lena, and I'll get us rolling.'

Their visitor left the piano and refilled three glasses while Jeff made up two more spliffs. The virtuous teenager sat down on the floor again, debating whether to finish his wine or share it between the others' glasses.

'What's your best memory of Lynn?' Madalena asked outright, looking from one man to the other.

'Jesus!' her brother exclaimed. 'Where did that come from?'

'Mine's winning the three-legged race with her at the MA juniors' sports day,' Jet responded without hesitation. 'When we nearly fell over about six times and were laughing so hard we could hardly run.'

His dad smiled. He hadn't been around to witness this spectacle, but his mind painted a picture he liked. It didn't mean anything to his sister, who was eager to move on.

'What's yours, *chico*? Pick one.'

The grieving husband shook his head, dragging on his joint and curling the smoke around through his nose and mouth. 'So many,' he sighed. 'So, so many... Probably the blowjob she gave me in the shower just before you were born, Jetto. Or the tennis skirt episode? That's one for you to learn from, mate.'

'What do you mean, one for me to learn from?'

'It was only the second night we'd spent together, and we very nearly didn't spend it together,' Jeff recalled, his heart rate accelerating as the inexcusable act reconstituted itself in his mind.

'Oh, yeah?' Madalena urged.

'Yeah. That's what I mean about something to learn,' he nodded, becoming serious. 'I'd had way too much to drink and thought I was invincible. God's gift, as they say... We got back to Lynn's room at Admin, and I pinned her to the wall. Literally. She couldn't move. Of course I didn't intend it at the time, but I was about to rape the girl of my dreams.'

Jet whistled, both shocked and spellbound. He had never heard this story before and was surprised by his father's lingering shame after so long. Clearly, the near-miss hadn't spelled disaster for their relationship, but he sensed a definite dose of impending doom from the emotional *raconteur*.

'Jeez, Dad. That's huge. This means I might never have existed.'

The former tearaway chuckled. 'I guess it does, mate. I never thought about it that way before. If that night had ended differently, there'd have been no "JL" tattoo, no "Together, Forever, Wherever" and...' his voice cracked, and the tears rolled down from his eyes, '...no hotel lobby shooting. Anyway... I was impossible to stop. Only one thing on my mind, y'know. And I must've been pretty aggressive 'cause your mum had to push me off, yelling at me over and over to bring me to my senses. It took me a long time to get the message, and when I finally did, it knocked me for six. I thought she was going to kick me out and never want to see me again.'

'God! That *was* serious. What did you do?'

Noticing Madalena seemed quite nonplussed by this story, Jeff exhaled through pursed lips. 'Whoa... So that's the special memory, right there. Lynn disappeared while I wallowed in my drunken self-pity. Then after a while, she called me into the bedroom. I remember it as clear as anything, the hot minx! She'd changed into her oh-so-short tennis skirt, and her hair was loose over her... Well, you can guess.'

The younger man gave an embarrassed laugh. 'Yes, OK. I get the picture.'

'My mind was all over the place, and I was crawling across the bloody floor, mate. Tongue dragging along the carpet, hard as a rock and ready to blow.'

'You even speak like you're singing a song,' Madalena chimed in, suddenly agog.

'It was agonisingly humiliating,' the singer continued, flicking his sister a subtle acknowledgement. 'But we made love in complete silence afterwards. It was magic. Pure magic.'

'So what's the blowjob story, but?' their guest blurted out.

Trust Madalena to spoil any tender moment! Jeff sighed, staring into space while he re-grouped. He was anxious to hold on to the happy memories he had conjured up for himself and his son.

'This bloke's induction.'

'Oh, for fuck's sake, Dad!' Jet cried out. 'Now who's the humiliator? Do you mind?'

'Not at all. Do you?' his father sniffed, the drug beginning to have the desired effect.

The former street girl was on the edge of her seat in anticipation now. This was her world; her stock in trade. This was Research and Development for her.

'What 'appened then? What's induction?'

Jeff cocked his handsome head, tossing his mane of thick dark hair. 'You remember I nearly missed his guy being born altogether?'

The former prostitute shook her head. 'Nah. Tell me, but. I wanna hear the blowjob bit.'

Her brother continued, taking a huge gulp of wine. 'When I finally got to the hospital, Lynn'd already been in labour for a couple of hours. I had a major fucking headache, what with coming off the plane and rushing through traffic from the airport. Wound up like a bloody spring, so Lynn suggested I have a shower and take some painkillers.'

'So far so good,' Jet chuckled, knowing this tale very well indeed.

'Then at the last minute, Lynn decided she was going to come into the bathroom with me.'

'Hmm...' the young man mumbled. 'Suddenly not so good.'

The widower laughed. 'Shut up, you. Drink your wine and hold your tongue.'

Madalena smiled, content with the relaxed ambiance that had settled in the Diamonds' apartment at last. 'Get on with the story, *chico*.'

'Well... To spare Jet the embarrassment, one thing led to another, and there we were enjoying ourselves, with Lynn having contractions every few minutes. It was amazingly scary but such an unbelievable turn-on at the same time. I can still remember how good it made me feel. Bloody selfish, now I look back on it, but she always knows exactly what gets me going.'

' Jesus, old man!' the sportsman shouted. 'Didn't you know you shouldn't do that sort of thing in front of a minor?'

'You're not a minor,' the visitor disputed.

'He was then! Less than... Listen and learn, boy,' Jeff teased, beginning to cry again as the memory triggered a deep longing.

Seeing his father descend into grief again, the youngster curled up into the foetal position, rocking back and forth. 'And so there I was inside Mum, with my baby hands over my baby ears, going "La, la, la, la, la" and wondering what all the slurping was about. No wonder I'm so warped.'

'Get outta here,' Jeff jeered, wiping his eyes. 'Yeah, right. Sorry to ruin your life, mate.'

The teenager huffed and raised his middle finger in response to the gratuitous irony. The mix of trepidation and thrill were still vivid in the superstar's mind, recalling how keen the couple had been to meet their newborn.

'But to finish off... When it was all over, Lynn started to laugh really hard. She'd been gripping my arse so tight that her fingernails had almost drawn blood, and she was in hysterics at the row of claw marks she'd left on each cheek. I didn't feel it at all because I was focussed on trying not to bring the house down while I came into her mouth.'

'Euch!' Jet winced. 'Too much information! It's amazing how I still let myself be born after such an experience. I'm like, "What the hell? I'm not going out there. Weird shit happens."'

His aunt was flabbergasted. 'How much longer before 'e was born?'

'About twenty minutes or so. You took ages, mate. Compared to your sister anyway. When she announced her arrival, it was a case of "Jeff, I think I'm going to have the..."'

The skilled storyteller made a fist, handballed an imaginary football into the air and then lifted his eyes to the ceiling, pretending to mark the ball as it dropped into his hands.

'"...baby." Oh, hello, Kierney! Welcome to the world.'

Madalena smiled. 'Ah! That's so cute.'

Her brother was on a roll, once more mellow and lost in happier times. 'But I think the best memory of all time was when we got back together after your mum's two years in exile, mate. In a room at the Sydney Intercontinental.'

'Yeah, that doesn't surprise me,' Jet replied. 'Sex again. Spot the recurring theme! You're more of a monster than I am.'

'Maybe so, mate, but this time you're wrong. Well, half wrong. It was the point when Lynn realised what we had between us wasn't gonna go away. I remember going to her hotel room and pushing the door open, not exactly sure what reception I'd get.

There she was, standing right in front of me, looking like an angel sent down from heaven just for me. I held my arms out...'

The bereaved husband closed his eyes and extended his hands in front of him, bringing the vision to life. 'And she walked into them. What an incredible feeling! It felt like I'd come home, after two years of not knowing if we'd ever get back together. Lynn said the same thing later on, when we talked about it. We just stood there, in the passageway of her hotel room, for what seemed like hours.'

'And then you had sex,' his son scoffed.

Jeff shrugged, still with his eyes closed. He took a last hard drag on the dwindling spliff before stubbing it out in the ashtray on the coffee table. Tears streamed down his cheeks, and he smeared them off with the back of his left hand.

'Enough about me... So what's yours, Auntie Lena?' he asked, offering his sister an ordinary cigarette.

The woman grinned. 'My best memory of Lynn was at your weddin', when she told me to ask you to dance with you to that song, "Where Are You, My Lovely?"'

The two men burst into a fit of laughter, much to the poor woman's confusion.

'"Where Are You, My Lovely?"' Jet repeated, catching his breath and coughing. 'That's hilarious!'

'What? Jesus fuckin' Christ, you two!'

'It's "Where Do You Go To, My Lovely?"' the musician corrected.

Madalena whined. '¡Ai! How'm I s'posed to know? You got what I mean, din't ya? It was good she told me to dance with you. She was always nice to me. Not like you shits.'

The cricketer tried to pull himself together. 'I'm sorry, Auntie Lena,' he gasped. 'I guess that's the song Dad needs now.'

His father slapped his knees, stood up and left the room without acknowledging the compassionate comment that resulted from his naïve sister's error. Heading straight into the bedroom he had shared with his beautiful best friend for so long, he closed the door, lay down and wept. It was indeed a good end to a shit day.

'Where are you, angel?' Jeff cried up to the ceiling. 'I need you with me. I can't stand this emptiness any longer. Take me with you. Please, baby?'

He turned onto his side to face Lynn's half of the bed, barely able to breathe. Oblivious of the door having reopened, he became aware of the room becoming lighter. He rolled over again to find his sister standing above him, as if he had been transported back to his childhood, in their squalid Stones Road flat.

'Bloody hell. Leave me alone, Lena, please,' he begged, so close to losing control. 'I can't talk to you now. Please go.'

Madalena took a step backwards. 'OK, *chico*. I get it. I just come to see if you was OK.'

'*Gracias, hermana mía*, but I can't deal with anyone right now. I'll see you *mañana*.'

The room darkened again as Jet's frame filled the doorway. 'Sorry, Dad,' he said, knowing he should have tried to stop his aunt from going in.

'It's alright, mate. Go to bed. I've reached the end of my tether for tonight. Fucked off to the high teeth with everything. We *brûléed* your mother today, and it sucks big-time. I'm stoned and I'm drunk, and I just want to forget this week ever happened. I want to wake up in the morning with Lynn lying here like she should be.'

'Night, *chico*,' Madalena said, starting to cry. 'Sorry I barged in. I wish she was still alive as well.'

'*Gracias, Lena.* I'm sorry for going off at you. *Te amo.* Sleep well.'

'Yeah. *Te amo también*,' his sister echoed, turning on her heels to leave the room.

Jet didn't leave with his aunt, instead sitting on the edge of his dad's bed. 'Do you want me to clear everything up?'

'No, mate. Cheers, but I'll do it later. I'll get up in a minute. By the way, I know what you came in here to do, so thanks for that. Thanks heaps. And for what you said earlier about the song title. You're absolutely right, and it hurts so much.'

Bart and Marianna gave the Diamonds a restrained welcome when they arrived at the farm before lunchtime the following day. Anna and Brandon were already lounging by the swimming pool when the downhearted foursome filed out, keen to strip off and jump into the cool water.

'How are you?' asked the pregnant former gymnast.

'Shithouse, to tell you the truth.'

'To be expected,' Brandon said, shaking the great man's hand. 'Are you sleeping?'

The widower scoffed. 'Sleep? What's that? How are you guys?'

The younger Dyson daughter and her husband smiled in sympathy, kissing their unusually unobtrusive sister-in-law.

'It's a bit weird for us because it feels like we're on holidays,' Anna answered. 'Nice weather, Mum and Dad here, time to catch up on reading and relaxing... It's like our bodies are on holidays but our brains are in mourning.'

Jeff nodded. 'I know what you mean. We had a big night last night, swapping memories while heavily under the influence.'

His eyes welled up, and he stopped speaking, gazing over at Jet and Kierney, who were already swimming laps. He didn't want to crowd them this weekend. As predicted, all four had woken with a seedy hangover this morning, with the aftermath of the funeral also taking its toll on their recovery. They had driven almost the whole way to Benloch without exchanging a word.

'Hey, Lena? Have you seen the gym' here?'

'Gym'? Like machines and...' his sister managed to stop herself before another swear word polluted the refined environment. 'Nah.'

'Yep. Come on. Let me show you around,' he invited, offering a hand to help the forty-six-year-old off the sun-lounger. 'Bring your towel. We can have a swim in there.'

This last piece of information confused the Sydney woman, not realising there was an indoor pool in addition to the glistening expanse of water she was currently surveying. She followed with a shy nod to the others.

'Auntie Lena should really go back home,' Kierney said to her brother, seeing the troublesome visitor leave with their dad. 'It's just an extra thing Papá shouldn't have to worry about. He can't relax with her here.'

Jet agreed, dipping under the water to escape further melancholy conversation. He wondered if any of them would have the chance to relax, given how raw their loss felt today. The young woman watched him swim off and chased after him.

'Listen to me!' she insisted, having caught up and cornered him at the far wall.

'I know. But what can we do about it? He won't give her to any of us to babysit. He asked her to leave yesterday. I overheard through an open window in the pub toilets. But then she got all stroppy, so he gave in.'

'Did he? Wow, I didn't know that,' the caring young woman sighed. 'Oh, well... Perhaps we can try and plant the seed in her head that she should go home, in the hope she'll raise it herself?'

Jet flicked water at his sister. 'Fat chance of that!' he snapped back. 'Madalena Moreno doesn't get hints. And I doubt if she'll leave before the memorial service. I heard Dad telling her he wanted her there.'

Meanwhile, Jeff and his sister had reached the entrance to the large, modern building beside the house, the flip-flop of their striding thongs reverberating through the cavernous sports hall. Madalena's eyes were wide with amazement at the various court lines marked in different coloured paint on the polished wooden floor.

The celebrity doubted whether the working girl had ever set foot in a sports centre before, let alone one so grand. 'Take a look at this,' he said, like a child in a toyshop himself.

The self-made billionaire flicked each switch in a bank of two rows on the wall. The power surge altered the air pressure as it whipped through the open space, and lights came on both above and beneath the water level.

The Sydneysider screamed. 'Bloody 'ell! That's fuckin' amazin'. All the colours. Wow-wee! Can you swim in it when they're on?'

'Sure. Absolutely you can. Get your kit off.'

Jeff adjusted the lighting so that only the underwater colours remained on, brightening and dimming in turn. He kicked off his thongs, removed his T-shirt and sprinted to the edge of the pool.

'Come on,' he shouted back.

'Is it deep?' Madalena called out, undressing on the run and skipping towards him. 'I need to be able to stand up.'

'You'll be fine,' he told her, as he had his toddlers all those years ago. 'This is the shallow end. It suits you.'

In complete ignorance of her brother's sarcasm, the dark-haired woman climbed gingerly down the ladder, complaining that the water was freezing cold. Jeff couldn't be bothered to listen to her whingeing and dived straight in. She watched him power his way to the other end without coming to the surface.

The tired man swam up and down, length after length, cleansing body and soul as best he could. Every now and again, he checked to make sure his sister hadn't drowned, before ducking under and enjoying the muffled sounds of solitude.

After the last few barren days, his mind had started producing song snippets again, as yet unsure if this was a positive or negative sign. He was in no way ready to move on, although he longed to be rid of the nauseous numbness and constant emotional turmoil.

The water slipping past his body felt curative, and raising his heart rate through exercise was so much healthier than through the panic he had experienced over the past week. Having blood pumping through his veins rather than rushing to and from his head was bound to reinvigorate him, even though his heart would rebel to the last.

Pausing at the opposite end to where the novice was paddling from side to side, he flattened his aching back against the pool wall and felt his tattoo itch again. 'Hey, angel,' he whispered, knowing how far sound carried in this luxurious echo-chamber. 'Welcome back.'

The widower let his body come to the surface and floated in peace, closing his eyes against the lights overhead. Before long, morbid themes began to flood his brain, ridding it of any restorative hope.

He found himself in a prison, searching for Lynn down endless stark corridors, and fought off the images by focussing on the many enjoyable hours he had spent with her in this pool. They had taught Jet and Kierney to swim here and had celebrated many birthdays and anniversaries over the years, including the momentous one of only six weeks ago.

'What do you feel like now?' he asked his dream girl, evoking an image of a weightless soul searching for a new home. 'Are you drifting or stuck in one place?'

His attention was snapped back to the present by his sister's shrill cry. He flipped himself onto his stomach and swam in a smooth front crawl down to the shallow end, where Madalena was ready for something new. About five metres from her, Jeff sank below the surface and grabbed her ankles, pulling her head under the water.

She struggled and kicked in all directions, but he refused to let go for several seconds. When the pair burst above the waterline again, gasping for oxygen, the larrikin's sister was fuming.

The woman lashed out, frustrated at his ability to dodge out of her reach so easily. 'You bastard!' she screeched. 'Why d'you do that? I wanna get out.'

'Then get out,' her brother shrugged. 'I'm not stopping you. I'm sorry, Lena. Just mucking around. Let's go back to the others. It must be nearly lunchtime by now.'

The pair towelled the excess drips off their bodies and slotted their feet into their thongs for the return trek to the outdoor pool, which was behind the H-shaped mansion. Madalena stared into every ground-floor window she could access, overawed by the grandeur of her surroundings. This house was even bigger than her brother's seaside home, which had taken several visits to find her way around.

Jeff jumped straight in to join his children and continued to swim lazily while their guest stretched out on a sun-lounger. They ducked under the water in a huddle for as long as their lungs would allow, before coming up for air and whooping with laughter. In the meantime, Marianna invited the wayward Sydneysider to join her and Anna, asking a series of easy questions about her simple life.

After lunch was served and eaten, the Diamonds encouraged Madalena to take a *siesta* while they drove out to their favourite place. She didn't take much coaxing, since the combination of exercise, fresh air and cold beer had already dulled her senses.

Coldwater Creek, the idyllic dam setting which Jeff and Lynn had come to know as theirs, was as tranquil as ever. The trio swapped updates on how each was faring and were pleased to be reminded that they were not alone in their anguish.

Kierney hugged her father, with tears in her eyes. 'It must've been terrible for you when *your* mamá died, 'cause you were completely on your own.'

'Not completely. I had Lena,' the charitable man responded, the expression on his face remaining unchanged.

'You were on your own,' Jet shared his sister's observation.

Their father chuckled. 'We didn't talk about it much, so you're right, I guess. It was mostly my choice though. I could've talked to her, or to Celia. I just chose to keep it to myself. I was pretty pig-headed in those days.'

'Did you talk to Mamá back then too?' Kierney asked.

The furtive celebrity looked around, winding his left index finger in circles next to his temple. 'Careful! Don't say that out loud.'

'Mamá, we love you!' the eighteen-year-old romantic yelled at the top of her voice. 'I hope you can hear us.'

Jeff reclined on the grass, buoyed by the young woman's willingness to embrace any concept with an open and enquiring mind. Whether their departed family member could hear them or not, it was therapeutic to express themselves in the wide expanse of nature.

'OK! So what's the plan?' his impatient son changed tack, always in search of the next chapter. 'Once next Saturday's over, I mean.'

The father sighed, rolling onto one elbow and fixing his son with a glum stare. 'Let's not get ahead of ourselves,' he urged. 'We need to move slowly through the molasses of this grieving process. I don't want us to make any decisions we might regret and have to unmake.'

'And maybe not be able to unmake?' Jet added with a heavy sigh.

'Exactly.'

Kierney's face paled. 'Do we have to talk about this now? Papá's right, Jetto. We're not ready for any big decisions.'

'Sure,' her brother agreed, knowing the Sensible Twins had outvoted him. 'What about smaller ones in that case? How long do you want me to stay in Melbourne?'

'Mate, as long or as short as you want,' the older man answered straightaway. 'When you're ready to go back to uni', you have my full support, whether that's tomorrow or in a year. You too, *pequeñita*.'

'Thanks, Dad. I don't know yet either, but I need to know what you want. And how are you going to work yours out, Kizzo? You've missed the start of term. You'll be disqualified.'

His sister giggled. 'I know. I'm going to defer a year, I think.'

Jeff nodded, secretly overjoyed at this news. 'That's fine. I wanted you to make up your own mind. Did you ring them and ask what your options were?'

'E-mailed.'

'Good girl. And they don't have a problem with it?'

'No. Not under the circumstances. Although I haven't officially pulled out yet. I shall though, now we've discussed it.'

'Listen, guys... What I'm thinking at the moment,' the sole parent began, resting his head back down on the rough sandy ground and staring up at the cloudless azure canopy, 'is that I'll come out to the UK after your summer term finishes, around your birthday. We could ride bikes, and I could watch you play cricket for a few weeks.'

Jet's eyes lit up. 'Wow! That sounds very cool. I'd love it.'

The father was glad to receive such an enthusiastic response. 'Kizzy, would you mind if I did that? It's just that we had the idea originally on the assumption that you'd be in Sydney, and your mamá was...'

'That's fine,' his daughter affirmed, without letting him finish. 'July's ages away. I have no clue what I'll be doing by then, but go ahead and make plans.'

The younger man sprang up all of a sudden, brushing the grass off his shorts and gazing around. Jeff's sixth sense assumed his son had drawn the short straw to raise an uncomfortable topic, especially when he began to pace around a little and exchanged surreptitious glances with his partner-in-crime.

Their father sat up. 'What's going on?'

'Dad?' Jet opened, red in the face.

'Yeah...' the empathetic man responded, wiping the smile from his face. 'Say what's on your mind.'

The nineteen-year-old coughed in embarrassment. 'This is hard for me to say. I mean, after our memories discussion last night and everything...'

Telepathy was a wonderful thing, the intellectual mused, tapping in to his children's concerns. 'About sex?'

While the baffled siblings stared at each other, open-mouthed, Jeff permitted himself a kind laugh. 'You want to know if I need it?'

Kierney nodded, and Jet's face assumed a deeper shade of crimson as he spoke.

'We want you to know that we'd understand if you went to see someone. You know... Like you did for me the other night. We realise you're not dead too.'

Jeff stood up and put his arm round the courageous lad. 'You could've sent me a text, son,' he cajoled, digging him in the ribs. 'I don't want you to find speaking to me this difficult.'

The strapping lad relaxed. 'It's not that difficult now it's happening. The build-up was worse.'

'Well... Thanks for the generous offer, but actually, I *am* dead too.'

'What? Don't say that!' Kierney's tone was full of consternation. 'What do you mean?'

'*Calmate, pequeñita*. It's just that since Mamá's been gone, I don't have the slighted interest in anything sexual. My libido's shutdown. And to be honest, I quite like it.'

The worried sportsman was unable to imagine a life without sex. 'Oh, my God. Do you think it'll change?'

'How should *he* know?' his sister snapped. 'He's never lost the love of his life before, you worm.'

Jeff grinned, adopting the same derisory tone in reply. 'Actually, *he* does know because I did lose the love of my life before, remember. I had exactly the same reaction when I found out your mamá was leaving for the US. It's shock, I guess. My physical incarnation's rebellion or some crap like that... Only this time, I'm not in a hurry for it to come back.'

'Sorry to shout at you, guys. I suppose it's one less thing for you to worry about,' his daughter suggested. 'Not like Auntie Lena.'

The songwriter laughed out loud. 'You know me very well, you two.'

IN MEMORIAM

Jeff Diamond and Gerry Blake returned to Sydney on the Monday after the funeral to attend a committal hearing for the man accused of Victoria Lynn Shannon Dyson Diamond's murder. Juan Antonio García had made his confession only two hours after being taken into custody and was charged the same evening in front of a magistrate. There were three charges in all; the other offences being intent to murder Jeffrey Moreno Diamond and possession of a firearm without a permit.

Bail was not offered to the Spaniard on two grounds: first, he had carried a life-threatening weapon in a public place; and second, he had confessed to having discharged it while aimed at the victim, leading to loss of life. The magistrate silenced the defence's objections, saying he was doubtful that García would have been able to afford bail.

The celebrity took exception to this comment, ever conscious of the insidious class war that waged in the Australian legal system. No-one else appeared affronted by the haughty judgement call, so he let it pass.

Defence countered that the Court would be denying the accused the opportunity to protect his family adequately. The judge chose to disregard this request too, seeing that García's family was not thought to be known to anyone connected with the crime.

Again, had he been representing the defendant, the famous egalitarian would have argued that any number of irate Lynn Dyson Diamond fans might be out to exact revenge.

But he wasn't representing the defendant, was he?

Far from it.

The defence lawyers revealed to the magistrate that their client was deemed mentally disturbed and that they would be seeking advice from an expert psychiatric witness. This was not such good news. For all his advocacy over the years on behalf of people suffering from mental illness, Jeff failed to find sympathy for the pathetic, beige offender.

Ironically, a story had appeared in the press this morning revealing that García's wife of over two decades was filing for divorce. By all accounts, she had been a lifelong fan of both superstars and couldn't bear being married to the man who destroyed a partnership which captured the hearts of so many people around the world.

Encouraged by scandal-hungry media pundits, Wendy García was outspoken about her husband's jealousy toward the Diamond family, telling of his regular criticism and insults against Jeff's immigrant heritage. However, she had stopped short of stating whether these obsessive misgivings might lead him to murder.

Rock star and business manager read this breaking story in The Age during their pre-dawn flight from Melbourne. At first, they had cracked a few jokes, bemused by the timing of the woman's damning statements. Yet the more the widower mulled it over, the more uncomfortable he became. In the car, driving away from the courts, he put in a call to Dyson Administration.

'Bart, it's Jeff,' he announced. 'Sorry to interrupt your meeting.'

He had decided to ring Big D to inform him of the results of the proceedings, while also sharing his opinion on these latest revelations.

'Good morning, Jeff. What can I do for you? Aren't you in Sydney today?'

'Yes, I am. We've just left García's hearing. It's mostly good news, you'll be pleased to know.'

The Olympian sighed. 'It's about time, after the furore from his wife in the papers this morning.'

'Precisely. That's what I want to speak to you about, sir. I'm pleased to hear your reaction. Have you got a few minutes?'

The two great Australians, who had gained enormous respect for one another over the years, were these days glad of the mutual support as they worked through the messy aftermath of Lynn's death.

Gerry Blake drove through the late morning traffic towards Surry Hills Police Station, where they were due to attend a post-committal briefing from the appointed Crown Prosecutors.

'Yes, of course. Fire away,' the booming voice blasted through the telephone.

Jeff took a deep breath and gave his alter-ego a half-smile as his chest tightened. Somehow his father-in-law still made him feel as if he were fifteen years old and in deep trouble.

'Well... As we expected, they're going for diminished mental capacity, which his wife is doing her best to affirm, but we'll talk about that later. Three charges: Lynn's murder, my intended murder, and he didn't have a licence for the gun.'

'Right-oh. The last one's somewhat incidental, I'm guessing,' Bart gave a sardonic chuckle.

'Indeed. Next, there was a total of four bullets fired, not three. One went into the couch to Lynn's left-hand side, but the other three were all fired into her body.'

The grieving husband moved the handset away from his face for a few moments while he rode through a sudden wave of emotion, putting the palm of his hand over the mouthpiece. Gerry reached out his left hand and shook his mate's shoulder supportively.

'Jeff, are you still there?' he heard his father-in-law say.

The widower coughed and spoke into the microphone again. 'Sorry, sir. This is still very fresh in my mind.'

'Certainly, Jeff. I apologise. Take your time.'

'Cheers. I'm OK,' the caller continued, breathing heavily and becoming quite nauseated. 'His first shot was the fatal one. Sorry, Bart. Hang on...'

The passenger signalled to his friend to pull the car over to the kerb, and it came to a smooth stop within a short distance. He had flung the door wide open before the handbrake was applied. All Gerry could do was to look on as his mate rushed to the brambles which lined the roadside.

'You alright, mate?'

Nodding and giving a quick thumbs-up, Jeff returned, stooping to retrieve the water bottle from the stowage tray. He stood tall and gulped in the fresh air. Lifting his mobile to resume the call, he picked up where he left off.

'I'm back. Sorry if you overheard any of that... Chucking up in the bushes, in case you're wondering. The bastard was damned accurate, even with the silencer,' the bitter man told his nemesis in Melbourne. 'And fast, I guess. He must've been practising.

'The first shot was spot-on, the second one went into her right shoulder and straight through into the cushion behind her, the third directly into the couch on the other side and the last one into her lower chest cavity.'

The caller heard Lynn's father breathing deeply too; a lengthy pause before the older man responded. 'So, were it not for the first shot, she may have survived,' he murmured.

The widower shook his head, staring into the busy traffic from behind his sunglasses. This conclusion hadn't occurred to him, but the elder statesman was probably right. One well-timed squeeze of the trigger was all it took to extinguish their loved one's life.

'Yep. Maybe,' he replied. 'Fucker got lucky. The last slug would've caused significant damage to vital organs though. Apparently, he'd had the gun for two years; never registered it, although he claims he did. Whatever...None of that makes any material difference to the case. The next steps are to prepare for the trial, which has been diarised for the end of April.'

'End of April?' his father-in-law exclaimed. 'Why so far away? It gives so much time for the newspapers to wreak havoc. Are you considering some sort of blackout or injunction?'

'Yep. I expect so. I'll request one, but I don't hold out much hope of stopping the rumour mill. This is supposed to be a free country. People are entitled to say what they want, and I don't want to stop that. April's not actually that far away really, sir. The QC told us this morning it'll take them at least a month to assemble the evidence, and that's for an almost cut and dried case. If it gets any more complicated, it'll take longer.'

'Very well,' Bart capitulated. 'I'll leave it to you. I just don't relish seeing endless conjecture about my daughter's killer plastered all over the newsstands. We need some privacy to grieve and get back to normal.'

'Oh, I hear you, sir,' the younger man said. 'I agree completely. I'll ring you and Marianna over the next few days to discuss it some more. But tell me... What do you think about the wife's decision to file for divorce?'

'What do I think?' the conservative stalwart snapped an angry retort. 'It's sleaze. What *can* we think about it? It sells papers, and she'll earn good money from our sorrow.'

'Perhaps, but I reckon it might be more dangerous than that,' the patient negotiator explained, bile rising in his throat once more. 'It could go either way. She'll polarise public opinion. People'll either sympathise with her and think García's a madman, in which case his claim of diminished responsibility is strengthened, or they'll sympathise with him 'cause she's mouthing off about him when he can't defend himself.'

A protracted silence greeted the peacemaker as he finished proffering the opposing arguments. The call was still active, according to the screen on his mobile, so he waited for his father-in-law to process this latest piece of disturbing conjecture.

'You're absolutely right,' the reply came eventually, issued in a defeatist tone. 'Whichever way, it weakens our case. I see what you mean now. What should we do?'

'Don't know yet,' the widower admitted. 'But that's the problem in a nutshell, Bart. It's not our case. It belongs to the Commonwealth. We're lucky the police want me involved, so we stand some chance of staying in touch with how it all develops. But it's not our case. Plain and simple.

'Gerry and I are meeting with the prosecution team shortly and we'll get their advice. I'm going to engage our own barrister to work with the Crown guys. Not sure how the land lies with a Crown case...

'And if the whole bloody thing falls in a heap, I can launch a private prosecution but wouldn't be able to sue the arsehole for a criminal matter. Weird, isn't it? The Queen versus García. Lynn's name isn't anywhere on the front page. She doesn't crack a mention until page three of this damned script.'

Bart's worldly and persuasive son-in-law never failed to find exactly the right words to illustrate a point. 'Bloody oath,' he coughed. 'This is sounding worse by the minute. What do you need me to do?'

Climbing back into the car, Jeff smiled at the Olympian's apparent deference. His friend continued to wait, taking the opportunity to listen to his own voicemail messages. The VIP patted the passenger's shoulder with his free hand, and the car moved off to re-join the traffic.

'Nothing, sir. Sit tight. I'll ring you later,' he reassured the older man. 'How's Marianna going?'

'Oh... Not too bad, thanks. Better since Anna got here. She's got someone else to speak to now. I'd rather not spend every minute of the day talking about it, and consequently I've lost my usefulness for the moment.'

The widower chuckled at the rare attempt at self-deprecating humour. Endurance was the Bart Dyson way, and he did it so well. In the face of such inconvenient adversity, one's only recourse was to climb back on one's horse, and everything in one's world was rosy again.

'All good,' the younger man said. 'I'll ring you later at home. Are you at Benloch or staying in the city?'

'In the city tonight. How's Kierney?'

'She's doing pretty well, thanks. In fact, how about having dinner with us?' Jeff asked, much against his better judgement. 'I don't know what Kizzy's up to, but she's trying to force-feed me, so I'll get a gold star for inviting you.'

Bart chuckled. 'Good idea. Thank you. Thanks a lot, yes. That'd be very nice.'

Gerry swung the hired Commodore into a space in the police station car park and turned off the ignition. His downcast client said goodbye to his father-in-law, terminating the call with a growl.

'Christ! What did I just do?' he turned to his business manager. 'Are you and Fiona free tonight? You've gotta help me out.'

The affable accountant shrugged, slamming the car door. 'Why should I help you out? You got yourself into this mess.'

Jeff scoffed. 'Mate, thanks for your support. And it's "Why should *we* help you out?" If you're serious about getting married, that is...'

The executive shoved his arrogant friend into the metal frame as they wrestled for space in the revolving door at the police station's front entrance. The physicality of their interaction diffused some of the tension which had built up over the journey.

'Will I get a smoke out of it?'

The reformed addict raised his eyebrows after a uniformed officer passed them in the corridor. 'Shut the fuck up!' he warned in a hushed voice. 'We're in an effin' cop shop. No smokes while Big D's in *da* house.'

Conductor, James Howard, and the indefatigable Kiley Jones laboured night and day after Lynn's funeral to create a memorial service fit for a megastar. Big names were flying in from all over the world, either to perform or simply to sit in the audience. Lynn Dyson Diamond was respected and loved by all, and her husband made sure he passed on each and every compliment to his children and to the Dysons.

Students from Melbourne Academy, both junior and senior schools, were keen to take part, as was virtually every artist and musician whose life had been touched by the gorgeous and generous celebrity, the apple of the public's eye since birth. Numbers swelled to such a degree that Kiley and James were forced to turn people away, at most able to offer them a part in the *Finalé*.

The battle for television coverage was fierce too, each company trying to outdo the other with the proliferation of cameras, length of promotional trailers and the credentials of presenters and commentators who had been hired to give professional insight and to impart personal secrets during the event.

The other phenomenon apparent to Jeff and his staff since the funeral was the incredible number of letters from women pledging their undying love. This in itself was nothing new for the good-looking, enigmatic celebrity, but these fans were all hellbent on looking after his physical needs despite his enduring love for Lynn.

The fun-loving business manager found it all rather amusing, teasing his old friend about booking in a few days' "R and R" over the next ten years, while he worked his way down the list. 'You're not as young as you used to be, old boy. You'll need a break to refuel the old tanks.'

Jeff was far from amused. The idea of spending time with another woman filled him with disgust, and he felt sick to think of these wildcats already on the prowl before Lynn was properly farewelled. What sort of fans did they consider themselves to be, if they didn't realise how all-consuming a part of his world she had been?

He was relieved to watch Jet and Kierney grow stronger as the days went by, now able to talk about their mother without succumbing to overflowing emotions.

Saturday afternoon's extravaganza was his chance to show the world once and for all what a dastardly act had been committed on the 16th of February 1996. With Cathy and the Dysons, he had catalogued his dream girl's long list of achievements and had designed a novel way to weave them into the programme.

Communiqués passing between their souls remained few and far between, but when they happened, they filled Jeff with fleeting bursts of joy. His dream girl was determined to stay close, he was sure. Whether this notion was true or whether he was completely deranged didn't bother him. Either way was OK, as long as the channels stayed open.

Even memorial services needed rehearsals, the professional lamented, crossing Alexandra Parade and starting up the steep hill towards the Sidney Myer Music Bowl.

By the time he reached the venue's entrance, Jet and Kierney were standing at the gates, having left the apartment early for a head-start on their father.

Disguised behind sunglasses and under a black baseball cap, the widower trudged up the steps carved into the hillside. His heart weighed a tonne, and his legs felt as heavy as lead while he stood marvelling at the multitude of picnic rugs and deck chairs already littering the grass beyond the perimeter.

Once inside, everywhere he turned, the grieving husband saw people he knew. His passage from auditorium entrance to stage was lined with a series of awkward stares and waves, impromptu tearful embraces and angry accusations.

Flanked by his popular offspring, the concert's host made his way onto the stage, where he was greeted by the two trusty orchestrators. His arrival interrupting musicians locating their positions and the choir practising their walks on and off the stage, a deathly hush smothered the hive of activity.

Jeff looked over to where the first violins were tuning up and made eye contact with Piraea Loudon, his daughter's closest friend. He waved, and she promptly burst into tears. Disappointed at the effect he was having on everyone, the dejected superstar lowered his eyes and began to run through the set-list.

When they reached the fifth item, the rock star's index finger stopped still. 'What's this? Shane Adams?' he asked James, anxiety building inside as soon as he saw the handwritten comments beside the song.

'He really wants to do it,' Kiley told him. 'The film's going to be released in two weeks' time, Jeff. Do you mind? It'd be great.'

The forty-three-year-old's head span, and he lurched a few steps backwards to the first row of seating, unsteady on his feet. He remembered only too well that the young chart-topper had been commissioned to record the title track from the deceased director's upcoming film, "King of Diamonds, King of Hearts".

'Jesus, Kizzo,' the widower gasped. 'Is Shane here? I don't know if I want to hear it for the first time in such a public forum.'

'You do,' his daughter insisted, sitting next to him and taking his hand. 'Really you do. You'll love it. Mamá told me she wrote it from words you used in her proposal.'

Jeff sighed, leaning back and smiling as best he could at his gorgeous gipsy girl. The flame-haired composer stepped forward and put her arm around the eighteen-year-old for moral support.

'I know, *pequeñita*. She told me too. I understand all that, but I want to talk to Shane first. Where is he?'

'I've sent someone to find him,' Kiley reported. 'Ben's here too, and John Betts arrived a few hours ago and will be here any minute. It's like the old days.'

James frowned. 'Minus one.'

Jeff shook his head and exhaled. This was difficult for everyone involved, and he wondered whether they had bitten off more than they could chew so soon after Lynn's death. Too late now, he sighed. Another shining example of his impulsiveness no longer reined in by his dream girl's good sense.

'Yep. Minus one,' he sniffed, brushing the outer corner of his left eye with the back of his hand.

Shane Adams and Jet Diamond were walking towards him, the teenaged sportsman towering over the skinny musician. Jeff remembered the days when their respective heights were very much reversed, and not so long ago either.

'¡El Jefe! How're you doing, man?' the singer embraced his idol. 'I am *so* sorry for Lynn's passing. I still can't believe it.'

'Cheers, Shane,' the celebrity responded, slapping his fellow guitarist on the back. 'I wish I could tell you things were different, but they're not.'

'Look, man, I won't do the song from the movie if you don't want me to,' the confident newcomer offered. 'We can stick to the original plan. I think you'll love it though. It's an awesome testimony...'

'Yeah. It is, but to *me*,' Jeff interjected in his typical authoritative way. 'It's a testimony to me. This is Lynn's gig, guys. Let's not lose focus just because there's a movie coming out. This is our chance to tell everyone how much we loved Lynn. It's got fuck all to do with me.'

Kiley blushed, agreeing with the humble star's justification and annoyed with herself for getting caught up in the hype. 'Jeff, you're so right,' she apologised. 'I should've thought of that. I'm sorry. Let's leave it the way it was.'

The celebrity nodded, taking the red-haired virtuosa by the hand. 'Thanks, KJ. I think that's the best idea,' and turning to the singer, 'You can do the other one at *my* funeral.'

Everyone fell silent except his long-suffering children.

'Papá!'

'Dad!'

Both kids registered their objections, bringing light relief to the sombre occasion. Jeff faked a wide grin, the significance of their outcry reinforced when both teenagers punched him hard on the arms and chest.

The turgid atmosphere had been well diffused, but at the expense of his children's precarious emotional state. Their father was seized by extreme guilt, hugging them both and stepping away from the production team and fellow artists.

'Hey, guys, I'm really sorry,' he said, desperate to make amends. 'I shouldn't have said that.'

Kierney was crying, and his son did his utmost to mask his pain with anger; a trick he had learnt from his father.

'No, you definitely shouldn't have,' the nineteen-year-old scolded, with eyes as dark as an ocean storm. 'Don't play the martyr with us, please, even if it is just for show.'

Jet's well-chosen words penetrated the star's core. Was that what everyone really thought? These kids were trying their hardest to give their mother the best send-off, and all he had to offer was to snipe from the sidelines. What a prima donna he had become in the last few minutes...

Behave yourself, you arsehole, he chastised himself.

'You're right, mate,' the great man agreed, utterly contrite. 'I'm very sorry. Kiz, are you OK?'

'I will be,' the pretty teenager shrugged. 'I just don't want to think about morbid things anymore. I want tomorrow to be as happy and joyful as we can make it. Do you still want that, Papá?'

Jeff put an arm around each child and bowed his head onto Kierney's. 'Yes, I do,' he promised. 'You guys are going to make fantastic parents, by the way. I feel very small right at this moment. It won't happen again, I promise.'

Arriving at the memorial service on Saturday afternoon and passing a sea of faces he recognised, Jeff felt as if he were travelling through Lynn's life at warp speed. He had watched her parents, her siblings and their families go in ahead of him, to a series of polite ripples of applause.

'Jesus, I hope they don't clap for us,' he said to the children.

'Just go with the flow, Dad,' Jet hinted, feeling his father quivering beside him. 'If they want to clap, they'll clap.'

The audience did far more than clap. As soon as those in the last few rows caught sight of the Diamonds at the rear of the auditorium, an initial wave of warm appreciation fast escalated to cheers, shouting and stamping of feet.

The threesome marched towards the stage in lock-step, both energised and perplexed by the extent of the reaction. Finally taking their places in the front row, they acknowledged the Dysons on the other side of the aisle.

No sooner had they sat down than Jeff was back on his feet. Beckoning for Jet and Kierney to follow him, he crossed sides to greet Bart, Marianna and the rest of the blond clan. The crowd gasped in bittersweet pleasure at the open display of support, and the concert's sponsor raised both arms to signal for quiet as the event got underway.

Everyone fell silent as the lights dimmed, leaving the widower in disarray. 'We're sitting in the same formation as our wedding. You're where I sat, mate,' he whispered. 'It's killing me, but it's kind o' nice too.'

'Sort of like coming full-circle,' Jet agreed.

The superstar's chest twitched with a sharp pain at this very moment; acute enough to make him inhale in pained surprise. The children watched him rubbing his left pectoral muscle, a smile spreading over his face. They made eye contact with each other in consternation, wondering whether this strange tattoo talk could be more than a figment of his hyperactive imagination.

Ben Jansen, another of Lynn's successful protégés, kicked off proceedings with one of the songs Jeff had written for his wife on their recent anniversary, "The Rest Will Be History". The upbeat opening song was followed by an address by Sir Bradley Morrison, who used his time to chart the superstar's career from primary school to high school.

The grieving humanitarian had requested that the service not concentrate too much on hits, medals or qualifications, but rather on the human qualities his dream girl exhibited in abundance throughout her life: her leadership as a child; her compassion for others; her interest in the world in general; and her sense of team spirit in both musical and sporting pursuits.

Bart and Marianna Dyson were the next to stand in the spotlight, speaking at length about their elder daughter against a backdrop of photographs from the late nineteen-fifties and -sixties, some of which Jeff and the children had never seen before.

In these pictures, Jeff recognised the girl of ten or eleven years old with whom he had fallen in love way too early, compelled to bide his time through tormented teenage years for her to come of age.

Musicians from the early days combined with present day members of the Melbourne Academy orchestra and chorus to perform a medley of their patron's hits, with Janice singing Lynn's part. While her children felt strong enough to join the throng on stage, her husband spent the whole segment staring at the floor, determined not to be drawn into the sadness of an era before he was even a blip on the starlet's radar.

The dreamer's avoidance was to be short-lived however. Straight after the compilation finished, Sir Brad turned to the sea of adoring faces again to announce the point in the young woman's life when everything changed. Projected behind the orchestra and on enormous screens erected in the gardens, the unforgettable video of "Everlasting" celebrated the beginning of one of the greatest partnerships in living memory.

Looking up to see himself and Lynn as reunited lovers on tour in Japan, the middle-aged performer went to pieces. For Jet and Kierney, the sight and sounds of their father wearing his heart on his sleeve in the public spotlight were every bit as heartbreaking as seeing their youthful parents so happy on the big screen.

Earlier that day, their dad had made them promise to ignore any distress he might exhibit, yet such a task was easier said than done. They knew how painful this event was for him, recognising the tumultuous response from the audience on his behalf.

The footage changed to edited highlights from the good-looking pair's wedding, the applause reaching new heights. Due on stage in less than a minute, Jeff fought to regain his composure well enough to stand and face the lively but respectful crowd. Following his cue from James Howard, he and the children rose to their feet and hugged each other.

Dressed in his favourite black leather jacket, the lonely figure walked across the stage to take his place in front of the rows of past and present Melbourne Academy students who knew the Diamond family so well. The sight drew audible gasps and some sobs from all around him.

Despite the circumstances, this was Jeff Diamond's territory. Close-ups of his handsome face were beamed to screens far and wide in close-up. Larger than life, albeit thin and drawn, he endowed his loyal flock with a broad grin.

The local hero raised his arms to silence everyone. 'Whoa,' he sighed, throwing his head back and inhaling to stave off the dizziness. 'You guys are fantastic! Thank you so much for coming out today, all of you. Hope the grass is comfortable out in the wilderness beyond.'

With this reference to the audience members spread around the Botanic Gardens, those in the reserved seating were overshadowed momentarily when a huge cheer from their friends outside the venue rose above their own ovation.

'I have to tell you this is not easy,' the seasoned orator went on, lifting his hands again in an effort to bring the proceedings to order. 'This is quite an ordeal for Jet, Kierney and me, and for the Dyson family down there, but we're glad we're here. And we're mighty glad you're here, more to the point.

'Your support for us over the last two weeks has been unbelievable, and we'd all like to thank you. This afternoon is all about allowing you to celebrate Lynn's life and to reflect on what she meant to you. Over the years, I read hundreds of your letters to her, and I know Lynn Dyson Diamond was adored and admired by a mind-blowing number of people.'

Another enthusiastic round of applause broke out, which Jeff again signalled with heavy arms to calm down.

'We love you, Jeff!' came a brash exclamation from somewhere in the first bank of rows, receiving an appropriately cheerful response from those around her.

'Thanks! I love you too,' the celebrity replied, wiping tears from his eyes. 'So... What was I going to say? Ah, yeah. I was going to talk a little bit about when Lynn and I first got together. As you could see up on those screens, we clicked. For any of you cynics out there... and I was one once... love is real.

'Elton John sings a lyric every now and again that goes something like, "In the instant that you love someone, in the second that the hammer hits, reality runs up your spine and the pieces finally fit." Well, I gotta tell you, that's exactly how it was for Lynn and me, and we damned well made the most of it. Every single day.'

The crowd went crazy, not only at the image the master communicator had conjured up, but also because the screens displayed the raw emotion brimming out of his eyes while he spoke. He was holding it together, but only by the thinnest of threads.

The veteran performer struggled on. 'But then I was going to talk more about later in our life, after the newness wore off and our relationship matured from heady, rebellious passion to the realities of family life and the highs and lows of two public figures who were committed to changing the world.

'I'm proud to claim that I was there in the wings when Lynn discovered who she really was: teacher, mother, mentor and friend to so many people of all walks of life. I was just saying to the kids the other night that their mamá was driven by an limitless desire to grow us all up.'

The widower did his best to laugh, and the multitude of ever-merciful fans helped him along. He dug his fingers into his eye sockets in an effort to stem the throbbing in his temples, taking several deep breaths. Gazing gazed down to the front row at his children, whom he knew were up next on the run-sheet, he was anxious not to upset them too much.

'Today's concert is a celebration of the adorable angel who filled all our lives with joy,' the speaker went on. 'I want to let you know there was nothing left outstanding between Lynn and me. Nothing I should've said to her. Nothing I wish she'd said to me. The kids and I miss her terribly, and she knows that. I'm sure she's missing us too, wherever she is. I just have to figure out what I'm going to do now.'

A unexpected silence chilled the air, leading the world-changer to regret baring his soul to such an extent. However, after the calculated ambiguity of his words sank in, the audience began to clap warmly and rose to their feet one by one to salute him.

'Thank you. Sit, sit, sit! Please don't make this about me. I have a bad habit of doing that, don't I, angel?' the humble man said into the microphone, eyes directed upwards and beyond the edge of the Music Bowl's roofline. 'This show's all about Lynn.

'When we were expecting these wonderful kids here, we discussed all those old-fashioned names like Constance and Prudence. And y'know, there's a good reason this type of name came to be, because they're the qualities we all need more of.

'Lynn Dyson Diamond was the most constant person I've ever met. We even thought of Equilibria 'cause her byword was "balance". But that was too "out there" even for us! Lynn never gave or took more than what was right. That's true wisdom. I always pretended to be smart, but baby, you were way smarter.'

Jeff looked up to the heavens again, standing eerily still for several seconds while the tears flowed. Before he knew what was happening, his children had jumped up onto the stage and were standing beside him, with the audience once again clapping and cheering. The emotional trio stood arm-in-arm and took a single synchronised bow.

'That's my cue to get off! Ladies and gentlemen, Ryan and Kierney Diamond...' he introduced the next segment with a flamboyant wave and exited stage-left to yet more rapture.

The orchestra scrambled to ready itself for Kiley Jones' baton, which called the musicians to arms with a flourish. The young stars stood side by side in the centre, ready to sing the song Kierney had written especially for this event.

This melodious tribute was backed up by a new and multi-lingual version of a hit which had captured the world's hearts when the family performed it to close the Feed Africa concert at Wembley Stadium in the UK.

Steve Christie, with Jeff's blessing, churned out one of his chart-toppers, co-written for the stunning record producer several years in advance of his well-chronicled challenge for her hand.

Several of Lynn's school-friends, who had also gone on to successful careers, banded together for a single number. The conductor then moved straight on to a spirited performance from the combined choirs owing to the soloists becoming too overwhelmed by sadness.

Afterwards, a professor from the Massachusetts Institute of Technology spoke about The Good School programme, another brainchild of the Australian beauty's, before the whole cast was to return to the stage for their *Grand Finalé*.

Jeff jogged back up the steps to shake the academic's hand and thanked everyone again for their support. His arm circled in an expansive gesture towards another of the couple's discoveries, who was already seated at the grand piano to the compère's right.

'To close tonight's show, I'm really stoked that Ben agreed to perform one of my musical love letters to Lynn. He's gonna do it way more justice than I could just now. It's a few years old, written for Lynn for our fifteenth wedding anniversary, but it's never been out in public before.'

The bereft songwriter paused, gathering his faculties. 'It's called "Original", and it's what Lynn means to me. Ben Jansen, everybody! Give it up!'

His introduction nearly drowned out by the audience's reaction, the handsome idol left the stage to the opening strains of the song his beautiful best friend had adored above any other. The audience sat in silence as the rich lyric was sung as only the soulful Californian could render, full of imagery and raw human emotion.

The *Finalé* rolled straight into the soaring strings of "World Children", the last track on what became Lynn's last album. Every celebrity guest, performing or otherwise, linked arms to give their all for the occasion. Even her husband managed to sing, or at least to mouth the words.

Footage from a recent family documentary showed the deceased musician rehearsing this very track with members of present day Melbourne Academy orchestra and chorus, which also included a contingent from the junior school.

Bart and Marianna took their places with their remaining children and the Diamonds at the front of the throng, and the song reprised as planned. Kiley Jones and James Howard also joined the family, completing the picture perfectly.

With a few closing words from Sir Bradley Morrison, the afternoon's concert came to an end. The platform emptied into the space behind the backdrop, where chaos reigned for many minutes while orchestra members tangled their instruments and music stands with each other, and stagehands rushed to clear everything away to make way for the evening's scheduled orchestral programme.

Cathy's team at Stonebridge Music had arranged a party for performers and special guests at a hotel in the city, and an extended complement of staff were busy loading stars into a convoy of hired sedans. Jet and Kierney joined their cousins, and their car followed their grandparents' to the function.

The widower was not with them, having broken ranks yet again. He opted to take the scenic route, filled with taciturn contemplation and maladjusted emotions. He decided to walk along Alexandra Parade, past Flinders Street station and on through the CBD.

He failed to divert on Collins Street, where he ought to have turned left. Instead, he continued northwards, up Exhibition Street, until he reached the apartment, exactly as the couple had done on their wedding night.

Sitting alone on the balcony, the distraught man wept anew, rubbing his tattoo from time to time as it stang. Strangely, he had no desire to drink or smoke, to play the piano, nor to write down the myriad lyric ideas that filled his head to bursting point.

'I just want to be with you, angel,' he sobbed. 'Where are you? We've given you a good send-off, and I know you'd have loved it, but I don't want you to go. Please don't go.'

His mobile rang, and his heart leapt to yet another joyful but erroneous conclusion. It was his daughter, enquiring as to his whereabouts.

'I'm at home,' Jeff replied, sniffing back the tears. 'Are you guys alright?'

'You gave us the slip again,' Kierney scolded. 'We're good. There are hundreds of people here.'

'That's good,' he smiled, interpreting her gentle tone. 'I'll run back in a while to pick you up. I don't want to stand around like I'm at a bloody cocktail party, with people trying not to say what they really want to say.'

The youngster laughed. 'It is exactly like that. We're with Bruce and Jazz, keeping our heads down. Jet really loved what you said about Mamá, by the way. I did too, but he was really moved. Are you OK?'

Her father let out a long groan. 'Yeah. *Sorta-kinda*. I love you, *pequeñita*. And that damned brother of yours. I'll see you in half an hour or so.'

Kierney hung up, resigned that it would be at least two hours before they would see the world's favourite husband at the party he had thrown for their guests. She pictured him silhouetted against the fading light over Melbourne's inner north and wished she could be with him. He had seemed unusually vulnerable on the stage earlier, and it made her wonder how long his wounds would stay so raw.

How long did it take to get over losing a soul-mate? Was it really worth loving someone at all, with the danger of losing him or her at any moment? She had listened to her parents having this very conversation a few times, never once thinking they would be putting their theories to the test.

KING OF DIAMONDS, KING OF HEARTS

"King of Diamonds, King of Hearts" was released on the first Thursday in March. The media company responsible for the worldwide release had done its best to control the hysteria which now surrounded this movie due to the sudden death of its writer and director.

On the one hand, the extra focus on the Diamond family in the week prior to the launch was like manna from heaven for the promoters. The hype that had built all by itself was quite enough to ensure massive box office receipts.

On the other hand however, the interconnected schedules for a whirlwind tour by the stars and production team, planned so carefully in advance, had since been thrown into disarray. After the opening in Melbourne, Lynn and Jeff were booked to fly to Sydney, Singapore, Tokyo and various European capitals before ending up in New York and Los Angeles.

In each city, there were to have been premières and parties and after-parties, interspersed with press conferences and numerous television and radio appearances. All in all, about two hundred hours of events had been left with no headline act.

The film's charismatic protagonist felt terrible for pulling out and canvassed everyone he could think of for some alternate ideas to make amends. There was simply no way he could fly solo around the world, spending hours parading along red carpets and talking about a movie which his dead wife had made about him.

It was wrong on so many levels, and to his relief, the majority of his entourage concurred. Fortunately for the film executives, the lead actors were more than happy to help fill the void the Diamonds had left, out of respect for the dearly-departed director.

'Are you at least going to watch it?' Kierney pleaded with her father as they ran round the streets of Carlton on the morning of the local opening night.

'I can't, baby. How can I say I'm not joining the circus, yet then turn up for my free glass of champagne?'

'That's ridiculous,' his daughter chided. 'Everyone would love you to turn up, and we'd make sure you stayed in the dark. People'll expect you to be there. Mamá made this film for *you*. Everybody knows that.'

The widower stopped, bending over and resting his hands on his knees to catch his breath. He was losing fitness rapidly, with his lifestyle now far less healthy than it used to be. He was also frustrated because his miniature was quite correct. Shane Adams' single from the soundtrack had gone straight to Number One in many countries, and perversely, its frequent spots on the radio were helping to prolong Lynn's existence.

'Damn you, *pequeñita*,' he cursed with a half-smile. 'You're my voice of reason now. I know I should go, but can you imagine what I'm going to be like? They'll have to put plastic sheeting over the carpet.'

His daughter giggled. 'You sound like a puppy who needs house-training. Please, Papá. Martin Day'll be there, and Tom Bingham. They're going to want you to be there. You *are* "King of Diamonds, King of Hearts" to them.'

'Argh!' Jeff groaned, impersonating his dream girl. 'Alright then, I'll do it. Yippee! Another outing for my penguin suit. I hope you'll be there.'

'Papá!' Kierney exclaimed, bumping into him deliberately. 'Of course I'll be there. I'm dying to see it. I've seen the rushes already and basically know the story, but I'm so looking forward to seeing the whole thing strung together. Apparently, the woman who plays your mamá is stunning.'

'Like you, baby,' her father sighed, stopping again and reaching towards his daughter for a hug. 'She was cast to look like you, Mamá told me. So far, I don't like my chances of getting through it, but I'll do my best for my two angels.'

The teenager kissed his chin. '*Gracias*. And one more favour.'

'Oh-oh,' her father smiled, suspecting a catch. 'What's that?'

'I'd like us to invite messieurs Day and Bingham for dinner afterwards. Somewhere private. One of those tiny restaurants on Little Collins, up the Harry's Bar end.'

'The Paris end,' Jeff gave the district its fashionable nickname, feeling the blood drain out of his head. 'You are scarily like your mother, *hija mía*.'

The young woman watched her father try his best to come to terms with her idea. 'No, I'm not,' she assured him. 'The request was in our letters, remember?'

The forty-three-year-old lurched towards the nearest tree and crouched down next to its sturdy trunk, becoming particularly dizzy. Kierney sat down on a patch of grass opposite, in the shade of an gnarly old oak, and waited while he processed this latest piece of Lynn's puzzle.

'When am I ever going to get control of my life back?' Jeff lamented, only half joking.

'Don't you think it's a good idea though? Especially as it's *la première* première. I wonder if those guys have ever been to Melbourne before.'

'Jesus!' the exasperated man snapped to attention, shaking his aching leg muscles out before they cramped solid. 'No, they haven't been here, and yes, OK, it's a good idea, angels. Anything you say. Life goes on, Kizzo.'

The pair walked the rest of the way back to the apartment hand in hand. Kierney changed tack and told her dad about a project in which she planned to involve herself as a substitute for her Sydney University courses. According to an associate professor who had contacted her, the multi-faculty initiative was intended to be run out of Melbourne University and would give her credits towards her chosen Bachelor's degree. Jeff listened to her enthusiastic chatter, and it calmed his wild thoughts.

'You can have control of your life back whenever you want,' the eighteen-year-old declared after a while, noticing the man beside her had gone very quiet.

Her father's pace quickened as they closed in on the city, the famous duo beginning to engender more and more interest from the general population. He had an air of impending doom about him, and the youngster lengthened her stride to keep up.

After five minutes or so, they reached the glass front doors of their apartment building. Several international students were hanging around in the lobby, waiting for their friends, and they turned and gaped as their penthouse neighbours let themselves in.

'Hi,' the cheerful young woman gave them a wave as the lift opened.

Once inside their apartment, she watched her usually forthcoming father disappear straight into the spare bedroom and shut the door. What had caused this uncharacteristic withdrawal? She had no idea whether their conversation had triggered positive or negative thoughts, since no words had been spoken for a good ten minutes. He needed space, Kierney figured. She decided to wait for an hour and then, if her dad hadn't reappeared, she would try knocking on his door.

This hour comprised the longest sixty minutes the gipsy girl could remember for quite a while. She logged on to one of the computers in the office and began checking e-mails. There was a funny message from Jet, who had returned to Cambridge the previous week. He had discovered a series of cartoons on a website and every now and again he would send one he found amusing.

His sister typed a serious reply, telling him what had happened. It was the middle of the night over in England, and she and Jeff would be at the cinema by the time her brother would retrieve his messages, so she deleted it without sending. If the problem hadn't been resolved by then, she would ring him for advice. At least writing the situation down in a way that would ensure he understood it had helped clarify in her own mind which action she should take.

Walking up to her father's bedroom door with two mugs of coffee, Kierney knocked. 'Papá, may I come in? Are you awake?'

'*Sí, pequeñita.* Come in.'

Cheered by his ready response, she nudged down the door handle with her elbow and carried their drinks into the room. For the first time after her mother's passing, she found the bed unmade and its occupant stretched out on the sheet, dressed in nothing but a pair of boxer shorts.

His hair was still wet from the shower, and his pile of sweaty sports clothing had been dumped on the floor. She had become so accustomed to finding him reading or simply staring at the ceiling, on top of undisturbed bedclothes and usually dressed from head to toe in black, that this previously commonplace sight warmed her heart.

'Wow! You're making the room bright today. *Es muy bueno.*'

On closer inspection however, the scene wasn't quite so promising after all... Having not seen her papá's upper body naked since the weekend at Benloch after the funeral, the teenager noticed how much weight he had lost. She could see his ribs clearly, his biceps and triceps had lost their former substance and definition, and there seemed to be a cavern of empty skin under his diaphragm where abdominal muscles had rippled.

Hoping her eyes didn't betray this new disappointment, Kierney chose not to mention her latest observation, simply placing the mug on the bedside table. She resolved to whip up a hearty pasta meal for them this evening, in the hope that he couldn't resist his favourite dish.

'*Gracias*, gorgeous. How're you going? Sorry I nicked off without an explanation.'

'That's OK,' the young woman lied. 'I told myself I'd give you an hour and then interfere some more.'

Jeff laughed. 'Good plan. Are you going to answer my question?'

'How am I going? Worried, to be honest. It's not like you to keep things to yourself. I wrote Jet a long e-mail and then deleted it 'cause there's nothing he can do from over there. And the story might've moved on by the time he reads it, so I decided to move the story on myself instead.'

Picking up his coffee, Jeff patted the other side of the bed, requesting his daughter sit next to him. 'OK, here goes, Ms Mover-and-Shaker... I'm in a quandary. Well, several quandaries actually...'

'What about?'

'You, for starters.'

'Me? Why?'

'Because,' the widower sighed, 'I need to stop depending on you and holding you back.'

Kierney pouted. 'You're not holding me back.'

'Hear me out, please. What I mean is that, at first, when you were upset and grieving and stuck like me, it was good for us to lean on each other. But now you're on the mend and busy making plans for the future, which is entirely good and proper.'

'So?'

'So I have to back off and let it happen without constantly reminding you that I'm not as well-adjusted to the future as you are. It's not that I'm ungrateful for all the little things you do... and big things... looking after me and making sure I'm not left in the corner banging my head against the padded wall all day. I am. Extremely grateful.'

'You make yourself sound like a demented fool,' his daughter laughed, using one of her beloved mamá's favourite expressions.

The handsome man leant over and kissed her cheek. 'But I am a demented fool,' he confirmed, finishing his coffee. 'Suzanne gave me a lecture a couple of days ago, and it's been playing on my mind. Then this morning, when you were going through all your Melbourne Uni' plans and how they'd count towards your degree, *et cetera*, I realised what Suze was saying is true.'

'What did she say?'

'She asked whether I was seeing a counsellor to help me work through the grief cycle, and I flippantly said you and Jet were my counsellors,' the intellectual responded, sounding tired again. 'She jumped down my throat, telling me you were too young for such a burden and that I should seriously think about getting professional help.'

The caring teenager gazed in front of her for a few seconds before turning to stare her father down. 'Well, I think that's crap,' she objected, smiling. 'After all these years as a family, supporting each other through anything bad or sad, I'm not prepared to throw that away now there's only you and me here. Do I look like I want to run away?'

'I hear you, *pequeñita*,' the superstar murmured, resting his head back against the headboard and closing his eyes. 'Thanks heaps, but Suzie is right to an extent. You have your own life to live now. You're not Lynn, and neither of us can expect you'll take her place. That's why I clammed up on the way home, 'cause the conversation I wanted to have belongs between Mamá and me. It's not your fate to become her substitute.'

'I know, but it's still very soon after Mamá died. If we were having this conversation next year or in five years' time, that'd be more of a problem. For now, I think we still need each other. I'm enjoying sharing the apartment with you, just the two of us. It's nice. Comforting to know we're here for each other. You don't crowd me at all. Do you think you do?'

'I hope not, but I expect I do. It's kind of you to say I don't, but can I ask you something?'

'Sure. *Dígame*.'

'You haven't once spoken about moving back into the house,' her father challenged. 'In all this time, you haven't mentioned the fact that most of your stuff's still over there. You're living in this temporary hotel in my temporary life while you're planning your permanent life. Don't you want to get back into the house and find your permanent life again?'

'Sometimes, yeah,' Kierney admitted. 'You're right. Sometimes it *is* frustrating not to have everything to hand, but it's convenient here too. Escondido's a long way away, so there's good and bad about both.'

Jeff shook his head. 'Jeez, Kizzy! You are so beautiful. So objective and circumspect. I love you so much.'

'But it scares you too, doesn't it?' his daughter whispered. 'Because you don't want me to replace Mamá in your heart.'

The grieving husband inhaled, ashamed to have once more leant on his empathetic progeny too heavily, emotionally speaking. 'No-one'll replace Mamá in my heart,' he countered. 'I don't want to replace her. And you have your own place in my heart, right next to hers and Jet's. My job now is to stop those places from blurring into one another, which I suppose is kind o' what you meant.'

The young woman nodded. 'Yes, but that's a nicer way of describing it. So what are your other quandaries?'

Jeff smiled. 'The house is one,' he told her, 'and my future is the other.'

'Your future?' she hesitated. 'That's on our minds too. Is there something we need to know?'

'Do you want to go for a drive?' he asked, sitting forward.

The youngster checked her watch. It was eleven-thirty in the morning, and she had planned to devote some time to researching her new project. She was curious though, and her dad seemed a little more settled, judging by the level of animation that had seeped into his demeanour.

'Where to?'

'Where do most of your friends live?'

'Why? Are we going to visit someone? All over: Camberwell, Hawthorn, Caulfield, Elsternwick...'

'So where would you like to live?' her father asked, tossing his car keys into her hands and heading into the bathroom.

'Papá, stop for a second!' she protested. 'What the hell are you going on about?'

Deciding there was no point shouting through yet another closed door, Kierney wheeled round and headed to her bedroom to prepare for their spontaneous excursion. Her mother often used to characterise the impulsiveness her mystery man used to show during their relationship's early days as "exciting but exhausting", and she was beginning to understand this state only too well. There were so many thoughts sprinting through his irrepressible mind that he sometimes appeared to grab hold of one before it had a chance to run away, only to have it amplify to demand his full attention.

'Do you want to drive?' Jeff asked, the lift doors opening in the basement car park.

His daughter giggled. 'Where are we going?'

'Is either of us ever going to answer the other's question?' the handsome man played with her.

'No, I don't want to drive, thanks,' she replied, raising her voice. 'I've given you an answer, so now please will you give me one?'

The Land Rover reversed out of its parking space and rolled towards the electric gates, which were already swinging slowly out of the way. For the first time since the tragedy, the expert driver put his foot down as the car approached the gates. The youngster hid her face in her hands, waiting for the bull bars to clang against the metal barrier.

Fortunately, her dad hadn't lost his touch, and the family's big black box on wheels muscled through the gap with centimetres to spare on each side.

'Woohoo!' Kierney cried out. 'My papá's back!'

Jeff grinned at her childlike behaviour and revved the engine hard as he paused for a break in the traffic on Little Lonsdale Street. 'This car just doesn't have the same "brush with danger" feel, does it?' he remarked. 'Now, what were all your questions? Where are we going? What am I going on about? Are we going to visit someone?'

'Is there something we need to know?' the teenager added, emphasising this as the question that weighed heaviest on her mind.

'No, angel, there's nothing you need to know yet,' a sincere voice replied. 'Not that I'm not constantly assessing, re-assessing, re-re-assessing it all. And by the way, I *will* come to dinner with messieurs Day and Bingham. Ask Cath to organise it, please. Somewhere quiet, as you say.'

His daughter sighed. 'Oh, fantastic! *Muchas gracias, Papá. Te amo.*'

'No worries. *Te amo* too. So here's a proposal for you, *pequeñita*... How's about we rent a house somewhere close enough to your mates, wherein we could move all our stuff while we figure out what life's going to be like in the longer term?'

'Would we be allowed to make it secure enough? It'd only take five minutes for everyone to work out where we are.'

'Yeah, I know. We'd have to fortify it somewhat, but it'd be good to be nearer the ground. And now you're not going to Sydney, you need somewhere suitable to hang out.'

'With my old man,' the teenager appended on the end of her father's sentence.

'Hopefully. But, hey... I'm not that old!'

'That'd be great. Are you really serious about this?' Kierney asked, smiling at his defensiveness. 'Jetto'd like it too, I think.'

'Absolutely. Escondido's completely lost its magic for me,' the widower went on, twisting the unwieldy vehicle round the narrow streets off Punt Road. 'It was perfect for us when you two were little: plenty of space to run around; drivers and nannies on hand. With the dogs, and that darned snooty cat, y'know... It was a superb family home, but nowadays it's too far away, in so many ways.'

'I completely agree,' the young woman said. 'It hasn't felt like home the few times I've been back lately. And actually, Jet hasn't liked going there for a while 'cause it's so far from the city. Perhaps it is time to leave it behind...'

'Cool. Let's ring Comprendo the Marvellous tonight and see what he reckons to the alternative,' Jeff suggested, pulling into a wide, leafy street which wound southwards towards the Yarra.

Kierney giggled at the nickname her brother had earned as a know-all child. 'Sounds like a plan. You've convinced me. So where are we?'

'Western boundary of Richmond, more or less. I've always liked it round here. And now you're driving, you can get anywhere without needing tram stops and train stations.'

'What about you though? You've got a lot of history tied up in the apartment. I hoped you'd be able to move back into your bedroom after a while. Do you really think you could leave all that behind?'

'I have to,' the sad man confirmed with a deep sigh. 'While ever I'm there, I still try and convince myself your mamá's coming back. I still expect to see her come round a corner at any minute, but I know I won't. It's just endless torture. I need to somehow get the idea through my thick skull that she's never coming back, and I'm pretty sure moving out's the only way I'm going to achieve it. As you said, I need to take back control of my life.'

The Discovery reached the river and crossed to the south bank. The dark-haired duo parked the car and strolled along the towpath until they came to a café which neither had tried before. The teenager pointed to a table on its own on the shady side, and her father took a seat on her instruction while she went inside to place their order.

An awestruck waitress arrived a few minutes later with two large panini and two sticky, sugary-looking muffins wrapped in greaseproof paper. After she had run away, the Diamonds could hear her through the open kitchen windows, shouting to the other staff about the town's most famous celebrities who were outside. One by one, prying pairs of eyes led several giggling girls to appear at the door, contorting themselves to get a better view.

'You have to eat at least one of each,' Kierney instructed, pouring two long glasses of water. 'You're getting way too thin. I could see your ribs earlier.'

'Yes, boss,' Jeff saluted. 'I'll do my best, boss. What was that about being in control of my life?'

The sultry teenager scoffed. 'Yeah, well... You're also doing very well at avoiding my questions today. Do you honestly think you can leave the apartment behind?'

'Jesus, gimme a break!' her father teased, chomping into his sandwich to avoid committing himself. 'Do you want me to eat or talk?'

'What did you say?' she giggled.

The songwriter threw his paper napkin at his tormenter before wiping his mouth with the back of his hand. 'We won't leave the apartment behind altogether,' he stated with considerable fortitude. 'It's yours and Jet's for whatever you want to do with it. My suggestion is to make it into two again, then you can have one each for when you move overseas.

'I'm going to ask someone to pack all Mamá's belongings up in boxes and store them somewhere, just so you're aware. All that material shit means nothing to me. That's another thing I was discussing with Suzanne: clothes, shoes, jewellery... That's just not who Lynn was to me. And you and the other significant ladies in her life should take whatever *mementi* you want from it all.'

The young woman nodded, struck by feelings of guilt. 'I understand. There *are* some things of hers I'd like to keep, if that's OK. And I'm sure we could make heaps of money from charity auc...'

The philanthropist was about to put a large piece of chicken into his mouth when he noticed his daughter cringe and stop in her tracks. He replaced the tasty morsel onto his plate and wiped his fingers.

Kierney smiled and took a deep breath in, waving at him to continue eating. 'Don't stop,' she said. 'I'm good. Just sometimes I catch myself saying something I'm not ready for, and then I feel terrible.'

'Yeah, *pequeñita*. I know exactly what that feels like. I do it too. Just leave that door slightly ajar. Y' never know...'

The eighteen-year-old's eyes filled with tears, but this time the attentive parent stabbed at the chicken with a fork and swallowed his mouthful down. It pained him to see her struggle, but he knew it was his responsibility to goad his children through this difficult period. His pectoral muscle affirmed his chosen course of action, and he smiled.

'Mamá says you're beautiful,' the proud father relayed. 'She'd love you to auction her stuff off for charity whenever you guys are ready.'

'Thanks, Mamá,' the teenager chanted into the air. 'I'm glad you can hear us. But, Papá, what about all the songs? And cards and letters and things? You have to keep those.'

'Sure. That'll all come with us to the new place. Those things are so special. Not clothes and earrings and make-up though. I'm not thinking of taking up cross-dressing.'

The youngster laughed. 'That's a relief! But what if Mamá doesn't want you to move?'

Sensitive to her sudden panic, Jeff put his hand on hers and squeezed it. 'It'll be fine, gorgeous. I haven't told you, but I do spend time in our bedroom some nights. I even fell asleep in there once. It freaked me out to wake up in our bed alone, so I'm not gonna do it again. She's not in there, Kizzy. She's with me. She's wherever I am.'

Kierney forced a smile. 'Do you really think so? How do you know?'

''Cause I can feel her all the time nowadays. I know you guys think I'm a nut-job, but I've cracked her code. When I do something she doesn't approve of, my thoughts get all messed up and music rings in my ears.'

'Does it? How?' the young woman asked, not knowing whether to take him seriously or not.

Jeff winked, putting the second half of his sandwich down and reaching for her hand. She stood up to let him insert her fingers inside his shirt.

'And when I do something she likes, this tatt' stings or itches like crazy.'

'I don't know if I can believe you,' Kierney owned up, stroking the hairy skin for a second or two before snatching her hand out again. 'I've never heard of anyone else communicating with dead loved ones like this.'

'That's fine. I don't expect you to believe me. It doesn't matter whether you do or don't. It's up to you.'

'I know... I'll believe you if you eat at least one of these,' his caretaker declared, pushing the dessert plate to his side of the table.

'You're on,' he laughed, fingers diving straight for a muffin and peeling off its wrapper.

'Wait!' Kierney shouted, raising a hand. 'What have I committed to if I say I believe you?'

'*Nada*,' the good-looking star grinned. 'Except maybe to humour me. So to get back on track, whether we stay in the apartment or move, I hope Lynn'll still be around. Does that answer your question, *señorita*?'

'Yes, partly. What makes you so sure she'll come to a new house with you?'

Jeff frowned. 'Good point, but I'm pretty sure she will. She's with me when I'm out.'

'Now? Can you feel her now?'

'Actually, no. Not right now. But a few minutes ago I could. You're playing well, *pequeñita*. You don't give in to me. I love that about you.'

Despite her father's encouraging words, Kierney became upset. 'I don't want you to hurt any more than you already do. I'm scared that if we leave Escondido and the apartment behind, you might leave Mamá behind too.'

Jeff gazed across the grass towards the river, his mind racing. His sage certainly had a point. He couldn't be sure. In fact, he couldn't be sure of anything.

'Kizzy, can I ask you another question?'

She inhaled, putting on a brave face. 'Yes. Course ya can.'

'D'you think I *should* leave Mamá behind? Honestly?'

'No. Definitely not. Well, not yet anyway... Maybe in a few years, if you're...' she gasped, annoyed at how she continually put her foot in her mouth.

'If I'm still here?'

'Yes,' the dejected young woman said. 'You keep reminding us that your old plan's still a distinct possibility, and Jet and I've accepted it'll happen at some point. We're just not sure when. And if you know, we'd be very grateful if you'd tell us.'

Jeff pushed his chair back over the gravel and stood up, screwing his paper napkin into a ball and dropping it onto his empty plate. 'Did you pay already?'

Kierney nodded. 'Where are we going now?'

'Where d'you wanna go now?'

'Oh, Papá!' the teenager slapped his arm hard. 'For God's sake, stop doing this! Where are we going?'

'To drive around the area a bit. You on board with that, boss?'

While the musician ferried his daughter along the wide suburban streets between Richmond and the river, through the suburbs of Cremorne and Burnley, he began to explain his last quandary. It followed on from her request to know when she and her brother could expect their father to follow his soul-mate.

'So would you like to know everything I'm thinking about or just the conclusions I come to?' he asked. 'I don't want to be a burden or for you to be my counsellor, but I do want you to be part of the decision-making process.'

Kierney frowned. 'Hmm... I don't know. Just me, or Jet too?'

'Both of you obviously, but Jetto's not here, in case you hadn't noticed,' the wordsmith joked. 'Or if you want, we can have this conversation together over the phone. Whichever is fine by me.'

'Is this how things were with you and Mamá? So open?'

'Absolutely. There's no other way, *pequeñita*. We never saw any point in hiding anything. What sort of respect does it show the other person? That you think they can't cope with the truth? Or that they're not worthy of knowing the truth? Or you're ashamed of the truth, so you'd rather not be honest?'

Kierney leant her head against the passenger-side window, gazing in wonderment at the gaunt but no less alluring communicator. He made everything sound so clear and so logical. Why did so many people not behave this way, in that case? And why, if relationships were this simple, did so many go wrong and so many people get hurt?

'Papá, how come you and Mamá got it, when heaps of other couples don't and end up getting divorced?'

Jeff shrugged. 'Good sex?'

'Argh!' the teenager groaned. 'I'm being serious.'

'So am I,' the great man answered, amused by her frustration. 'Sorry, baby. Good sex goes a long way towards making things work. But OK... Have you heard the expression "The whole is greater than the sum of its parts"?'

His daughter nodded.

'Well, in my humble opinion,' the intellectual declared, using his best professorial voice, 'if you remember you're worth more as a couple, or as a family or team or government, than you are as a bunch of individuals, then it should focus your mind on not getting hung up on what *you* want. We need to focus on what everyone wants, even if it means someone has to compromise.'

'Alright. I get that. That's how we've always been. But why don't other people do this?'

The famous Jeff Diamond, negotiator and world-changer *extraordinair*, thumped the steering wheel so hard with his left fist that it sent a judder through the whole car. 'Christ! If I knew how to solve that problem, we'd have world peace by now,' he replied, verging on angry. 'Why d'you think I've spent the best part of twenty years flying around the world trying to get overgrown kids to play nicely in the playground?'

The ambitious youngster laughed out loud. 'Right! So that'll be my job too,' she vowed, sitting up straighter. 'When I'm at the UN… I'm going to preach the gospels of openness and collaboration for the greater good.'

'¡Excelente!' her father encouraged, shaking her right shoulder. 'Nothing would give me greater pleasure than to see that happen.'

'Oh,' Kierney let out a plaintive cry.

Jeff watched his gorgeous gipsy girl gulp, her jaw tensing up as if she were trying not to cry. 'I know what you're thinking,' he said. 'That I lied.'

'Yes. And that you might not be here to see me do it,' she added, tears rolling down her cheeks.

The driver stopped the car at the roadside. He leapt out, ran around the back and along the grass verge to open the passenger door.

Hugging his daughter tight, he cried too. 'I *will* see you,' he promised. 'You just have to believe I'm with you, whether you can see me or feel me or just remember me. Same as Mamá. You can think of us together, looking after you from a distance.'

The evening's dinner with two acclaimed Hollywood actors, Martin Day and Tom Bingham, was a complete success. The Americans had jumped at the chance of a guided tour of Melbourne from the Diamond father and daughter team.

Safe behind tinted glass, they cruised down the majestic, tree-lined boulevard to St Kilda, along which clusters of coloured lights flickered on every bough, then returning in a wide arc via the Yarra River and the Melbourne Cricket Ground.

'Melbourne's not a tourist city *per se*,' the local celebrity explained. 'It's a city for living in. Sydney's amazing for visitors: the harbour and the bridge; that's all stunning stuff... But Melbourne's where you go to be part of life. Sport, music, theatre, it's all in Sydney too, yet somehow I feel more involved in Melbourne. Like it engages me more.'

Kierney sat in the back seat, next to the heart-stoppingly sexy Martin Day, who had charmed and amused her over dinner. She listened to her father providing a running commentary to the live footage of his adopted city and knew he wasn't doing it for their guests' benefit alone. The man on whom the film's central figure was based had more than lived up to expectations in the flesh.

And for Jeff's part, he asked no questions about the screenplay. Not one. Kierney knew he would cogitate on the whole thing for hours... perhaps days... but it was clear he had no inclination to discuss it with the two stars.

It was after one o'clock in the morning before the Diamonds dropped the actors back to their hotel, receiving invitations to visit their homes whenever they next flew to Los Angeles, New York or Paris. The engaging philanthropist gave them his sincere thanks, all the while hanging on to his daughter's shoulders. He breathed a sigh of relief when the sultry pair waved their guests into the lift.

'I hope tonight wasn't too painful,' the teenager said, cuddling in to his side as they strolled back to the car. 'Was it?'

'No, baby. It was fine. Entirely the right thing to do. Were you bored with Martin Day sitting next to you all night?'

'Desperately! Can't say I was, no!'

'Thought not. I was dying to ask him what it's like making love to a bag of bones,' Jeff smiled, referring to the actor's current relationship with a top-flight supermodel.

'Papá! You're terrible,' Kierney's eyes widened. 'Is she really that skinny?'

The rock star's smile vanished. 'I seem to remember comments from you on that topic earlier.'

'I didn't say you were a bag of bones,' his daughter defended herself. 'Just that you need to eat more or you'll *become* a bag of bones.'

'Or Mamá won't find me attractive?'

Kierney's right hand reached over to touch the driver's left bicep, gently squeezing it, as he unlocked the car door and opened it to let her climb in. 'I'll say no, she won't,' she agreed, ''cause then you might start looking after yourself a bit better.'

The eighteen-year-old turned away and stared through the windscreen, afraid she had gone too far. She regretted her attempt at a humorous dig at her papá's former glory.

'It's OK. I know what you're thinking.'

'What am I thinking?'

'That Mamá's not even a bag of bones anymore. Neither of us looks that shit-hot, do we? And that all this is one hell of a stupid game.'

His daughter shrugged. 'Not really, but I agree with you. It does all seem so false. Maybe it'll be better when we move.'

'Yep,' Jeff shook his head. 'Let's get home and phone your brother. Thanks for a great evening, gorgeous.'

Back in the apartment, Kierney retreated to her room on the pretext of changing into her nightdress. After locking the door, she lay on her bed and cried her mixed-up emotions out, picturing her dad doing the same while making coffee. She felt better for the short intermission, even finding a smile to take back into the lounge room.

'Jetto!' Jeff greeted his son. 'How're you going, mate?'

'Hey, Dad,' a sleepy voice squeezed itself out of the small speaker. 'I'm well, thanks. How are you? Wasn't it the première of "KoDKoH" last night?'

'Yes, it was,' his sister chimed in. 'It was amazing. Tough but amazing.'

'Oh, hi, sis'. I didn't know you were on the line,' Jet laughed. 'Don't sneak up on a bloke like that. I could've said something nasty.'

'Doesn't normally stop you. The movie was great, Jetto. It's really a strange story in its entirety, isn't it, Papá?'

'Yes, indeed,' their father confirmed. 'I need some time to digest it properly. I could barely concentrate, to be honest. It still astounds me that your mamá'd even make such a film about me, let alone make its theme so cryptic. When does it open in London?'

'No idea,' both kids answered at once, following their reply with subdued laughter.

'Mamá would be ashamed of us,' Kierney moaned, half in jest, 'not knowing such important dates in our calendars. Will you go and see it, Jet?'

'Of course I shall. With a box of tissues secreted about my person. I've even got someone lined up to go with me.'

'*Excelente*,' Jeff approved. 'Someone someone? Like smoke smoke?'

Kierney frowned, staring at the telephone. 'What are you talking about?'

'He means a significant other,' her brother explained with a smile in his voice. 'Don't you know anything?'

'That's enough, mate. Be kind to each other. It's been a long day here.'

The man in Cambridge apologised. 'Just someone, that's all. Why are you both ringing me anyway?'

Jeff cleared his throat. 'Mate, we've had an idea…'

'Papá's had an idea,' the young woman interrupted, 'and I like it.'

The kind-hearted celebrity ruffled his daughter's hair, guessing she was exhausted. 'Don't show your hand too early, *pequeñita*,' he smiled. 'Keep 'em guessing.'

'Guessing what?'

'We're moving to South Richmond,' the younger sibling blurted out. 'Somewhere near the river, on the north bank.'

'Really? Why?'

'Mate, I can't go back to Escondido,' Jeff explained. 'You knew that, didn't you?'

'Yes.'

'And the apartment doesn't feel like home anymore either. It's like purgatory, halfway between somewhere and nowhere. Like a motel on the outskirts of hell.'

'Papá, you're exaggerating,' Kierney moaned. 'It's not that bad! That's not what we talked about.'

'OK, Constable Censorship, I apologise. Perhaps we should wait to have this discussion when I'm less of an arsehole.'

'You're always an arsehole,' his son teased. 'Tell me your plan, and I'll agree to it. Speaking selfishly, Escondido's too far out of the city these days. Richmond would be ace! You mean a proper house?'

'Yes, mate. Don't think our thought police'll go for an improper one!' Jeff said, nudging his daughter. 'I want to know your thoughts about Escondido though, now and long-term. Open to any suggestions, so speak up.

'I'm ninety-nine-point-nine percent sure I'll never want to live there again, and I completely understand your comment about it being too far from the city. I've whinged about that since we moved in! As I said to Kizzy earlier, Mount Eliza was perfect for us when you two were young: close to the beach; safe behind bars, y'know…'

The young woman laughed. 'Like a zoo.'

'Quite,' their dad smiled. 'An open range zoo, I hope, without people gawking at you all the time.'

'Yeah. But we were growing out of it, regardless of what happened to Mum,' Jet took up his father's argument. 'Even before I came over here, it was a real pain to drive all that way home from whatever I'd been doing. And you guys weren't even staying there much recently, were you?'

'Nope,' Jeff agreed. 'That makes me feel better about my intentions. Baby, d'you think the same thing?'

Kierney nodded. 'Yes, I do. I actually like living in the apartment, but Richmond would be just as nice.'

The rock star reached his hand over to rest on his daughter's. 'Cool. Let's explore this idea further then. What facilities do you guys want in your new home?'

'Fully-equipped gym',' their British correspondent jumped in, 'Olympic-sized pool, three-kilometre go-kart track, recording studio, bar staffed with topless waitresses…'

'Dream on, Jetto,' his sister groaned. 'I've seen pictures of your digs over there. How about a small pool, one tennis court and a bar where you make your own drinks with or without clothes on?'

'Steady, *gorgeousita*,' the forty-three-year-old chuckled. 'The topless waitresses were the only thing that caught my attention on his list.'

Kierney pulled a face. 'Argh! Men! Anyway, it's really late, and I'd like to get to bed in the not too distant future. Are we going to talk sensibly about this or not?'

'Sorry, Kizzy,' their father relented. 'OK, mate, listen up… Here's the deal: I'm not proposing to sell Escondido or the apartment, but I am proposing to close the house up. And most likely, depending on permits, *et cetera*, it'll make a whole heap of sense to divide this place back into the original pair. Then you could have one each for your city hideaways.'

'Why would we need city hideaways if we're living in Richmond?' his son challenged.

'Richmond's only going to be rented, mate. I'm not thinking permanent solution here. There's no point buying another big house when you guys'll be getting your own places soon, most likely in other cities or even other countries.'

Tears filled Kierney's eyes, but her brother spoke first.

'Dad, that tells me you're not planning on living anywhere long-term,' his voice cracked too. 'What is long-term in your mind? A year? Five years? Six months?'

Jeff shuffled his chair closer to his daughter's, and she nestled in. It was a half-hearted gesture on her part, and her father knew it. He couldn't shirk his responsibility. They had put him on the spot.

'Jeez, guys, I don't know. And that's not side-stepping the issue either. I really don't know. Some days I feel OK, and others I feel like absolute crap. I know I owe you more certainty, but I can't give it to you. I want to see you guys on your feet, settled and happy, then I'll deal with me. Until that point, I honestly can't give you a better answer.'

Kierney turned her face towards her dad's stubbly cheek and kissed it. 'Thanks for being honest, Papá,' she said, wiping her eyes. 'Jet, are you still there?'

'Yes. Although I wish I were there with you. So the trick is, Kizzo, to stay bewildered and grief-stricken for as long as we can.'

Their father couldn't help laughing. 'I was waiting for you to say something like that, mate.'

'So what will you do with Escondido?' the young woman asked. 'After all our stuff's out?'

'Up to you two. There are several options: lock it up and leave it empty until you guys decide what you want to do with it, or give it to an organisation to make use of.'

'One of the charities?' Kierney asked. 'Like a respite home or something?'

The philanthropist nodded. 'Yeah. Or a retreat for The Good School. All worthy suggestions considered, topless waitresses included.'

'Oh, yeah!' agreed the voice from the other side of the world. 'But seriously, that's an ace idea. At least it'll be put to good use that way, and we'd be able to visit from time to time. What'll happen to Ross and June?'

'Whatever they want,' Jeff answered. 'I spoke to June last week, to make sure everything's OK. She asked me what I was planning for the house and if I wanted them to move out, and I told her definitely not, unless they wanted to.'

'What did she say?' Kierney asked, fond of the Scottish couple who ran the household with military-style precision.

'For the moment, they want to stay and help out. I'll take them for lunch or dinner next week, to tell them what we decide. Then I'll let them choose. Whatever happens, they'll be well looked after.'

'I don't doubt that, Dad,' his son said. 'If the house gets used for something, they might as well stay on.'

'Yep. Although it might be too much for them,' the considerate employer added. 'They'd have to get extra help if it becomes some sort of group home. There are heaps of possibilities to consider, but generally I get the sense that you're at peace with all this. Are you?'

Kierney nodded. 'I am.'

'Jetto?'

'Yeah. Me too. So what sort of place do *you* want to live in, Dad?'

'And don't say a motel on the edge of heaven,' Kierney interjected, almost playful in her overtiredness. 'Please answer seriously.'

'Sure, baby,' Jeff agreed. 'I'm sorry to give you such a hard time. I want somewhere secure and reasonably private, not huge but big enough to move around in.'

'Topless waitresses?' the young man laughed. 'Please?'

'Be serious!' the songwriter whined. 'And we're also going to rent a dog.'

'Rent a dog? Where can you rent dogs from?' his son asked, incredulous. 'What happens when you travel?'

'I don't know,' the widower replied. 'I only just thought of it. It's only a germ of an idea at this point.'

'Kizzo?' Jet raised his voice.

'Yes?'

'I'm happy for you to do my third of the choosing.'

'Quarter,' Kierney corrected, leaning against her father's arm and stifling a yawn while she rubbed the front of his shirt. 'I expect Mamá's going to have a say too, isn't she?'

Jeff smiled. 'Don't go there, baby. I know you guys think I'm batshit crazy with all this tattoo business. You don't have to go along with my weird notions. Just give me licence to get through this any way I can.'

His son sighed. 'Sure thing, you senile whack-job. I have to go soon. Send me some house pictures, please. When's all this likely to happen anyway?'

'Not for a few weeks, mate. After the trial. We might look in on some places if we like the sound of them, but no great rush.'

Jeff's left hand hovered over the telephone, about to terminate the call. 'No-one got any other news? Thanks heaps, guys. I love you so much, and please don't worry about me. Live your life, Jetto. Enjoy yourself to the fullest.'

'OK, Papá,' Kierney agreed. 'Have fun, bro'. I'll keep you posted.'

The man in Cambridge signed off. 'Cheers, both. Love to you two too.'

'*Adiós, hijo mío.*'

The musician's long index finger pressed down on the button, cutting the call off. He sat back on the chair and let out a loud groan.

'I'm so sorry, angel. I really am. I'm fucked.'

'You are,' the sympathetic teenager nodded. 'Are you alright if I go to bed?'

'Yeah. I'm tired too. Sleep well, gorgeous. Wake me up if you want to run in the morning.'

'Cool! That's the best thing you've said for a while. *Buenas noches.*'

With a quick kiss on the lips and a hug around her father's shoulders, Kierney left for her bedroom. Jeff continued to stare at the telephone, pondering the consequences of their conversation. Why was life so complicated? Why couldn't he leave things the way they were?

Perhaps he shouldn't be so quick to regain control after all... His daughter was happy in the apartment. Maybe all he had to do was bring her things up from the house and carry on living a few doors from hell until he decided otherwise.

ADIÓS A ESCONDIDO

The night after the "King of Diamonds, King of Hearts" première, Jeff took Lynn's Maserati out for a spin. Its engine was reluctant to start after almost a month stationary in the basement, but within five minutes and as many kilometres at speeds well in excess of the legal limit, it remembered what a nice car it was. The purr of the motor combined with the itching of his tattoo enveloped the confused man in an uncanny serenity.

The lonesome rock star had spent most of the previous night and a good part of the afternoon sitting on the balcony, mulling over the movie's plot. He was surprised how much he remembered, marvelling at the power of the subconscious brain.

Had the tempest of their early years really seemed so prodigious and other-worldly to Lynn? He posed the question outright on several occasions but had so far received no reply from his ghostly companion. It was obviously not something he was meant to overanalyse. He could hear his wife's voice telling him to enjoy it as a testament to his love; a line she had used a number of times while she had been filming.

The keys to Escondido lay loose on the seat to his left, along with his mobile, and a six-pack of pale ale and a bottle of Sauvignon Blanc were warming up in the passenger footwell. Every time Jeff accelerated or decelerated, they shunted backwards and forwards with the momentum of the car. Kierney and Dylan had gone out for the evening with friends and weren't expected back until after midnight, which had given her father a chance to make a few telephone calls without risk of interruption.

One of these calls had been to the husband and wife team who managed the magnificent hideaway residence in the gateway to the Mornington Peninsula. Gone were the days when the Diamonds needed a posse of drivers and nannies to help their lives run like clockwork.

Jet had been correct in his observation that they had spent precious little time there for the last two years, even choosing to hold Lynn's fortieth birthday party in the city. This fact pleased the master of the house, for it meant they would most likely have come to the same conclusion about its fate as a quartet as they had yesterday as a trio.

'Come for dinner, Jeff,' June had requested, delighted to have her boss return to the family home.

The widower had declined, saying he didn't want to put them to any trouble. The couple were under no illusion that the great man was telling the whole truth, but agreed readily to his counter-offer of a few drinks after dark. Little did they know he was only coming to say goodbye.

'Hey, Regala,' the bereaved star whispered into the air as he got out of the car and shut the door quietly. 'Some signs'd be good, if you're here.'

Nothing happened.

The small inset lights embedded in the solid walls around the courtyard had been illuminated for his arrival, and they shone like tiny stars in the remains of daylight. A stiff sea breeze was chilling the temperature down fast as night drew nigh, and the harsh screech of seagulls could be heard in the distance.

Walking towards the huge, wooden double doors which smelled as if they had been freshly oiled, the tall man raised the key to the lock, hearing footsteps on the gravel driveway behind him.

'Jeff,' Ross greeted him. 'Welcome home.'

The superstar turned around, stepping backwards through the creaking portico. He extended his right hand to the retired air force officer, who grabbed it like a long-lost friend. In the older man's eyes were a thousand questions that his employer hoped he would not have to answer tonight.

'How're you going, Ross? And June?'

'Very well, thank you. How are you, more to the point? And Jet and Kierney, how are they?'

'The kids are great, thanks. Jet's back in the UK, studying hard and partying harder. Kizzy's with me in the apartment. She decided to defer uni' for a year.'

'That's nice. She's a caring young thing, that one.'

'You're not wrong there,' Jeff agreed. 'Thanks again. I'll tell her you said that.'

The housekeeper hesitated for a second before continuing. 'What are your plans here this evening? You're still welcome to come in for drinks, either now or afterwards.'

'Ah, yeah! I forgot, mate,' the forty-three-year-old frowned, returning through the door and marching past his loyal employee to the radiating sports car. 'Why don't you take these and put them in the fridge? I'll see you in an hour or so, and I can give you an update of where things are at.'

He handed the alcohol to Ross, who accepted them as a signal to take his leave. The younger man was spooked a little at finding himself alone, and he paused for a few seconds before stepping over the threshold into the home he and Lynn had designed during their first year of marriage. A surge of poetry tumbled into his head as he started over the flagstones towards the front entrance.

'Whoa!' he shouted into the air. 'What's that all about? Is it good or bad that I'm here, angel?'

The front door opened with a sharp cracking noise, indignantly letting its owner know that it hadn't been used too often in recent weeks. As a rule, Jeff remembered, June entered through the back door whenever she came in to clean or to stock up with provisions.

He hoped she hadn't bought food for him tonight, since it would be wasted. Closing the door behind him, his shoes made a familiar noise as they paced across the marble tiles on their way to the kitchen. He stopped in the hallway to peer up the stairs, and a shiver ran down his spine.

Where should he start? The proud father pictured Kierney as a toddler, climbing the steps one by one, holding onto the banister that she could hardly reach. He couldn't face going up there straightaway, suddenly nauseated. He leant against the wall at the junction of corridors leading to the office, recording studio and gymnasium in one direction, and to the kitchen and laundry in the other.

The house felt like someone else's home. It was as if he were an intruder, not recognising anything clearly anymore. The only break in the silence was the soft sound of rain falling on the cover of the swimming pool beyond the patio doors.

Jeff took off his jacket and laid it on the workbench, alongside his keys. 'Are you here, baby?' he asked into the air. 'Aren't you supposed to be making dinner or something? Isn't that what wives are for?'

Again nothing.

The grieving husband sighed, tears welling up in his eyes. He opened the refrigerator, which thankfully did not contain anything fresh, and removed a bottle of lager.

'In fact, you don't have to cook tonight, angel,' he continued, twisting off the crimped metal cap and tossing it into the bin under the sink. 'We've been invited over to the Monroes'. Where would you like me to take you? Come on a tour of *chez nous*, Lynn, please.'

The persistent lyric floating around his mind began to take shape. It was a song about Escondido, first and foremost, but also about the myriad questions he grappled with these days, the answers to which his children most needed.

'Come into the lounge room, will you?' he called out. 'I've got something to play for you. Please, angel?'

Fuelled with the typical burst of autopilot energy that tended to take hold when a lyric or a poem demanded to be given form, the artist strode into the large, open living room, with its sumptuous white leather couches and walls painted in calming pastel shades. He flicked on a couple of lamps and lifted the top of the piano stool, taking out a notepad he knew would be there.

Opening the lid of the gleaming, white instrument which had been complicit in the creation of so many platinum-selling masterpieces, he sat and picked out some chord structures, humming the tune which couldn't wait to be written.

As the piece developed, genial faces bore down on the singer from the kaleidoscopic paintings of Ethiopian Suri tribeswomen that hung above the fireplace and along two walls. They confirmed his beautiful best friend's absence, their dark brown eyes engaging his own through a sheet of salt water.

Jeff forced a smile in return for their sympathy. The women and girls from the Omo tribe, whom the family had got to know during one of many trips to the country's fledgling irrigation schemes, had shown Lynn and Kierney how to decorate their bodies with leaves, flowers, fruit and animal skins for festivals and celebrations. So enamoured by their harmonious way of life, the Diamonds had commissioned this series of paintings from photographs taken by their cameraman.

Purged of creativity for the time being, the widower flipped over the page and started a list of items he wanted removed from the house for new purposes. He began by adding these same, stunning works of art, with an arrow pointing to the abbreviation "NGV" for the National Gallery of Victoria. Underneath he wrote "piano", and then a question mark, before crossing the word out. The instrument should stay until they decided how the house might be used.

The skin under Jeff's tattoo twitched, making him jump. 'Hey!' he crooned. 'So you *are* here. What took you so long?'

Buoyed that he was no longer on his own, the musician picked up his empty beer bottle and headed back towards the kitchen, choosing first to divert left, past the stairs and into the office. It was unusually neat and tidy, with no piles of correspondence requiring attention. Those piles were now at the apartment and they still needed attention.

The lost lover hurried to close the door before an image of Lynn sitting at her desk had the opportunity to imprint itself on the backs of his sore eyes. How many hours had his dream girl spent in this room over the last eighteen years? She had done such an amazing job to bring so many of his preposterous dreams to fruition, and all while he was swanning round the world chasing yet more.

How many ground-breaking telephone calls had been made from this room? And how many important faxes, e-mails and letters had been written with Jet and Kierney playing happily on the floor or running like whirling dervishes from one end of the house to the other? He couldn't begin to count.

'A whole lot, angel. Thank you. Did I ever say that before?'

'*Bueno*,' Jeff said, feeling the strange sensation again, this time twice. 'I hope I did, but I mean it, baby. You did some bloody awesome things. I'll make sure everyone knows. Where to now?'

Turning about, his head was clearer when he entered the kitchen for the second time. He removed another bottle from the fridge, slid the patio doors open at the back of the house and walked out to the barbecue area by the pool.

This time, it was the toddler Jet who occupied his thoughts, jumping off the diving board and larking about in the water, followed by the weekends they spent here with touring musicians such as Rod Stewart, Garth Brooks and the outlandish Elton John.

What an oasis this house had seemed back then! A chance to behave like ordinary folk with other extraordinary stars. Hell! Bill Clinton had even come to dinner once, playing the saxophone to Lynn's accompaniment after a long and fruitful discussion on funding an HIV vaccination program in Africa.

Terror gripped him at the prospect of climbing the stairs, even though his guardian angel seemed to be accompanying him. Jeff checked his watch: after eight o'clock. It wasn't fair to keep Ross and June waiting too long, so he took a deep breath and dragged his heavy, unfit legs up the twenty steps which swept in an arc from hallway to landing.

Wobbling and light headed by the time he reached the top, he grabbed the end of the smooth, curved rail with his left hand and steadied himself. He took a seat on the highest step, where the children used to wait for him after picking up on the sound of car tyres on the gravel driveway.

No matter how many nights he had been away, he always received the same, exuberant welcome. Lynn would ask the patient pair to sit still while their papá put his bags down and gave Mamá a big kiss. Only then were they permitted to call him upstairs to tuck them into bed and say goodnight.

'Christ, I miss you so much,' Jeff wept into his hands. 'We were so happy. All of us. That bastard García, he ruined everything. We had so much to do; so many years of happiness waiting for us. And now look...'

The desperate man's left hand formed the shape of a gun, and he took aim at an imaginary figure downstairs in the entrance hall. A growl of agony burst from his angry lips, loud enough to bounce off the marble floor.

A man playing a boy's game.

He wasn't self-righteous enough to deny that he too had dreamed about killing as a boy, and even once or twice as an adult. Yet he never would have stooped so low as to shoot an innocent party at point-blank range, regardless of how much hatred or jealousy lurked inside him; especially not someone as beautiful and virtuous as Lynn Dyson. Why ever would anyone want to shoot Lynn Dyson?

The lost boy stood up and yelled into the upstairs darkness. 'You fucking waste of a life, Jeff Diamond! Where were you? Could never resist a fast car, could you, you fucking bastard? You're no better than he is. A man playing a boy's game. Fuck you, Juan Antonio García! And fuck me too. Lynn, I'm sorry I wasn't there to save you. I'm truly, truly sorry.'

A host of despicable characters from the angry man's childhood rushed into his head at once, along with his father-in-law and several other rivals he had encountered later in life. He tore into the children's bathroom and vomited into the toilet, coughing hard as he cried.

Perched on the side of the bath, waiting for this latest bout of rage to subside, Jeff's gaze wandered around the paraphernalia belonging to his teenagers. Hair product of various sorts, anti-pimple lotion, a man's razor with a black handle and a delicate, pink lady's razor sitting side-by-side. Two toothbrushes in a glass near the taps, and a selection of brightly-coloured towels.

A pair of Jet's board shorts still hung over the shower screen from the first few days of the New Year, before he had returned to Cambridge the first time, back when he still had a mother. They were stiff with rigor mortis too, and the analogy turned the father's stomach anew.

With nothing left to bring up, he drank three glasses of water in rapid succession in an effort to expel the bile less painfully; a trick he had taught himself as a lonely, fire-fuelled adolescent.

'D'you mind if we don't go into their rooms, angel?' the grieving husband enquired. 'I don't want to like what I see. I want to leave all this behind.'

The song he had written half an hour ago, downstairs at the piano, instantly replayed in his head at a raucous volume and much too fast.

'Right!' the composer shouted in bitter amusement. 'Have it your way, Lynn. I'll take you in, but I hope you don't expect me to stay long. You're still in control, lady. Right from the word go, you were in control. And I wouldn't have had it any other way. I love you so much. You always were good for me. And way too good *to* me.'

Kierney's bedroom door was open, but the curtains were closed. Jeff switched on the light and paused in the doorway. How long had it been since they were last here together? The day before her driving test?

On her eighteenth birthday, no doubt, when the proud parents had dined outside by the pool with three of her friends and the quirky but devoted Dylan. They had all stayed the night, the girls in a spare room further down the hall and the weird and wonderful lovebirds in this very room, cavorting quietly so as not to wake her parents.

'Kizzy's going to be fine, angel, don't you think?' the musician asked his wife.

She had turned down the volume on his song, having got her own way. Right on cue however, his pectoral muscle flinched again. The grateful father rubbed it affectionately.

'Thank you. That was the clearest signal yet. I'll try to be less of an arsehole to her. She's good at slapping me down, but I promise I'll try harder to stay positive when I'm around them regardless.'

The same sign came again. Good. Jeff allowed his heart to lift a little, entering his son's bedroom on the other side of the house, with its view out over the bay. It had also been tidied since the teenager was last in residence but retained its distinct "air de bomb-site".

Or perhaps this was how his mind insisted on remembering it? Jet had never been one to worry about aesthetics. "Mess is only skin deep," he would claim, whenever his mother requested he clean his room.

'What a beautiful boy he was, eh, baby?' the father requested another confirmation, eyes panning across the space their firstborn had occupied from two years old. 'Three parts you, one part me. He's definitely going to be OK. He's a smart one, despite the cheek and charm. We built strong, ethical children, Lynn. Good people. Good people who won't let other people down. Like you, angel.'

Jeff slumped down onto his son's bed and wept again. *Not like me*, his twisted mind taunted. *I let you die*. Jet worshipped his mum. He wouldn't have let her die.

Sensing himself sliding dangerously down the happiness scale, the widower forced his brain to focus on the list he had started at the piano. What else should he bring back from the house before it was closed up? He would empty the kids' bedrooms.

Everything they held dear must come to Richmond, or wherever the family ended up finding a suitable home. Mess replication was a necessity for them to feel at home in their new place. Ever since they were tiny, the Diamond children had only known this house as a real home; particularly Kierney, who had been but a few months old when they moved into their brand new seaside *hacienda*.

One room remained on the grand tour. The master bedroom was situated on the south-western corner of the house, with a sheltered, stone balcony outside a pair of shuttered French windows. Even in his state of extreme distress, the world-changer still loved this room best of all.

There were pictures of Paris spread out across one wall: L'Ile Saint Louis, Montmartre and the cafés near la Sorbonne, along la Boulevard Saint Michel and in the narrow side streets of the Latin Quarter. Jeff Diamond's favourite place in the entire world.

Above the headboard was a large, black and white portrait of the Fantastic Foursome that had been taken for the couple's tenth wedding anniversary. Clustered in a combined hug, they gazed down on the bed where the soul-mates had fallen asleep after making love night after night for seventeen of their twenty-three years together.

Along the opposite wall from Paris were two parallel but uneven lines of photographs of the children, one per year of their lives. They had been painstakingly selected from the hundreds snapped by the doting parents or from those donated by friends or family; funny ones, stiff school ones, the sporty and the musical. This had become known as the "mug-shot wall", and beside each picture was a mark scored into the paint to indicate how tall its subject had been on that particular birthday.

This chronological account of their growing offspring had been Lynn's idea, based on a significant theme for their relationship: always make the most of the unrelenting passage of time. No less predictably, remembering her mantra in the present day, Jeff found himself crying again, though these were calmer, less angry tears he was shedding now. Tears tasting of love and not bile.

'All these mug-shots'll have to come with us, won't they?' he asked, sniffing back the last of the latest batch. 'I'll put them up in the new house, but probably not in the bedroom.'

His tattoo itched. '*Excelente*,' he chuckled. 'We're getting good at this, angel, aren't we?'

The grieving husband's eyes examined the rest of the room as he turned on his heels. The walk-in wardrobe, which at some point would need to be cleared out, looked exactly the same as he remembered, even down to the pile of laundry in one corner. Whose job was it to empty this?

He knew there were many items of her mother's clothing that Kierney would love, and probably Michelle and Anna too. Was it unfair of him to ask them to purge the room of its contents and make decisions on what should happen to each garment?

Thankfully, the couple had auctioned off Lynn's wedding dress for Childlight after they had celebrated five years together. Instinct suggested the stunning gown of ivory satin with its long train and laced-up bodice was not something he would want stashed away in Richmond, but then he wondered why not. He smiled as he recalled how it had stood up for itself in their hotel room after he helped his new wife out of it with awestruck eyes on that happiest of nights. And then again at the gasp it drew from them both when they laid eyes on it again the following morning.

'I'll ask your mum to decide what to do with all this,' Jeff announced into the air, gazing up towards the ceiling. 'You still here?'

Their king-sized bed, still swathed in dark green satin sheets, beckoned its former occupant cruelly to lie down, making him feel sick again. He almost succumbed to its trap, such was his level of exhaustion at this moment, but the knots in his stomach and the lack of sensation anywhere else convinced him to turn away. He could think of nothing worse than falling asleep on their marital bed, then waking up with the impression that his beautiful best friend was downstairs making coffee and would be returning forthwith for some joyous, rampant sex.

Jeff's head began to spin the title track of Lynn's last album, on which he had sung backing vocals. Complete with comic antics and attempts to censor his most provocative of gestures, video footage of their efforts in the studio had winged its way around the world's media outlets to a public who never ceased to crave more from the stars who could do no wrong.

'I *will* find you,' he whispered, the potency of memories educed by this catchy hit knocking the breath out of his lungs. 'I promise I shall somehow. As yet I haven't figured out when or how though. It'd be a whole lot simpler if you'd come back to me. To us, Lynn. The kids still need me around. Hope you understand, because there's nothing I want more than to be with you. Nothing, God damn it. *Nada*.'

The celestial music decreased in volume and slowly receded until the widower could no longer hear it. He turned round and left the simple luxury of their boudoir, raising his eyes to the landing ceiling and to the covered channel through which a security grille could cordon off their sleeping quarters.

It was a tip he had harvested on his dangerous travels in South Africa, where many families slept in what could only be described as a cage, garrisoned against the violent criminals who regularly ransacked middle-class houses while the residents lay petrified in their beds. It was the wanderer's way of assuaging deep-seated fears that his family might be targets for the western Sydney gangs in which his father had been embroiled.

The superstar couple had designed their home in such a way that the children's bedrooms and theirs were all in close proximity, allowing the occupants to drop down a chained barricade of high-tensile metal bars if an intruder managed to gain entry into the house. Mercifully, it had only ever been used for demonstration purposes, and a couple of times by their gadget-obsessed son to show off to his friends before he had faced his mother's wrath for playing with something that was most definitely not a toy.

'Jeez! You scared him that day, angel,' Jeff remembered, smiling into the dark corridor beyond his daughter's bedroom door. 'But it worked. It never happened again. You scared me too. I wish I could've protected you better from that fucking maniac. I should've kept you locked up here every day, safe from stupid Spanish arseholes with guns.'

The previous melody rang in the widower's brain once more, this time so loud that the tune was barely recognisable. Crumpling onto the floor and propping his back against the landing wall, he put his hands over his ears in an attempt to silence the torturous noise. He knew it was his ghostly dream girl's way of ridding his mind of such self-reproach, yet its intensity drove him berserk.

Emerging from this shock, the exhausted widower thought he could hear his name being called by a female voice from downstairs. It was not his wife's voice, and luckily, his lonely psyche didn't try to trick him into thinking it was.

'Jeff, are you alright?' came the high-pitched, lilting voice of June Monroe. 'Jeff? Are you upstairs?'

The songwriter took another quick look around the bedroom before heading for the staircase. The short, grey-haired woman, a retired nurse who had been the Diamonds' housekeeper for the last three years, had her hand on the banister at the bottom, while he gripped it at the top.

'G'day, June. I'm OK. How're you going?'

'Oh, thank heaven for that,' the woman sounded breathless. 'You've been so long, and the house was so dark and silent. I'm afraid we were beginning to fear the worst.'

'I'm sorry,' he said. 'I didn't mean to worry you. What time is it?'

Jeff glanced down at his watch while the lady downstairs answered, both telling each other the time. It was almost nine o'clock. Only two hours, he calculated. Was this the length of time it took for people to fear the worst? Little did she know...

'Is there anything you'd like done?' the kindly Scot enquired, wringing her hands. 'You're still welcome for that drink, you know.'

'Thanks very much. No. Don't think so. I'm writing a list of things to get moved to the city. I'll come over in a while and explain what's going on. I just need a few more minutes up here, if you don't mind.'

'Oh, of course. Sorry to disturb you. We shouldn't interfere.'

'You're not interfering,' the chivalrous celebrity lied, before making a snap decision. 'Actually, one thing...'

'Yes?'

'I'm going to swap cars tonight. Please could you ask Ross if he could make sure everything's in the Aston? Papers, *et cetera*. I'm leaving Lynn's car here.'

Jeff watched his reliable staff member blanch on hearing the sophisticated singer's name from her husband's mouth for the first time since meeting her fate.

June grabbed at the banister again, seeming to lose her balance. 'Oh, it's so sad, isn't it? I promised I wouldn't cry while you were here, but it's impossible not to feel bitter about what happened. I'm so sorry.'

'Don't worry about it,' the widower replied, forcing a smile. 'I cry every five minutes, without fail. Give me ten or fifteen more, and we can all drown our sorrows.'

The elderly woman smiled up at her charming employer, who was looking thin and drained. The tears came again, and she turned away, embarrassed.

'Right you are,' her voice croaked. 'We'll see you when you're ready.'

Hearing June's shoes clip-clopping along the tiles in the kitchen, the superstar turned back to the master bedroom. Another five minutes in their former sanctuary would be enough. He was glad to have come back to Escondido but also felt justified in his resolve to vacate. His mind was convinced he was not supposed to be here anymore.

Jeff opened the French windows towards him, into the spacious area at the foot of the bed, and twisted the catch on the heavy wooden shutters. They squeaked open, expanded wooden frames sticking on the bottom edge, as they always had. Stepping out onto a balcony strewn with dead leaves, the abnormal unkemptness reassured him that the house had not been expecting them back.

A sudden doubt occurred to the resolute rocker that Lynn may have been sorry to abandon their *hacienda*, and he was momentarily filled with guilt. In many ways, he was sorry too. They had created this heavenly hermitage, and now he was about to liberate it to new occupants, whoever they might be.

His chest twitched again. Jeff leant over the roughly-rendered balcony wall and surveyed the gardens in front and to each side of his vantage point. To his extreme left, he heard tinkering in the garage, imagining the fastidious housekeeper giving his employer's nearly-new Aston Martin the once-over.

Beyond the dense line of shrubs and trees was the bay, choppy and as cold as a bad omen surrendered by the windy darkness. To his right, by contrast, were the swimming pool and tennis court, the floodlights of which had seen so many lively capers.

'I'm not going to miss any of this, Regala,' the mournful man vowed, lifting his eyes to the clouds. 'It means nothing to me without you here. I kind o' wanted to feel something, given how fine our life was here, but it won't happen. Is that wrong? I don't even feel regret. Just numb and ready to let go, like it's not ours anymore.'

Jeff lit a cigarette and flopped down onto one of the deck chairs, peering along the distant coastline. The smoke was whipped away to the right on a strong, southerly sea breeze. Across the pitching expanse of water, he could just about make out the twin lighthouses of Queenscliff on the opposite side of the narrow channel connecting Port Phillip Bay with Bass Strait and ultimately the Antarctic Ocean.

'Angel, thanks for being my lighthouse for all those years,' the forlorn poet spoke into the wind. 'I'm going to leave Escondido shortly and I'm not planning to come back. Is that OK with you?'

The widower's cigarette had blown out. Reaching into his trouser pocket to pull out his lighter, Jeff succumbed to an almighty muscle contraction over his heart, stronger than any signal he had previously received. He re-lit the cigarette and took a long drag, rubbing the tattoo hard and grimacing.

'Hey! That hurt!' he laughed, filled with elation. 'What did I do to deserve that?'

The stinging sensation happened again, although not quite as intense. Jeff squashed the spent stub in the ashtray and closed his eyes as they began to cry yet again. He would need to finish up very soon because the Monroes were waiting for him in the cottage across the driveway, on the other side of the courtyard walls. The ramparts, as Jet had often called them.

'Lynn?' he requested. 'When I drive away, please tell me you're still with me. And soon. I need to know I'm not going to be leaving you here. I need to know that when the kids and I find somewhere else to live, you'll still be around. Can you do that, please, angel?'

With the tattoo smarting for a third time, Jeff's mobile burst into life against his thigh, sending his heartbeat racing again. Standing up, he fished the handset out of his other pocket and checked the glowing screen. It put him in mind of a mini lighthouse. He was right; it was Kierney.

'Hey, gorgeous. How're you going?'

'OK, thanks. Where are you? I can hear the wind.'

'I'm sitting on the balcony at Escondido,' he replied, feigning calm and collection. '¿Y tú?'

'Escondido?' his daughter yelled in surprise. 'What are you doing there?'

'Having a cigarette and a good cry. I'm saying *adiós*.'

'Wow,' Kierney whispered. 'Are you alright? When did you decide to go?'

'Spur of the moment. I'd been thinking about Mamá's film and about moving to a new place. Our conversation with Jet last night, y'know…'

'Yes, I know, but I didn't think you wanted to go back at all.'

The tired man continued. 'Yeah, me neither. In the end, I thought I'd better come over and test whether I really want to come back or not, before I ruled it out completely.'

'And do you?'

'Nope. There are some things I'm going to have shipped into town, like the Omo paintings in the lounge room and some photos of you guys. But I have to tell you, I don't feel much for anything else. Where are you?'

'I'm in the car park downstairs and saw Mamá's car's gone,' the teenager said. 'I was ringing you to say I think it's been stolen. Did you take it?'

'No,' the comic feigned ignorance this time. 'What do you mean, stolen?'

'Papá, you did take it, didn't you?' she whined. 'Don't mess me around. You didn't walk to Escondido.'

Her dad paused. 'Can't recall.'

'Papá, for God's sake.'

'Sorry, baby,' he capitulated, stepping inside and out of the gale, tugging the shutters closed. 'I'm winding you up. I took it because I wanted to swap it for mine.'

'Thank you,' Kierney sounded perturbed. 'At last, a straight answer. I was worried. Did you leave me a note?'

'Yes,' Jeff couldn't help smiling. 'And I've got my licence and plenty of petrol, and my phone's charged. You'll see my note on the coffee table. I trust you'll find it exonerates me nicely. I didn't expect you back so early.'

'Dylan and I split up,' she declared without ceremony but with a certain sadness in her voice.

'Oh, no. How come? Are you alright?'

'Yes, I'm fine,' a brighter voice affirmed. 'I've wanted to do it for a few weeks now. We had a long talk and agreed to see how it went as friends. I feel a bit empty but not too bad.'

The superstar's watch told him it was now almost ten o'clock. He needed to return home to his daughter, and therefore Ross and June would have to wait. His inscrutable dark-haired gipsy girl was making another brave foray into the adult world, and he ought to be by her side to help make sense of things, like a good parent should.

'Kiz, I'm leaving in ten minutes or so. Hang tight. I was planning to have a drink with the Monroes but I'll make that another night.'

'OK, that'd be cool. Thanks, Papá. It's all good though. Don't drive ridiculously fast because you think I'm upset. I'm not really.'

'Good girl,' the empathetic man praised her maturity. 'If you want to go to bed, I'll see you in the morning. I wasn't going to stay long anyway. *Te amo.*'

'*Te amo también.* Say hi to June and Ross from me.'

'Shall do, *pequeñita*. Oh, and thanks for worrying about the car,' he added. 'I'll see you in an hour or maybe a bit more.'

'Great. Drive carefully. *Adiós.*'

'*Adiós.*'

Slipping the telephone back into his trouser pocket, Jeff pushed the French windows tightly shut and bolted out of the bedroom, turning for one last look before flicking the light off. Kierney's call had come at an opportune time since it presented him with the perfect excuse not to string out his visit. The kindly couple would surely not be looking forward to drinking at this hour.

The celebrity loped down the curved staircase and grabbed his jacket and keys from the kitchen. He then tore the top two pages off the notepad, leaving the remainder on the counter with a scribbled message on the front page, thanking June for keeping the house in such good order. The rain had stopped, but the wind still blew hard, seeming to suck the door closed behind him.

'*Adiós*, Escondido,' its owner said, gazing up at the arched, *Gaudiesque* balconies of the guest bedrooms above and then back down into the courtyard. 'You are a *great* house. You made us very welcome, and we were very happy here.'

The man of the house paused to dip his hand in the simple stone fountain on the way to the pair of three-metre-high wooden gates which led to the driveway and to the other houses on the property. He tasted a palmful of the Mornington Peninsula's finest mains water before scooping up another and dousing his face with *aqua manantial* that had no origins whatsoever in the mountains of Andalucía.

Jeff's chest itched again. The lady of the house appreciated the fact that he had taken the trouble to say goodbye to the house properly.

'You're welcome, angel,' her husband whispered, wiping glinting droplets off his jacket.

Re-energised either by the purifying ritual or by Lynn's positive feedback, he sprinted over the gravel to the old Californian bungalow occupied by the Monroes. Their two dogs yapped annoyingly at the sound of the doorbell, and the songwriter spied June's shape approaching through the frosted glass.

'Come on in, Jeff,' she invited, waving her boss through to the lounge room.

'June, thanks,' he replied, towering over his housekeeper. 'Sorry to've taken so long.'

'That's no trouble, really. We're not early-bedders these days, dear.'

The celebrity shook hands again with Ross, who had joined his wife in the hall. The keys to his Aston Martin sat on the telephone table in their hallway, on top of a white folder. His request had been fulfilled to the usual standard, and it made the carefree beatnik in him smile.

'Actually, I won't stay, if you don't mind,' he continued, following the couple into the living room. 'Kierney just rang to say she's home early. I'd hoped to sneak out and back before she noticed I was missing, but I didn't count on spending this long in the house.'

'I don't want to leave her at home on her own too long. Why don't you pick something you'd like to see in the city? Theatre, concert or anything... And let me know when you'd like to come up. I'll book a hotel room for you, and we can all go out to dinner. Kizzy'd love to see you again.'

The famous negotiator perched on the edge of the couch, making a fuss of the Monroes' boisterous Jack Russell terriers.

'Not to worry,' the retired warrant officer replied. 'We suspected it might be getting too late. We'd love to catch up in Melbourne, thank you. That's very kind. How is everything in the house?'

'Mate, everything's perfect in the house, but it doesn't feel like home anymore. We haven't made any firm decisions yet, but the kids and I will almost certainly not be moving back here. They're off doing their own thing now. Jet's going to be in the UK for at least another eighteen months, and Kierney wants to be closer to uni' and her friends.'

'I see,' June murmured. 'That's a real shame, but I'm not surprised. We have been wondering whether there are too many memories for you here.'

Jeff nodded, tears pricking the back of his eyes. 'That's part of the reason too,' he agreed. 'This house is our marriage, our family, but things just aren't the same now. I don't feel anything in there. I expected not to and I've confirmed it tonight. We're going to rent a house in South Richmond or Burnley. Close enough to the city but at ground level. When you come up to Melbourne we can talk through the details at length.'

The master communicator hesitated, letting his comments sink into the couple's minds. He knew they would refrain from asking any selfish questions tonight, although they would be burning inside.

'Whatever happens, I'll make sure you guys are well set-up,' he added. 'You can stay as long as you like here. I'm not selling up or anything drastic like that. The kids and I need some time to work out what our life's going to be like, and neutral territory's important for that process. The trial's next month too, which'll be a nightmare for all of us, and I'm going to ask Lynn's mum to make some decisions about all the clothes upstairs and the other personal stuff.'

June breathed in deeply again. It was painful to hear the generous beauty's name coming out of her husband's mouth, even though he seemed relatively composed.

'Are you going to the trial?' Ross hazarded.

'Yep. I'll definitely be there, and probably Gerry too. Kizzy wants to go, but I haven't decided if I want her to listen to all the gory details.'

June's expression brightened. 'How are the children now? Please say a big hello from us.'

'I shall. Thanks. Jet's going well. He's back at uni' and adjusting pretty well. We speak to him two or three times a week, but already he's showing signs of not needing so much contact. Kierney's OK too. She said to say hi, sorry!

'I'm holding her back something chronic. She feels obliged to babysit me all the time, which I'm trying to put a stop to. Y'know how she is... She's gorgeous and extremely helpful.'

'They've always been such fantastic kids,' the older man agreed. 'They're a credit to the two of you.'

'Thanks again,' his employer smiled. 'We think so, but it's always nice to hear it from someone else! And credit to you and everyone who surrounded them, don't forget. Anyway, I'd better go. I've stayed out longer than my curfew allows, so I'll have to pay for it with a run tomorrow morning.'

Both housekeepers chuckled, Ross first looking to his wife for permission. 'I'm glad to hear you haven't lost your sense of humour in all this heartbreak. That would've been a terrible pity.'

Standing up, the songwriter shrugged. 'It's a defence mechanism more than anything, mate. Forcing myself to behave somewhat normally. Give me a ring when you decide when you're coming up to town.'

The grey-haired couple raised themselves off the couch to embrace the companionable star, who hoped curtailing his visit at the last minute hadn't left them too much in limbo. Not in the habit of leaving people high and dry, he trusted Lynn's death wouldn't make them think differently.

Jeff left the modest cottage with the keys to his new car. He had only taken delivery the week before Christmas, and the ensuing tragedy had prevented him from putting it through its paces until now.

Tossing the keys up and down in his hand as he walked, Lynn's last million-seller played in his head. Was the CD still in the car? The prospect of listening to the entire album made his heart-rate soar in a mélange of apprehension and appetite.

The vastness of the garage and workshop amplified his footsteps, and its meticulous array of tools and maintenance equipment seemed to belong more to the shed itself than to the man who had paid for it all. True to form, Ross had already moved the Maserati inside and covered it.

The departing driver tapped its bonnet. '*Arrivederci, Maz,*' he murmured. 'Don't get too lonely.'

Climbing into the vehicle parked next-door, Jeff felt his left pectoral muscle twitch again. He leant over to open the glove compartment and fished out three CD cases. Through dim shadows cast by the overhead courtesy light, his dream girl's face beamed up at him from the coveted album cover. He kissed it, love surging to warm his lips.

The showman flipped the plastic case open and found it empty, so he turned the key in the ignition. His ears were assailed by a sophisticated rock'n'roll riff from the penultimate song blaring out through the sound system.

'Good evening, ladies and gentlemen,' he announced, turning the volume down a little while he steered the car out of the garage and along the driveway.

No doubt Ross and June would be standing like sentries in their doorway to wave him off. He didn't want to behave too much like a lovesick lout, even though this was *his* sports car, outside *his* house, and he was at liberty to behave exactly as he chose. Regardless, Lynn Dyson was travelling with him, which in itself demanded a certain decorum.

The musician clicked back through the tracks until the disc was at the beginning before switching the CD player off temporarily. The charcoal grey Aston Martin prowled stealthily toward the gates, illuminated only by its sidelights, as if stalking some nocturnal prey. Under his right foot, the engine felt as wound up as the driver, poised to rush onto the open road and blow some cobwebs away.

Sure enough, the Monroes were waiting together at the end of their garden path. Seeing the long-married couple arm-in-arm, Jeff was gripped by a pang of jealousy. He rolled down the window to shout a friendly goodbye.

'Thanks heaps, guys. See you in a week or so. Keep well.'

The electronic gates swung open on his approach and began to close as soon as the powerful car passed through. For possibly the last time, Mount Eliza's favourite son drove sedately and unnoticed along the quiet roads between beach and highway, past the picturesque strip of shops which the family had frequented hundreds of times over their seventeen years as residents of this sleepy municipality.

Jeff recalled how the local shopkeepers would love their celebrity neighbours to come in and chat, especially when the children were young. They used to be offered free coffees and muffins in every café as though their presence would attract extra customers, particularly the all-important tourist dollars.

The wealthy couple often despaired whenever their money was refused. Didn't everyone know that, out of the growing number of yuppies calling the hamlet home, the Diamonds were the most able to pay? Good luck charms, their kids had been labelled on several occasions.

'*Sayonara*, Mount Eliza,' the forty-three-year-old whispered, circling the sleepy village and heading up the hill to join the Nepean Highway.

The clock on the dashboard said ten-twenty. Jeff cursed as tears pricked at his eyes, feeling both guilty for leaving Kierney alone in the apartment and lost and lonely after saying farewell to their family home. In compensation however, the tattoo burned like fury under his shirt.

'Thanks, angel. That's just what I need. This is tough as,' he sighed, reaching over to switch the CD player back on. 'Did you hear Kiz and Dylan split up? Sad, huh? Welcome to the real world, poor thing.'

The sound of his stunning wife singing only for him washed through the cabin and made the widower cry even more. He pulled over into the service road that ran parallel to the highway, wound the window down and lit a cigarette.

Late-night traffic whooshed past, competing with the well-known song, and he moved the disc on to the third track; his favourite from this record. The upbeat but romantic track had been his fortieth birthday present, instantly spiriting him back to the trip he and Lynn had taken with their son to appraise Trinity College in Cambridge, not long after the big birthday bash she had thrown for her black stallion.

The grieving husband remembered their intimacy that night in their hotel room, his beautiful best friend lamenting how young Jet was to be heading overseas to university. After an initial, sympathetic agreement, he had reminded her that in reality the blond sportsman was a couple of months older than she herself had been when her parents shipped her off to California.

'Jesus, angel... What I'd give for a two-way conversation with you!' Jeff spoke to the voice crooning through the speakers. 'You too probably, wherever you are. I love you. I still miss you so, so much.'

The driver nudged the car into first gear, looking over his shoulder for a gap in the oncoming traffic. He pressed his foot to the floor, and the rear of the car fishtailed on the wet, oily road surface. Easing off the throttle, he turned the volume up higher and sped toward the city with both front windows open.

The car's untapped power compensated in part for its owner's acute sense of loss. This was something he could control, he realised; a facility sorely lacking in recent weeks. It was now time to reclaim it, bit by agonising bit.

The top-floor apartment was totally quiet when the night owl stepped out of the lift. Kierney had left the lamp on in the entrance hall, and a note was affixed to the light switch: "Please wake me when you get home. Kx".

It was already after eleven o'clock, yet the father was happy to read her request because he too needed to talk. Tossing his leather jacket and car keys onto the bed and slipping his shoes off, he padded down the hall to his daughter's bedroom and knocked on the door.

'Come in, Papá,' the youngster's drowsy voice invited. 'What time is it?'

'Late,' Jeff whispered, bending over to kiss her forehead. 'Are you sure you want me to wake you up?'

'Yes, it's fine. I'll make some tea.'

'No, I'll do it,' her father insisted. 'It's too cold to sit on the balcony, but we could sit by the kitchen doors and look out. I want to hear what happened with Dylan and whether you're alright.'

'I'm OK. Really. I've been preparing myself for a while. I want to hear about Escondido.'

The pair walked arm-in-arm through to the northern side of the flat. Kierney sagged obediently into a kitchen chair on her father's instruction, ready to spill the boyfriend blues beans.

'There's not much to say, Papá. It's got nothing to do with Mamá passing away or you being sad, or even Youssouf Elhadji. We grew apart. I'm ambitious to go interstate and overseas, and he wants me to stay in Melbourne. Dylan never wanted me to go to Sydney Uni', so when I deferred, he thought we'd be staying together and both go to Melbourne Uni'. But I've got other plans that don't have him in them.'

'Ah, yeah? Does that mean there's someone else on the horizon then?' her father asked, sensing a certain excitement. 'Or closer than that?'

In the gentle lighting from the bulbs in the extractor fan above the stove, Jeff thought he could discern a slight blush. This cute reaction warmed his lonely heart, since it represented another sign that his daughter was on the road to recovery.

'A bit closer,' she admitted. 'Nothing's happened yet, but someone I met at uni' asked me out the other day, and tomorrow I'll say yes.'

Jeff leant forward and planted another kiss on his daughter's forehead. 'Very honourable of you,' he praised. 'You're a good person, Ms Diamond. Ross and June said so too. They were asking after you and send their love.'

'Oh, thanks. How were they? Nervous?'

'Yeah. I think so, but you know them... They'd never say anything as direct as that. They asked if everything was alright in the house, which was definitely code for "Are you going to kick us out?"'

'Oh, no,' Kierney sounded disappointed. 'What did you tell them?'

'That we hadn't made up our minds yet, and I'd make sure they were OK, whatever happens,' her dad recounted. 'I told them they can stay there as long as they like.'

'Good. Not that it's any of my business.'

Jeff smiled. 'Of course it's your business. You feel an obligation to them too, which is again honourable. I've suggested they look for a show or movie they want to see, and that I'd put them up in a hotel so we could go out to dinner somewhere together.

I think they were happy with that. We can talk specifics then. I didn't want to stay and have a drink with them after you rang. I was worried.'

'Thanks, Papá,' his gipsy girl grinned back. 'I hope you're not worried anymore. I'm fine. I'm just a bit scared that I'll keep bumping into Dylan, and he's bound to find out if I'm seeing someone new.'

'*C'est la vie*, baby. It won't be the first time. And it'll happen to you too, somewhere down the track,' the supportive former man-about-town intimated. 'You might find you're jealous if you see him with someone new too. So what's his name, this new bloke?'

'You know him,' the sheepish youngster offered.

'Do I? How? Someone who doesn't want you to stay down here?'

Kierney let out a coy giggle. 'Oh, shut up! We haven't got anywhere near that far yet. I've only had one coffee with him. It's David Ekwensi.'

Jeff pulled a face as if to say he disapproved. David hailed from Nigeria and currently occupied a lecturer's position in Melbourne University's Economic History department. He had been involved with various African aid budgeting and expenditure management processes over the past couple of years, proving a reliable source of practical wisdom.

'No. I can't allow it,' he responded in mock disdain. 'He's way too old for you. What do you think you're playing at?'

But his daughter was wise to his intonation. 'Knock it off. I know you like him. It was your comment about Youssouf Elhadji that made me rethink, to be truthful. I've always really admired David and just never thought he'd be interested in me.'

'So you went out hunting?' Jeff teased. 'You little tramp! You enticed him into your web, Ms Spider. I'm proud of you.'

The handsome man beckoned to the dark-haired beauty to stand up, and the two hugged each other close. 'You're growing up so fast,' he grumbled, thrown back to his deliberations in the car on the way home. 'Don't take any notice of me. I'm just the dad who doesn't want to see you get hurt.'

Kierney stood on tiptoe to kiss her father on the lips. 'Don't stress. I'm not sure if it'll go anywhere. I was ready to break it off with Dylan anyway. He and I definitely weren't going anywhere. Now, tell me what happened at the house. How did you feel when you were inside?'

'So where's David taking you?' her dad asked with a straight face.

'Papá, I've changed the subject.'

'And I'm changing it back again.'

'We had a deal,' Kierney frowned. 'Please tell me. I want to know whether it's made you change your mind about living there.'

Jeff swallowed the last mouthful of his tea and focussed his gaze on the Macedon hills beyond the airport, overlooking the suburbs laid low on the plains south of the dividing range. He took a few moments to collect his thoughts on some of the healthier observations he made while at Escondido.

'Negatory. I don't want to live there,' he confirmed. 'There was nothing there that told me it missed me, and I didn't see anything that made me feel like I needed to be there either.'

'Where did you go? More tea?'

The widower nodded. 'Please. All over, except the studio and the gym'. Oh, and I didn't strip off and go for a swim.'

'Really?' Kierney giggled, shivering at the very idea. 'That's good. Did you go in your bedroom?'

'I did,' came a heavy sigh. 'I looked at the mug-shot wall and went into your bathroom and threw up before sticking my head in your rooms... I sat and had a cigarette on the balcony and had a quick chat with Mamá, then turned tail pretty quickly. That was about it.'

'I'm not sure you're telling me the whole truth, but OK,' his minder complained. 'Was it traumatic?'

'A little, gorgeous. I expected to feel more but I didn't. I did write a song though, on the lounge room piano. One of those lyrics that pushes its way out of my eyes.'

'Ugh. Yeah, I know that feeling. But what about Mamá?' the teenager asked, placing two mugs of fresh, hot tea on the table. 'Did you get any clues if she wanted you to be there?'

'Who knows? There were a few times I got the impression she was OK with everything. I asked her to let me know if she'd left with me when I drove away, but then I put her album on loud and let her sing to me, so I never really gave her a chance.'

Kierney saw her dad's expression change as soon as he had stopped speaking. 'Was that her?' she cried out. 'I saw your shoulder twitch!'

Jeff couldn't stave off the tears, more due to his daughter's excited reaction than because he had received another message from his dream girl. 'Yep,' he nodded, rubbing his shirt above its breast pocket. 'Did you see something?'

'Yes! Your left side moved really quickly, like this...'

The young woman demonstrated the spasm she had observed, also starting to cry. The grieving husband reached for her hand, and the pair sat at the table shell-shocked and baffled by the peculiar phenomenon. He wasn't entirely comfortable with Kierney believing that tattoos could talk. She didn't need another complication in her life.

'I wish I could feel Mamá with me too,' she sobbed. 'I still miss her so much.'

'I bet you do,' her father said, inviting her to sit on his lap. 'And she misses you, baby. There's no doubt about that. Perhaps if we'd got you guys tatts as well, you'd be having similar interactions with your mamá. Don't get too upset, angel. It's most likely pure fantasy on my part. Perhaps I'm just willing it to happen, and my body's learned to play along?'

Kierney leant against her father's shoulder. '*Gracias*. We'd have had to have "JeLyJeKi" as our tattoo. Do you remember that? It would've stretched as we grew bigger. I feel better now, but I really needed to cry. Sorry to go all weird on you. What was it like driving the Aston after all this time?'

'Very cool,' Jeff responded, kissing her cheek. 'You're not weird, by the way. We need to give each other the space to express our grief, however it comes out. I wish you could talk to Mamá too, although it's not that fulfilling, to tell you the truth. It's mostly asynchronous. D'you know what that means?'

'*Sorta-kinda*,' she smiled. 'Not like a normal conversation. One after the other, with gaps.'

The amused intellectual squeezed her shoulder. 'Exactly, clever clogs. Not spontaneous. That's why I was so pleased to see your note when I got in. I needed to cry too.'

'*Excelente*. So it's all good,' Kierney agreed, stifling a yawn.

'Tired?'

'No,' she pouted, using a little girl's voice.

'Well, I am. Can I be excused our run in the morning?'

'We could go now, and then we wouldn't have to go in the morning,' his daughter suggested, standing up and carrying their empty mugs to the sink.

Jeff groaned and stretched his arms up in the air. 'No way, lady,' he said. 'I'm in and I'm staying in. End of story.'

Father and daughter left the kitchen and headed to their respective bedrooms, kissing each other in the hallway.

'Hey? D'you mind if I invite Michelle and Alan over tomorrow night?' the widower asked as he pushed his door open and flicked the light on.

'No. Of course not,' Kierney's response was genuine in its enthusiasm. 'Why?'

''Cause I need to talk some more and don't want to use you any more than I do already.'

'Oh, OK. Do you want me to go out?' the teenager looked disappointed.

'No, I hope not,' Jeff hugged her. 'Unless you and Dave want to hook up! I'd love you to be there if you can. It's just that I don't want you to always be the person I unload on.'

'But I like being the person you unload on,' the young woman objected, thumping her dad's chest. '*Buenas noches,* Papá. I'm glad you got some answers.'

'*Gracias, pequeñita.* Me too. Sweet dreams of David.'

Kierney gave him a dismissive wave, smiling in embarrassment. 'And you with Mamá.'

Blowing his daughter a kiss, the widower stepped inside the spare bedroom. As soon as he was confident the youngster was behind a closed door however, he slipped across the corridor into the master suite. Sitting down on Lynn's side of the bed, he put his head in his hands and wept his full tank of wretchedness dry.

The chapter of Castle Diamond, the Escondido era, was at an end, having carved yet another chunk out of the great man's hollow heart.

END OF PART ONE; VOLUME ONE

CONTINUED IN

A LIFE SINGULAR
PART TWO; VOLUME ONE
ARRIVING IN 2020

Lorraine Pestell

A Life Singular
Part One; Volume One
2020©Copyright Lorraine Pestell
AUSTRALIA

SHAWLINE PUBLISHING GROUP

www.indieauthorsaust.com.au